CITY OF WOMEN

CITY OF WOMEN

DAVID R. GILLHAM

AMY EINHORN BOOKS
Published by G. P. Putnam's Sons
a member of Penguin Group (USA) Inc.
New York

AMY EINHORN BOOKS
Published by G. P. Putnam's Sons
Publishers Since 1838
Published by the Penguin Group
Penguin Group (USA) Inc., 375 Hudson Street, New York,
New York 10014, USA • Penguin Group (Canada),
90 Eglinton Avenue East, Suite 700, Toronto, Ontario M4P 2Y3,
Canada (a division of Pearson Penguin Canada Inc.) • Penguin Books Ltd,
80 Strand, London WC2R 0RL, England • Penguin Ireland, 25 St Stephen's Green,
Dublin 2, Ireland (a division of Penguin Books Ltd) • Penguin Group (Australia),
250 Camberwell Road, Camberwell, Victoria 3124, Australia
(a division of Pearson Australia Group Pty Ltd) • Penguin Books India Pvt Ltd,
11 Community Centre, Panchsheel Park, New Delhi–110 017, India •
Penguin Group (NZ), 67 Apollo Drive, Rosedale, North Shore 0632,
New Zealand (a division of Pearson New Zealand Ltd) • Penguin Books
(South Africa) (Pty) Ltd, 24 Sturdee Avenue, Rosebank,
Johannesburg 2196, South Africa

Penguin Books Ltd, Registered Offices:
80 Strand, London WC2R 0RL, England

First published in the United States of America by G. P. Putnam's Sons 2012
Copyright © 2012 by David R. Gillham

"Amy Einhorn Books" and the "ae" logo are registered trademarks
belonging to Penguin Group (USA) Inc.

ISBN 978-0-399-16152-0

Printed in the United States of America
1   3   5   7   9   10   8   6   4   2

BOOK DESIGN BY AMANDA DEWEY

This is a work of fiction. Names, characters, places, and incidents either are the product of the
author's imagination or are used fictitiously, and any resemblance to actual persons, living or
dead, businesses, companies, events, or locales is entirely coincidental.

While the author has made every effort to provide accurate telephone numbers and Inter-
net addresses at the time of publication, neither the publisher nor the author assumes any
responsibility for errors, or for changes that occur after publication. Further, the publisher
does not have any control over and does not assume any responsibility for author or third-
party websites or their content.

ALWAYS LEARNING   PEARSON

To Ludmilla

Take hold of kettle, broom, and pan,
then you'll surely get a man!
Shop and office leave alone,
Your true life's work lies at home.

—COMMON GERMAN RHYME OF THE 1930S

"Who will ever ask in three or five hundred years' time
whether a Fräulein Muller or Schulze was unhappy?"

—HEINRICH HIMMLER, REICHSFÜHRER OF THE SS
AND CHIEF OF THE GERMAN POLICE, CIRCA 1941

BERLIN

1943

ONE

THE BLIND MAN TAPS his cane rhythmically. Three taps, three taps, three taps to gain the attention of passing Berliners. He is a cadaverous sentry with a shaved pate under an old soldier's cap, selling pencils from a canister strung about his neck. A pyramid of dots is stamped onto the armband he wears, and his round black goggles are like two holes poked through the day, letting the night bleed through. Sigrid fishes out the coin purse from her bag as she emerges from the U-Bahn stairwell, and drops a few groschen into his cup. "Bless you," he rasps in answer to the jangle. "Please choose a pencil." She thanks him, but when he turns his head in the direction of her voice, something behind the blindness of those goggles seems to mark her. She puts the pencil into her handbag and crosses the street at the signal.

Tickets for the matinee are three and a half marks now. Up fifty pfennigs. But Sigrid pays the increase without complaint. Today's feature is titled *Soldiers of Tomorrow*. The poster casement displays eager, towheaded boys in soldierly Hitler-Jugend outfits, charging across a field with wooden rifles, practicing gymnastics, or peering down the barrel of a heavy-caliber machine gun, under the smiling instruction of an army officer. But what's playing makes no difference. She's not here to see a film.

Inside, the usual wartime patrons greet her ticket purchase with vacant appraisal. The lobby smells of mildew and unswept rugs, and the once-grand chandelier lighting is dim and spotty with missing filaments. The sweets counter is empty. Nothing to sell, like the rest of the town. The coat-check porter is reading a sporting magazine to ease his boredom, since the heating is poor, and the weather is far too raw for anyone to shed their overcoats. But there's a crowd waiting for the ushers to open the doors to the auditorium. In a city where the food is bad and getting worse, where rationing has emptied the shop windows, in a city slowly suffocating on the gritty effluence of another year of war, movie houses are still places to spend a few marks without cutting coupons from a ration book, or waiting one's life away in a queue.

Ashen-faced pensioners are bent over their canes. Factory women between shifts, with their hair tied up in turbans, pass a single cigarette among themselves. Hard-eyed street whores are on the lookout for takers among the off-duty soldiers. Hausfrauen clutch their heavy purses on their laps, and wait patiently, relieved to escape their children and the duties of home for a few hours.

To all the patrons, Sigrid Schröder speaks only silence.

She is a stenographer in the applications department of the Gitschiner Strasse Patent Office near the Belle Alliance Platz. Still with her looks, she likes to think. Her hair is still thick and flaxen, underneath the scarf she ties over her head. Her body still strong and favorably proportioned. She is not displeased when she looks in the mirror, she simply seldom bothers to. The years of war have redefined her in very restricted terms. She is a number on a pay book, on a booklet of rationing coupons, a face on an identity card. She is Frau Schröder, a kriegsfrau. The wife of a frontline soldier. Her name is merely something to which she answers.

Following the pattern of the threadbare runner, she mounts the stairs to the mezzanine, which overlooks the horseshoe shape of the central auditorium. Sometimes the whores escort their customers up there for their transactions. It's more private, and the ushers never seem to mind. They're likely hoping for a tip. Sigrid has learned to pay them no heed. She, too, counts on the balcony's sparse population during matinees.

Discovering that the old uncle in the usher's uniform has found a spot for a nap in a seat by the door, she ignores the number on her ticket and takes a seat in the last row against the wall. This is the seat of her memory.

The first winter of the war was bitterly cold. The most frigid temperatures in decades gripped the city. In January, thermometers plummeted to minus twenty degrees, and people joked grimly that Berlin had been traded for Siberia in the nonaggression pact with the Soviets. But by the end of the month, humor was running thin, even in Berlin, along with the coal supply. It was the sort of cold that followed you inside, that searched your clothes for gaps and penetrated you slowly, until it crept into your heart and chilled your blood.

In the bedroom, she would huddle for warmth with her husband, but when her hand ventured to explore the territory below his waist, he would shrug away her touch. "Sigrid, please. I have a long day ahead of me tomorrow" was his usual response. Afterward, she would stare through the frigid darkness above their bed until sleep smothered her.

"Is it because of the miscarriage?" she finally asked him one night.

"I must get my sleep, Sigrid," was his eventual reply. "And so must you. We'll talk about this later."

But of course they never did. Since the war had started in Poland, Kaspar's work hours had been extended at the bank, and he had become moody and silent. Several men of the staff had already been called up, and he was sure that his turn would come soon. Sigrid tried to picture him in uniform, with a rifle in his hands, but the picture seemed too absurd. He was nearly thirty-five. Surely there were plenty of younger men the army would prefer. And though this rarely happened, Kaspar's mother agreed with her. "You have important duties to fulfill at the bank," the old woman declared confidently. "The government understands that we must keep some of our best men at home in order to keep things running." At which point Kaspar would observe them both from an interior distance, and politely request more coffee in his cup.

The teaser curtain rings open, and the lights dissolve. Sigrid removes her scarf. The show begins with footage of a military chorus launching into the "Horst Wessel Lied." A jumble of voices rises in response from the auditorium. Audience members are encouraged to join in the singing of patriotic songs. That's what the sign in the lobby reads, but with no one around to report her, Sigrid remains silent. After the numbing shock of the Sixth Army's defeat at Stalingrad—an army that had smashed through France only a few years before—the Party's been engineering an upswing of patriotic fervor. More flags, more slogans, more posters smothering the walls. But under the surface, an acidic dread is eating away at the official convictions concerning victory. In the first week of February, regular radio broadcasting had been suddenly preempted by a Wagnerian funeral march. Reichsmarschall Goering made a solemn announcement from the Air Ministry. The men of the Sixth Army were said to have fought to the last bullet. A few weeks later Goebbels broadcast from the Sportspalast, and declared that the only answer to their sacrifice was Total War. *I ask you: Do you want total war? If necessary, do you want a war more total and radical than anything that we can even yet imagine?* The audience in the Sportspalast roared with frenzied ardor. But most Berliners responded with bewildered silence. Stalingrad was supposed to have been the greatest victory for the Wehrmacht since the fall of Paris. The Red Army on the Volga was reported to be in tatters. How then could this have *happened*? Three hundred thousand German men dead or taken prisoner. *How did it happen?* A question often posed in a whisper but left unanswered.

A panic of newsreel images shutters across the screen: troops leaping over shell craters, a tank crushing a stone wall. The onslaught toward victory in the East continues, at least in the movie houses. She breathes in solemnly. Kaspar is there now. He was conscripted two months before the *Aufmarsch* into Russia, and is now stalled somewhere to the south of Moscow with a few hundred thousand other German husbands. She thinks about him nightly as she goes to sleep. Fears that he is suffering in the elements, but cannot quite wish him in the bed beside her. Does that make *her* as cold as the Russian winter? Maybe just her heart, she thinks.

A flamethrower belches a stream of burning oil. A chorus of rockets squeals into the smoke–encrusted air. A heavy machine gun rattles. But Sigrid closes her eyes to all of it. She craves this square of darkness like an addict. Only sleep offers her such sanctuary from the present world. Alone in the darkness, she reopens the past, and returns to the instant before Egon had spoken his first words to her.

Listen to this, she hears him say from the empty seat beside her, though she knows it is only a whisper of memory.

The mezzanine had been an icebox that day, but the simple sight of this man who was not her husband had drawn her toward him not her husband, as if she had just found an unexpected source of heat. He was sleekly barbered and wearing a cashmere coat with the collar turned up, striking a dandyish note that was incongruous with the rawness he exuded. Something in his expression was unruly, and his posture was defined by a confident animal brawn.

She had come to the cinema to find an empty space in the day. War movies were best, because attendance was usually weak, so she had bought a ticket for the matinee of *Battle Group Danzig*, in order to find a crevice of solitude. To find a fissure in her concrete routine, where she could escape the racket of office typewriters. Escape the noise of her mother-in-law's complaints and the wordless criticisms of her husband's glances.

The house lights were still up. She couldn't help but steal a look at the man as he brooded over a copy of the *Morgenpost*. He looked out of place, but intentionally so. A premeditated outsider. Is that what had prompted her to disregard the number on her ticket and choose a spot only two seats away from his? His eyes had captured and then released her. Then nothing. Only the newspaper claimed his interest as she adjusted her scarf and settled herself in the seat, trying to build her walls out of the empty space. A stout Berliner occupied a seat at the front of the balcony, his hat clamped down over his ears as he stared in obedient anticipation at the curtained screen. She inhaled the tang of smoke from the projector operator's cigarette above her head. Beside her, the man who was not her husband grunted to himself and turned a page in his newspaper. She found that she, too, was sitting in obedient anticipation, her palms clammy. Was she expecting something? There were many reasons why she should not be planting herself so close to a stranger. Any number of reasons, not the least of which was that she had just made some small effort to conceal her wedding band in the way she folded her hands. A thin, unadorned ring of electroplated gold on the third finger of her right hand. As unadorned as the marriage itself.

"Listen to this," she heard the man say suddenly, without preamble, without introduction, as if they had been in the midst of a conversation. His voice was deep, as if scraped from the rock of a cave. "'Physician of true German stock, fifty-seven years old and a veteran of the Cameroon campaigns, fervently desires marital union with a modest and frugal Aryan female, who is strong and healthy, blessed with broad hips for childbearing, and who is repulsed by nicotine and cosmetics.' My God, now, *there's* a catch," he said, and grinned, showing her his smile for the very first time. "Don't tell me you're not tempted."

"No, I think not," Sigrid replied, even though she knew she shouldn't be answering. Even though she had no business doing so. "I'm afraid I once owned a tube of lipstick."

"Well, *this one*, then. I know *this one* will set your heart pounding. 'Aryan widower of property, age sixty-two, wishes male progeny through matrimony with a young, fertile Aryan mate, in order to preserve an old family name from extinction.' There you have it. An old family name, yours for the taking." He read on. This old man and that old man searching for pure-blooded Aryan bedmates, but Sigrid was not fully listening. Instead, she was watching the slight twitch in his jawline as he spoke. A thin tremble of muscle that she felt repeated as a shiver beneath her skin.

He smiled again, but this time with scrutiny. He gave her his surname, which she would soon learn was false. "But I insist you call me by my forename. Egon," said the man who was not her husband, offering his hand. "I know that I am a terribly rude man, interrupting your privacy this way. But I hope you'll forgive me. I saw your face, and I simply had to hear the sound of your voice."

She glanced at the outstretched hand, as if she might ignore it, but the smile was too much. Open. Easy. Carnivorous. Even more appealing for its sharp splinter of pain. She took his hand. It was warm, and she felt the strength of his grip. "So now you have heard it," she said.

That same day he took her to a café that smelled of boiled sugar, balsam oil, and pipe smoke. It was a small place in the Savignyplatz with leaded casement windows where she could hear the clank of the S-Bahn trains as they passed. He bought her coffee and an apple torte, and amused her by eating most of it himself. But mostly what he did was listen to her as she bounced from topic to topic, with anxious release. Small topics, which turned into larger ones. Peeling potatoes for supper turned into the stagnation she felt living under her mother-in-law's roof. A memory of her father's love for fancy cakes turned into his desertion and the emptiness she felt at her mother's deathbed. She would suddenly become aware of how much she was talking and apologize, but the depth of his eyes encouraged her to continue. When she realized how late it was, she became flustered. But again he only smiled, crushed out one of the many cigarettes he had smoked, and paid the bill. That night she could not forget his eyes. Could not forget their easy desire, their brute intelligence. Even as she lay beside Kaspar in their bed with the clunking mattress springs, she felt as if Egon was still watching her.

Two days later, she bought a ticket to *Aces of the Sea*. He met her in the lobby. She extended her hand, and he took it, but kissed her cheek. Briefly, but with intention. Up in the mezzanine, sitting beside him, she found that she did not dare look into his face. The teaser divided, and the silvered images stormed onto the screen with an edge of static. She stared dutifully at the screen as the Ufa newsreel erupted with a blare of trumpets. Footage of artillery caissons and tanks. Polish army prisoners formed a soup line inside a fenced-in pasture. Gangs of old Warsaw Jews with bristling beards were paraded in front of the camera. They gazed out from the screen, blinking with anxiety. When the movie began, she stared straight ahead at it. But to her the heroics of the submarine fleet in the North Atlantic were nothing but a distraction of noise and flicker. Her eyes shifted furtively to the periphery, her mind now bent on the man who was not her husband, whose hand she felt suddenly touch her face.

The first time he kissed her on the mouth, she shoved him away. The second time he kissed her on the mouth, she kissed him back. The theater was dark. On the screen a U-boat captain sighted a freighter through his periscope as Egon calmly guided her hand to the center of his trousers.

"Do you feel that?" he whispered.

"Yes."

"Then you know what it's for."

Her memory, at that instant, is disrupted by an intrusion. Some piece of the present forcing itself into her consciousness. She is aware that someone has filled the seat beside her, though she does not immediately open her eyes. It's a problem these days. A woman by herself. Soldiers off duty. Usually it's nothing much to rebuff them. A few pointed words, and if words don't work, she's started carrying a fish knife. She makes an attempt to hold on to the heat of the past, but when she hears the girl's pressured whisper, her eyes snap open.

"Please say that we came here together."

"What?" Sigrid blinks.

"Please, Frau Schröder. Say we came here together. That we've both been here since the beginning of the film."

It's Frau Granzinger's duty-year girl. What is her *name*? A thin, long-limbed specimen with an oval face and soot black hair under a wool beret. Her eyes are so overtly charged that they give off an electrical shock. Sigrid starts to speak, but something prevents her. Maybe it's the sight of the two men marching around the horseshoe of the auditorium below, their electric torches slicing up the darkness of the aisle. Several members of the audience complain when the beams hit them in the face, till one of the men shouts, "Sicherheitspolizei! Lights up!"

A grumble broadens across the theater as the house lights are raised and the film shudders to a halt, but it quickly dies when the men start checking papers.

The door to the balcony opens and a figure enters. Inside the borders of the Reich, the security police wear plain clothes. In this case, a long khaki raincoat and a slouch hat. He wakes the sleeping usher unceremoniously, and the old man staggers to his feet, spluttering, "Yes, Herr Kriminal-Kommissar," and "No, Herr Kriminal-Kommissar." The Sipo man dismisses him with a wave and examines the papers of a young Fräulein who had been necking with her boyfriend, a callow Luftwaffe Flakhelfer. "What's this *about*?" the Flakhelfer demands to know, in order to exhibit his bravery in uniform, but the Sipo man simply ignores him, and the boy's bravery ends there. A glance down, and then a glance up, and the Herr Kommissar heads straight for the row where Sigrid and the girl are installed. Sigrid feels the girl grasp her hand tightly, but breaks the grip. "Take this," she whispers, pressing her ticket stub on the girl. "*Quickly*. Put it into your pocket."

GEHEIME STAATSPOLIZEI.

That's what's stamped on the small aluminum warrant disk hanging from a chain. It's what all agents of the Gestapo carry. The man allows it to dangle over his fingers just long enough for its meaning to sink in, and then flips it back into his palm. He has a hard jaw, and not unhandsome features, but there is a kind of animal fatigue entrenched in his face. A sleeplessness in his eyes, as if they have been burned open. "Papers," he says, talking to the girl first. She says nothing but digs out her identification from her shoulder bag and hands it over. The man squints at it. Does not hand it back. "Papers," he says to Sigrid, extending an open hand.

Sigrid swallows as she opens her bag. Once, on an electric tram going up the Friedrichstrasse, it took her three minutes to find her identification in order to satisfy some glowering police sergeant. It was the longest three minutes of her life. But this time she has no trouble. Her identity booklet has become slightly dog-eared from overuse. When she hands it over, she makes sure that she touches the Herr Kommissar's finger with her own. Just a graze of contact, but enough to elicit the snap of a glance from the man, before he trains his attention on her photograph stapled to the gray cardboard. "Frau Schröder."

"Yes," Sigrid confirms.

"You know this young female?" he asks with a nod toward the girl wedged in beside her.

Does she hesitate? She seems to hear the words before she realizes that she is speaking them. "Yes. She's serving her duty year with my downstairs neighbor."

"Her duty year?"

"Surely you're aware, Herr Kommissar, of the requirements for youth these days? She's found work as a domestic, caring for the children of a mother of six. A recipient of the Mother's Cross."

"Really? How commendable," the man replies flatly. "And I suppose that the two of you have been sitting here since the beginning of the film?"

"We have," Sigrid replies simply.

"And the ticket window will recall selling you your tickets together?"

"We purchased our tickets separately, Herr Kommissar. She paid for hers, I for mine. I can't tell you what the ticket window will or will not recall about it."

A frown shadows the Sipo man's face. Then he looks down at the girl. "May I see your ticket stub, please? Fräulein?" His voice is not polite.

But the girl does not blink. She removes Sigrid's ticket stub from her pocket and hands it over. He examines it without altering the shape of his frown, and checks it against the number of the next empty seat. "Frau Schröder," he says to Sigrid without expression, "this young lady is in the wrong seat."

"Is she?" Sigrid responds innocently. "Well, to be truthful, Herr Kommissar, we preferred these seats in the rear rather than those down front, so we could chat and not disturb anyone. I know it's against the rules, but we women do like to chat, so we moved." She gives a lightly pleasant shrug. "Is that the crime you're investigating, Herr Kommissar?" she inquires. "Shall we move back down to our original seats?"

His eyes lock onto hers, and she knows she must hold his gaze without hesitation.

"Tell me, Frau Schröder," the Sipo man begins, with only the barest edge to his voice. "What is this young woman's name?"

Sigrid does not budge. "Her name?"

"Yes." He nods. "She works for your neighbor. You've come to see a film together. Surely you know her name."

Sigrid's mind speeds back to Frau Granzinger's introduction of the girl on the stairs of their apartment block. There *must* be a name stuck somewhere in her head.

"Frau Schröder?" the Sipo man prompts.

"Fräulein Kohl," she announces. The name pops out of her mouth.

The Herr Kommissar's eyes flick up from the girl's identity card, still in his hand. A muscle in his jawline grows taut as calculations are made behind his eyes. "And her given name?"

"I'm sure I don't know," Sigrid answers. "Child, what is your given name?"

"Ericha," the girl replies tersely.

"*Ericha,* Herr Kommissar," Sigrid informs the man. "To answer your question."

A pause. Again the calculations are made behind the shield of his gaze. Another plainclothes man swings open the balcony door. When the Herr Kommissar looks at him, the fellow shrugs loosely. No luck. The Sipo man's frown gains definition for a moment. But then he swallows a breath. Sigrid feels the painful force of his eyes for only an instant before he hands back their papers. "Enjoy the show, ladies," he tells them, and then marches from the balcony with his man trailing.

Sigrid exhales deeply. She realizes that even in the drafty theater, she is clammy with sweat. This time it's she who clenches the girl's hand, and it is the girl who breaks away.

"Thank you," the Fräulein says, as if the words might choke her if she does not dislodge them quickly.

"Don't thank me," Sigrid informs her.

"No, I must."

"Actually, what you *must* do is tell me what this is about."

"I'm sorry, but that is what I *cannot* do."

"No? I stick out my neck, and then I can't ask why?"

"I won't impose any further, Frau Schröder. Once the film starts up, I'll leave you to your solitude."

"Oh, you *will*? You'll leave me to my *solitude*? That's a very thick word from someone who doesn't know me from a lamppost."

The girl adjusts the strap of her shoulder bag, as if preparing for sudden departure. "I can tell about people."

"Tell?"

"What they're like. On the inside." She shrugs. "I've seen how you are. Around the apartment block. You hold yourself in. You hold yourself apart."

Sigrid absorbs a mild wave of dismay. "Ah. So you're a Gypsy, I suppose? You have the Menschenkenntnis." This is meant as sarcasm, but the girl gives her a close look before facing the screen.

"I have certain instincts. Call them what you wish, but I'm usually right," she says. "At least, I was right about you."

"Don't be too sure. I might decide to call the Herr Kommissar back at any second and recant."

But now the girl only smiles. "I thought I was going to pee myself when he asked you my name."

Sigrid lifts her eyebrows at this remark. "Yes, well. It's a good thing for you that I have my father's memory for such things." At that moment the house lights darken and the projector rattles back to life. The images on the screen return after a bright flicker. "I'll be going now," the girl whispers, but before she can rise, Sigrid clamps a hand over her arm. "You'll do nothing of the kind. Do you actually think that the Herr Kommissar and his comrades are done? They'll be standing outside the theater right now, just to see who comes bolting out of the door. No. Whatever this is about—and I'm not *asking*, mind you— but whatever this is about, you will sit here with me for the duration of this film. You will be properly inspired by the heroic effort of the Hitler Youth Battalion No. 47 to work a field radio. And then you and I will take our leave and catch the next Elektrische down the Uhlandstrasse to our building, where, if you have any sense, you will do your chores, have your supper, and go straight to bed. Is that understood?"

The girl looks like she might argue, but then doesn't. Both of them turn their faces to the screen, and stare at it in silence. Hitler Youth boys crawling on their bellies with wooden rifles. Sigrid shakes her head at herself. Her grandmother had always clucked at her for being too impulsive. Too rash. "Unbesonnen" was the word she used. A person easily seduced by the thrill of reckless behavior. "Just like your mother," the old lady would declare with resignation. Her Grossmutter did not dispense compliments, and Sigrid had always taken it as an unfair scold. But, sitting in the mezzanine of this disheveled cinema, having just rescued this sooty-haired girl from the Gestapo's attention, she cannot deny the pulse of exhilaration she feels at her unbesonnen behavior.

The film ends with the predictable salvo of martial music. The lights go up halfway. Everyone stumbles listlessly out of the exits, emerging into the thickening afternoon light. Sigrid looks across the street at the Gestapo Kommissar and his men standing around a large black sedan. He lights a cigarette, and the light colors his face as he cups the match. One of his men says something to a pair of uniformed Ordnungspolizei officers who have joined them. It must be a joke, because the Orpo men laugh. Ericha takes Sigrid's arm as if to prompt her forward. "We should go," she says firmly, "or we'll miss the tram."

By the time they have traveled down the Uhlandstrasse, the light is failing, the sky has gained an edge of slate blue, and the streets have darkened. On the No. 14 Elektrische tram the ghost light glows green. They don't speak as the tram rumbles down its track, but sit, sharing silence with the rest of the passengers. The greenish air raid lamps have turned the windows into sickly mirrors, but Sigrid avoids her reflection. Only after they disembark and the tram makes the circle toward Schöneberg does she finally ask, "How did you know to find me in the cinema?"

The girl wraps her coat tightly around her body. Sigrid notes that it's missing buttons. "I was waiting across the street," she replies. "I happened to see you go in. It was luck, really. Just luck."

"And who were you waiting for?"

"Someone."

"A man, I suppose."

Ericha hesitates for no more than a breath. "Yes."

"But he didn't show."

"He did not."

Sigrid suddenly stops. "Is this how it's going to continue? Me dragging out every word from you?"

Ericha turns and looks at her but does not answer.

"Don't you think that I am owed some sort of explanation?'

"Owed?" Ericha repeats, as if the word is foreign.

"*Owed*. I put myself in danger on your behalf this evening, without knowing a single reason why I should."

The girl nods. "Because that is your nature."

Sigrid sighs, exasperated. "So you know me so well from nodding to me in the stairwell. How is that again? Ah, yes. Because of your second sight," Sigrid says caustically. "You can read people's minds. Fine. I can't. You must give me an explanation. Tell me what you were *doing*."

But the girl only smiles with regret. "My business is not your business, Frau Schröder. Besides, even if I told you, it would only be a lie. You must trust me in this matter," she assures Sigrid. "The truth is not something that you want to hear."

TWO

T HE NO. 8 T-LINE BUS lumbers south, stuffy with people on their
way home from work. A middle-aged Bürger reluctantly surrenders his seat to Sigrid, and she sits with a cursory nod of gratitude,
quickly walling herself off from the busload of her fellow Berliners. At
the patent office they make a joke about her. She is an unassailable bas-
tion they say, calling her Fortress Schröder just loudly enough so that
she must pretend not to hear them.

Staring at nothing as the gray day sinks into a purple evening, her
eyes look past her reflection in the window glass to the curious patch-
work of bombing damage along the bus's route. Windows boarded over
and bricks blackened in spots, but the buildings still occupied. A vacant
lot where the remains of a block of flats had been pulled down. The
British Royal Air Force had made a target of Berlin the year before. The
newsreels had shown rescue crews digging survivors from the rubble,
but not the bodies they had also dug out. Sigrid remembers the sight
of the dead laid out like bales of rags on the sidewalk. She closes her
eyes to the street. Sometimes she envies the blind man with his black
goggles. There's so much he does not have to see.

By the time she climbs down from the bus, the twilight is drowning the streets, darkening the granite façade of Uhlandstrasse 11. It's

a narrow, middle-class apartment block of the sort that's common to the district. Her husband had grown up on the fourth floor, 11G. Even now the flat remains in her mother-in-law's name. Living here had started out as a temporary arrangement to "economize" after Kaspar married her, but that was eight years ago. The smell of boiled cabbage ambushes Sigrid as she steps into the tiled, hexagonal foyer. The first time she had entered the building was on her wedding day. Kaspar and she had been married at the registry office in Berlin-Mitte, then took the U-Bahn to the Uhlandstrasse, with Kaspar toting the entirety of her life's possessions contained in two rather worn suitcases. Ahead of her on the steps, he set the cases down on the well-scrubbed granite landing and opened the door to the foyer with a comic élan, then turned and, without warning, lifted her off her feet, causing her to squawk with surprise. "Kaspar, what are you *doing*?"

"It is the husband's job to carry his bride over the threshold of their new home," he answered, smiling. "Don't you know?"

But when he crossed the foyer with Sigrid in his arms, and was suddenly faced with the multiple flights of stairs ascending farther and farther upward, he paused gravely. Sigrid laughed. "Well, go on," she prompted. "What's keeping you, husband? It's only a few stairs."

"I thought this building had a lift."

"Did you? How? You grew up here."

"Yes, and I always imagined a lift."

She laughed again contently. "Then put me down, put me down," she said, smiling. "Carrying one's bride across the threshold of the foyer will quite suffice for German common law, I'm sure." When her feet touched the floor again, her arms were still hung around his neck, and she kissed him. He smiled back at her. Though she could tell that the kiss in a public area had made him uncomfortable. "Go," she commanded lightly. "Go, husband. If you want to carry something, then carry your bride's luggage over the threshold."

She remembers watching him take up her bags with gallant

obedience and climb the stairs with them. It was a feeling she so seldom experienced in her life. A feeling of home. Of coming home after a long journey. And here was her husband, taking up her bags. In that instant, she decided that she *had*, in fact, made the correct decision by marrying Kaspar Schröder. And that she was so relieved, so very relieved, that she would *no longer* have to live on her passion alone, as her mother had done. She would, instead, have all the things her mother disdained. A clean floor swept by her own hand, good bone china, a good German kitchen, a meaningful but uncomplicated routine, and a man in her bed to share the simple intimacies at the end of the day, without heartache, without the squalid Sturm und Drang.

What a relief it was.

Eight years later, as Sigrid steps in and shakes raindrops from her scarf, the stingy foyer is dank as a pit, its tile hexagon disintegrating at the edges. On the wall, the official notice board, maintained by Portierfrau Mundt, is festooned with bulletins from the Reich Rationing Office, the Reich Medical Office, the Security and Aid Service, the Air Defense League, the Winter Relief Fund, and the Social Insurance Bureau. Sigrid ignores them as always, and starts up the grueling helix of stairs to the top floor, passing the buckets of sand and water at each landing, just in case a British phosphorus stick someday finds a home on the roof.

At the door to 11G, she heaves a sigh and turns her key in the lock. Entering the flat, she is met by the smell of coal smoke. Her mother-in-law must have just lit the coke stove. Just enough briquettes fed into its belly to make it through the evening with a draft of heat. Sigrid removes her coat and scarf. The short entrance hall leads into an incommodious box kitchen. Then come three rooms and one bath barely large enough to fit the cast-iron tub. Newsprint is stuffed between the double-hung windows to deaden the buffeting winds gusting in from the lake districts, and the window glass is taped up against bombings.

"Mother Schröder?" she calls out, smelling the old woman's bitter cigarettes. Her mother-in-law appears from the kitchen, toting an iron tureen with pot holders. "You're late," the old lady declares. Even after all these years, she still uses the formal address with her. "Next time, I'll start without you, and you can scrape out what's left."

Stuck into a chair at the table, she listens to her mother-in-law grouse about a downstairs neighbor. It's hard to separate the incessant noise of her complaints from the incessant burble of the cheap Volksempfänger wireless in the next room. "You'd think the Luftwaffe has won the war for us single-handedly to hear her tell it," the old lady grumbles. "And all because that *boy* of hers, who barely has the brains to blow his nose, somehow learned to work an airplane." Mother Schröder's face is gaunt, well chiseled. Her hair once blond, now wintry white in its helmet of hairpins, her eyes hot as stoves. "You know, I tried to convince Kaspar to sign up for the Luftwaffe before he was conscripted. He could have had a position with the Air Ministry right here in town, I'm sure of it. A man of his abilities. But, of course, men do not listen to women," she declares with remorse, the lines around her mouth deepening. "He could have been making a true contribution to the war effort with his intellect. But instead what do they have him doing? Marching with a rifle. As if there aren't a hundred other men, less gifted, who couldn't be doing that in his place." She clucks over the foolishness of it all, and then gives Sigrid a look. "You're not eating."

"I don't have much of an appetite."

Another look. "We don't waste food. It's immoral. Not to mention illegal."

"I'm not wasting it. I'll put it in my thermos. It'll keep until tomorrow," Sigrid says as she stands and lifts her bowl from the table. "But if you think I've transgressed, feel free to ring up the authorities. I'm sure you can get a job at a ball-bearing plant after they haul me away for soup crimes."

"Of course. *Disrespect.* That's all you ever have to offer." Her mother-in-law shakes her head in resignation. She removes one of her acrid cigarettes from a packet beside her soup bowl. But as she lights it up with a spirit lighter, the wireless snags her attention. "*Ah.* This is a new song," she announces. And for a moment, the old woman's expression lightens its starch. She fingers the notes in the air, and hums tunelessly along with the radio songstress. *Sing, nightingale, sing—a song from the old days—touch my weary heart.* Until the broadcast cuts out with a spurt of static and is replaced by a sharp, syncopated beep. Quickly Sigrid is up and tuning the dial on the wireless, until she catches the strident warning voice of the Flaksender announcer. *A large force of enemy bombers has entered the territory of the Reich, on course for grid square G/H. To repeat: Enemy bombers currently on course for grid square G/H, Gustav/Heinrich.*

It's the signal that the British bombers have crossed the line into the Mark Brandenburg, and are coming for Berlin.

Sigrid gazes bleakly at the wireless, but Mother Schröder is already bustling about, firing off orders. "Turn off the gas line, and see to the fuse box, daughter-in-law. And the *blankets.* Don't forget the blankets. I'm sure those dreadful benches haven't gotten any softer on the backside."

THE TENANTS PACK themselves into the cellar with grumbles and rubber-stamped frowns, but without any embarrassing panic. They have learned to soldier through the routine. They are armed with their air raid bags, their Volksgasmasken, their water jugs, and heavy blankets. They pick up the same vinegary prattle, as if they had left it behind during the last raid, but it's easy to tell from their faces that the return of the bombers in strength after so many months has soured their stomachs. This is not supposed to be happening. They have been *assured* by the proper authorities that Berlin's air defense rings have now been so well armored that they are simply impenetrable. So how *is it,* then, that the British Air Gangsters have regained such traction in the skies? It's an unanswered question that hangs in the cellar air like the stink of mildewed sandbags and mice droppings.

Sigrid is impatient for the bombers to come. To finish their business and allow her to be on her way. Around her, the tenants hem her in with their stale bodies, their stale complaints. If she hates the Tommies at all, it is because they have forced her down into this goddamned hole again. A wail from Frau Granzinger's infant closes in on her. Trapped. How did she ever become so trapped?

To her left, her mother-in-law is darning the toe of a stocking while griping to a trio of her kaffeeklatsch women about a recent injustice. A rude grocery clerk or a shop girl's poor grammar. Some damned thing. Even as they are squeezed into this dank basement, awaiting the onslaught of the British bombers, the old lady can't manage to shut off her spout. Her cronies nod in frowning agreement with baggy chins as they tend to the mending in their laps. They cluck their tongues in sympathy and bite off loose threads.

Sigrid turns inward. Certainly she no longer thinks of the future, because every day the future proves itself to be a duplicate of the present. So instead she roots through the past. She spots him for a moment in the corner of her mind. Not on their last day together, in a sweaty flat in Little Wedding. But on their first day. His voice preserved in her head.

Do you feel that? he said.

Yes.

Then you know what it's for.

The dangling light in the cellar flickers, then dims, a signal that the main event is coming closer, but no one comments. It's said that air raid shelters develop their own personalities. Some timorous, some fatalistic, some raucous, some prone to panic. It's a tough crowd in the bottom of 11 Uhlandstrasse. No raid hysterics here. Someone has tacked up a sign: CRYING FORBIDDEN. Across the room, Frau Mundt's husband offers Sigrid a lascivious wink as he chews the stem of his pipe. The Herr Hausleiter Mundt. He is the porter and the Party's Hausobman for the building. An Old Fighter who once a month dresses up in his dun brown Sturmabteilung getup and cycles off to get soused with his chums at the local SA beer hall. He's set up a game of Skat on a card table with a pair of his drinking cohorts. In the event that a bomb comes through the roof, their job is to sledgehammer the layer of bricks that opens up an escape route into the next building. They grunt and spit tobacco and chortle, and scratch their rumps, but they're relatively harmless. The real danger is the Hausleiter's *wife*. The Portierfrau Mundt. It's *her* connections to the Party that count, not the old man's. She has caught her husband's wink in Sigrid's direction, and now scrutinizes Sigrid with flinty, unforgiving eyes.

Sigrid turns her head away. To her right, the eternally harried Frau Granzinger struggles with the youngest members of her brood. One who fidgets and one who fusses. The infant in her arms is only a peanut, and the rest are squirming in this dank cellar, mad for attention with only one mummy to share. The woman scolds and coos at them in succession.

Sigrid thinks of the touch of his hand on her skin under her clothes. The mad connection of their bodies. *Wait, not yet, not yet*, his words burning in her ear. His pulse invading her. *Not until I tell you.*

She tasted blood as she bit his lip, her skirt hiked up, his mouth burrowing into her neck, his hands searching, traveling under her blouse. She had no resistance to offer, only her own need, only her own rage, like that of an animal out of its cage. The film projector muttering mechanically above them, beaming sterile, blue-white light. The old man at the mezzanine rail had turned his head to stare at them. A piece of silk ripped, and her back arched. He entered her, one nylon-clad leg hooked around his thigh, his trousers sagging to his knees as he thumped into her, pounding her against the velour cinema seat. She gazed blindly at the silvered dance of images on the screen. She begged him, commanded him, her mouth raw with demands. But then her words broke up and there was nothing but the shrieking inside her, which she bit her own knuckle to contain.

Near the door to the cellar, Frau Remki coughs coarsely, and the Portierfrau Mundt makes a performance of shielding herself from contamination by germs, or perhaps from the contamination by Frau Remki herself. The old lady is Sigrid's fourth-floor neighbor. Once Hildegard Remki was the queen of the block. Her husband was a dentist, and she could afford mink fur collars and luncheons once a month at the Hotel Adlon, along with new shoes and a private tutor for her son, Anno, to learn the piano. When it was her turn to act as hostess for the kaffeeklatsch, it was always with the English sterling coffee service, and the Meissen porcelain. Even Mother Schröder deferred to her taste in chanson singers on the radio. *Don't you really find, Petronela, that Marika Rökk has the superior vocal cords? I know you're fond of that Swedish woman, but don't you really agree?* But all that changed when her husband was thrown out of his practice because he was a Social Democrat. When he died, suicide was rumored. And then Anno was conscripted into the army and killed in the Balkans. Now Frau Remki is the block's pariah. Thin and threadbare as a ghost, she wears only mourning black. Looking into her eyes is like staring through the windows of a bombed-out building.

More screaming from Frau Granzinger's hobgoblins. In a jealous effort to displace the smaller creature from the coveted position on its mother's lap, the larger one, with the piglet's nose, has started to bawl with a forcible vengeance and pinch its mother's arm repeatedly. The harried Frau Granzinger attempts to combat the attack by increasing the volume of her scolding, but it's a losing battle. She quite suddenly capitulates, and shovels the crying infant over to Sigrid with a beleaguered appeal. "Please, Frau Schröder. Take the baby, won't you?" And before she can refuse, Sigrid is holding the child as if it were a time-fused bomb that has dropped through the ceiling. She feels the unaccustomed weight of the squirming baby, feels the sticky pressure of the gazes of the cellar's denizens as the infant begins to wail in earnest. She coos ineffectively and tries to readjust her hold, but to no avail. The child's crying is like an air raid siren. Only her mother-in-law's intervention ends the ordeal. *"Tsst,"* the old woman clucks caustically as she drops her sewing into her basket in exasperation. "For pity's sake, hand her to *me*," she commands, and plucks the child from her daughter-in-law's grasp. "Honestly, there are times when I think it's a *blessing* you never had a child of your own. It's obvious that you don't have a *whit* of maternal instinct," she announces.

And there it is. The dirty truth out in the open for all to know, like soiled linen hung from the windows. Sigrid clutches the strap of her air raid sack, feeling her face heat even in the cold. "Yes. Quite a blessing," she agrees, glaring at the whiteness of her knuckles.

Her mother-in-law, however, carries on, oblivious. The baby has calmed immediately in her no-nonsense grip. "I see your new duty-year girl has gone missing again. What is she up to this time?" she demands curiously of Frau Granzinger. Sigrid shifts her eyes to see Granzinger grimace, then wave off the thought. *"Don't ask,"* she groans. "It's too ridiculous."

"Don't tell me," the multiple-chinned Marta Trotzmüller chimes in mischievously "Don't tell me that she's got a bun in the oven *already*?" Granzinger's previous girl turned up pregnant by an SS man from a Death's Head Company, and was whisked off to a Fount of Life home in the Harz Mountains.

"Who knows *what* she does." Granzinger sighs. "You know, in the beginning she wasn't so bad. A little moody, perhaps. A little mürrisch, but at least competent in her work. She could change the baby's diaper without fuss, and wash a dish without leaving bits of schmutz along the edges like the last one did. And she could manage bedtime without argument or tears. So I thought maybe finally I've had some luck. But then suddenly she starts to evaporate. I send her out with the shopping bags, and she disappears for hours, and comes back with no explanation. The queues were long, is all she says. The trains were slow. That's all. And when I raise the roof about it, she just stares. It's really too incredible. I hardly see the creature," Granzinger complains, perfecting her frown. "Except at supper, of course. She always manages to find her way to the supper table."

"Maybe she has *better* things to do than change diapers," Marta Trotzmüller suggests with ladled nuance, but the joke is wearing thin.

Frau Granzinger only shrugs. "I suppose she thinks so. But I swear, when I was her age, I would never have *thought* of disobeying my elders. It simply would not have crossed my mind."

"You should get rid of her. *Complain*," Mother Schröder insists. "For God's sake, Lotti, they awarded you the Mother's Cross. You shouldn't have to put up with such insults."

"Yes," Marta Trotzmüller agrees fervently. "That's right! An insult. That's what it is, all right. You should complain to the Labor Service officer."

"Exactly so," Mother Schröder agrees, as if it is all too obvious. "If looking after your children doesn't interest her, perhaps she'd prefer a year in the Land Army. Have them stick a pitchfork in her hands and let her muck out a stable before she sits down to the supper table," she insists. "That'll cool her engines considerably, I'll wager."

Sigrid thinks of the girl occupying the seat bedside her in the cinema. *Please, Frau Schröder. Say we came here together.* Oddly, she has some inclination to defend the girl from this onslaught from the kaffeeklatsch. The same inclination, perhaps, that has caused her to tell a lie to a security policeman. A stranger's impulse to step in and protect a child from a bully? Perhaps, in the end, she thinks, that's all it was.

Talk in the cellar abruptly dies at the eruption of the Luftwaffe's air defense guns. Even at this distance, the arsenal of cannons and pom-poms mounted atop the gargantuan Zoo Flak Tower causes a tremble in her heart when unleashed. It is the signal that the RAF bombers have arrived. The dangling cellar light quakes. Faces turn upward to the rafters as the carpet of thunder unrolls.

"Wellingtons," one of the old farts announces with a scowl. As if he can tell the difference between the engine of a Wellington bomber and a beer belch, or between a sack of sand and his great fat ass. But whatever they are, Wellingtons or no, they are close. Beside Sigrid, Mother Schröder clicks her tongue mechanically at the fretting baby as the whistling begins.

It's said that if you can hear a bomb whistle, then you're safe. It's the bomb you don't hear that rips the roof from your building, pulverizes the walls, and buries you alive in a heap of smoldering slag. Still, the whistling builds up inside you like a scream. You can't help but hold your breath.

Sigrid winces as the first explosion shudders through the cellar and the children's wailing builds in pitch. Fingers of dust filter down from the rafters. People cough and snort. The overhead lamp sways. More bombs fall. More whistling and more bombs and more dust. This is how time passes. Who knows how long? Minutes? Hours? Then, with a deafening thunderclap, the lights black out, and even this tough crowd bellows, because, for a heartbeat, the darkness is solid. Death, Sigrid thinks. This is death. This is how death comes. But then the lamp flickers back to life. Its weak, swaying bulb illuminates the baldly stunned faces. They glare at one another, blinking through the cascades of dust, bewildered, perhaps, by the fact that they are still in one piece. "Well, that was a close shave," someone observes with a laugh. "Such jokers they are, those Tommies and their bombs." But the banter stops when the Portierfrau Mundt gives an angry squawk. "Curse that devil Churchill!" she declares. "May he rot in his grave before this war is over!" Typical Mundt performance. And everyone replies with the silence of a well-trained audience. Until a boney black rage rears up from the bench beside the door.

"Churchill? *Churchill?*" the voice echoes incredulously. "Never mind *Churchill*. Curse that devil *Hitler*! *He's* the one responsible!" All eyes snap to the rising black-clad figure of Frau Remki. She shakes her skinny fist, her narrow face pinched with rage and ruinous grief. "*He's* the one who's murdered my boy with his war lust! My son! *Gone!*" she cries. Eyes as wild as spiders. "He should never have been a soldier, but that devil decreed it! *That devil*," she repeats, her breathing growing coarse, but then her face sags. "Anno was such a beautiful baby. Don't you know?" she asks, though the women around her recoil from the question. "So very *beautiful*," she explains. "And he slept like an angel, too. Never a night of colic. No trouble at all. But now he's been torn to pieces, and I have nothing. Not even his body to bury. Not even *that*. Only a broken metal tag with a number on it. That was all our *beloved* Führer saw fit to return of my only child!"

Another blast shakes the cellar, and the lamps blink frantically. But by this time the rest of the shelter's inhabitants must welcome a bomb blast or two, if only to silence Frau Remki's suicidal indictment. And indeed when the light sputters back to a low-wattage glow, the woman has sunk back down to her place like a pile of rags. The thudding explosions grow more distant, but the cellar remains a densely silent place, like a room full of drunkards with painful hangovers. Only the children cry. Finally, as the drone of the attack fades to nothing, the wail of the children is overwhelmed by the wail of a siren. One long, aching howl, signaling that the RAF has crossed over the line into Hannover-Brunswick airspace, and that Berlin, that vast, rambling city, is all-clear.

———

The explosions had seemed so close in the cellar, so intimately connected, that Sigrid half expects to be greeted the next morning by a streetscape of destruction. But as she walks to the bus, the damage appears modest in their block of the Uhlandstrasse. A few buildings with blown-out windowpanes. A roof, pockmarked by splinters of flak shrapnel from the Zoo Tower guns, is being patched by a gang of workers up on ladders. A crack here, a hole there. Some smoke hovering farther up. Then she turns the corner and is faced with a scene that no roof and window gang could hope to mend. The façade of the white brick apartment house with the pretty garden terraces has been sheared off completely, exposing the interiors within. There was a time when she imagined Kaspar leasing them a place in this building, with its fanciful scrollwork and clean, whitewashed face. She had often speculated about what the flats might look like on the inside, and now, thanks to the Royal Air Force bombardiers, she can see them clearly. The wallpaper from floor to floor is pinstriped, floral print, woodland. The family pictures are hanging askew. Furniture is coated with plaster dust. Two women and an old grandpa struggle in the morning drizzle to carry a horsehair settee over the rubble to the curbside, where they have piled a few lonely, surviving possessions. A coffee table. A toilet seat. A dining-room chair. A chipped soapstone bust of Beethoven. The maestro scowls at the rain as Sigrid passes. The air smells burned and bitter. She tastes ash and keeps on walking. It's a chilly morning under brackish green skies. Her scarf is tied over her head. Her breath frosts lightly as she spots her bus lumbering down the street toward her stop. She enters the end of the queue and concentrates on nothing as she stares at the back of people's heads.

There aren't many buses running in Berlin these days. Petrol is a military priority, and the Wehrmacht has commandeered hordes of city vehicles. But the No. 8 T-Line bus, with its dingy coat of BVG yellow, still rolls onward, three times a day, from the Badensche Strasse to the Alex and back, as part of the clockwork of the city. More Berliners pack the aisles as the bus trumbles onward. An odor of human dank deepens. A familiar bouquet by now. It is the smell of all that is unwashed, stale, and solidified. It is the smell that has replaced the brisk scent of the city's famous air. The ersatz perfume of Berlin, distilled from all that is chemically treated and synthetically processed. Of cigarettes manufactured from crushed acorns, of fifty-gram cakes of grit-filled soap that clean nothing. Of rust and clotted plumbing. Damp wool, sour milk, and decay. The odor of the home front.

Passengers on the bus are lumped together like potato sacks. A few aging men with their newspapers, though mostly the city has been left to its women. Under the new conscription decrees, regiments of husbands, uncles, and brothers have been mobilized and Berlin has become a city of women. They fill the bus, as always, concentrating on their knitting or clutching their heavy handbags in their laps, while the advertising placards extol the virtues of the Ski-Nelly brassiere with extra wide straps, and Erdal shoe polish. But last night's return of the bombers has had its effect. There is an undercoating of tension hidden by the masks of business as usual slapped on people's faces. The newspaper headlines are high-strung and victimized. AIR ATTACK ON BERLIN WORKING-CLASS DISTRICT and AIMLESS BOMBING OVER BERLIN RESIDENTIAL AREAS the morning editions cry. The *Morgenpost* claims to know WHAT CHURCHILL INTENDS TO BOMB IN BERLIN.

She writes a few words to Kaspar on the special stationery issued by the Feldpost, using her purse as a desktop and her father's Montblanc fountain pen. She has grown rather proficient at this, learning how to anticipate the agitation of the bus ride and lift the nib of the pen to keep from creating a blot. She does not mention the bombing, because she knows the censors would scratch it out in any case. So all she writes is that she and his mother remain healthy and well, and that she is quite busy at the office. All is in order. What else can she say? Recapping her pen, she folds the letter away, and leans back her head, closing her eyes.

Do you feel that?

Yes.

Then you know what it's for.

At the Ku'damm she transfers from the bus to the underground.

The U1 on the B line. The U-Bahn train that traverses the city's belly from the Uhlandstrasse, past the Schlesisches Tor and across the River Spree to the station at the Warschauer Brücke. It's usually a quick enough ride for her, five stops to Hallesches Tor. But then, at Anhalter Bahnhof, something happens. The usual crowd pushes on from the commuter trains, and the doors have been closed to the platform, but the train does not move. Nobody talks. Why bother? Delays happen. It's all part of the war. Then the door to the carriage is rolled open, and two men shove their way in. Snap-brim hats and long overcoats. They come to a halt in front of a woman in a threadbare outfit and a kerchief over her tousled brown hair. Her face is colorless and gaunt, she stands hanging from a handrail. "Papers," one of the men demands. The timber of his voice cuts through dreary silence. It is an official voice. A voice of authority. "Papers. Show me your papers."

The woman's posture goes rigid. She glares for a heartbeat and then spits solidly into the man's face. "*Shit!*" he swears, smearing the spittle from his eye. "You ugly bitch!" The crack of his hand, as he slaps her face, galvanizes the attention of the carriage. A middle-aged hausfrau across the car leaps to her feet, but then she freezes.

"Geheime Staatspolizei," the man in the leather trench coat assures everyone, displaying his aluminum warrant disc for all to peruse. He is fat. Fatter than any Berliner living on a lawful share of war rations should be. "This creature is a Jewish parasite, and is of no concern to any good German," the fat man declares. "She has boarded public transportation in violation of the law, *and* has appeared in public without the Judenstern *that she is legally required to wear*." The Judenstern. A cloth badge in the shape of a yellow star with six points, and the word "Jude" machine-stitched at the center in mock Hebraic lettering.

The carriage remains silent. The standing hausfrau suddenly looks hunted and slouches back down into her seat. Most eyes turn to the carriage floor. The fat man appears satisfied with this. He nods to his partner, who shoves the woman in the kerchief out of the car, and then rolls the door closed behind them.

No one speaks until the train begins to lumber out of the station, when the hausfrau, now clutching her handbag, tries to redeem herself as a good German by blustering, "Dirty Jewess, delaying the train. Now we'll *all* be late."

Eyes dart back and forth, but the only replies are a few loud coughs and the rattle of newspapers.

———

TWO DAYS AFTER the coupling in the back row of the cinema, he took her to a room at the top of a dingy flight of steps. Inside, he dropped his trousers in front of her, while she was still only half out of her coat. She froze up at the sight, one arm out of her sleeve, her eyes dropping to his exposure.

"Take a good look," he instructed her, "before we go any further. You know what this means."

Still staring. Somehow it answered the questions that had been building. His covertness. All the hidden thought she detected behind his eyes. But all she said was, "It means you're missing a small flap of skin."

"It means more than that, and you know it. This is exactly what all the race laws have been written to prevent. "

She did not budge a muscle as she lifted her eyes to his face "I don't care."

"No? You are so eager to become a blood traitor to your race?"

"I already have become."

"That was in the dark. This is in the light. You know what happens if we are found out. An Aryan female fornicating with a *Jew*, much less a *criminal* Jew who doesn't wear the Judenstern? It could mean prison for you, *if you're lucky*. If you're not, they'll drop you into a camp, where you'll be breaking up rusted batteries with a wooden mallet."

A small breath inhaled and then exhaled. She had seen the newsreels of labor camps, for the work-shy, for politicals and habitual criminals. They weren't exactly a secret. For an instant she tried to imagine such a fate. Tried to imagine herself in a rough barracks, smashing those batteries. A prisoner in a striped smock. A race criminal. But the heat she felt rise up in her simply scorched the image from her mind. "Then we must not be found out," she answered, and dropped her coat onto the floor.

THREE

BUILDINGS ALONG THE BROAD AVENUE of Unter den Linden are veiled by acres of camouflage netting festooned with artificial branches to fool Tommy into thinking he's flying over the Spreewald instead of the middle of the city. But the area around the Hallesches Tor is much like it has always been. It's a glum working-class slice of Kreuzberg known for its rowdy beer halls. Not a place she'd ever walk at night, but during the day it's not so bad. Off-duty soldiers loiter about the U-Bahn station, smoking and calling to the girls. Berliners troop off to work across the Belle Alliance Brücke, which bridges the Landwehrkanal's slow, murky green current. The U1 exits its underground tunnel and rumbles up a long stretch of elevated track toward Rummelsburg, throwing off sparks from its wheels. Only the tangy smell of smoke betrays the recent visit by the RAF bombers. A smell that will linger for days.

She enters the patent office building through the Alexandrinenstrasse door. On the wall there is a dark bronze memorial plaque listing the names of all those patent officials killed in the last war. Across the hall, one of the building porters is tacking up a poster. A leering green face with a hooked beak and drooping, malevolent eyes wears the six-pointed star on his lapel like a boutonniere. *This is the enemy of our blood!* the caption decries. *Show him no mercy!* She gazes at the poster blankly, then joins the queue to have her identity card checked by the aging policeman at the desk.

THE STENOGRAPHIC DEPARTMENT is a drab and cavernous affair of flat gray paint and hardwood floors worn smooth. Footsteps can boom into the high ceilings like cannon fire. A photograph of the Führer is hung without irony beside the official air raid alarm instructions. *Stay calm. Obey the warden. Keep gas masks ready.*

Fräulein Kretchmar arrives, clapping her hands together like the village schoolmistress. "Come, come! No time for frivolous chitchat. To work!" she scolds the roomful of women. "Think of our troops fighting the Bolsheviks. *They* have no time to waste with such twaddle, and neither do we!"

Sigrid adjusts her chair and removes the hood from her typewriter, easing herself into her standard position in front of the keys. Then, from across the room, she gets a seductively conspiratorial wink from a dusky-eyed brunette. This is Renate Hochwilde, the closest thing she has to a friend here, or anywhere else, for that matter. During their midday break, she recounts the tale of Frau Remki's outburst. Renate shakes her head and sighs. "She's a goner." They are sitting outside in the grass above the Waterloo Ufer on the lower bank of the canal.

"Her husband was in the last war. He was decorated," Sigrid tells her. "An Iron Cross, First Class."

But Renate only shakes her head. "Makes no difference. The last war? That's ancient history. It's *this* war that counts. And you don't lose your mind like that without consequences." She says this and stretches her back languidly. Dark, luxurious curls. Feline eyes. A well-built body. Men go insane for her. "You can be *sure* that somebody has already rung up the gentlemen of the Gestapo."

Sigrid shrugs. "Certainly," she must agree, "that's the likelihood."

"So keep your distance, is my advice. That's what I'd do."

"It's what we all do."

"And is that so bad? To look out for yourself? Besides, what exactly should you be doing that you're not?"

Shaking her head, Sigrid digs into her rucksack. "I don't know. Nothing. There's nothing I can do, I suppose."

"And what should you feel *obliged* to do, anyway? Did you know this woman so well?"

"I helped her with shopping a few times. That sort of thing." The morning has produced a flaccid sunshine, but it's revitalizing after the hours under the fluorescent lamps of the patent office. Sigrid is happy to feel even this weak sunlight on her face. She closes her eyes to it. "It's my mother-in-law who's known her for ages."

"Ah. Dear Mother Schröder," Renate pronounces archly. "And is *she* rushing off to plead this crazy woman's case?"

"Not as of this morning."

"No, I would think not. For once the old gorgon can give you a lesson worth learning. Are you still fighting with her?"

"Always."

Renate produces a cucumber from her bag and bites into it. "I don't know how you stand it," she says, chewing. "I think if I had to live with *my* mother-in-law under the same roof, there'd be blood on the floor within a week. Hers or mine, I'm not sure. The funny thing is that Oskar feels precisely the same way about her." Oskar is Renate's husband, a driver for a staff officer posted in France. Supposedly, he is aware of his wife's myriad trysts, but makes no objections. "He doesn't care," she insists. "He has a wife whose picture he can show about. He adores the children, and I'm sure he gets plenty of what he needs from those pretty mademoiselles."

Stretching like a cat, Renate purrs over the thought of her latest bedmate. "Oh, he's very *appealing*. Very *fierce* eyes," she says. "Older, you know. Younger is hard to find these days. But still with the body of an athlete. And, of course, fabulous under the sheets."

"Um-hmm." Sigrid nods. "Well. Aren't *all* your conquests?"

"I suppose," Renate replies airily. "But I like this one. He's polite."

"You mean he holds the door for you?"

"I mean, he's not simply interested in *his* pleasure."

"How virtuous. What's he do?" she asks. "For a living, that is."

Renate takes another bite from her cucumber and chews dutifully. "I'm not sure, really. He has a firm of some sort in the Potsdamer Platz. But we don't talk much about it, as you might imagine. In fact, we hardly talk at all."

"Married?"

Renate shrugs. Who cares? "Shipped off to the country with the *kinder*, where it's safe. The family abode is in Zehlendorf, but he keeps a cozy little flat off the Potsdamer Platz. For *business*," she says.

Sigrid smiles, but as she watches the wands of the willow tree float on the canal's marble green surface, the smile wanes. She treasures Renate but is frightened by her as well. Frightened by all that desire, the bottomless hunger. "Should I envy you?" she asks.

"Envy?" Her eyebrows rise. "Why?"

"Why? You have no fear of your own *appetites*."

To which Renate replies with a laugh. "Well, in truth, it is *I* who should envy *you*. Isn't it? All that self-control."

Tell me something no one else knows.

On the bus ride home, Sigrid stares through the window. Stares into the past stowed inside her head.

There is nothing to tell, he'd answered. *I have no secrets.*

She divided her life into two sides of a mirror. On one side of the mirror was her true life with Kaspar and his mother, which felt false. Every morning, she left the flat with Kaspar, as he was off to his work at the bank. They traveled together as far as the Nollendorfplatz, at which point he would give her a pat on the arm and wish her a pleasant day. Her part-time job at the patent office was not as rewarding as she pretended, but it gave her an excuse to be absent from her mother-in-law's flat in the afternoons when she was asked to work "extra hours" for the war effort. Who wasn't working extra hours now, anyway? And when that excuse wore thin, there were always the films. A matinee with a friend from the office. *Renate Hochwilde is her name. She's one of the other stenographers. Her husband's just been called up*, Sigrid would explain. *I think she's lonely.* Mother Schröder would frown at the idea of such excursions when there was plenty of cleaning to do, but then she frowned at everything. And Sigrid took over washing the supper dishes so that her mother-in-law could sit and listen to the wireless. Rosita Serrano's cool, clear voice singing "La Paloma." She would scrub the skillet and think of the sound of Egon's voice. The heat of his breath on her skin.

On the opposite side of the mirror was the life that felt true. A rendezvous in front of the cinema. Then off to the cramped one-room flat, belonging to a "friend." The stairs creaked forlornly on their way up, and the hall smelled of failing plumbing and hardship. This had become their routine. But when she asked him her question—*A friend? What kind of friend?*—the answer was None of Her Business: the name of a land so much more vast than the simple boundaries of a hardscrabble district in eastern Berlin. He still listened to her when she talked, but now she suspected he was simply using her talk to camouflage his silence.

Outside, the air was frigid. Inside, they had generated their own heat. The windowpanes were smeared with condensation. From the knot of blankets she gazed at him as he lit his cigarette, dragged in the smoke, and then exhaled it sloppily. She liked to see him stand naked so casually. Kaspar was different. He never undressed in front of her. And after their business in bed was concluded, he redressed under the covers, before slumping over to his side and collapsing into sleep. Kaspar would never allow her to gape at his ass, standing by a window. He would never turn and show her his member, hanging at rest.

"You look thoughtful," he told her.

"Just thinking about how far away you are from the bed."

He gave her an uneven smile that was more interior than exterior, and climbed back onto the mattress. Taking a drag from his cigarette, he blew smoke toward the ceiling.

"I think a circumcised cock is an honest organ. It looks so naked. So unsheathed," she told him, drowsing her hand over it. "It has nothing to hide. All men should have such an honest cock." And then she said, "Funny, that word still feels so strange in my mouth."

"The word or the organ?"

"Ha!" She laughed and slapped her hand against his arm. "If you're worried, I'll confess that I've come to love the taste of both."

And now he laughed, too, but she could tell that there was something secret behind his eyes. This was nothing new. She'd seen it many times, and had always been able to ignore it, but wondered now if there would come a moment when that would change. She leaned over and kissed him thickly on the mouth, and he kissed her back, holding his cigarette up in the air. Was it politeness? No ashes or embers dropped on your lover's delicate flesh? Or perfunctory. Kissing her to the depth required before he could return to his smoking? These were the types of questions with which she battered herself, but only when they were together. Or when they were apart. Just another sample of the minutiae of their connection that would roll around like a marble for days in her brain. Moments before, his mouth had tasted of her. Had tasted of the last place his mouth had been, between her thighs. But this kiss tasted only of tobacco.

AT NIGHT, she came home to 11G. Shelling beans or peeling potatoes for supper, while her mother-in-law fussed over her roast or her chops. The radio masked the silence between them. And when Kaspar came home from the bank, he would kiss them both on the forehead, then go change into a sweater. She was never required to return his kiss, which was a relief, because she feared that she would be incapable of kissing without passion after her hour with Egon. At the table, she was also relieved that she was not required to contribute to the talk. Mother Schröder would yammer on. Kaspar would grunt with polite interest at appropriate moments. So it surprised her one evening when her husband turned his eyes on her and asked, "How was your day?"

She felt caught, as if the thoughts inside her head had just been turned inside out for all to see. As if Egon had suddenly taken a chair at the table.

"*My* day?"

A mildly wry smile. "Yes. *Yours*," he assured her.

"It was fine," she answered, and then waved away the question. "Uneventful." For an instant, she was convinced that he *knew* about everything. That she had been fooling no one. But then he only nodded. "Good," he said, and went on with supper. At bedtime, he gave her the same chaste kiss as always before settling his head onto the pillow. She turned and faced the wall, staring at her memory of Egon's face.

There was no part of herself from which she forbade Egon. She was unlocked. Undefended. An open gate. In the aftermath she was shellacked in sweat, though the windowpanes were sticky with frost. She shoved the wet strings of hair from her eyes, and stared up into his face, which hung above her like the sun. She felt herself smile in simple reflex. "I want you to tell me something."

"Tell you?" His face was arranged into an easy, sated expression, but some fragment of caution had entered his voice. "Tell you what?"

"Tell me something no one else knows."

"There is nothing to tell," he answered. "I have no secrets."

"You have nothing *but* secrets," she pointed out. "So tell me something."

"My name is Weiss."

This was not exactly what she had in mind. "What?"

"My name is Weiss," he repeated, and rolled onto his back to pick up his cigarette pack, the paper crinkling as he rummaged about inside. "It's the name that I was born to."

"I see. So, your name is Weiss," she said.

"Don't sound disappointed, Sigrid. That's an explosive bit of intelligence. Not many know it."

A breath. "It's a very sharp name," she observed, trying to make the best of it. "It sounds like the swish of a saber blade. *Weiss*," she said, demonstrating with a whoosh.

"A Jew's name," he pointed out blandly, and lit up.

"No. It is *your* name."

"Precisely my point, Frau Schröder."

She didn't like it when he addressed her in this way. Didn't like the scorn it veiled. Perhaps it was her punishment for squeezing a secret from him. So was it *her* retribution when she suddenly said, "Tell me about your wife."

He breathed in the question slowly with his cigarette smoke, and then released his response with a frown. "You won't enjoy this game, Sigrid. I promise you that. You will not."

"It's not a game. Only a question."

No words, only smoke.

"You have nothing to say?" she inquired, drawing the blankets around her. "Or is it that you have no interest in me, beyond what I offer below the waist?"

"Above the waist as well," he answered in a grimy voice. "You've got quite a set."

It might have aroused her to have heard this a moment before. But now that she was angry, it sounded only crude. She frowned blackly to herself. "Yes. I must have made an irresistible target. Another unfulfilled hausfrau. One among many, no doubt. Stupid in my desires."

"If you're intent on torturing yourself like this"—he shrugged—"I can't stop you."

"Tell me her name."

Shaking his head. "Sigrid."

"It's a question, Egon. Only a very small one for a mistress. What do you call your wife?"

"I call her by her name."

"Which is?"

A small breath of concession. "Which is Anna."

Anna. Sigrid takes the name inside herself, and consigns it to an interior vault. The name of her lover's wife. "Where is she?" she asked. Nothing. "You have forgotten, perhaps? *Now, let's see . . . where did I put my wife?* Should you search your coat pockets?"

Egon exhaled darkly, then answered. "She's in Vienna. Her parents are there."

"How long have you been married to her?"

"Six years."

"Six years." It might as well have been a lifetime. It might as well have been a century in comparison to their six frantic months. Six months, one week, and what? How many days? How many hours? How many minutes left? "And does she know?"

"Know?"

"Does she suspect that you so easily slip off your wedding band?"

"I don't wear a wedding band. I don't care for symbols of ownership."

"How convenient for you. And you have children?"

"*Sigrid,*" he says, glowering.

"Should I assume that the answer is yes?"

"I wouldn't think you'd be in such a rush to assume *anything* at this point."

"But you *do,* though. *Have children,* that is."

"I have daughters," he admitted. "Two."

"Ah. You see that wasn't so difficult. A straight answer."

"How old?"

He was up, out of the bed. His bare feet padding across the crooked hardwood floor. "How old?" she repeated.

"Five and three."

"And they have names, like most children?"

Uncorking a bottle of schnapps on the battered sideboard, he poured out a glass. Only one glass. "These questions of yours, Sigrid. They have nothing to do with us."

"No?" said Sigrid, her voice strident.

He faced her, leaning naked against the sideboard's edge with the drink in his hand. "What we have," he told her, "is private. Just between you and me. If you must have the words, fine. You know that I love you."

"Are you certain of that?"

"But this love is not to be made public. It would be an insult to our feelings to expose them to the hostility of the world."

"It was public enough in the back of a movie theater."

"That was fucking."

"Rather than love. I see." Sigrid nodded. "And your wife?"

"Not our subject, Sigrid."

"You love her, too?"

He inhaled smoke. "Differently from you."

"Hmm. I wonder what that means."

"I don't ask you about your husband."

"Well, you *can*."

"But I don't wish to. Why must he exist for me?"

"Because he exists for *me*. I go home to him and have you between us every day. The lies I must tell." She shook her head at the lies stored inside of her brain. "The lies I must remember."

"Your lies are not my responsibility," he said. "Your *choices* are not my responsibility."

"You have no feelings for me. Not really. If you did, you couldn't say such things."

"I love you intensely, Sigrid. Touching you is like sticking my hand into a fire."

"Sounds very painful for you," she replied in anger, but also knowing that it was true.

"But my wife. My children. They're quite simply none of your business. None of *our* business."

The words hit her with the weight of stones. For an instant, and not for the first time, she felt herself to be utterly alone. Alone, as if she lay dead in her coffin. The feeling emptied her completely, even of tears. It was also the end of his words for the day, even after he returned to the bed. To her body. As her punishment, his articulation was withdrawn, and afterward there were only grunts and mumbled half words. She was always helpless against this, and raged inwardly at her own stupidity. All his rough terrain had caused her to forget just how vulnerable he was to pain. She cursed her own hubris, her own frantic desire to be everything to him. To blot out wives, children, histories. To render them all without consequence.

Then at the door he had whispered, "Please don't."

"Don't what?"

"Let your smaller emotions taint what we have."

She gazed at him for a moment, and shook her head. Quite without a drop of fight remaining, she propped herself up against the pillar of his body, and said, "There are times, Herr Weiss, when I could simply murder you."

"Well," he answered calmly, "for that you'll need to stand in quite a long queue."

Suddenly she nearly laughed. She glared up into his face. "Longer, you think, than the queue for milk?"

He raised his eyebrows. "Longer than milk, shorter than meat," he said, and then kissed her.

. . .

COMING HOME from the patent office, she thinks, for an instant, that she *sees* him. Sees him at the bus stop across the street from the zoo. This happens now and again, causing her heart to flood. She conjures him out of the brisk air of the present. Fleshing her memory into a man on the corner, or sitting at a café window. But, of course, it isn't him. It isn't him at all. How could it be? He is gone. Escaped into the world beyond the boundaries the Greater German Reich. She sometimes allows herself silly fantasies that, in her old age, she will travel abroad as a widow, and find him sitting at a café table in Barcelona or perhaps Cairo. She will turn the corner and discover a finely silvered version of him wearing a beret. An Egon Weiss she will finally be able to claim.

Entering the flat in the Uhlandstrasse, she hangs her scarf on a peg when her mother-in-law appears wearing a black smirk. "You saw the door?" the old woman inquires.

Sigrid glances at their door. "Saw it?"

"Not *ours*," she gruffs. "Frau Remki's. It's been sealed. They sealed it up after they took her away."

"*Who* took her away?"

"*Who?* Who do you *think*, dear child?" *Dear child* is not a pleasantry in Mother Schröder's mouth. Sigrid pastes her eyes to her mother-in-law's expression, then peers into the hall. Frau Remki's door has been sealed with four white-and-black adhesive-backed stamps bearing the eagle over the hooked cross and encircled by a ring that reads CLOSED BY THE GEHEIME STAATSPOLIZEI. A fifth stamp covers the keyhole.

"Three of them arrived with their pistols out. But, of course, she had beaten them to the punch. A spoiler to the last," says her mother-in-law. "They had to carry her out feet first."

Sigrid shakes her head as if to clear it. "*What?* What are you saying?"

"I'm saying she followed the same path as her exalted husband.

A suicide." The old lady shrugs. "Probably the smartest thing she ever did," she concludes, then crosses over to the stove and lifts the lid on a large steaming pot. "Soup's nearly ready," she announces. "You should put the plates on the table."

Sigrid stares. "Was it Mundt?"

Sniffing at the soup. "Mundt?"

"Was it Mundt who *denounced* her?"

"How should I know?" Her mother-in-law picks up the ladle and stirs the pot. "Why don't you go below stairs and ask her? Knowing Ilse Mundt, she'll be happy to brag. Now kindly put the plates on the table, will you? I'd like to eat my supper."

FOUR

AT A TRAM STOP, the conductor must clear the aisle to make space for a soldier propped on crutches who is boarding without the benefit of a right foot. Several passengers compete to give up their seats for him, but he politely refuses all offers, face flushing. There was an invasion of Berlin after the Aufmarsch into Russia. An invasion by an army of mutilated and crippled young men. A year ago they said the war was all but won. The Party press secretary announced that the Wehrmacht's victory in Russia was now irreversible. THE GREAT HOUR HAS STRUCK! CAMPAIGN IN THE EAST DECIDED! roared the headlines in the *B.Z.* EASTERN BREAKTHROUGH DEEPENS. THE SPIRES OF MOSCOW ARE IN SIGHT! Reports over the wireless were triumphant. Soviet Army Groups Timoshenko and Voroshilov were encircled! Army Group Budyonny was in chaos! German boys would be coming home by Christmas, and everyone was going to be rich. In the cafés, Berliners leapt to their feet, saluting the radio announcements, and booming out the "Deutschland" and "Horst Wessel" lieder. Russian-language phrase books crowded the bookshop display windows for those pioneers soon to resettle in the East, and for practical minds expecting a flood of Russian-speaking servants. But then came winter, with rumors of unbearable cold. Cold that froze engine blocks and turned motor oil to sludge. The phrase books vanished from the shops, along with such items as soap, tooth powder, sewing needles, eggs, and wool socks. And though many boys did return home, they did so missing limbs.

The soldier must hop to one side at the next stop to allow for more passengers, and finally accepts a seat simply to get out of the way. Once he is settled, Sigrid notices that everyone carefully avoids looking at him. But the young man does not appear to notice. He sits, lost in his own stare, as if he is still facing down a frigid wind sluicing off the steppes. She thinks of Kaspar. The letters she receives in the Feldpost from him are flat, oddly factual, and really rather dull. *We had hot soup today. Beans, potatoes, and a bit of ham. It really wasn't too bad.* Or, *The cough persists. Perhaps I shall ask the Sanitäter for a gargle.* But when she pictures his winter-chapped face, a vast distance fills his eyes, until she allows the routine rustle of an ur-Berliner's newspaper to sweep the image away. Final victory continues to fill the front page, but the back page is crowded with black-bordered hero's death notices. *Fallen for Führer and Fatherland* under an iron cross. Black borders to match the number of black armbands worn on Berliner coat sleeves.

She only felt guilt for her infidelity after it had ended. In the heat of Egon's grip, she was so boiling over that she sometimes transferred her passion to Kaspar's body in sudden spasms of desire in the bed they shared at 11G. Kaspar's reaction was always one of surprised participation. He was not a bad lover, her husband. He possessed his own kind of well-rehearsed power, and certainly had always been attentive to her body. She has never had any complaints. And when her brimming desire for Egon would secretly slop over her rim, Kaspar always entertained her instructions. But he never took root inside her. She could always separate herself from him when their coupling was through, and listen to the mild saw of his snore without interest. Without guilt. Only after Egon was gone and Kaspar remained did her betrayal cause her pain. So she tried to camouflage her guilt with the overeagerness of her wifely laugh and her solicitude at the supper table. Or subsume it in the binding vacancy that settled between them as they sat listening to the radio. But it was really only after he was conscripted and the army stuffed him onto a train rolling toward the Eastern Front that her guilt eased. If he was a soldier, then she was a soldier's wife, and could play that role without torment.

At the following stop, she squeezes past the wounded boy's crutches, and hurries off the tram. It is not a short trip to her mother's grave. It's a train ride to Schmargendorf, and then a tram, and then a long hike. Head down, she walks beneath the bare poplars following the course of an old limestone wall. Like most of Berlin's cemeteries, this one is an antique, a crowded garden of tombstones and looming marble funerary tableaux from a previous century. Many graves are overwhelmed by weeds, the flotsam growth of ungoverned flora, ancient flat-faced headstones caked with moss, choked by vines. Obelisks and mute stone angels blackened by wreaths of the city's soot. But to the north of the Misdroyerstrasse gate they are still burying people. The graves are fresh. Mounds and mounds of newly interred German boys shipped back from the East in pine. Officers only. Lower ranks are buried where they fall, and all that comes back to the families is a letter from the Army Information Authority, and if they're lucky, some personal items. A watch. A pipe. A photograph. Half of an identity disk. Paper flags decorate the ground beside the granite markers. Small flapping swastikas. Sigrid skirts a funeral that is in progress. A clot of family members in black, raising their arms in weak salute as a crew of laborers lowers a plain pine coffin into the earth on ropes. The clergyman in his stiff white vestment is booming out a raw-throated version of the "Horst Wessel Lied." A dozen yards farther down, workers with spades are busy cutting out more graves from the clay.

One day a month, she makes the trip here to discharge her responsibilities. Her mother's grave, she finds, has fingers of dying vines clinging to the marble, and a spiky thicket of pigweed popping up at its base. She pulls out the gloves and old gardening shears from her bag and starts trimming it away, kneeling on a sheet of newspaper so as not to soil her nylons. So much overgrowth. Had she missed a month?

There are times she thinks of her mother, lying silent in death below her, staring up through empty sockets at the darkness of her coffin. Can she see through that darkness? Can she feel the weight of the daughter above her, on her knees trimming weeds?

All arms and legs, she hears her mother saying.

They were still living in the airy, garden flat in the Südgelände. Her father's engineering practice was doing well. A turbine contract from AEG had provided for regular trips to the shops and daily stops at the neighborhood butcher.

"Eat," her grandmother commanded, rough as ever on the surface, but there was an urgency underneath. Her voice resilient with an under-pinning of duty and . . . *what*? Concern, perhaps? Not really affection, but something of the same species. Sigrid was fourteen and skinny as a pole the three women of the house, as Poppa referred to them, were sharing the kitchen table. "All arms and legs," her mother announced. "Remember? I was the same way before I developed," she said, as if speaking in code. But Sigrid knew what she meant. Breasts and hips. A woman's body like her mother's, all curves. "Eat," her grandmother said, repeating her command. "The both of you." She had placed steam-ing bowls of her famous pea soup with salted pork in front of them, and large cuts of white bread. Sigrid eagerly picked up her spoon. Her grandmother's pea soup was her very favorite. "Put some meat on your bones," the old woman advised, "before people start thinking we're starving you to death here."

Sigrid glanced to her mother for permission, and received a quick wink. *Let's humor the old lady*, the wink said. The Grossmutter. A loud and cranky engine normally, a solid piece of diesel machinery that would till the fields, or plow you over. Either one with efficiency. But that day, as her mother joined Sigrid in devouring those bowls of soup with salt pork, the trio of women formed a comfortably faultless triangle.

Suddenly, her mother leaned over and nuzzled Sigrid with a kiss. A smile ignited her face, and Sigrid felt herself blush with surprise and happiness. It was not the sort of thing her mother was likely to do. Only when she was in a perfect mood.

A year later, the stock market crashed, trips to the shops ceased, and Grossmutter was dead. A stroke took her in the kitchen, like the drop of an ax blade. Her body was shipped off to a plot beside her husband in Hanover. They said good-bye to the old woman's coffin on platform B of Lehrter Bahnhof, just the two of them, because Poppa had deadlines, and simply could *not* leave the office unsupervised. Her mother was a slop bucket of tears spilling over, while Sigrid hid hers.

After that, it was her mother's job to cook, but that didn't work out well, so it became Sigrid's job instead. Meanwhile, business for her father's firm died, too, when AEG canceled its contracts. Sigrid somehow linked the two events in her head. Her father started spending evenings at the office, then some nights stopped coming home altogether. Then one morning in late March, the day after a terrible rainstorm, he left his key to the flat on the kitchen table and never came back.

There were certain formalities to observe after a certain period of time. Telephone calls placed to his embarrassed secretary at the firm. A visit to the local police precinct, where the Wachtmeister at the desk treated her mother like a foolish woman who had just lost her husband. A solemn discussion with her father's partner in the firm. A solemn discussion with the manager of their bank. A solemn discussion with their landlord. Sigrid blamed her mother's cooking. *"Why couldn't you have cooked better for him!"* she'd bellowed. It was the first time she had ever raised her voice to her mother in her life. But her mother only gazed back at her flatly. "Why couldn't have you been a better daughter?" she asked. The same day, her mother cleaned out her father's wardrobe, and gave everything to Winter Relief. Soon after, she started selling things off. Every day, when Sigrid came home from school, there would be another empty space somewhere in the flat. The furniture went first. The fancy dresses went next, and then the pots and pans, dishware, flatware, knickknacks, Meissen, books, everything her mother could lay her hands on. Though, only as a last resort did she empty the contents of her jewelry case, her eyes filling. *That,* thought Sigrid with a mix of bitterness and satisfaction, seemed to pain her mother more than parting with her husband. And, of course, the garden flat in Südgelände was now far out of their reach, so her mother found a dustbin in the Salzbrunner Strasse where the WC was down at the end of the hallway and was often clogged. There they lived alone. And that's how it felt. Both of them together. But both of them alone.

Making her way along a graveled path toward the gate, with her sack of garden tools, Sigrid notices a couple occupying a granite bench near an untended landscape of forgotten graves. They are seated close to each other, yet something seems to separate them. She looks away and keeps walking. But then behind her are voices. Raised voices. She can't help but turn back to look.

The girl is standing now, and the fellow bent forward from the bench, holding her hand as if he might have to prevent her fleeing. He looks innocuous in the drab, shapeless coat and hat that is the civilian uniform of all Berliner males these days. The girl is in a dark, too-large coat with a wool beret pulled over soot black hair. Sigrid does not immediately recognize the creature until she spots the girl's awkwardly stiffened posture as the man jumps to his feet and kisses her full on the mouth. It's the duty-year girl, Fräulein Kohl. Sigrid finds herself staring, oddly transfixed. The Fräulein does not exactly resist, but neither does she exactly respond. Then she turns her head toward Sigrid, and even from the distance that separates them, Sigrid can feel the grip of the girl's glare. It chases her away. She turns quickly and starts hiking toward the street, as if it were *she* who'd just been caught in a moment of intimacy. The footsteps she hears crunching on the gravel behind her are hurried and growing closer.

Frau Schröder.

For several steps Sigrid does not slow, but then she hears the Fräulein appeal again, calling her name, and she stops. Turns about. The girl swallows a breath. Close up, Sigrid is reminded again how young this girl is. No lines on her brow. A touch of baby fat in the oval of her face. Eighteen, perhaps. Nineteen. Certainly no older. "Fräulein Kohl," she says blankly.

"Frau Schröder, I must ask you, please, not to mention to anyone what you just saw."

"And what *did* I just see, Fräulein Kohl?"

"That man and me."

"You mean the man who kissed you?"

"I know that you have no reason to do me any more favors, but I ask you to *please* keep this under your hat. It could mean trouble for me." Sigrid looks into the girl's electric eyes. It's obvious that asking for favors is a painful exercise. Sigrid blinks. Takes a breath. Why is *she* the one feeling cornered? Looking toward the bench, she sees that the man is still there, watching them.

"He's married, I take it?"

"Married? I really have no idea." Ericha pauses as if she must make a quick calculation, and then she says: "But that has nothing to do with it."

Sigrid looks down at her in confusion. "I see. Well. In any case, Fräulein Kohl, *your* business is not *my* business. I am not a gossip, if that's what you are worried about. So, if you'll excuse me, I must catch a bus." She turns and starts walking.

"Ah. Frau Schröder," the girl begins as she catches up. "Do you mind if I walk with you?"

Sigrid keeps moving, but gives a glance to the rear. The fellow on the bench is staring after them with obvious frustration. "Won't your friend object?"

Ericha glances back as well, but for only an instant. "He'll survive," she replies. And then, "You have someone buried here?"

Sigrid looks the girl over quickly. "Yes," is all she says. And then, "My mother."

Ericha nods. "I never knew my mother," she volunteers flatly.

"No? I'm sorry."

"Don't be. She didn't die. She just gave me up. I was raised in an orphanage in Moabit." Outside the gate, Sigrid turns and starts to follow the soot-stained wall down the Misdroyerstrasse.

"I'll be leaving you here," the girl tells her.

"I beg your pardon? So I continue to be your convenient shield, without a breath of explanation."

"Don't be offended. I'm only trying to protect you."

"Protect me from what? It seems you have things backward. *I* am the one who's been protecting *you*."

"I must go."

"And what about your duty, Fräulein?"

Blankness. "My duty?"

"Yes! Your *duty*. Have you forgotten about that word?"

"You don't understand."

"Well, at least you're quite correct in *that*. I *don't* understand. But what I *do* understand quite well, Fräulein Kohl, is that you have responsibilities to discharge. And if I recall, Frau Granzinger has not yet given up *her* children." Why is she suddenly angry?

The girl absorbs this with a barely noticeable flinch. Her expression remains unchanged.

"I'm sorry, I don't know why I said that," Sigrid tells her.

The girl shrugs. "It makes no difference. People often behave in hurtful ways. Why try to explain it? Thank you for the morality lesson, Frau Schröder. It was most helpful. Good-bye," she says, and turns and walks away.

"Wait," Sigrid calls after her, but the girl only quickens her step.

. . .

SHE IS LATE returning to the patent office and is summoned by Fräulein Kretchmar into the hallway. Kretchmar scowls, her eyes hard as bullets behind the rimless pince-nez. Her graying hair tightly pinned. Her Party membership badge fastened to the lapel of her charcoal suit. "You were *late*, Frau Schröder, returning from your midday break."

"Yes, Fräulein Kretchmar."

"By fourteen minutes, Frau Schröder."

"Yes, Fräulein Kretchmar. My apologies. Of course, I will make the time up."

"That is not the point, Frau Schröder. We are at war here in the Reichspatentamt, just as surely as the soldiers at the front are at war, only we have our battlefields here at our desks. Now, what do you suppose would happen if our soldiers were late in responding to a call to arms, hmm?"

"Chaos, Fräulein Kretchmar."

"*Chaos*, Frau Schröder," Fräulein Kretchmar confirms with fervor. A favorite theme of hers. "Your work has always been exemplary. We both know that. We both know that you are a cut above most of these young women, who are only marking time till they reach the wedding altar. But that does not excuse you from the rules. If it happens again, I'll have no choice but to report you to Herr Esterwegen. Do you understand that?"

"Yes, Fräulein Kretchmar."

Silence. Fräulein Kretchmar's scowl remains unaltered. But then she says, "Very well, you may return to your desk."

"Yes, Fräulein Kretchmar. Thank you."

But no sooner does Sigrid turn than Fräulein Kretchmar calls her again. "I am aware of the general opinion of me, Frau Schröder."

Sigrid looks back at her.

"Among the women. That I'm a shriveled-up spinster." Fräulein

Kretchmar's expression is still hard as granite, but the muscles in her jaw twitch slightly. "No, you needn't deny it. Its something I've come to terms with long ago. But from *you*, Frau Schröder, from you I expect better. It's not easy being a female in my position. My work must be perfect. *Better* than perfect. I am the sole female in authority in this office, and if one of my stenographers comes back fourteen minutes late from her midday break, it not only reflects poorly upon *her*, it reflects poorly upon *me,* and upon every woman here. Upon every woman in the Reich. We are all responsible to each other for our actions, Frau Schröder. As one woman is judged, so all women are judged. "

Sigrid holds her gaze for a moment, then nods once. "Yes, Fräulein Kretchmar," she says. "I understand."

RAIN COMES IN the afternoon, but dwindles by the time she leaves her bus. Marching down the Uhlandstrasse toward her block, Sigrid can see that the soggy band of clouds is breaking up, revealing a sheet of blue steel sky. Good weather for Tommy. Bad weather for any Berliner trying to get a decent night's sleep. Untying her scarf, she passes the bombed-out apartment house. The collection of salvaged belongings has long since been hauled away from the curbside, but the family pictures still hang askew on the exposed walls. Grandma and grandpa in their frame, staring out at a world they never imagined possible.

A detail of foreign workers are hauling rubble and tossing it into the rear of a cart drawn by a sagging dray. Their boss is a tubby work leader in the Labor Service, but they are not so well fed as he. Their clothes are ragged and stained. She hears them gabbling among themselves. Something slushy and Slavic. Their jackets bear a large white letter. P for "Polnisch." They grunt with the heavy work. Their faces are hard and their expressions raw. They struggle with the chunks of bomb-scorched masonry as the boss puffs on his cigars and complains to an equally well-fed police meister about the results of a local football match. Both offer Sigrid a perfunctory nod as she passes, but the workers look at her sightlessly, all of them sharing the same covenant. They do not see her, she does not see them. A conspiracy of blindness.

WHEN SHE ENTERS the apartment block, she finds a crowd filling the steps of the top-floor landing. "What is this?" she asks Marta Trotzmüller.

"They've come from the SS Economics Office," the woman replies with puckish excitement, "for the *auction*."

"Auction?"

"Didn't you see the sign?"

There's a spattering of applause, as the paper stamps are broken by Frau Mundt's husband under the supervision of a tubby bureaucrat in a steel gray uniform with a death's head on his cap. She spots her mother-in-law in the front rank.

In the kitchen of the flat, she tries to remain deaf to the burble of voices next door, and instead concentrates on the potatoes she is peeling. Blackish brown and rubbery with age. She watches their skin curl and then drop away into the scrap bucket in the sink. By law, scraps must be saved. The Party collects them for pig slop. How funny Egon would find that. Before she knows it, she is thinking of his face, his touch, and feels a finger of warmth in her belly. But then she hears the front door creak, and she shoves all thought away as her mother-in-law enters, struggling with the weight of Frau Remki's Telefunken wireless set. Sigrid glares at her in shock. Mother Schröder glares back in defiance, and kicks the door shut behind her with the heel of her shoe. "Don't you start, daughter-in-law," she warns. "Don't you dare start. I don't want to hear any of your sermonizing."

"But how could you *do* that?" Sigrid begins anyway.

Mother Schröder frowns. "Do *what*? What's my horrible crime? It's a radio."

"A radio that belonged to one of your oldest *friends* until she committed suicide."

The old woman plunks the heavy wireless onto the kitchen table, and huffs, her face flush. "Why must you always side with anyone but me?" she demands. "You heard what she said in the cellar. The woman was a traitor."

"Maybe that's what Frau Mundt calls her."

"It's what *everyone* calls her, because it's what she *was*."

"I can't believe you can speak like this. You knew her for over twenty years."

"And for over twenty years she was a toffee-nosed bitch who thought her turds didn't stink. I can remember when her husband, *the gallant war hero*, bought her this radio. She played it just loudly enough to let everyone know what she had. That was always her way. Flaunting her possessions. Always the higher grade. Always the new coat every winter, while the rest of us patched ours. Only the *balcony* flat was good enough for her. But when your husband's father died, it took her three days to manage the walk across the hall to offer me her 'condolences,' and of course with a fancy cake she'd *bought* from Oswald's. So don't you lecture *me* on Hildegard Remki, my good girl. Everyone in that cellar had troubles of their own, and plenty of them. I've lost a child, too, you know. Kaspar's little brother. He was just a tiny little baby, and he was beautiful. God took him from me when the influenza came, and it was like a knife in my heart. But I did my mourning in *private*; I didn't go vomiting it out in public. But of course, *as usual*, the eminent Hildegard Remki had to flaunt. Her grief was so much *deeper*, you see. So much more profound. So much more *important*. She had to open her trap, only this time she had to pay the piper. And if I have her precious radio, what's the difference? She won't be listening to it any longer."

Sigrid stands frozen, a damp, half-peeled potato in one hand and the paring knife in the other, stunned by the sheer vehemence of the mother-in-law's outburst. She watches the old woman brush a frazzled white hair out of her face, clutch the heavy mahogany wireless to her breast, and hulk it out of the kitchen. Sigrid stares after her, breathing in and breathing out. Only a shaft of milky light draws her back to the sink, where she returns to the peeling of the potatoes.

A few minutes later, she pauses when a hash of radio static is followed by music. Lale Andersen singing, *Everything Passes, Everything Goes.* Then she lowers her eyes toward the sink's drain, and continues peeling.

The next day, when she returns from work, the door to the Remki flat is standing open. She cannot resist the impulse to peek inside. The emptiness draws her in. She stands in the front room, where Frau Remki once set her sterling service on the mahogany coffee table. Nothing is left now but the hardwood of the floors mottled by holes from carpet tacks. Kaiserreich lithographs of the Rhineland? No trace beyond the shadows on the wall, where the frames had hung, and a twist of picture wire knotted around a nail. The noise of Sigrid's heels on the floorboards echo largely in the barren space.

IN A WEEK'S TIME, however, the place has been repainted, a sign that someone important is moving in. And Sigrid must squeeze past the furniture being hauled up the stairs by Frau Mundt's husband and a gang of his cronies from the beer hall. They huff and puff and sweat as they lug the lengthy leather couch, the silk-upholstered armchairs, the heavy oak dinner table, and rolled tapestry carpets. The bronze relief portrait of the Reich's First Soldier and Führer of the German Volk, Adolf Hitler.

Of course, there's a portrait of the same fellow hanging in Sigrid's flat, too. It's a stationer's print in a cheap tackboard frame. Her mother-in-law had it hung over her chair. "Don't drop it, for God's sake," one of Mundt's pals jokes as they negotiate the stairwell railing with the heavy bronze plaque. "We don't want the Gestapo crawling up our arseholes." He guffaws and then swears sharply as he nearly loses his grip. This, just as the new mistress of the flat appears. The fellow's face darkens as Mundt's husband berates him roughly. "Bauer, you dunderhead. Watch your *mouth*."

"Beg pardon, gnädige Frau." The old beer-swiller begs demurely. But the flat's new mistress appears not to hear him. "Haven't you brought the china up yet?" she demands of Mundt's husband with a frown that pinches her face. "I told you I wanted the china. I'm sure I said that."

Mundt's husband clears his throat. "It'll be up next, gnädige Frau." he assures her. "The very next thing." Then he takes it out on his chum. "Come on, meathead! Keep moving! Do you think the lady has time to waste?"

She is young. Couldn't be more than a couple of years into her twenties, with glossy, honey brown hair plaited into a crown of braids. Her eyes are blue and as large as lakes. A cherub face and a milkmaid's body. Pretty and quite pregnant. Several months along, to judge by the large bulge covered by a simple print maternity dress cut from top-quality linen.

"Frau Schröder, isn't it?"

Sigrid looks up. "Yes," she answers with a politely blank expression.

"I am the Frau Obersturmführer Junger," the girl announces, and glides forward with an outstretched hand.

"Very pleased," Sigrid tells her, and moves forward as well, but not a hair farther than is required to take the Frau Junger's plump white hand. It takes a certain type of female to introduce herself to a new neighbor by her husband's rank in the SS. *The Frau Obersturmführer.* "Welcome to the building."

The Frau Obersturmführer gives her a single military shake. "Thank you," she responds without inflection. "Your husband is serving, isn't he?"

Sigrid stares, her eyebrows arched. "I beg your pardon?"

"I asked if your husband is serving."

"Well, yes. He is."

"On the front line?"

Her teeth clench lightly. She feels her face heat. "In the East," she answers, "with the Ninth Army."

The Frau Obersturmführer nods. "Ah. Very good." And her lips pucker into a tight little smile. Very good. As it should be. "*My* husband is also in central Russia. Eighth SS-Kavallerie-Division," she announces, as if this obviously trumps Sigrid. "He commands an anti-banditry company, and is a holder of the German Cross in gold."

"I see," says Sigrid, stretching her face into a pleasant mask.

"I'm really so proud of him," the Frau Obersturmführer declares, her round face glowing. "Really so very proud."

Escaping into the flat, Sigrid thumps the door behind her, only to discover her mother-in-law crouched down on the floor in the living room with her ear pressed against the speaker of Frau Remki's wireless. This is the standard position for listening to the forbidden broadcasts of the British Broadcasting Company. Sigrid clears her throat loudly and takes no small pleasure in watching the old crone jump out of her skin. "That's a crime, you know," she says.

"*What's* a crime?" The old woman quickly snaps the radio off and lights up one of her cheap Aristons. The air goes bitter as she expels smoke. "Going deaf or growing old?"

Sigrid drops her bags on the sideboard. "Hörsig's had our number on the board, so I got some carp. Doesn't look too bad."

"Still no codfish?"

"No, you'll have to wait for Army Day for that."

"Fine," Mother Schröder responds flatly, distancing herself from the radio as she stands. "I'll put water on for the potatoes. We should get them prepared," she announces, crossing into the kitchen, cigarette still poking out from between her lips.

Sigrid slips off her coat and shivers. The flat is chilled. She crosses to the coke stove and dumps a few briquettes into the firebox from the scuttle, taking advantage of the temporary weakness of Mother Schröder's position. "I met our new neighbor," she says, picking up the day's mail. Nothing unusual. An invitation from the German Association of Music Lovers. Something from the Dairy Society of Mark Brandenburg. "Just now," she says, "on the landing. She's very young."

Mother Schröder glares at the coke stove, but makes no protest. Resting her cigarette on the edge of the counter, she frowns as she dumps a few shrunken potatoes into the metal colander. "Yes, and I understand she is with child." This fact is tossed at Sigrid like a hand grenade tossed by a soldier. "Unless I've heard incorrectly," the old woman adds.

Sigrid swallows and walks over to the sink, opening the hot water tap, though the water still runs cold. "Don't worry. Your hearing is still good enough for gossip. She's really quite the ripe little plum." She plops the fish on the cutting board. Brownish blood has soaked through the newspaper in which it's been wrapped, and colors Sigrid's fingers.

"When is she due?" her mother-in-law asks with mock innocence. "Did she mention?"

"She did not, nor did I inquire. All she wanted to know was if Kaspar is at the front."

Mother Schröder's face suddenly tenses. "She asked about Kaspar?"

"She asked if my husband is serving on the front line."

"And what did you tell her?"

Sigrid squints at the intensity of her mother-in-law's question. "I told her the truth. Why? What should I have told her?"

But Mother Schröder only shakes her head and turns back to the potatoes. "Just watch your words, daughter-in-law," the old woman warns, scrubbing the potatoes roughly. "The wife of an active-duty officer in the SS. She may look ripe, but that's the kind of plum that bites back."

For a moment they are quiet as Mother Schröder dumps the last potato into a bowl. Sigrid removes a knife from the drawer and slices a grayish fillet in half. "So," she ventures, "what did they have to say?"

Her mother-in-law scowls. "What did *who* have to say?"

"You know who. The radio."

The old woman looks hunted. She shakes her head. "Nonsense," she says. "Pure nonsense."

Sigrid takes a step closer. "Pure nonsense of what sort?"

"The same sort of ridiculous rumors one can hear in the queue at the fishmonger's," the old woman says, facing the sink. Then her eyes dart to either side, a reflex so involuntary and commonplace that Berliners have given it a name: the German glance. "They say that the Bolsheviks have launched an offensive against our forces outside of Moscow," she admits in a low voice, meeting Sigrid's eyes for only an instant. "But surely it will be repulsed. His generals may have failed him at Stalingrad, but the Führer will not permit such a thing to happen again. We can, I think, be most certain of that."

THAT NIGHT THEY'RE down in the cellar again, but the Brits have targets in the northern districts in mind. The true purpose of the raid seems to be to establish the young Frau Obersturmführer Junger as the new queen of the block. The rain of bombs is only background music. She beams beatifically at one and all. Shares her bratwurst. Coos at Frau Granzinger's child and cradles the infant like a Madonna. Even goes so far as to read aloud a portion of a letter from her SS-Obersturmführer husband at the front. "'My treasured wife,'" she begins. "'You must remember that regardless of how painful our separation may be, at this most sacred time in a woman's life, that we are fighting to create nothing less than a new world. And that the sacrifices we make at home, as well as here on the field of battle, shrink to triviality when compared with the Führer's Great Purpose. We fight not for mundane conquest but for the very survival of all that is good and true and pure.'"

By this point Sigrid is praying for a bomb to hit. Fortunately the all-clear sounds before her prayer is answered. The residents gather themselves together and shamble toward the steps with the usual post-raid prattle. "Looks like the Tommies will have to try harder next time; we're still among the living." "Who knows? Maybe they ran out of bombs." Sigrid notes that Fräulein Kohl has appeared in the cellar tonight, holding the restless little Granzinger infant as if it were a lit bomb while squeezed into the benches. She glares at Sigrid as if this is somehow *her* fault .

I HAVE SOMETHING for you.

Her mother-in-law has uncorked a bottle of peach brandy to share with Marta Trotzmüller, but does not bother to invite Sigrid to join them. Just as well. Unlike the harried Frau Granzinger, Marta is of the same generation as her mother-in-law. The Kaiser's generation. And after a few snorts of brandy, they begin to unravel the spiderweb of their past. Back in days when the Pariser Platz was filled with smartly appointed carriages, and Berlin was the stomping ground for the mustachioed officers of the imperial guard regiment.

Sigrid is sitting in the bedroom in the chair, where Kaspar always draped his trousers at night, putting some greasy cream on her hands and shoulders.

There are letters that she has kept. Recklessly. Foolishly out of some girlish sentiment. They are tied with a silk burgundy-colored ribbon and stashed in a cigarette tin. He would never post them, of course. But he would leave them in her coat pocket, in her bag, to find on the train ride home. Or the next day when she opened her purse before work. Raw, animal scribbling, often dedicated to the torture to which she was subjecting him. His *need* for her, flowing through the ink across the pages. Her culpability in the matter of his brutal sexual despair when they are parted. He calls her a siren. A Lilith. A succubus.

But also an Aphrodite. The Angel of his Flesh. Foolish little names that always left her disproportionately senseless. Now and again she removes the letters from the tin and holds them. When she's alone in the flat or the old woman is passed out, she holds them just to feel their weight, but never reads a word again. She doesn't need to. They are all printed in fire on the walls of her memory. And all she need do to see his face, to hear is voice, is close her eyes.

I have something for you, he told her.

"Something?" She tried not to sound hopeful. He had never given her a gift of any kind.

"Yes. Sometimes I write to you when you're not with me. Sometimes at night," he said, and reached over to the side table, where he plucked a small envelope from beneath a monstrous volume of Goethe's *Theory of Colors.*

"You mean," she asked, "a love letter?"

A shrug. Call it what you like. She crinkled open the envelope, trying to restrain her excitement. No one had ever written her a love letter. When she opened the page and read it, she could hear his voice as if from a distance, even though he was right next to her. The words both murdered her and made her whole. She touched his face as she read, just to feel him. And felt the kiss of his lips on her fingers. When she finished, when she reached the last word, she was no longer trying to hold back the tears from cooling her cheek. She gazed openly up into his face. Then raised her mouth to him and whispered her love into his ear. It was the first time she had used the word with him in a direct sentence.

He reacted by kissing her briefly. Brushing hair from her forehead. "It's just a letter, Sigrid. Just what I've been thinking."

She felt suddenly confused. Suddenly at risk. Something had gone off course in his voice. He dumped himself onto his back and blew smoke at the ceiling.

"Why did you marry your husband?" he inquired.

A blink. "Why?"

"You're surprised at the question?"

"I am," she admitted, "a little."

"You said that I should ask about him."

"I said that you *could* ask about him."

"So you married for love? Is that correct? You loved him?"

She rearranged her face to accommodate her answer to this question. Perhaps she couldn't quite imagine that he was so quickly turning the word against her. "Well. In some ways, yes, of course."

But he cut her off. "Of course? Why, of course? You think it's required?" Another puff from his cigarette. "You think it's something ordained by God?"

"I don't think I like this conversation."

"You know what I believe? I believe God is a confidence man. And that love is his favorite swindle."

A moment later, he was back on the bed, pushing into her. Pumping himself into her as if she were the holy repository for all his perfect sacrilege.

———

When Sigrid was fifteen, during a time when the Nazi Party was still merely a political curiosity in Berlin, there was a chubby old lady named Steinberg, who lived above the dingy flat, which Sigrid shared with her mother in the Salzbrunner Strasse. The old lady was losing her sight, so Sigrid would help her with cleaning and laundry and shopping after school dismissal, and for this Sigrid earned a few marks. It wasn't so bad. Since her mother had taken a secretarial position at a Kreuzberg Blaupunkt factory to pay the rent, their flat always felt like an empty grave when Sigrid came home, so she didn't mind having another place to be. Sitting in Frau Steinberg's small living room, she often read the books that lined the shelves, sometimes aloud for the old lady's benefit. She knew, of course, that Frau Steinberg was Jewish, but had never given this fact any great thought. On the mantel was a picture of Herr Steinberg in uniform with a medal pinned to his tunic from the Kaiser's war. At Christmastime, Frau Steinberg distributed sweets to the children in the building. And if there was a tiny copy of Jewish scripture inserted into a small brass knickknack tacked to the front door frame, it didn't seem to bother the neighbors much.

Then one afternoon, Frau Steinberg's son arrived. His name was Fabian. He was not very tall, but physically very strongly built, with dark, lustrously palmated hair. There was a brawniness under the suit he wore, and when he smiled, Sigrid felt her stomach flip. When her mother met him, she saw a look on her mother's face that made her highly suspect. It was the look usually reserved for the jewelry counter at KaDeWe. And Fabian's look in return was not much different. It caused Sigrid a twinge of jealousy, the way they smiled at each other. And she certainly didn't like the way her mother questioned her at supper. *So you say he's a salesman?*

Of some sort.

And he's come back to Berlin?

Only temporarily, Sigrid had answered, though she had made that up.

Did you see the shirt he was wearing? That was real silk.

Sigrid frowned. She had paid no attention to his shirt.

He must do well, don't you think? But at this point, Sigrid could tell that her mother was now talking to herself, not to her daughter.

Dinners and outings followed, with Sigrid present. Then dinners and outings followed *without* her present. It made Sigrid angry, and to get back at her mother, she started copying her father's mannerisms: fortifying herself behind printed words at the supper table, answering questions with a dull, ironic huff of breath followed by a flat grunt of disapproval, all in attempt to conjure her father's ghost and sting her mother with the memory of her absent husband. But her mother simply ignored her and talked about the French automobile that Fabian had bought.

A Renault the color of ripe cherries.

A huff of breath. Not even a German car. Followed by a flat grunt of disapproval.

Then there was a morning when Sigrid woke up at first light only to find Fabian leaving their flat. She stood there, clutching her dressing gown closed over her flannel nightclothes, staring at him in shock. He only smiled his smile in return, and chirped, "Be smart at school today, blondie." He had started calling her that. "Study hard."

A few moments later, her mother came bustling into the room, in a pale blue satin nightgown, with a flimsy lace top that left her bosom largely exposed. Sigrid had never seen her in such a thing before. Her mother stopped dead at Sigrid's stare, but only for the length of a breath to recalculate. Then she hurried toward the kitchen. "You're up early," was all she said. Sigrid said nothing.

In fact, Sigrid said nothing for the rest of the day. It was only after dinner when her mother was boiling coffee that she blurted out the words. "Are you going to marry him?"

Her mother offered her the thinnest of glances as she lit up a cigarette.

"Marry whom, Liebchen?"

Sigrid frowned. "Herr Steinberg, of course," she blurted. "*Fabian.*"

Her mother formed an odd smile shaped around something sharp and painful. "Liebchen," she began, drowsily, then spewed out smoke. "That would never happen."

"Why?" Sigrid had demanded. "Because he doesn't love you?"

And now a flash of pain colored her mother's eyes. "Oh, no. I'm sure he loves me."

"Then *why*?" Sigrid was a little afraid now. Afraid of what was coming.

"Because of *you,* of course."

"Me?"

"He's a Jew, child." And then her voice became blandly incredulous. "I could never permit a Jew to become your father."

Sigrid saw Fabian perhaps a week later, standing out in the street in front of their flat. But her mother only closed the shades. "I've spoken to Frau Schultz across the street. She needs help with her housework, and will pay two marks a day."

"Frau Schultz?"

"The money will come in handy. Look at you, you're growing out of your clothes," her mother observed with a dim reproach informing her voice. "Soon you'll be popping out of our blouse."

"But Frau Schultz is *mean,*" Sigrid complained. "And she has that nasty dog who always nips my ankles."

"You'll learn to live with it. I've learned to live with plenty worse, believe me. She's expecting you to start tomorrow."

"I don't think Fabian ever loved you," Sigrid announced. "And neither did Poppa." Her eyes were suddenly burning with tears. It was the cruelest thing she could think of to say. Her mother only gazed back at her with a kind of wretched disdain, but all she said was, "Don't make any problems for old lady Schultz. Or it'll be *my* bite you have to worry about."

Good. For once you are staying out of trouble, Sigrid hears herself observe. Returning home from the patent office, she has met Fräulein Kohl outside the building, shepherding Granzinger's two middle girls up the steps. She finds that she is inexplicably happy to see the young woman, though she does not dare show it.

"Go on. Go on up," the Fräulein directs the children without sympathy. "You know the way, I think, by now."

"Mutti will be cross if you leave us alone again," the piggy-faced child points out.

"And I'll be cross if you don't do as you're told, and we don't want *that*, do we? Now go. I want a word with Frau Schröder."

The little piglet frowns. She looks like she might want to challenge her orders, but decides not to, and the two children bounce up the steps.

"A word?" Sigrid asks.

"Will you do something for me? Frau Schröder?"

"You mean something *else*?"

The girl removes a parcel from her pocket, tightly wrapped in brown butcher's paper and tied with twine. "Would you hold this for me? Just for a few days."

"Hold it?" Sigrid feels a small pinch in her belly. "What does that mean, 'hold it'? Hold it for what? What is it?"

"Something that I would prefer not to have just anyone open. I have very little privacy, you see. Frau Granzinger is regularly searching through my things."

"And how do you know I won't open it as well? Because of your intuition again?"

"No. I think you might open it. But better you than her. Anyway, it won't be long," she says. "I'll take it back in a few days."

"No. No, this doesn't feel correct."

"It's *not* correct, Frau Schröder. In fact, it's very *in*correct. But never mind," the girl tells her, and replaces the parcel into her pocket. "Never mind. I'm sorry to have bothered you." She turns her back to Sigrid and heads up the steps.

"Wait. Child. You needn't simply walk away," Sigrid points out.

But the girl only shrugs as she opens the doors to the foyer. "No? Why not? Either you do something or you don't. That's what I've learned," she says, and disappears into the building.

Climbing the steps alone toward 11G, Sigrid fills her head with a memory. The first time Egon asked her to deliver an envelope for him, they had just made love. Afterward, she lay collapsed on her back, her head on the mattress. Where had the pillow gone? He reached over to retrieve his cigarettes from the end table, and then lit up, leaning beside her on one elbow.

"Don't tell me your husband has ever done *that* for you," he said, exhaling smoke in a stream. "That takes some true craftsmanship." She didn't answer, and he didn't seem to expect her to. "So, Frau Schröder. There's something you can do for *me*," he told her.

She let her head roll over so that she was looking into his face. "In payment for your fine craftsmanship?" she asked.

"Tomorrow at noon, there will be a man waiting on the main platform of Schlesischer Bahnhof. I'd like you to exchange packages with him."

"Packages," Sigrid repeated.

"Yes. I'll give you the package for him. You bring back his package for me."

A stare.

"Very simple, actually," Egon told her. "It won't take you thirty minutes. You can do it on your midday break."

She took the cigarette from his fingers. "Am I permitted to ask questions?"

"It's a small business transaction. That's all."

"But illegal," she said, and inhaled smoke.

"Will you do it?"

Exhaled. The smoke plumed upward. "Of course I'll do it. I think you know that I'll do anything you ask of me."

"Good," he said, and reclaimed his cigarette.

THE PACKAGE ITSELF was a sack of Karneval brand rock sugar candy. When she looked at Egon for an explanation, he simply said, "Don't eat any. You could break a tooth." When she opened the drawstring and shook a sample of the contents into her palm, a shard of glimmer appeared among bits of the amber rock sugar. She had never owned a diamond, but assumed that this is what one looked like.

When she gave Egon the box of Weike Garde cigars, which she had received in return for the sack of rock sugar candy, he dropped the box on the end table and sat on the bed, pulling off his shoes.

"No trouble?"

"No," she answered, draping her coat over the flimsy cane-back chair. "The gentleman was just where you'd said he would be."

One shoe hit the floor. "Good. What did he look like?" The other shoe hit the floor.

"Skinny. Head shaved. A black Homburg and a gray mustache that was waxed."

Egon nodded to himself. "Good," he said again, yanking out the tail of his shirt, then peeling it, still buttoned, over his head.

"So. What's in the cigar box? Cigars?"

"You didn't look?" he asked. Then shrugged. "Only money. A few marks to get by on." And then he asked, "Did you enjoy it?"

"You mean my secret mission?" she asked, unbuttoning her dress.

"If we were mobsters in Chicago, you'd be called my 'bagman.'"

"'Bagman'?" Sigrid repeats. Incomprehensible. "So we're mobsters now?

"Tell me the truth. It didn't give you a thrill, Frau Schröder, to be disobeying the rules?"

In fact, it had. Her heart had pumped excitedly as she had made the exchange. It had happened so fast, she had barely realized that it was over when the skinny Berliner disappeared into the crowd on the platform. But all she tells Egon is, "I'm already disobeying the rules. With you, you great monster."

Egon grinned, and stood long enough to unbuckle his belt and drop his trousers. "So you'll do it again?" he asked.

But Sigrid didn't answer him. They both knew the answer to his question. So instead she turned her back to him and showed him the clasp of her brassiere. "Undo me," she whispered lightly.

OPENING THE DOOR to her mother-in-law's flat, Sigrid smells camphor balls. "Frau Mundt has posted a notice from the Party," Mother Schröder announces as Sigrid removes her coat and scarf.

"A notice?" she asks, still distracted by her own memory.

"A collection for the war effort," the old lady says, "of winter clothing."

Sigrid glances at the striped dress box from Tempelhof's that her mother-in-law is filling. "And do we have any winter clothing left worthy of collecting?"

"As usual, your attempts at humor are ill placed."

There were always collections being made. SA men rattling tins for Winter Relief in the rail stations. Hitler Youth collecting pots and pans door to door for scrap metal drives. Sigrid digs through the pile on the table. Last year it was the same. Scarves, old gloves, some rabbit-fur collars. But this year it's also the gray-blue houndstooth coat the old lady had worn before the war, and a long black wool cape that Sigrid had bought for herself before she'd quit her job at the telephone company to get married. None of Kaspar's clothes. Kaspar's bedroom wardrobe has become something of a shrine to her mother-in-law since he was called up. "And I am contributing my sable hat?" Sigrid asks. It is the only expensive gift that Kaspar ever bought for her. Russian sable. It was their fifth wedding anniversary, after he had been promoted to the position of authorized signatory at the bank. She had picked it out from a shop window in the Unter den Linden.

Mother Schröder grabs the hat like it's an old cleaning rag. "You mean *this*?" The old woman shrugs, tossing the hat aside. "Fine. You want to keep it, go ahead. Let our soldiers turn to ice. Forget about the fact that your *husband* is at the front right now, doing his patriotic duty. You must have your important hat."

Sigrid takes a breath. "No," she replies, returning the hat to the heap. "It makes no difference," she says, and realizes that this is true. Let it return to Russia.

That evening, per Frau Mundt's notice-board instructions, Sigrid places the striped dress box and the pair of coats on the landing for official collection by the Portierfrau's slovenly husband. She notes that across the hall, at the door of the Frau Obersturmführer's flat, are a pile of coats and a wicker basket full of furs and wools. Also, two pairs of skis complete with poles, which are added to the inventory by a lean, dark-headed man supported heavily by a cane, who steps out of the flat just as Sigrid is taking her mental inventory. Her surprise must register clearly on her face, because he lifts his eyebrows and asks, "Did I startle you?"

He looks to be in his early thirties, not so much older than she, wearing a dark wool cardigan, with a patch at one of the elbows, over a white linen shirt buttoned at the collar. His face is evenly proportioned, with patrician features. What used to be called an "officer's face." But his gaze is like a gun sight, as if he is looking at her down the bore of a rifle. When she does not respond, he stacks the skis neatly against the wall. "Well. Shan't be getting much use out of these anytime soon. Ski-ing, as I recall it, requires *two* legs," he tells her, and turns his weight on his cane to reenter the flat.

"Wait. I'm sorry," Sigrid hears herself suddenly say.

Again he takes her into his sights. "You're sorry? For what?" he says mildly. "That you were impolite, or that I am a one-legged cripple?"

"Both," she answers. She can feel a sudden thickening in her blood. A certain dryness at the back of her mouth. It's not that she feels stripped by his gaze, more like annihilated. "Are you in pain?" Sigrid asks, feeling her face heat.

"Yes," he answers. "Are you?"

"Me?"

"You look it," he tells her. "In pain, that is."

"Yes," she hears herself answer suddenly.

"Then you should do something about it. I could help you."

"Help me?"

"Relieve the pain."

She swallows. Absorbs the force of his stare. "No. Thank you."

The man fixes her with the gun sight a moment longer, then shrugs. "Well, you should do *something*, gnädige Frau," he tells her, opening the door to the flat. "I have my pain, and what can be done about it? Stitch a leg back on after it's been blown off? Not very practical. But you? What's your excuse?"

THAT NIGHT, Sigrid lies awake, staring up at the darkness of the ceiling. She's still awake with a wire of tension in her body. Her palms are clammy. It's been so long that she's even *thought* about doing this that she's hesitant. Will she remember how? Shoving off her covers, she gingerly tugs up her nightdress and lets her fingers go seeking. They come up dry at first, but then she feels the dampness. Her body slowing, arching. Tightening. She must bite her wrist to silence her cry. Her cry for the man who has turned her past into a treasury, and her future into an ash pit of hope.

It's Saturday. Her day for the dairy shop and greengrocer. So she swallows some belladonna with a cup of sour chicory coffee, eats a slice of tasteless rye bread, and hurries out the door, only to be intercepted at the top of the stairs. Frau Mundt, the porter's wife, is decked out in her best Nazi fashion. The blue-black Frauenschaft uniform, complete with the felt fedora and swastika pin on the lapel of her overcoat. An ensemble she is known to wear any time she visits the Party's district office in the Jägerstrasse.

"'Morning," Sigrid offers quickly.

"*Heil Hitler*," Mundt reminds her.

"Yes of course. Heil Hitler. I'm sorry, but I'm on my way to Brodheker's, before they run out of milk."

But Frau Mundt makes no move to clear the stairwell. "Perhaps you did not see the notice," she announces, in a tone a bit too sharp for a Saturday morning.

"Notice," Sigrid repeats. "I'm sorry, *notice*? I don't know what you mean."

"*Donations*, Frau Schröder," Mundt replies with a thin frown. "Of warm clothing for our men in the east, struggling against the Bolshevik enemy. Your husband among them, I believe. They were to be placed on the landing for collection."

"Yes. Oh, yes, of course. I put out our donation last night. Right here at the door. A box and two coats."

"*Is that so?*" Mundt replies dubiously with pursed lips. "Well, then. I suppose we have a *mystery* on our hands, Frau Schröder. Because my husband, the Herr Hausleiter, picked up no such donation. The only clothing left on the landing was that at the Frau Obersturmführer Junger's door."

Sigrid gives the door a glance. "Well, then there must have been some mistake. Perhaps it was all mixed together in error."

"No. No error was made. I spoke personally to the Frau Obersturmführer on this subject first thing. All of her items were accounted for."

Sigrid heaves a breath. "Then you're correct, Frau Mundt. It is a mystery. Since you're so *positive* that your husband couldn't possibly have mixed one set of coats with another, then I recommend you speak to my mother-in-law. Perhaps she can explain it." Mundt shoots her eyes in the direction of Sigrid's door. Maybe she's not quite so anxious to tangle with the *elder* Frau Schröder. "*Go ahead.* She's in the kitchen boiling diapers for Frau Granzinger. You know, in the spirit of the people's community. But I'm sure she'll be quite happy to discuss the matter with you. Now, you'll excuse me, please, I don't wish to miss my bus," she says as she squeezes past and dashes down the steps.

"Very well, Frau Schröder," the woman calls after her with an arch tone. "I shouldn't want to *delay* you. But be aware. This isn't just about a few old coats. The Party pays very close attention to the proper expression of the National Socialist spirit. Do you hear me, Frau Schröder? *Very close attention.*"

Outside, Sigrid must pass Mundt's husband, sporting his dung brown SA kepi and greatcoat, which bulges at the belly as he piles another stack of coats onto the bed of a three-wheeled lorry. He gives her a gusty whistle. "So, she reamed you good, did she?" he says, and grins. Sigrid frowns and does not answer, causing the paunchy old hog to snort. "Don't worry about it. I'll make sure she simmers down. No trouble. Just remember that your old Uncle Mundt always takes care of his pretty ones." He winks and then cackles, showing a mouthful of brown teeth.

Most Berlin display windows are filled with empty boxes now. The signs above them read DECORATION ONLY. "Nur Antrappen" is how it is worded. Berlin has nothing left to sell. It has been reduced by the years of war to grinding coffee from acorns, to drinking wood alcohol mixed with chemical syrup, and to filling up shop windows with nothing but "Nur Antrappen." The dairy shop's window is lined with milk bottles, filled with salt. Inside, maybe a few liters of actual milk will be available for those who queue up early enough. Not whole milk, of course, but skim, a thin, bluish white fluid. By the time Sigrid gets there, the sign has already been put out. NO MORE TODAY. So much for that. Now she must hurry over to the greengrocer's, hoping to pick up a few green onions plus a questionable cabbage head and three and a half kilos of graying potatoes. That will be dinner for the week, plus the few kilos of war bread that her red paper ration cards will allow. But before she steps into the grocer's she sees someone stepping out. The young Fräulein Kohl, still with her wool beret stuffed over her soot-colored hair. On one side she carries a shopping sack sagging with the weight of produce, and on the other, tucked under her arm, a striped dress box from Tempelhof's secured with twine, and two coats. A gray-blue houndstooth and a long black wool cape. Sigrid stops dead. *Fräulein Kohl,* she starts to call out, but then swallows it. Some instinct is at work she cannot quite name. The girl continues her striding progress. Sigrid hesitates for an instant longer. Glances from side to side. Then falls in a discreet distance behind, and follows the girl's eastwardly march.

The march ends two blocks farther, a short stretch of unremarkable pavement, at a spot where the street curves around the tall Litfass column smothered with tattered advertisements for products no longer available: Miele vacuums, Miele-Ideal, RM 58, and Miele L, RM 90. Dralle's Birch Hair Water. The pretty blond Fräulein leans, smiling, against a birch tree trunk. Afri-Cola, with a palm tree on the bottle. *Good and German!*

The building is an old double-story gray brick monstrosity from the previous century. The street-level windows off the tobacconist's are grimed with dust. Their display cases empty. The light-bleached sign on the glass reads CLOSED FOR INVENTORY. The top-floor windows are boarded up, and the bricks blackened by smoke.

Sigrid watches the girl set down her burdens long enough to unlock a door tucked beside the shop. Then she gathers it all back up and vanishes inside.

So what is it? A black market in used clothes? Maybe so. Certainly there's a market for everything in Berlin these days. Sigrid looks around and goes into a small Konditorei at the corner, where she orders a cup of coffee too tasteless to finish, and watches from the window. Maybe half an hour passes before the girl reappears on the street, without the dress box or coats, and with the contents of her shopping sack substantially reduced.

Sigrid stands, digs a few groschen from her coin purse, and drops them on the tabletop.

FIVE

Something odd is going on in my building."

Renate is smoking a cigarette. She holds it in a confidential manner, like a film star, close to her lips. "Odd? In what way odd?"

Sigrid hesitates. Perhaps she's making a mistake. She may use the intimate form of address with Renate, but just how far does that go? Renate cocks her head to one side at Sigrid's silence, puffing languidly. "What is it, strudel?" she inquires.

"There's a girl, on her duty year, come to work for Frau Granzinger. Helping her with the children."

"And you've fallen in love with her?"

"No. *What?*" It takes Sigrid a moment to hear that. She shakes the question off with impatience. "Renate, please, for once no jokes."

"Well, what is a person *supposed* to think," Renate replies, slightly bemused as she expels smoke. "You look so painfully serious. What else could it be but love?"

"She's involved in something. I don't know what. But something illegal."

"*So?* Half of Berlin is involved in something illegal, and the other half *wishes* it was. It's how to survive."

"No, I don't mean stoop transactions at the greengrocer's. I mean something . . ." She does not quite have the nerve to speak the word.

But Renate, it appears, does not flinch. "*Political*," she says with a direct gaze.

Sigrid breathes in. Looks back toward the flow of the canal. They are sitting on a bench, wrapped against the cold. "We had put out some clothing. You know. For our men in the East. Old coats, gloves, and things of that sort. But before the Hausobman came to collect, the girl made off with the lot of it."

"You mean she *stole* it? How do you know this?"

"I saw her in the street. She took it all to an address in Moabit. Also food from her shopping sack."

"Well, then, she's hiding somebody," Renate announces flatly.

Sigrid gives her a slightly uncomfortable look, as if she is experiencing an unexpected pain in an unexpected place. "Yes. I think probably so."

"You *think*? What else could it be? A boyfriend would be my guess, trying to dodge the army. Or maybe he's deserted."

"But what would a *boyfriend* do with a lady's winter cape?"

"I don't know. What is the army going to do with my fitch fur jacket? I didn't ask. They wanted it, so I gave it to them. Who knows? Maybe the boyfriend likes to dress like a girlfriend. It could be his disguise."

"Very unlikely," Sigrid says. She is watching the wands of the willow tree float mournfully on the dark surface of the canal.

"Did you have any trouble with your Hausobman over the clothes?"

Sigrid blinks. Glances back at her. "No. A little with his wife. Nothing too serious."

Renate exhales a breath. "Then forget about it," she advises. "What's she to you, anyway?"

Sigrid exhales stiffly. Rewraps her half-eaten sandwich in its crinkled wax paper, and says, "I don't know. Nothing, I suppose."

"So mind your own business, dumpling." Renate says this with a smile, but her eyes mean it. "Anyway, this is all far too serious. Let's leave such silly Quatsch behind. I have a gift."

Sigrid blinks. "A gift," she starts to protest, but Renate raises her palm.

"Not for *you*. For your dear Mother Schröder. This should make your life easier," Renate says, and slips a packet of cigarettes into the pocket of Sigrid's coat, giving it a pat. "Bulgarian. Real tobacco, sugar cured. She'll love you for it."

Sigrid releases a small, restless laugh. "No. She'll hate me for it. But you're right. She'll take them," she says. "It seems I'm always thanking you."

"*Phhtt*. Forget about that. Besides, it's Gerhardt you should thank. Not me. He's the king of contraband."

THE GERMAN WOMAN DOES NOT SMOKE.

That's what the signs read across the city. Restaurant and café owners have been banned from selling cigarettes to their female patrons. But the campaign has come to little effect, at least in Sigrid's fourth-floor flat in the Uhlandstrasse. The old lady continues to foul the air with her Aristons, at forty pfennigs per packet of five. Above her chair in the front room, there is a permanent brown stain on the ceiling from decades of low-grade tobacco.

Sigrid enters the flat while her mother-in-law scrubs potatoes over the sink.

"Here. A present for you," she says, and places the packet of Renate's cigarettes on the kitchen table.

Mother Schröder quits her scrubbing. Gazes hungrily. "Where did those come from?'

"Bulgaria, I believe."

"You know very well what I mean."

"They were a gift."

Eyes shoot up, appraisingly. "A *gift*?"

Sigrid frowns. "From my friend at the office."

"Ah." The old lady dries her hands on the dish towel and nods now with understanding. "Frau *Hochwilde*," she pronounces. The whore.

"Look, if you don't want them, that's fine." Sigrid grows impatient. "I'll put them away. I'm sure they'll come in handy someday."

"No, *I'll* put them away," Mother Schröder suddenly insists, and snatches the packet from the table. "Knowing you, daughter-in-law, you won't remember where they *are* in a week's time." Slipping the packet into the pocket of her apron, she returns to the sink and shows Sigrid her back. "By the way, that girl stopped by for you."

Sigrid lifts her eyes from the mail. "Girl?"

"I can't think of her name, if I ever knew it. But you know who I mean," she insists, as if perhaps her daughter-in-law is being willfully obtuse. "The duty-year creature for Lotti Granzinger. The one who looks like trouble. Mark my words, I can spot the type."

Sigrid drops the mail on the table and pours a glass of water from a pitcher in the icebox. "And what did she want?" she asks with a neutral voice before she takes a drink.

"How should I know? I'm not a mind reader."

"No," Sigrid agrees, thinking, *And thank God for that.*

THE FRONT ROOM of Frau Granzinger's flat is cramped with heavy, veneered furnishings. A worn woven carpet. A colored print of the Führer, rendered in pastel, prewar issue, is hung centrally on the wall, where it is surrounded by photographs of the husband and children. The slightly pudgy Herr Granzinger in his army forage cap and service uniform poses with their two oldest boys, also in uniform. A chubby trio in feldgrau. A Volksempfänger radio sits on a lace doily atop a laminated bureau. The only piece of furniture in sight with any value is a glass-fronted cherrywood curio cabinet. On prominent display inside the top shelf is the Mother's Cross of Honor in gold, awarded by the Party. The framed certificate reads *The most beautiful name of the heart is Mother! Honor Card of the German Mothers rich in children.* And then, above a swastika, *Protecting the German Mother is the honorable duty of every German.*

A herd of children stampede about Sigrid, whooping and shrieking. Sigrid stands rigidly in the middle of the room. Through the door to the kitchen she can see a pot steaming on the stove, tended by the two eldest girls, a pair of sullen things in their teens. One stirs while the other cranks the wringer and hangs dripping nappies on the line. Frau Granzinger is stationed by the bassinet jammed into the corner of the room, waging war against soiled diapers with her infant.

"No, Frau Schröder, I'm sorry," she is saying, "but Fräulein Kohl is *not* here. In fact, she is *often* not here. Especially when I could use her most. *Fredi, stop that, this instant! Leave your sister alone!*" she commands. "Last week I had the laundry room booked. And what happens? She doesn't show. I had to make do with *these two*," she says, nodding toward the daughters. "And neither of them have the brains God gave a flea."

Sigrid flinches at a childish shriek as two of the wild spawn do battle over possession of a toy. The male child in a Jungvolk's "Pimpf" uniform is delighting in ripping the head from his sister's doll. "I tell you truthfully, Frau Schröder," Frau Granzinger declares gravely, "I had more help with the children when our little dachshund was alive. At least Pooki could keep them entertained. Now it might as well be Red Indians on the loose." She shakes her head as she extracts the newly diapered infant from the bassinet, who immediately begins to wail. "Unless she mends her ways, I may be forced to speak to someone about that girl." There's a crash, as the Jungvolk boy now attacks an enemy trash basket and pretends to bayonet it with a wooden rifle. *"Friedrich! What did I say? You leave your roughhousing for outside!"*

Sigrid steals a breath. "Perhaps, Frau Granzinger," she suggests over the din, "perhaps *I* could have a word with her. I mean, I can certainly understand why you're having trouble, but she may find it easier to talk to me. As a neutral party," she says, though she knows how that will be translated: as one childless woman to another.

"Friedrich! Leave your sister alone, you nasty little scrapper!" Frau Granzinger squawks, and then shakes her head with exhaustion. "You're welcome to try, Frau Schröder. As you can see, I'm at the end of my tether. But let me warn you, she's stubborn as a goat, that one. And far too much of an independent thinker for my tastes. No wonder they booted her out of the BDM."

Sigrid nods sympathetically. "Ah. Is that what happened?" The BDM. Bund Deutscher Mädel, the female Hitler Youth.

Frau Granzinger crooks the crying baby over her shoulder and starts pounding the infant for a burp. "They thought that under the right influence she would come around. You know what Hetzblätter fills a girl's head with at her age. But as you can *see*"—the woman quits her mechanical pounding long enough to fling her hand out in a gesture of resigned disappointment— "she is nowhere to be found."

A sharp clang of metal comes from the kitchen, as one of the daughters burns her fingers on the lid from the pot of boiling diapers, and drops it with a cry of pain. "God in heaven," Granzinger groans. "What *now*?"

WHEN ERICHA KOHL APPEARS at the door to Sigrid's flat just after suppertime, her face is tense and even more pale than usual.

"You talked to Frau Granzinger," she whispers tersely. "What did you *say* to her?"

Sigrid frowns. "Shut up, will you?" she answers flatly. "I'll be asking the questions from here on out. Now go get your coat and meet me downstairs by the front door. And if anyone asks, you and I are going to the cinema. Because we love it so."

THE STREET IS a smear of darkness where only pinpoints of blue and red float and bob. According to the blackout regulations, no light is permissible that can be detected from a ceiling of five hundred meters. Curbstones are striped with whitewash, steps are marked with phosphorous zigzag patterns. People negotiate the sidewalks with pocket torches filtered by colored tissue paper, or, for the stalwart Party comrade who wishes to distinguish himself from a lamppost during blackouts, a lapel pin with a fluorescent swastika. One can buy them from vendors on the street for sixty pfennigs each.

Sigrid switches on her torch to pay for their tickets under an unlit marquee. When Ericha attempts a word, she shushes her curtly. Inside, the latest edition of the *Deutsche Wochenschau* newsreel casts a sputtering of light and shadow across the screen. A Waffen-SS man in a steel helmet is tramping across a stretch of frozen ground, navigating his way through a dozen corpses lying stiff as plaster, dusted with snow, as if they have been brushed with confectioner's sugar. *More evidence of Bolshevik atrocities*, the narrator announces in a bludgeoning tone.

"May I speak now?" Ericha whispers.

"When I say so," Sigrid snaps back at her, glaring up at the field of bodies. The two women are planted in the rear of the balcony. Empty but for an old Berliner hausfrau who is snoring loudly.

"No one can hear us," Ericha insists.

"How do you know? How do you know *anything*?" Sigrid suddenly bursts out. "How old are you, anyway?"

"I'm nineteen."

"Nineteen. Still a girl."

"There are boys dying at the front who are no older."

"That's different."

"*Why* is it different?"

"*Because they are boys.* Boys become soldiers. It's the natural way."

"And girls become *what*? What is the natural way for them? To become livestock. That's how the brown swine see us. On our backs with our legs spread, and then the same when we're giving birth. To them that's our only purpose. They have made us whores to motherhood."

"*Quiet.*" Sigrid burns. "I haven't brought you here to debate. I may not be a Party member, child, but I'm still a good German," she warns. "And regardless of what your 'instincts' may tell you, I have my limits."

Ericha glares, then slumps sullenly back into her seat. Stares up at the newsreel. "We'll see."

"You came to my flat this afternoon," Sigrid says.

"Yes."

"Why?"

"Treasonable reasons, I'm sure."

"More humor like that, and I stand up and walk out right now. Is that what you want?"

Ericha still stares at the screen. "*You* are the one who brought *me* here."

"Not for nonsense."

The girl exhales dully. "I came by because . . . I don't know. I just wanted to talk. That's all. It gets so stifling in Frau Granzinger's flat. Sometimes I have to get *out* before I am suffocated to death by the odor of diaper dirt."

"Well, you should know that Frau Granzinger is keenly aware of your delinquency. She said that her dachshund was more help with the children than you are."

Only now does Ericha turn her eyes, a trace of anxiety filling them. "She said that?"

"She said that, and plenty more. I understand you were dismissed from the BdM?"

Sharp glance. "So you *are* tied into the gossip mill. Yes, it's true. I was tossed out."

"Why?"

"I realize that you haven't known me for very long, Frau Schröder, but do you actually need to ask that question? Do I strike you as the ideal of National Socialist maidenhood?"

"Was it because of a boy?"

"You mean because they call it the 'Mattress League'?"

"Is that what happened to you? You lost your virginity?" Sigrid asks bluntly.

Ericha returns the question with a probing glare. "I didn't lose it, I gave it away," she answers. "But, no, that's not why they booted me. I refused to sing a song."

"A song?" Sigrid repeats flatly.

"The 'Horst Wessel Lied.' Since I was in grammar school they've forced me to choke on that bloody thing, until one day I simply refused to sing it." She shrugs. Casually. "And so that was the end of my glorious career in the Bund Deutscher Mädel."

Sigrid shakes her head. The "Horst Wessel Lied" is a grandiloquent ballad of blood and thunder, penned by the Party's most celebrated martyr, and officially sanctified as the sacred anthem of National Socialism. "You're lucky it wasn't the end of more than that."

"So I've een told over and over. In any case, I was given a choice. A duty year as a domestic or the Land Army."

Sigrid stares back.

"First," the girl tells her, "I went to a woman in Charlottenburg whose husband was a manager at the Borsig plant. She wanted me to take her children to the zoo while she bedded down her boyfriends. That wasn't so bad. I liked the zoo. There's a splendid Siberian tiger in the Raubtierhaus. But then one day her husband came home from the factory unexpectedly. End of the story. Then next, a woman in Rummelsburg, who would leave her children to me so she could drink herself into a stupor. I could have dealt with that, she only occasionally became violent, but then she fell down a flight of stairs and snapped her neck. So now it's Frau Granzinger's."

"Well, it won't be Frau Granzinger's much longer if you don't buckle down and get to work."

"That's why you brought me here tonight? To give me a lecture?"

"No," Sigrid says. "It's not." She breathes in. "I want to know who you're hiding."

Ericha's head snaps around. She goes stock-still.

"I know that you stole the clothing from in front of my door," Sigrid tells her. "I saw you coming out of a grocer's with them, and I followed you. Is it the man you were with that day in the cemetery? Has your sweetheart decided to hide out from the army?"

Ericha still has not budged the smallest muscle. She looks frozen in place. When she speaks, her voice sounds very far away, as if she has fallen down a well. "Did you tell anyone else?" she asks.

Sigrid thinks of Renate. "No," she lies.

"Are you going to?"

"I don't know. That depends on what you have to say."

"I have *nothing* to say," Ericha replies in a thin voice.

"And that's not an acceptable answer," Sigrid flares. "Now, either you tell me what you're up to, or I'll—"

"You'll *what*? Denounce me? Ring up the police and have me arrested?"

"You think I *won't*?" Sigrid is gripping the sides of her seat, as if she might suddenly spring from it. But now Ericha nearly smiles.

"That's correct. I think you won't," she says.

"Then tell me what you're *doing*," Sigrid demands. "If I'm so trustworthy in your eyes. If your instincts are so *infallible*. What have you got to lose?"

"Why do you want to know?"

"Because," Sigrid answers her. And breathes in. "Because I think you are a child. Because I think your tough shell is a child's façade. And because I think you're in trouble far above your head, whether you've realized it or not."

"And what if I am? Why should it matter to you?"

Sigrid steadies her stare. "I wish you could tell me," she says. "Because I'm sure I don't know."

The girl goes dead silent, and then starts to rise.

Sigrid's brow knits. "What do you think you're doing?"

"Leaving," the girl declares, but Sigrid seizes her by the arm and pulls her back into her seat with a bump.

"You'll do nothing of the kind, I assure you."

On the screen Carl Raddatz has just fervently embraced Kristina Söderbaum, but their kiss in resplendent Agfacolor is forestalled by the arching wail of an air-raid siren. First one howl, then another. And another, building to a siren's song.

"*Shit*," Ericha hisses through clenched teeth.

The floor lights in the theater blink on and the projector stutters out. Berliners busy themselves by shoving impolitely toward the exits. Outside, Sigrid takes Ericha's arm, and feels the girl tense. A policeman is directing people into the nearest public shelter, which is actually the U-Bahn tunnel across the street. The crowd funnels itself down the steps, where the air goes thick with human sweat and track grease. And then when the guns of the Zoo Flak Tower go off, the recoil sounds like iron balls rolling across a concrete floor above their heads. It's the signal that Tommy will be above them soon. Yet everyone is reasonably calm, or perhaps simply resigning themselves to the routine business of death dropping from the skies again.

The bombers come and make their noise, and even when the lights blink out briefly, no one gets hysterical. Crying forbidden. The Berlin citizenry toughening up. Several men pass around a cigarette. Their wives take out their mending. People look for comfortable places to settle. Remarkably, a train passes by, though it doesn't stop. Lit faces in the windows telegraph past, like creatures from a ghoulish dream. Tommy is not close tonight.

"No bonbons for us tonight," one of the men pipes up. "Churchill's after the Siemens factory," he declares with confidence.

How is it that these men think they know so much? Sigrid cannot help but wonder. Did Churchill ring them up in advance and say, *Relax, gents. I'm heading for Spandau.* One of the wives steals the thought from Sigrid's head, and speaks as much aloud, followed by some harsh laughter on the part of the fellow's chums. Sigrid smiles with mild satisfaction, but when she looks at Ericha leaned against the wall, the girl is staring into a dark hole.

"Fräulein Kohl?"

Nothing.

"Ericha?"

Still nothing.

Sigrid takes breath. "There is no reason to worry," she assures. "The old fool's right. We're not the target."

"I'm not worried. The all-clear will sound soon."

"Ah," says Sigrid. "More Gypsy soothsaying." She says this mildly. But the look Ericha fires at her is anything but mild. "*What?* What's the matter?"

"The girls in my BdM troop," Ericha tells her in an emotionless voice. "That's what they used to call me. The Gypsy."

"Really? Well. I'm sorry. I didn't mean anything by it."

A pause. "*They* did," she says.

As the all-clear siren bawls its single note above them, Ericha goes mute and remains so, even as the crowd climbs the station steps and emerges into the darkness of the street. She has taken on the quality of a somnambulist. Not so unusual for a Berliner these days, but the transformation is so sudden that Sigrid feels uneasy.

"*Look,*" she whispers, latching onto Ericha's arm, "I know I'm often harsh. It's how I am. But striking yourself dumb won't remedy the situation."

Ericha raises her eyes. "Nothing will remedy the situation, Frau Schröder. We are all of us stuck in this mess, until the day when the last standing bricks in this town are turned into rubble. That's the only remedy we can expect. A clean slate. Counting upward from zero."

Sigrid stares, half baffled, half mortified. "I think you have gone mad, child," she whispers.

Ericha does not disagree. "Mad enough to surrender. Come with me, Frau Schröder, and I'll show you what you'll soon regret seeing."

A low bank of cloud cover glows crimson above the burning factory district to the northwest. The stench of chemical-rancid smoke perfumes the air. A fire brigade pumper clangs past them. A few shadows hurry down the opposite side of the street. They hurry, too, until they reach the curve in the nameless street and the *Litfass* pillar guarding the empty windows of the tobacconist shop.

"Last chance to turn back," Ericha informs her. "Are you sure?"

"*Yes*, I'm *sure*. Now, open the door, will you please?"

Ericha inserts the key by touch in the darkness. The door opens with a complaint of rusty hinges. Only when they are both inside, and the door is closed and locked behind them, does she tug the chain on a dangling lamp, dimly revealing a narrow corridor with a decrepit carpet runner smelling of burned wood. "This way to Ravensbrück, Frau Schröder," she announces.

Sigrid recoils.

Ravensbrück is the concentration camp for women, north of Berlin on the Havel. A favorite spot for the Gestapo to send females arrested for political crimes. "Is that a *joke*?" Sigrid frowns.

"You'll find out," Ericha replies, then turns and starts climbing the steps.

SIX

S THIS STILL A FLAT?" Sigrid asks when they reach the top. There's a residence plaque by the door, with a number, but no name, only an impression in the paint where a nameplate had once been tacked. But Ericha hushes her and knocks. Twice. Then three times. The hallway is thick with shadow and stinks of fire rot. The old woman who opens the door is a hefty old Berliner mare, with deep-pocketed eyes and a voice like a shovel full of cinders. "You scared the shit out of me," she declares crossly, then clamps her eyes on Sigrid. "Who's this?"

"A friend," Ericha tells her. "She's here to help."

"Help? Help how?" The old woman squints with animal suspicion. "By gossiping to her friends about what's none of her business?"

"My name is—" Sigrid begins, but the woman chops her off sharply.

"I don't need to know your name, gnädige Frau, and you don't need to know mine."

"Auntie, please," Ericha pleads aggressively. "You can trust her."

"No, *you* can trust her," the woman snorts. Her face drops into a deeply furrowed scowl. "But I suppose I've got no other choice in the matter. You're both here, so you may as well come in."

The door opens to a squat room crowded with furniture. The air smells of cat piss and lye soap. Sigrid starts to cover her nose, then quickly stops herself. Cats scurry away to their hiding places, except for a giant tom, enthroned on the shelf of a bookcase with a few dirty ledger volumes. The old woman shuts the door behind them and shoves the dead bolt closed.

"This is the lady I told you about. Who gave me the clothes," Ericha says.

"The clothes . . ." The old eyes squint. "Oh, you mean the one with the fancy fur hat. Quite a thing," she tells Sigrid as she shambles across the room.

"Do you . . ." Sigrid starts, still trying to knit this together. "Do you wear it?" To which the old woman cackles.

"*Wear it?* Oh, *yes.*" She nods mockingly and poses, as if modeling the sable on her grizzled gray mop. "I wore it just yesterday to the *opera*, don't you know. *Die Fledermaus,*" she declares with a faux grin, which quickly drops from her face.

Giving the tomcat a gentle shove from the bookcase shelf, she snorts at the absurdity. "It's all right, Hektor," she informs the tom, "you've done your job." The cat hops down, and the old woman reaches around and pulls what must be a latch, because the bookcase squeaks and swings out on a hinge, revealing a door in the wall.

"Handy little construction, isn't it?" the old woman points out with wry pride. "My husband, may he rest, could be handy at times."

"Where does it lead?"

"You saw the tobacconist on the street? That used to be our business, till the old fool fell asleep at his desk one night with a lit cigar. He was always afraid that his employees were stealing from him, so he blocked off the entrance to the attic stockroom from below and built this door in our flat." The old woman shrugs as if tossing away the thought. "Now I use it to board my *special guests*. I call it the Pension Unsagbar," she says. The Pension Unspeakable. "Not exactly the Hotel Adlon, but better than the alternatives." The first face Sigrid sees, as the door is opened, is thin and peering. An old man staring back with

watery, suspect eyes. Then an old woman whose face is as white as powder, her skin mapped with lines, her mouth set in a distant scowl. She
gazes out at Sigrid's entry into the cold, dank space in the way ghosts
must watch the living. Ericha steps up and announces, "This lady has
come to help. She can be trusted." But she addresses the inhabitants of
the space as if she might be speaking a language they do not understand.

Her body is tight. Her muscles clenching up. A ball of iron is forming in her belly. Sigrid opens her mouth, because there must be some
words she can find to speak, but then she fails to find a single one. She
can only attempt to blink away a sodden shock that has trapped her as
if it were a net dropped from the ceiling.

Swiveling her gaze, slowly, she takes in three children, pale and
hungry in the eyes. A little girl with a liquid gaze from under the sable
ring of Sigrid's hat. Twin boys in clothes far too large for them. They
couldn't be much past the age for kindergarten, huddling with blankets in the unheated attic room. A middle-aged Frau slowly rubbing her
hands for warmth, her eyeglasses held together by a twist of wire. The
Judenstern has been ripped out from her ragged coat by the stitching,
but a shadow remains.

Tricked.

Sigrid feels suddenly tricked. Fooled into passing through a door
and being confronted by this illegal world.

"Just as I warned you, Frau Schröder," Ericha breathes. "Was I
wrong?"

"So! You have gone *mad*," is all Sigrid says to the girl, as they reenter the street. A quick march down the sidewalk, following the sickly
blue beam of her pocket torch. Trying to walk off her anger and fear.
The cold in her belly and the heat under the skin. She allows Ericha to
fall in step with her, but does not permit her to breach the barrier of
silence she erects.

Sigrid carries her silence with an edge, in the same way she carries the fish knife. The sidewalk pavement glows blue from her pocket torch. "Frau Schröder, you must slow down," Ericha complains. "You'll fall off the curb in this darkness, and break your ankle."

"Shut up," Sigrid hisses back. "Just *shut up*. I'm unimpressed by your concern for my welfare, considering the vat of shit you've just dropped me into."

"*I* dropped you? Oh, no. I was only following orders, Frau Schröder. You were the one who insisted on knowing who I was *hiding*. If it's a vat of shit, it's one you climbed into on your own."

Sigrid frowns with anger at the sidewalk. "Are they all Jews?"

"Mostly, but not always," Ericha tells her. "Sometimes they're politicals. Or homosexuals. Or religious. Or all three. It makes no difference. The idea is to stop them from falling into the hands of the Gestapo."

"By sticking them up in the attic of a burned-out building?"

"Auntie's is only one link in the chain. We keep them moving."

"And the police are not bright enough to catch on?"

"Sometimes it works. Sometimes it doesn't. Sometimes the channels break down. Sometimes a mistake is made, or there's just bad luck. Or sometimes there's a betrayal." She says this in an offhanded tone. "That's why we don't trade in names. Names are not safe. They come as strangers and they leave as strangers."

"Strangers," Sigrid repeats. "And how do you feed these strangers without ration coupons?"

"It's difficult. Perhaps the most difficult thing. It helps now that I'm shopping for Frau Granzinger."

"You mean you're *stealing* from your employer's food coupons?" Sigrid says. But if this is meant as an accusation, Ericha doesn't appear to notice.

"A few less potatoes. A loaf or two of bread. Some sardines in a tin, maybe? It's nothing. She gets plenty of coupons, believe me. The NSV is very generous with recipients of the Mother's Cross. Her children do not go to sleep hungry."

"So you mean to say that you've become an accomplished thief."

"I mean to say that stealing is sometimes a moral imperative."

"Ah, such large words. I wonder if the Gestapo will be intimidated by them."

"If you're trying to scare me, Frau Schröder, I can assure you that I'm already properly terrified."

"*No*, I don't believe you *are*. This is a 'crusade' of some sort for you, little one. But have you really thought about the consequences?"

"I know all about consequences, Frau Schröder."

"I doubt it. But I wasn't just talking about you. What about the consequences to others? The old woman, for instance, whose flat we were in. You called her Auntie."

"It's what she is called."

"What about *her*?"

"What *about* her? She's made her choice. Just as I have."

Sigrid issues her a hard look, then turns away. "Lunacy," she whispers.

"Yes," Ericha agrees. "Absolute lunacy."

"How long have you had them?"

"This group? Only a few days."

"And you don't know where they come from?"

"No, I'm not *meant* to know. That's the way it works. None of us know more than we absolutely must."

"And who are 'none of us'?"

Ericha pauses, but then answers. "Others, Frau Schröder. Others with more courage than you or me. But I do my best. And when I have to, I lie. And when I have to, I steal."

A light sprinkle begins to fall. Sigrid pulls out her scarf and ties it around her head. "That doesn't make it right," she says.

"Maybe," Ericha replies. "But I think what's right and what's wrong is a much larger question now. Larger than a few rationing Marken."

"And you keep them there, in that awful attic, without respite. Like prisoners?"

Ericha shrugs. What else is she supposed to do?

Sigrid shakes her head. "They have no sunlight."

"During the day there is light that filters through the holes in the roof. Along with the cold, and sometimes the rain. At night they hang up blankets so they can light their candles."

"And where do they go to the *toilet*?"

"Twice a day, Auntie opens the door for them to use the WC, one at a time. It's the most dangerous times for everyone. She has a brother, a Party man, who likes to drop by unannounced, and would not be amused to find a Jew in the WC. At night, if they must, they pee in a bucket. We've hung a blanket for privacy."

Sigrid swallows a breath, shaking her head as she runs her hand over her forehead. But the silence between them is a sponge that soaks up the weak spattering of rain.

"So?" Ericha finally asks. "What are you going to do?"

"Do?"

"Is this the point where you ring up the police?"

"No," Sigrid admits grudgingly. "If it gives you pleasure, you were right about me to that extent. I'm not going to ring up the police."

"Then what?"

"Then what? Then nothing, Fräulein Kohl."

"Oh, no. I'm sorry, Frau Schröder, but you don't get off the hook that easily. You wanted to know all. I warned you, but you insisted. The moment you walked into that room, you committed yourself."

"Oh? Is that how it works?" Sigrid asks caustically. But Ericha only nods.

"Yes. Morally. That is how it works."

"I see. Your moral imperative."

"You told me earlier tonight that you're a good German," says Ericha. "Now is your opportunity to prove it. That's all."

"I don't require a lecture on moral principles from a nineteen-year-old."

"No. No, you who are older and so much wiser, you actually imagine that you can simply close your eyes again and everything you've seen will vanish. Go back to your flat, Frau Schröder. Go back to your job, go back to your routine. Convince yourself that there is nothing you can do, as the police drag their victims from their beds."

"There *are* criminals in this world, child, not just victims," Sigrid says. "There *are* people who commit crimes and deserve arrest."

Suddenly Ericha's eyes cool. "Last spring, there were three girls from a Jewish school for the blind, none of them more than ten. A colleague was trying to move them into a safe house we had at the time in Friedrichshain, but something happened. Maybe they were spotted by someone who denounced them. Maybe they simply stood out too much. But when the Sipo grabbed them off the street, it made no difference how it happened. Only that it had. Three little girls never coming back. So tell me, please, Frau Schröder, what crime do you imagine they had committed?" she asks. "Other than the crime of Jewish blood?"

"You have no right to address me in this way," Sigrid says, suddenly angry. "You are so incredibly naïve."

"*Really?*" the girl says, steaming. "Because I value morality?"

"Because you think that choices are all *yes or no*, and that there's *no room* in between."

"Untrue," Ericha says. "I have learned that fact quite well. Compromise is the lesson of the day. It's easy to do. A pregnant woman with a yellow star must walk in the freezing rain because Jews are barred from public transport. *Just don't look.* A man is beaten by the police in front of his children. *Don't look.* The SS march a column of skeletons, in filthy striped rags, down the middle of the goddamned *street.* But *don't look,*" she whispers roughly. "You avert your eyes enough times, and finally you go blind. You don't actually see *anything* any longer."

"*Enough.* I've had *enough* of this." Sigrid starts to turn away, but the girl grips her by the arm. "Let go of me, please," she commands tightly.

"Do you listen to the BBC, Frau Schröder? If you *do*, then you must know what's in store for the people in Auntie's attic, if the Gestapo lay their mitts on them."

Sigrid feels her breath constrict. "The British have always been full of atrocity stories," she replies. "In the last war, too. It's part of their propaganda."

Ericha fixes her closely with overcharged eyes, as if to examine Sigrid from the inside out. "*Now* who's being naïve?" the girl asks.

Sigrid gazes back at her, blinking raindrops from her eyes.

"Make your choice, Frau Schröder. Unlike those in the attic, you still have that privilege. Yes," she says, "or no."

THAT NIGHT, SIGRID gazes into the darkness above the bed, and the darkness stares back.

Egon had continued to use her for his black market exchanges. Different places each time. Different faces, too. A tubby Berliner mensch in a greasy hat waiting on the Wittenbergplatz U-Bahn station. A gaunt fellow with very thick eyeglasses and a cloth cap at the Kottbusser Tor stop, squinting at a copy of the *Deutsche Illustrierte* with a wounded infantry Landser on the cover. A whiskered old man who smelled of sour cabbage, waiting on the Prinzenstrasse platform. Always men and always stops on the U1 B line.

"I try to make it convenient for you," he told her. She had delivered another sack of rock sugar, but this time had been handed a simple kraft paper envelope, filled with twenty-mark notes.

"You must be rich by now," she'd said, crouched behind him on the bed, unbuttoning his shirt.

"All Jews are rich. Don't you know that by now?"

She frowned. "Don't take it that way. It was only a joke."

"Would you like me to be rich?" he asked, allowing her to remove his shirt.

"I don't care," she answered, brushing her lips across his skin from his neck to his shoulder. "I don't care about money." She could feel him breathe in and then out.

"That's quite a luxury. It's all I can think about."

She stopped. Did not pull away, but felt something clench inside. It hurt that *she* wasn't all he could think about. But more than that, it reminded her of the family he must be feeding and clothing with the money she collected for him in these U-Bahn transactions. The family that was None of Her Business, yet laid a deep and secret claim to him.

"What?" he asked.

"Nothing," she answered. But when he shifted toward her and stroked the hair from her face, she did not let him catch her eyes, for fear that he could too easily read the thoughts that were written in them.

"Do you love me?" she whispered with heat into his ear, when he was inside her.

"I love you," he huffed.

"And you choose me? You choose me over her?"

"I choose you," he told her, a growl in his throat as he increased the rhythm of his advance. *"You."*

But even as she gripped him. Even as she tried to draw him so deeply inside of her that he would never escape her embrace. She knew that his choice was only a breath of air.

"Frau Schröder. Heil Hitler and good morning."

Sigrid turns at the awkward sound of that particular combination, and is faced with the Frau Obersturmführer's dimpled smile and pregnant belly. "Yes. Good morning," she replies, issuing a smile in return. "And Heil Hitler," she adds for good measure.

"You're going out?" the young woman inquires smilingly. She is wearing a simple but well-cut dressing gown. Blond locks drape her shoulders. Just looking at her makes Sigrid feel like an old rag.

"Yes. To work," Sigrid says, and locks the door with the key.

"So I understand that you met my brother, Wolfram."

Sigrid feels something staple her into place. She thinks of the lean man with the gun-sight gaze. "Yes," she says. "I did."

"Well"—and this is said delicately—"I hope he didn't *impinge* upon you."

"Impinge upon me?"

"Yes. I hope he didn't *impose* upon your good nature."

"My good nature." Sigrid raises her eyebrows. "No, no, he neither impinged nor imposed."

"It's just that Wolfram, the poor man, it's just that he's been through quite a lot," the Frau Obersturmführer informs her.

"Yes. His leg." Sigrid nods. But the woman squints back at her.

"Oh, yes. His leg. That, too. In any case, if you ever feel that he's been *presumptuous* in some way, please don't hesitate to inform me. Will you promise?"

"I promise," Sigrid says, maintaining an even tone.

The woman's blazing smile returns. "Wonderful. I feel so much better now that we've had our little talk. This Sunday, you should stop by in the afternoon for coffee. That is, if you're not otherwise engaged. I'm sure I would find your company most enjoyable."

"Really?" She hears herself ask the question.

"I shall expect you at one," the Frau Obersturmführer informs her.

AT THEIR MIDDAY BREAK, she tells Renate, "I'll have to miss our lunch today."

"Really?" Renate arches an eyebrow. "Should I be jealous?"

"Only of the war effort," Sigrid replies. "I promised my mother-in-law I would volunteer at the Party office to help sort out clothes from the collections."

"Ah, yes. She's a member of the club, isn't she?"

"The lady pays her dues. That's all I know."

"Doesn't that entitle you to a few more ration coupons?'

"Oh, yes. One shoe more per year. Color of my choice, as long as it's brown."

"Well. At least sorting through coats might help some poor front-liner keep warm."

"That's the idea," Sigrid says, sighing, and shifts the weight of her armload of files. *Warm under a blanket. She can feel his body next to her, still. Smell the scent of sex mixed with the musty wool. The deception of peace in her heart. She had fallen in love with Egon while he slept.*

Renate pauses. Files a folder and then gives her a look. "Do you miss him?"

Sigrid flinches. Caught. The flash of Egon's face across the back of her eyes. "Miss him?"

"Kaspar," says Renate.

Kaspar. Sigrid opens her mouth but nothing sensible seems to come out of it, and Renate waves her off. "Never mind, never mind. A stupid question to ask. I'm sorry," she says. But for a moment, her expression has let slip its usual bravado. "It's only that I surprise myself. I mean, I know that my darling husband is likely screwing everything in and out of a skirt. But sometimes I'm still just *frantic* for him."

She frowns, then shrugs it off. "Never mind. Makes no sense," she announces, and then frowns again. "Women are such goddamned idiots," she whispers bitterly.

———

The No. 8 is packed, but a young Landser from a reserve regiment politely surrenders his seat to her. When the bus heaves to a halt unexpectedly, the passengers lean as a body to peer through the windows. Shouting and cries. Whistles screeching. SS Death's Head troops, armed with machine pistols, are herding a band of civilians out into the street in front of an apartment block. The women are clutching their children. The men are clutching their suitcases. All of their faces are paper white. An old man wears a long white beard and a skullcap. When he falls, an SS man kicks him with his boot, over and over. A curly-headed girl screams at the violence, and suddenly the SS are kicking them all, cursing at them as they are driven into the rear of a transport lorry. Then it is over. The rear of the lorry is clamped shut, and the Death's Head kommando piles into a massive Opel Blitz troop carrier. The vehicles veer into a horseshoe turn and speed away.

A hefty female police auxiliary in feldgrau coveralls steps up and waves the bus forward with stout authority.

Passengers settle back into their seats. Back into the grayness of their routine bus ride. But Sigrid realizes that she has bitten into her knuckle until it has started to bleed.

As her mother-in-law salts the potatoes boiling in the pan, she makes an excuse to go up to the Granzingers'. She returns a borrowed baking dish, with a slab of her mother-in-law's bundt cake on it, with real sugar icing. The children are so excited by the prospect of a sweet morsel that Frau Granzinger must hold the baking dish above her head to make it to the kitchen. That's when she takes Ericha by the arm.

"I've been thinking," she says to the girl.

Ericha's eyes lock onto hers. "Yes?" Sigrid flicks her eyes to Frau Granzinger, surrounded by her gaggle as she removes a large cake knife from a drawer. "Tell me," Ericha whispers.

"Friedrich, wait your turn!" Frau Granzinger snaps.

Sigrid hesitates.

"Tell me, Frau Schröder. Did you come here to bring cake?"

"Ilse! Watch your brother, he's made a mess. *Frau Schröder.* You must stay for a slice," Granzinger insists.

"Yes. Yes, of course. Thank you," she calls back. And then returns to the question in Ericha's eyes. "I came up here," Sigrid says, "because you said I must make a choice. And against my better judgment, I have made one."

SEVEN

THEY'RE CALLED "U-BOATS," Ericha tells her. Those in hiding. "Submarines," because they are submerged, and must run silently to avoid detection and destruction.

A teenage girl and her little brother are the latest guests to arrive at the pension. The girl has not removed the Judenstern, sewn, yellow and black, onto her coat. Ericha helps her with a penknife, cutting the threads with concentration. The next day, Sigrid uses her last blue ration coupon to purchase a quart of skim milk for them, which she hides on the outside windowsill of her bedroom, where her mother-in-law is unlikely to find it. But when she brings it to the pension, the brother and sister are gone. She doesn't ask questions, though the questions are bursting inside her. Where did they go? Who were they? Where were their parents? But Sigrid keeps her mouth closed. The milk goes to a pair of middle-aged women instead, who quote Shakespeare to each other as if quoting from the Bible.

But at night, lying in her bed, Sigrid cannot help but fill in the blank spots. She imagines the teenage girl sneaking a glance at the boys in her school, perhaps, stealing a drag from her father's cigarette. Imagines the girl's little brother kicking a ball down a cobbled street beside a canal. Chalking his games on the sidewalk. But these normal lives, which she conjures for the U-boats, are her secret. Her secret war against her own fear. It helps to steady her. Helps to stop her from dropping things. A bowl, a file of papers, her comb as she looks blankly at the reflection in the mirror, and suddenly loses strength in her fingers, as if she has had to divert it elsewhere. To some interior spot of resistance.

That's the way it is at first. Hiding people is much more draining. Much more terrifying than the games she played with Egon's black-market exchanges. She sometimes thinks she may blurt something out at the office that will give them all away. Worries that she brings home the smell of their fear to her mother-in-law's flat. She wakes in a silent panic one night, and is compelled to peer into the wardrobe to see if she has actually stashed a U-boat there, or if it was simply a dream.

But after a month, something begins to ease. She begins to make pathways in her head to accommodate the Pension Unsagbar. Auntie begins to call her Frau Blondi, because it has become necessary for her to have a name. After more than a month, a kind of machinery begins to take over. Her muscles grow used to the routine of breaking the law. She stops dropping her fountain pen, and has quit allowing dishes to slip from her fingers. She finds a small closet in her head, in which she can shut away the fear of hiding an attic full of contraband people from the Gestapo, and begins to mimic her old, bland addiction to routine.

Meanwhile, the machinery works. U-boats in, U-boats out, passed to one anonymous contact after the other. The parcels of black-market goods handed off at cafés or on U-Bahn platforms. Cigarettes, hard sausage, food coupons, powdered eggs, the currency of underground survival. Unnamed faces, fearful glances, anger and disbelief and grateful tears. All part of the procedure of daily life.

Ericha approves. "You're not such a hausfrau any longer," she informs Sigrid with satisfaction.

"Is that a compliment?"

No answer to that question. "I need you to do something for me," she says instead. "But it could be dangerous."

"You mean *more* dangerous?"

"Yes," Ericha agrees. "That's what I mean."

"Well, what *is* it?"

The girl expels smoke from a bitter-smelling cigarette. "A pickup."

TAKING A STEP back when the bus grinds up to the curb, Sigrid adjusts the copy of the *B.Z.* midday folded in a rectangle under her arm. When the passengers climb down, she watches their faces anxiously. What should she be looking for? A spark of fear? Defiance? Anticipation? Or simply the blankness of habitual suffering?

She realizes, to her own embarrassment, that she is also observing features. Noses with a hook? An Oriental shadow to the eyes? How he would laugh at her for that, she thinks. *Of course, my dear little shiksele. Look for the kosher snout.*

The last passengers disembark, and the Berliners crowding the curb pile aboard. She feels a twinge of panic. This is the third bus that has arrived without results. Has she missed them? Is she waiting at the wrong stop? Has something gone wrong?

She looks at her wristwatch. Not much time left before she is due back at the patent office. Can she wait another three minutes? Another two? How long until someone notices that she has not boarded a single bus? How long before she starts to stand out? She glances at the old man at the news kiosk, filling his pipe. Had she caught him watching her? But then she sees a woman approaching the stop with her two little girls in tow. There is nothing overtly distinguishing about them. The woman is probably around Sigrid's age, wrapped in a heavy, shapeless wool coat with a felt hat. They have no suitcases, no bags, they have simply themselves. And maybe that's it. Maybe that's why Sigrid is suddenly sure that she has been waiting at the right spot, after all. The children are hurrying to keep pace with their mother. The woman grips their little hands as if *they* are her luggage to carry. Not as a burden but as the only possessions of value she has left to her.

Sigrid gazes until she feels the woman's eyes lock onto hers, then she steps forward and changes the newspaper she is holding from her right arm to her left. That is the signal, which answers the guarded question darkening the woman's eyes.

"Excuse me, can you tell me the way to the zoo?" the woman asks, her voice controlled, but her face bleached by the effort.

"Yes," Sigrid answers as trained. "It's not far. I'll walk with you there."

"I'm sorry," the woman whispers thickly. "I was afraid to take the bus."

"It doesn't matter."

"I was afraid I would see someone I knew."

"It doesn't matter," Sigrid repeats. "You're in friendly hands now. But we must move quickly."

The U-Bahn carriage rocks with the rigor of the steel rails. Its dim thunder covers them like a blanket, covering any need for conversation. The woman sits with the older girl beside her and the younger on her lap. The children have frothy curls and deep brown eyes. Faces like hearts. The older sits in quiet imitation of her mother's self-possession. The younger rests her head on her mother's shoulder, and carries a small wooden tiger, with most of the stripes worn off. When required, the woman gives them brave smiles. Sigrid observes covertly, as if watching some small, inexplicable ritual: a mother and her children. Then looks away and absorbs the high-pitched keening of steel at the turns. The carriage bumping. Exhausted faces across the aisle colored by the low-wattage light. A poster featuring a German mother with her towheaded Kinder as she tucks a baby into its crib. *German women who are child-rich show the same dedication of body and life as the frontline soldier in the thunder of battle. Protect the children,* it commands, *the most valuable possession of our Volk!*

She does not take them to Auntie's pension. Only to the coffee bar inside the Bahnhof Zoo, where she seats them at a table and heads back outside to the street. The blind man's there, at his post under the bahnhof clock, and she drops a few groschen into his cup, as planned.

"Bless you," he rasps. Black goggles as dead as night.

"They're inside," she tells him.

"Yes. That's good. You should take a pencil."

"I should what?"

"You've done your job. Take a pencil and go about your business."

"You mean I'm to leave them there alone?"

"They are not alone, gnädige Frau," he says, "and neither are you. Now take a pencil and *go.*"

THAT EVENING SHE FLEES to the cinema after supper. The back row of the mezzanine smells of floor mop solution. The newsreel features footage of American soldiers taken prisoners by the Afrika Korps in the Kasserine Pass. The narrator contemptuously describes the American troops as mongrels. But Sigrid finds the faces of the young men heartbreaking. With sand in their hair and sticking to their skin, they stare into the camera like motherless children. She has taken to listening to the forbidden broadcasts while her mother-in-law is at her kaffeeklatsch, hunching by the radio in the standard position, with her ear pressed to the speaker. According to the BBC, the British have hounded the panzer armies in North Africa across Libya to the border of Tunisia. Of the war in the East, they say that, in the face of continued Red Army assaults, Ninth Army has evacuated positions south of Moscow near the city of Rzhev.

On the cinema screen, a squad of panzer grenadiers grin for the camera as they ride the turret of a Mark IV tank across a frozen white field. She allows herself a moment to imagine Kaspar's face. She pictures him now gaunt and unshaven. His helmet crooked, frosted white, like those of the men in the newsreel. Only without the smile for the camera. Instead, she draws a mild frown of appraisal on his lips.

And suddenly Ericha is beside her.

"Good evening, Frau Schröder."

Sigrid blinks. "You're late, I was afraid something had happened."

"Something did happen. But I'm fine."

"You're not going to tell me *what*, I suppose?"

Ericha confirms this by ignoring the question. "You did well today," she tells Sigrid. "Thank you."

Sigrid shrugs. Shakes her head as she stares up at the screen. "No thanks are required. I was anxious as a cat."

"Still. You did what was needed. Our cargo was safely delivered."

"Cargo? Is this how we must speak now?" she asks.

"I can't stay long."

"I thought you would be coming back with me."

"No. Something came up."

"Something happened, something came up." Sigrid frowns with frustration.

"I've left a wrapped parcel in the laundry room. There's a loose brick by the wringer. You'll see it. I scratched it with a pfennig."

"Scratched it?"

"I need you to pick it up and bring it to Auntie's tomorrow night. I'll meet you there at half past seven."

"And if there's a bombing raid?"

"Then the night after. Or the night after that." Ericha starts to stand, but then doesn't. "So how did it feel?"

"Feel?"

"You know what I mean. How did if feel to *act*?"

"It felt terrifying," Sigrid answers. "I felt like I was testing fate at every step."

The girl almost smiles. "Good. That's how you're supposed to feel. It's what keeps us out of the dungeons in the bottom of the Prinz-Albrecht-Strasse."

HER MOTHER-IN-LAW has begun to interrogate her about her whereabouts. *Going to a picture show? you say. What's it called? Who's in it? What's it about?* All questions designed to trip her up; to expose her in some way. Obviously the old woman suspects something, though exactly what, it's difficult to say. Some kind of unsavory behavior. So Sigrid has launched a counteroffensive. She's begun babbling at length over dinner, about this film and that. About how gifted is Zarah Leander, how lovely is Ilse Werner, how hilarious is poor Heinz Rühmann, how stern is Otto Gebühr, his face chiseled from a slab. In order to keep the plots straight for these films she never actually watches, she has begun memorizing the extracts in the back of Kino magazines, which she buys, dog-ears, and then leaves about the flat as proof of her cinematic devotion. Finally her mother-in-law gives up a groan. "Enough, enough. If I was so interested in such nonsense, I'd be wasting money as well at the ticket booth. But enough, please." She surrenders.

That night, when Sigrid returns from the Pension Unsagbar, the old lady does not question her.

Emboldened, the next night Sigrid gathers a quarter stick of chemical stretch butter and two tins of powdered milk from her mother-in-law's pantry, and totes them in her shopping sack to Auntie's, along with a head of brownish cabbage and two greasy fish fillets from Hörsig's, which Auntie fries up in a skillet and carves up into bites, as the cats go mad at her feet. But the cats are out of luck. At this point there are half a dozen people in the Pension Unsagbar to consume the feast. A scrawny middle-aged man with a large black mole on his face who habitually cracks his knuckles and wonders aloud what time it is. Of course, no one in the Pension Unsagbar owns a watch any longer. Watches have been sold long ago. Then there is a young husband and wife with three boys and an old grandpa, whom they all call "Opa." The husband and wife are so desperately grateful for her help. "To keep the children fed, you understand," the husband repeats over and over. But the children themselves eat quickly and covertly, as if they fear that the bites of fish and the few chunks of dried fruit may be stolen from their hands. The grandpa just stares backward at a world that no longer exists, or forward at a world beyond his comprehension. When Sigrid offers him a slice of bread with some gelatin spread, he blinks his watery pink eyes and waves it off, saying only, "For the young people."

Ericha touches her on the shoulder. "It's time," she tells her.

At the door, Sigrid gazes at her fretfully. "Where are they?"

"*They?*"

"The woman and her two girls. Where are they? *Were they caught?*" She asks the questions from the back of her throat, as if she would rather swallow the words than speak them.

"You liked them, did you?"

"I just expected to see them here."

"Don't worry. They're safe enough. Auntie's is not the only place we use. There are others willing to lend us a room or a bed or an attic for a night or two when necessary. I had to move them to accommodate this lot we just took in."

"So they won't be coming *back*?"

"That all depends on how things work out," Ericha tells her. And then she says, buttoning her coat, "I'd be careful, if I were you."

"Careful of what?"

"Careful of your emotions. You can't afford to form attachments."

Going down the steps of the stairwell to the street level, Sigrid catches a shadow of a glance. "What?" she inquires.

"Nothing," says Ericha.

"No, you gave me a look. What is it?"

"It's nothing. Only sometimes I wonder about your motives."

"My motives? What on earth do you mean by that?"

"I mean you're getting older."

"Why, thank you, little one. How kind of you to note that."

"Well, you are. You must be close to thirty by now, and without any children. Perhaps you need to be a mother, even if it's only to strangers."

"And perhaps you need to concentrate less on nonsense. You're so smart that you think yourself into knots. Besides. Just ask anyone. I haven't a germ of maternal instinct. So no more theories, please."

"You never talk about your husband," Ericha says.

Sigrid swallows sharply. "I do."

"No. You don't. Other women talk about their husbands constantly. So it makes me curious that you don't."

"I suppose I am not 'other women.' What's private to me is private."

Ericha gives a drilling look. Then turns away, and unlocks the door that leads to the street. "I'm sorry. I won't ask again. Did you bring the parcel?"

Sigrid looks back blankly. "Did I?"

"From the laundry room."

"Oh. Yes. Remind me to give you a groschen for the next time. I had the devil's own time finding your penny scratch." She reaches into her coat pocket, and retrieves a parcel in brown paper. "What is it?"

Ericha unties the twine as her answer. Then pushes aside the brown paper to reveal a stack of worn and crinkled bank notes of varied denominations that have been passed, well used, from hand to hand. "A withdrawal from our bank," she says.

Sigrid stares in the pale wattage of the stairwell bulb. "Where did this come from?"

"People who make donations to us rather than Winter Relief."

"There must be close to three hundred marks here."

Ericha does not respond to this. Instead, she says, "You should have a key."

"What?"

"A key to Auntie's door."

"And I'm sure your Auntie would be less than pleased at that idea."

"Don't misjudge her just because she can be thorny. It's her way. Believe me, if she didn't find you trustworthy, she wouldn't be letting you past the landing," Ericha tells her.

"Is this a test?"

"No."

"Is this your way of measuring my commitment?"

"No. It's not a test."

"It is, because with Ericha Kohl, everything is a test."

Ericha shakes her head. "Never mind. If you don't want the responsibility, then you don't."

"I didn't say that."

"You didn't say one thing or the other."

"Fine. If you give me a key, I will take a key."

Ericha reties the parcel of bills.

"What's it for?" Sigrid asks.

"A bribe. An important document." After tightening her knot on the parcel, the girl replaces it in Sigrid's handbag.

"What are you doing?"

"Giving it back to you. You'll need it. Our contact will be waiting for you in the cinema tonight at quarter past seven. Rear mezzanine."

If we were mobsters in Chicago, you'd be called my bagman.

"I'm not sure I wish to do this," Sigrid says.

"Maybe not. But you'll do it anyway," Ericha tells her confidently.

"Oh, you think so?"

"Yes. Because it's a test. And you can't resist passing tests."

Sigrid frowns. "Why can't *you* do it?"

"Because the man you'll be meeting knows me. I was in the BdM with his daughter."

"His daughter?"

"His brainless daughter. I bloodied her nose."

"I won't ask why."

"So, you'll do it."

Sigrid takes in a sharp breath. "My God, I'm going to be late getting back to work."

"So, you'll do it," Ericha repeats.

"Yes, yes, I'll do it," she squawks. "Now, open the door," Sigrid commands. "Quickly."

SHE IS ONLY a few seconds short of returning late to the patent office. Fräulein Kretchmar gazes at her, as she quickly removes the cover of her typewriter. The woman's mouth opens, as if she might speak, but then she doesn't. Sigrid breathes in, then breathes out.

Coming home at the end of the day, she finds her mother-in-law down on her hands and knees, scrubbing the kitchen floor, plunging a stiff-bristled brush into a pail of dirty water with a sickly-sweet odor.

"My God." Sigrid frowns. "What *is* that smell?"

"Pine needles," the old woman replies, slapping the brush onto the floor. "Stewed pine needles. It was on one of my radio programs."

"Well, at least it's not the soup. Have you put it on yet?"

"Just now. Watch where you're stepping, will you? If you leave footprints, *you'll* have to clean them. Not I."

Sigrid enters the kitchen. Lifts the lid on the soup pot, sniffs the contents, then replaces it. No meat. A little over half a kilo per week per person permitted by their allotted ration Marken does not allow for many meaty soups. But she can smell the aroma of cigarette tobacco. And not the odorous ersatz brands, either, but the real thing. Renate's gift. She considers mentioning it, just to wheedle, when the old lady suddenly announces, "Your new friend stopped by."

She steps out of the kitchen. *"Friend?"*

"The Frau Obersturmführer Junger," her mother pronounces

archly. "She asked if you could come at *two* on Sunday, rather than one." A pointed glance out of the corner of her eye as she scrubs. "I told her you'd be *delighted*."

After supper, she informs Mother Schröder that she is going to the cinema as she walks out, closing the door behind her before any argument can slow her down. She clatters down the steps, listening to the noise of her flat-heeled shoes on the worn wooden planks, and bursts out the door as the twilight glooms the streets. The air is stiff with cold, but she breathes it in with a mix of relief and trepidation. In her bag is the parcel of banknotes.

She has stolen one of her mother-in-law's Aristons from the packet, and lights it with a match from a paper box as she walks. The tobacco is so bitter that at first she feels she might retch. She pauses by a poplar tree to overcome her light-headedness, and then forces down another drag. This time the smoke sticks to her throat. Then, as she expels it, she spots the figure in the bleakness.

A man across the street.

It's not that she recognizes his face. His face is obscured by the down-turned hat brim and the upturned collar. Perhaps it's his posture that causes her heartbeat to shorten. The slightly dangerous slouch. Hands hidden in his pockets. The tilt of the head. And most of all his stillness. That stillness within him that she could never quite touch.

It's as if she can feel herself rooting to the spot. She does not move, and neither does he.

The No. 14 Elektrischetram hums up the Uhlandstrasse in the opposite direction, and after it passes, no one is standing across the street. No one at all.

IN THE CINEMA'S BALCONY, Sigrid finds the father of the BdM girl whose nose Ericha bloodied. He's a nervous bureaucrat, with multiple chins that ripple when he frowns. Opening an envelope, he exhibits the contraband he's brought to market. In the light from the screen Sigrid can read the title on the cardboard document cover. BOMBEN-PASS. A passbook for bombing victims. Tensely, she slides him the paper parcel in exchange. The bureaucrat yanks open the parcel wrapping and thumbs through the marks. Then he nods curtly. Transaction completed.

The bureaucrat scurries away, but Sigrid stays. She breathes deeply. The film assaults her ears with music. It rushes sharp gray-white light past her eyes. But she is concentrating on the darkness. Is he out there? Waiting for her? Buried in a row of seats, an escapee from the solitary prison of her memory? She searches the blackness. Waits. But then the house lights are raised. A scattered collection of Berliners, thickly wrapped in coats and scarves, are on their feet, milling toward the exits like somnambulists as the porters herd them down the aisles.

No one buried in the seats. No one waiting. No man. No ghost.

The last time she acted as Egon's bagman, she was carrying a tin of Malzkaffee in her purse. She was posted in the spot by the stairs as instructed, and was waiting on the skinny Berliner with the homburg once more. But she was looking at her wristwatch, because the man had not yet arrived, and she would soon be late in returning to the office. She tried not to appear anxious or out of place. But then a Sipo agent in a raincoat turned up on the platform, with a uniformed Orpo officer trailing. When the Sipo man started stopping women—women only—and asking for their papers, she felt a burn of nausea in her belly. Her eyes darted back and forth. No sign of the skinny Berliner or his black homburg. Perhaps he had spotted the Sipo men before her. Perhaps he had been tipped off. Perhaps they had already arrested him and were now searching for his accomplice.

A train whooshed into the station. It was headed the wrong direction, but Sigrid turned and stepped onto it anyway. She tried to keep her breathing level. It seemed to take a lifetime for the train to get under way, and when at last it rumbled forward, she had lost sight of the Sipo agent. Had he boarded the train as well? She stood tightly clutching the handrail when someone touched her on the shoulder, and she spun around with sparks in her eyes.

"*Excuse me*," a young boy in a Hitler Youth uniform said, obviously startled by her reaction to his touch. "But I thought . . . I thought you might like to sit down."

She glared at him, and then glared at the vacant seat he was offering her. "Ah," she breathed finally. "Thank you."

Your instincts are good. You made the right decision.

She had clamped the tin of Malzkaffee onto the table that afternoon, and announced to Egon that she was through with being his bagman. "Look at my hands, how they are shaking just talking about it. I could barely get through my work for the rest of the day. I'm sorry, I'm simply not cut out for this, Egon."

He took her hands in his and settled her onto the bed opposite him. "Don't worry. Your instincts are good. You made the right decision."

"Don't try to charm me."

"I'm not."

"I can't do it any longer. I'm just a hausfrau. That's all."

He took a deep breath and expelled it. She knew what he was doing. He was calculating how to handle this. How to handle *her*. "Let me get you a drink," he said, and left her slumped on the bed as he headed for the bottle in the cabinet. She picked up his cigarette smoldering in the ashtray and took a puff. Its bitterness bit into the back of her throat.

"Here. Take this."

"I shouldn't," she said, accepting the glass. "I'll smell of alcohol when I get home." But she took a swallow anyway, and closed her eyes as the heat flowed down to her belly. He flopped down on the bed, with a jangle of springs, leaning his head against the wall, and picking up his cigarette. "I'll get someone else," he said.

She looked over at him. "Will you?"

A shrug. "Of course I will." And then he looks away from her, examining the rising smoke. "What else can I do?"

When Ericha appears in the cinema seat beside her, she jumps.

"You did it," the girl whispers.

"What?"

"You did it. You made the exchange."

"Yes." Sigrid frowns. "Yes, I did it. A bombing passbook."

"A *blank* bombing passbook. We can type any name we like on it."

"Now all we need is a typewriter."

"You have a typewriter at your job."

"I see. So I am to be the secret agent at the Reich Patent Office. I have a typewriter, yes, but I also have a supervisor standing at my back."

"Never mind, then. There are other typewriters," Ericha tells her. "You're upset."

"No. I just can't stand to sit here any longer. Please, let's go."

The old usher opens the door for them, but also blocks it, clearing his throat with intention. "Evening, gnädige Frauen. Enjoy the film?"

"Give him some money," Ericha instructs in a whisper. "Ten marks."

Sigrid obeys, digging the money from her purse.

The old man grunts his thanks and clears the way for them with ersatz gallantry.

"You pay him off?" she asks Ericha as they hurry down the steps.

"Not me. *You*," she answers, but then says, "It's a good spot for transactions. It's worth a bit of wire to protect," she says, then asks, "What's the matter?"

"Nothing."

"You're lying," Ericha tells her as they reach the bottom of the steps, but leaves it at that.

The trip back down the Uhlandstrasse is filled with silence. The silence of the images inside Sigrid's head. His face. The weight of his eyes. The lightness of his fingers on her cheek. But as they enter the building, they are overrun by Frau Granzinger and her brood. *"Fräu-lein! Where have you been?"* Granzinger demands. Sigrid sees something in Ericha freeze up, and she is abruptly reminded of the girl's youth. "I told you, did I *not*," Granzinger is blaring, "that I had an appointment tonight?! And look at me! Here I am dragging all these children with me, because *you*, my duty girl, were nowhere to be found *as usual*."

"Frau Granzinger," Sigrid starts to intercede, but the woman sharply waves off her interruption.

"Please, Frau Schröder. Don't defend her. I realize you have taken an interest in this muddleheaded thing, and I won't ask why. But, *please*, tonight keep your explanations to yourself. Now *upstairs*. All of you!" she booms at her brood. Then to Ericha she adds with a glower, "And that includes *you*, Fräulein." Stuffing her hausfrau's bag, the size of a serving platter, under her arm, she finishes with Sigrid. "And to you, Frau Schröder. *Good night.*"

Climbing the stairs to the flat, she discovers Mother Schröder smoking in her chair, listening to the Italian Air Force Orchestra in concert on the Telefunken. The frequency band glows amber. "So. You've found your way back again. Lucky me," the old woman says, and tips back a swallow from her glass. A fruity schnapps is her favorite, but sometimes she resorts to cooking sherry.

"Lucky you, lucky me," Sigrid replies, and begins to unbutton her coat when the music is suddenly interrupted by a sharp, syncopated beeping.

THE TOMMIES COME, and the raid lasts for just under two hours, though it seems timeless. Never ending. The thunder of the bombing is numbing after a while. Nothing too close, like a chorus of war drums. Granzinger's children are as difficult as usual, but this time Sigrid has placed herself well away from the source of the tempest. She tries to concentrate on her knitting. It's a scarf for Kaspar from wool she had wound up after unraveling a ragged sweater. But then another night of theater begins, as the blond Frau Obersturmführer regales the assembled audience with tales of the holy struggle in the East as reported by her husband's latest Feldpost letter. Across the narrow cellar Ericha drills Sigrid with a stare while clutching one of Granzinger's squalling bundles, appearing as if she has been chained to the bench like the family dog. " 'Today we're hunting a gang of Bolshevik killers,' " the pregnant Frau announces stridently. " 'A bloody band of thieves, who'd been murdering Germans to steal their rations bag. We tracked the swine through the snow, but in the end, all we found were their corpses. They had taken the coward's way out, of course, when they realized we were closing in. All but one. A Jew, ugly as a toadstool, who'd been too cowardly to pull the trigger. My men begged me to allow them to dispatch him on the spot, and I will admit, my darling wife, that I was sorely tempted to permit them to have their way. But I could not. Instead, I reminded them that we Germans are not the murderers in this war, and that we would leave the slaughter of the unarmed to the Jews and Reds. Later on, true to form, the Jew tried to make his escape with a stolen loaf of bread. At that point, I gave the order to fire. He had left us no other choice.' "

Even the Frau Obersturmführer seems to hesitate at this point. She scrutinizes the letter in her hand, with a hint of uncertainty. Then swallows before finishing. " 'Until we are reunited, my darling one, you are, as always, at the center of my soul.' " With a breath, she folds the letter closed. *Heil Hitler,* " she offers as the closing benediction.

The cellar has settled into a silence as hard as stone. And then from the stone comes a high-pitched note. It is, in fact, a *song.* Frau Obersturmführer Junger has started *singing,* in a girlish soprano, a slightly off-key but nonetheless sweetly insistent rendition of that most sacred Party hymn, the "Horst Wessel Lied."

Eyes dart about, some of them covertly appalled. Crying is forbidden—and so is singing, the sign should say. They may be thinking that, but they remain too canny to say it, and then there's Mundt. Portierfrau Mundt, who is canny as well. Canny enough to seize an opportunity. Her voice is like a frog's, perhaps, but she starts croaking along during the chorus. It's a signal everyone gets. Soon the song is spreading. Voices gathering into a thick cacophony of National Socialist caterwauling, as tenant after tenant receives the message and jumps in. Mundt searches the ranks with her eyes, looking for laggards. She peers narrowly at Sigrid, but too bad, Sigrid is already singing. She has even beaten her mother-in-law into the fray, who is playing catch-up with some of the lyrics. *Sorry to disappoint, you venomous old snake,* Sigrid replies inwardly to Mundt, but then looks over at Ericha, and sees to her horror that the girl's mouth is clamped shut as tightly as a virgin's knees.

Sing! She telegraphs the command into the girl's skull. *Sing, for God's sake!* And maybe the girl *is* a mind reader, because, with a frigid glare in Sigrid's direction, she suddenly opens her mouth and bellows the lyrics.

At the song's end, there is ruckus of cheers and applause, and arms are tossed up for the inevitable chorus of *Heils!* Sigrid throws up her arm as well, but her *Heil* is not nearly so vehement as Ericha's, who is glaring at her now with a mix of scorn and defiance.

Shortly thereafter the drone of the bombers fade, and the all-clear sounds.

"Ha! We drove those cowardly air gangsters away!" Marta Trotzmüller feels compelled to trumpet. But as quickly as it had surfaced, the room has lost its taste for bravado. Compliments are showered appropriately on the Frau Obersturmführer, of course, and she is catered to on her way up the steps, but beyond that, there's mostly just grumbling about the lateness of the hour, as all over town, weary Berliners file out of their cellars, and those who still have them lust for their beds.

EIGHT

Across the hall Sigrid twists the bell and thinks, *When was the last time I rang this bell?* When she returned a glove Frau Remki had dropped on the stairs? She pictures Remki's colorless expression and waxy gaze. Like a corpse long before her suicide. But now the door opens and it is the Frau Obersturmführer smiling, showing all her teeth, aggressively alive.

"*Ah*, Frau Schröder. How wonderful," she announces. No *Heil* this time. Only, *How wonderful.* She wears another sensible, well-cut maternity dress, but somehow looks bigger in it than she had on Friday. Could that be? Her skin is well scrubbed and without a single blemish. Her eyes as bright as lightning strikes. Sigrid stands in the threshold, stiff like a shop mannequin, holding the plate of gooey rye-flour sugar rolls. "Good afternoon, Frau Obersturmführer. I'm late, I should apologize."

"*Ah, Quatsch*," says the girl, forgiving her immediately, still beaming. "A few minutes only. And we are all so busy these days. Please, come in. There's someone here I'd very much like you to meet."

Someone to meet? Sigrid does a poor impression of the Frau Obersturmführer's glowing smile and steps inside. Any trace of the flat's former occupant has been eradicated. Instead of Frau Remki's stolid Kaiserreich mahogany, the furnishings are blond oak with padded silk upholstery. No more tidy Viennese lithographs. Sigrid surveys photographs of men in uniforms, clustered about the bronze relief of the Führer mounted above the hearth.

"How kind," the Frau Obersturmführer remarks. "You baked us a treat?"

Sigrid blinks. Then glances down at the plate in her hand. "Oh. No, not me. Some sugar rolls my mother-in-law made for her Sunday kaffeeklatsch."

"Well. We'll hope she doesn't miss them, then."

Sigrid smiles again blankly. She is looking with polite hesitation at the woman filling one of the silk upholstered armchairs. Hair flat and straw blond with ringlets of ash gray. Body thin as a steel rod. Face, angular, and her eyes are banked with a lifetime of slow-burning anger. Ruined, Sigrid thinks. A ruined woman.

"Frau Schröder, may I present Fräulein Kessler," the Frau Obersturmführer announces formally. "My sister."

The woman offers her hand like a bony insect queen. "Half sister," she corrects, with a baring of teeth that passes for her smile. "So very pleased."

Sigrid shakes the outstretched hand, and then to fill in the strained silence that follows, the Frau Obersturmführer busies herself by relieving Sigrid of her plateful of rolls and waddling off to the kitchen. "Please. Sit," she chirps. "I'll go see to the coffee." Compared to the steely wreck of her *half* sister, she appears childlike.

"Oh. Can I offer you help?" Sigrid inquires a bit too hopefully, but the Frau Obersturmführer won't hear of it.

"No, no. *Sit. Talk*," she commands affably. "I shan't be a moment."

Sigrid sits.

"So," the woman announces briskly, "I understand you are a typist."

A brief look informed by the not-so-hidden disdain in Fräulein Kessler's voice. "I'm a stenographer for the Reichspatentamt," Sigrid answers.

A shrug. "Isn't that what I said?"

Sigrid absorbs this. "And you? Do you work?"

"I'm a nurse."

"Really."

"In the women's ward of Sankt-Gertrauden Hospital."

"You must find that rewarding."

"Must I?'

"To heal the sick."

"It's mostly dumping bedpans." Fräulein Kessler lights a cigarette from a tarnished sterling case. "Do you mind?" she asks, exhaling blue-white smoke. More of a challenge than a question.

"No."

"Would you like one?"

"No, thank you. I don't smoke."

"A good German woman."

"So you are staying with Frau Junger?"

"A bomb fell on my flat. An air mine, they told me. That's why *I* am here," Fräulein Kessler explains wanly. "Do you want to know why *you're* here?"

Sigrid pauses. "I beg your pardon?"

The woman languidly taps her cigarette over a small red glass ashtray. *"You're here as bait,"* she informs Sigrid in a mock whisper.

Sigrid's eyes level.

"To entice me out from under my rock," the woman explains.

"And what does that mean, Fräulein Kessler?"

"It means, Frau Schröder, that since my dear half sister has been saddled with me, she needs to find me a keeper."

"A keeper," Sigrid repeats.

"Yes. Like in the zoo. I'm a dangerous animal, you see."

Sigrid stares. "But . . . I'm sorry, I'm a bit confused. You're living here?"

"If you can define it as *living*, yes."

"But . . . Excuse me again. I thought I had met Frau Junger's *brother* . . ."

"Ah, so you met Wolfram, did you?" Fräulein Kessler nods with relish. "Oh, yes, and I'm *sure* he met *you*. You're just his type."

Sigrid swallows some tiny pulse of heat, and blinks.

"Wolfram *travels* a great deal since he returned from the front, but he *stays* here from time to time," the woman says. "And he's *my* brother. Not hers," she corrects with an unpleasantly bent smile. "I'm not sure if he's found a woman in the area yet," she says in a tone of assessment. "But he will. Even with half a leg, he's still ten times the man of the average specimen of his gender."

Sigrid finds herself wanting to ask, *What happened to him?* But with a rattling of porcelain cups on saucers, the Frau Obersturmführer reappears from the kitchen, still smiling as she bears a large tray over the swell of her belly. Sigrid jumps up to assist her. Strudel and lemon tarts surround Mother Schröder's rye flour rolls on a rose-pattern china platter, causing the rolls to look quite proletarian. And when the Frau Obersturmführer pours the coffee, Sigrid nearly swoons at the aroma. "I've been saving some real coffee," the Frau Obersturmführer admits coyly, "for a special occasion. No cream, I'm afraid. But I can offer you a little skim milk?"

"No, thank you. Just black."

"Very good. My father always said you can trust a person who drinks coffee black."

"I'll have milk," Fräulein Kessler injects.

But the Frau Obersturmführer's smile does not crack. "Of course you will, Carin," she says, and then turns the smile to Sigrid, passing her a delicate porcelain cup and saucer. "My sister, Frau Schröder," she explains, "has made a hobby of contrariness."

"Not a hobby, Brigitte," the woman inserts bitterly. "A career."

Sigrid takes the saucer in her hands. "And is there much of a living in that?" she asks.

Silence. Fräulein Kessler glares at her thickly for a moment, tipping her cigarette with a thumb, then, "Ha!" she snorts. "For once, Brigitte, you are correct," she announces. "I don't hate this woman."

———

The windows have been broken out of the tobacco shop. "Vandals," says Auntie with a shrug. "Children like to break things." Propaganda from the *Litfass* column has migrated to the boarded-up window spaces. A sloppy line of posters featuring the same stalwart army front-liner, over and over, advancing a swastika banner: *We will be victorious!*

The woman and her girls are still absent from the attic, but a youth with a narrow, hawkish face has appeared. Over one eyebrow he has a gash that has partially scabbed. Auntie makes an attempt to tend to the gash with some sulfur powder to help it mend, but he shoves her hand away. He is not interested in mending, he tells her. Issuing Sigrid a stiff stare, as if he might spit, he says, "You look like an authentic Aryan," his youthful voice cracked by anger. "It must amuse you to dirty your hands with Jews."

"He's angry," Ericha explains later, as they walk down the steps to the door at street level.

"That much I noticed."

"First he lost his father to an SS aktion. Then his sisters to a catcher."

Sigrid shakes the word around in her head. "And what does that *mean*? A *catcher*?"

The shattered crystal of Ericha's eyes sharpens. "Jews working for the Gestapo," she explains simply. "Jews who hunt Jews."

A blink. Sigrid stops on a step to stare.

"It happens, Frau Schröder. Don't look so shocked. There are some who've made a profession of it."

Absorbing this, Sigrid draws a breath and then continues. "You seem to be rather well informed about this boy," she observes, "for a person who asks no questions."

"I didn't ask. He spilled it all out after showing up on Auntie's step, bleeding. He's been traveling alone for weeks, on nothing but a stolen factory worker's pass, dodging the SS, dodging the Feldpolizei patrolling for deserters. No money and no food beyond what he could grab. I don't think he meant to insult you. He's grieving," she says, "frightened."

Sigrid gives a small shrug. "What he looks to me is *dangerous*."

Ericha does not disagree. She throws opens the dead bolt on the door. "I'll try to get rid of him soon," she says.

Back at the Uhlandstrasse, they part company at Frau Granzinger's door, and Sigrid listens to the racket of the Granzinger brood echo through the stairwell as she climbs the steps to the next floor. At the door to 11G, she is searching her bag for her house key when the door to 11H swings opens across the landing.

"Oh. It's you."

Sigrid turns and is met by the sight of the half sister, the bony Fräulein Kessler, standing staunchly in the threshold, wearing a well-starched housecoat, her hair parted severely.

"It *is* me, Fräulein Kessler," she confirms.

"I thought it was Brigitte," the woman says. "She went to the shops hours ago."

Sigrid stares politely, ready to turn away, until the woman takes a short step forward.

"You know, I almost find you interesting, Frau Schröder," the woman declares.

"Yes. You don't hate me."

"Ha!" Fräulein Kessler ejects a laugh. She shakes her head, still wearing her version of a smile. "You don't understand how uncommon an experience that is for a woman like me." Then her smile loosens slightly. "Or perhaps you *do*. You're an outsider, Frau Schröder," the woman announces, as if stating an essential fact.

"You think I am?"

"Oh, I *know* it. You wear it like a sign. You and your little feline friend. The duty-year girl slaving for the Fatherland's gift to motherhood."

Sigrid's gaze thickens. "She's just a lonely child," she assures the woman. "Not really a friend."

"No? Is that right? Well, I'm a bit surprised. Because I thought she *was* a friend. Perhaps a very close friend."

A silent beat.

"Come now, Frau Schröder. Surely you're aware of stairwell gossip, aren't you? You and your little black alley kitten are quite an item. All these old biddies just eat it up like hash."

Sigrid takes a breath. "Fräulein Kessler."

"*Carin,*" Fräulein Kessler informs her in a deadpan tone.

Another pause. "Fräulein Kessler. I'm aware that you have some difficulties with your current situation. And I'm aware that you apparently enjoy attempting to shock. But if you're going to ask me if I *am*, or if I am *not* a lesbian, I would greatly appreciate a direct question."

The woman's facial expression remains unchanged, but something is breaking up behind it. The cynical shallows of her eyes have deepened. "Very well, then. Are you a lesbian, Frau Schröder?"

"No, Fräulein Kessler. I am not."

The woman gazes, then draws a breath through her nostrils. "I see," she says with scratch of regret.

"I'm sorry if that disappoints you," Sigrid tells her.

"Disappoints me?" Fräulein Kessler shrugs. "No. Honestly, it's relief. I thought for a moment that I might be required to actually work up some unfortunate feelings, Frau Schröder," she says, placing her hand on the door to her flat to close it. "And I'm quite sure that I don't recall how to do so."

THAT NIGHT, Sigrid finds that the boy with the hawkish face is gone. She does not hide her relief.

"I won't ask where you sent him," she tells Ericha.

But Ericha only inhales, and then exhales. "I didn't send him anywhere. He simply vanished."

"What?"

"Auntie found the latch open on the bookcase yesterday morning, and money missing from her purse, along with a jackknife and a dozen food coupons she had stashed in a kitchen drawer."

Sigrid stares. "Well. Maybe it's for the best."

"For the best," Ericha replies, "until the Gestapo get their hands on him."

"Then we can only hope he does the right thing. Isn't that what you called it?" she asks thickly. "He struck me as the type who wouldn't be taken alive."

"So, Frau Schröder. You've become an expert in such matters?"

Sigrid lets an eyebrow rise. "What choice have I had?"

Renate glows with delight. "My, my. Imagine *that*. No wonder the little SS madonna was so interested in you. She was playing at matchmaking. She was hoping you'd ignite the lady's pilot light."

They are strolling down the banks of the canal. "It was really very sad," Sigrid tells her, and accepts a drag from a cigarette. The creamy foreign tobacco is too high quality for her to take. It makes her queasy.

She hands the cigarette back, shaking her head. "She must be very isolated. And very frightened, I think."

"Considering what the law says on the subject, she had *better* be," Renate observes. "I heard about a woman on my block, the wife of a Party man, no less, who was sent to Plotzensée with a ten-year sentence for—*you know.*"

Sigrid expels a breath. "Have you ever?"

"Have I ever?"

A shrug to the left. "Been with a woman?"

"Oh, God, no." Renate laughs brightly. "I require a throttle in order to put my engine into gear." And then a look with raised eyebrows. "Why? Have *you*?"

"What, *me*? Of course not. When would I ever find the time?"

A blink. And then again Renate laughs aloud. "You are so very entertaining," she declares.

"I'm so very pleased you find me amusing," Sigrid says, frowning. "So now would it be permissible to change the subject?"

"Oh, very well, then," Renate agrees. "Enough about you, let's talk about me. I'm afraid that my liaison with Gerhardt is running thin."

"Oh? The wife catch on?"

"Nothing so dramatic. What was once inventive and energetic has become stale and repetitive."

"Ah. Repetitive. The poor foolish man. So what now?"

Renate releases a sigh that floats along with her for several steps. "I don't know. Sometimes I think I could use a rest."

"Hmm. Renate Hochwilde without a man to bed," Sigrid murmurs. "Hard to imagine."

This is said lightly, thoughtlessly, but Renate looks at her closely.

"You know, Frau Schröder," she says after a moment. "There are times that I suspect you don't really like me very much."

Sigrid opens her mouth to protest, but, "Never mind," Renate tells her quickly. "I'm sure I'm being stupid. Let's just walk." But as they walk, a train passes above them on the elevated track, weighting the air with its iron thunder. Sigrid feels herself close off. Fortress Schröder. It's her secrets, she realizes. The secrets of the Pension Unsagbar walk between them. The secrets of Auntie's guests in a narrow, windowless room, huddling under blankets, peeing into a bucket. Every day separating Sigrid, not only from Renate, but from all who do not share that knowledge. Separating her by one more unspoken word, one more degree of silence.

NINE

S HE FINDS THAT SHE is eating less. Cabbage stew loses whatever taste it might have had. Boiled potatoes are lumpy as paste in her mouth. She cannot help but think that every bite of food she takes means one bite less for the people in hiding. As absurd and emotional as it may be, she cannot escape the idea that an inverse relationship is at work. More for her means less for them. At the midday break, she leaves her butter-spread sandwich uneaten, thinking she might save it, but then the bread goes green, and she curses herself for wasting it. *Combat spoilage*, the posters outside the dairy shop command. *Now more than ever!*

At the Pension Unsagbar, the woman and her two girls have reappeared as residents, moved back from wherever Ericha had been storing them. There's also an old man with thin white hair and blue veins popping from his temple. The old man is as worn out as an old broom, and never speaks to Sigrid. He nods politely and formally, but never says a word, and avoids eye contact. Only Ericha elicits a whisper from him now and again. He offers a "Thank you, child" when she presents him with a coat that does not have the outline of his Judenstern to betray his identity. The children's mother, on the other hand, is quite forthcoming. She plays at sock puppets with her girls with exquisite delight. She is always grateful for the help provided to her, genuinely and deeply. Yet she seems to be able to retain a certain central calm; a certain control over herself, as if she is determined that she will not become a victim.

Sigrid finds herself thinking about this woman and her girls. Not meaning to, really, just suddenly wondering, while she's doing the supper dishes or sitting on the tram—what was their life? Whence have they come? How is it that they were forced to submerge?

So on the next night she visits the pension, with a few tins of tuna fish and a stale loaf of rye, she asks the question she knows she is not supposed to ask.

"What is your name?"

The woman turns her face sharply, as if Sigrid has just stuck her with a pin. Blinks. But then she smiles. She is not a beautiful woman on the surface. Not like the plates in the fashion magazines. Her hair is kinked and reddish brown; her nose is slightly bent, as if it might have been broken years before and not quite healed properly in line. But her eyes are dark caramel, and there is a quality in her smile, in her face, that draws Sigrid in. It is confidence, perhaps. A beautiful confidence.

"Weiss," she answers. "I am Frau Weiss."

Sigrid's expression does not alter at the pinch of panic in her breast. "Frau Weiss," she repeats, and offers her hand. "I am Frau Schröder."

The woman must struggle slightly in order to take Sigrid's hand, shifting the weight of one of her sleeping daughters on her lap. The same kinky hair as her mother's, but another face completely. Sigrid compares it to Egon's broad cheekbones, and the match causes her mouth to go dry.

"Very nice to meet you," Frau Weiss tells her, then laughs without much humor. "Is that still an appropriate thing to say in this situation? I should be saying how grateful I am for people such as you. People with the courage," she says.

Her smile dims. She touches her lips to her daughter's forehead. "I can't imagine what would have become of us. Such unbelievable stories one hears. One simply cannot imagine . . ." The woman's voice trails off, but then she raises her eyes again. "I thank God that the human spirit is not dead."

Weiss, Sigrid is thinking. It's such a common Jewish name. How many thousands of people carry the name Weiss? It's only a meaningless coincidence. This could not *possibly* be *the* Frau Weiss. This could not possibly be that same invisible Anna, wife and mother of daughters, who had divided her from Egon. She glances down at the sound of the child's murmur. "How old is she?"

"My Ruthi?" she smiles. "Only three. But she's so big. Tall like her poppa."

Tall like her poppa. Tall like Egon. She looks up from the child's face to the woman's. Can she ask? Is it beyond the pale of etiquette when speaking the language of submarines? Where *is* her poppa? Where is your husband? But the question must be printed across Sigrid's brow.

"We don't know where their father is," Frau Weiss says to her, quietly, her eyes dropping as she calmly grooms her daughter's hair. Her husband had received a letter, she explains, from the jüdische Gemeinde, ordering him to report to the Levetzowstrasse Synagogue in Moabit. It was a spot that had been converted into a transit depot for those awaiting what the SS termed "evacuation." "Of course, we were no longer so foolish about words as we had been," she says. "So we decided the best thing was for him to go into hiding." Frau Weiss takes a breath at the absurdity of it all. "Though we were still naïve enough to believe that I would be spared because of Liesl and Ruthi. What a dream world that was." And then she raises a light smile. "But fortunately we were able to wake up to reality a moment before it was too late."

Sigrid swallows. "You have a slight accent," she notes.

"I was born in Vienna," the woman replies. "Liesl was born there, too." This is the older girl with watchful eyes and reddish hair, whom Ericha has escorted below to Auntie's toilet. "My good soldier, Liesl.

She has been such a help to me. So strong and so protective of her little sister. We named her for my mother, and she seems so much like her," the woman says, then something in her goes silent, even though she continues speaking. "So odd. So absurdly funny in a way. I have lived my entire life thinking that I was Viennese, only to discover that *actually* I am a Jewish parasite." She shakes her head, as if remembering some bitter foolishness. "We left in '38, after the Anschluss," the woman recounts, as she strokes the sleeping child's head. "We thought it would be safer in Berlin. Isn't that funny?"

Sigrid cannot prevent herself from asking, "Your husband was with you? In Vienna?"

The woman raises her eyes as if to view Sigrid more closely. "No," she answers mildly. "He had come to Berlin ahead of us. There were preparations to make, you understand. *Contacts* to be cemented. He had spent a great deal of time here on business over the years. The truth is," she says, as if this might be a secret she is sharing, "even when we lived in Vienna, he could never stay away from Berlin for too long. This city was his first love."

"Thank you, Frau Weiss. I'm sorry," Sigrid says. "I really shouldn't be prying."

The woman pauses, machinery working behind those caramel eyes. And then she says, "Anna. My name is Anna." She offers Sigrid her hand, and Sigrid must force her muscles to keep moving. She must force herself to swallow her shock and accept the offered hand.

"Sigrid," she replies, clearing her throat of obstructions, swallowing the perfect terror of serendipity swelling her throat.

At that moment, Ericha appears with the older girl. Holding her hand. Speaking in sweet tones. "This young lady is prepared for bed," she announces. And inserts the smallest of glances between Sigrid and the girls' mother. The child settles quietly on the cotton ticking folded on the floor for bedding, and lays her head down on a pair of small, perfect hands, folded together. But there's a deep watchfulness in the little girl's gaze, as if perhaps she is reading minds. Sigrid turns away, as Ericha tucks her in with a worn wool blanket.

Down in the street, the twilight is ashen and sharply cold. As Ericha locks the door behind them, Sigrid shivers. Wrapping her arms together for warmth, she steps toward the curb. She needs a bit of space to think. She must be clear first. Clear about what she can believe. There are one or two threads that are hanging loose. Egon had said it was his *wife and children* who had received the letter from the jüdische Gemeinde, not him. But it would be just like him to turn that around. To *underscore* his responsibility to his family when making his exit. It doesn't mean that the scenario she is building in her head can't be true. And if it *is* true. If the Fates have spun this thread, and she has just met Egon's wife, Egon's daughters. Then perhaps anything is possible. Paradise or apocalypse, or something of both.

"So, I'm still waiting," she says to Ericha.

"What?"

"For a key."

"Ah."

"Have you changed your mind about that?"

Ericha examines her with cool penetration. Then answers, "No. No, not at all. Take this one," she says, dangling the key from a small beaded chain.

"But that is yours."

"I have another. Take it."

Sigrid stares at the dangling thing. Then accepts it. Inserts the key into her pocket.

CLIMBING UP THE STEPS TOGETHER, she parts with Ericha at the third-floor landing. On the last set of steps, she thinks of the faces of those little girls in Auntie's pension. Thinks of the shadow wife. Or is Sigrid the real shadow wife? The shadow wife of a man who is himself little more than a shadow.

Why don't I feel guilt?

The days had grown warmer. The one-room flat where he took her was beginning to smell of a winter's worth of closed windows. When she wrenched open one of the sashes, the noise of the world outside spilled inside.

"Why don't I feel guilt?" she hears herself ask.

"Why should you?" he replies.

"I'm betraying my husband," she answers the open window. "Betraying my marriage. And yet I feel no guilt. What does that make me?"

She'd found him waiting for her on the bed, shoulders slumped against the wall. Still dressed. His shoes still on his feet. She watched him reach for the bottle of schnapps, a cigarette squeezed between his fingers. The schnapps sluiced into his glass. "I'm not your confessor, Sigrid," he tells her.

She smeared sweat across her brow with her palm. Her words were like sawdust in her mouth. "No?" she says blankly. "Why not? Don't I deserve a little absolution?"

"Guilt is one of God's little swindles. And a waste of time."

"Yes, well, you can say that, can't you, because you're barely human."

Egon released a loud hoot at this. But with the predatory tone he advanced upon her next, informed her that he was growing impatient with her foibles. "You stood in front of a bureaucrat and signed your name under a franking stamp, Sigrid," he instructed her with a grim light in his eyes. "You're part of a legal agreement. A name on a file in a municipal registry."

Turning to him, she asked, "And is that the story you tell your wife, too?" The words tumbled out. She suddenly had no desire to censor herself. "You tell her that she's simply part of a legal agreement? That her children are nothing but the result of a marriage license?"

"Go! *Get out!*" he bellowed suddenly, spilling his schnapps on the bedclothes. "If you don't like being with me. If it's tarnishing your immortal soul, then *go!* Go back to the bank clerk. Spread your legs every third Tuesday, then masturbate in the dark after he's asleep, if that's what your *conscience* dictates!"

Her body vibrated as if she were a taut wire plucked by a finger. She blinked. The color had drained from the room. All she saw was the gray of his eyes that matched the gray of his face, the gray of the walls, the gray of the window light reflected by the glass in his hand. She felt her words emerge in ether. "Why must you be so crude?"

"*Crude,*" she listened to him repeat.

And then winced as he shattered his glass on the floor. She jumped back a step as if to save herself from his pounce, as if she could. As if she could save herself from the force with which he hurled himself into her body. As if she could shout or shriek or cry out, as if resistance were something she could claim, as he ripped her skirt, tore open her chemise. Her head swam. Her body pinned to the wall. Something fell and broke. He entered her and she swallowed a cry as he bit into the flesh of her neck. "Take. *This*. Back to. Your marriage bed," he rasped.

Later. Later that night. Looking in the mirror before bed. The welt was the size of a five-mark piece. Pink and purplish, with a raw red corona. She marveled at his madness. To mark her so. To claim her with his teeth like an animal. To care so little for laws and rules and any definition of decency. To act so far beyond the pale. She marveled at his courage.

On the fourth-floor landing of the building in the Uhlandstrasse, Sigrid returns to the present. She has stopped at the top step, and finds herself gazing sightlessly at the door to her mother-in-law's flat. She feels a dragging resistance at the thought of taking a step further. But if this *is* his family that the Fates have tumbled into her hands, then she must hold them tightly. They are a link to him. A conduit. And something else. Her power over them is her power over him. The invisible thread of synchronicity connecting them, like the seam that threads the darkness to the day.

She turns when the door across the hall opens, and out steps the slim, dark-haired man with his cane. The brother, now dressed in an officer's uniform heavily embellished with combat decorations.

"I'm sorry. Did I startle you again? I seem to be making a habit of taking you by surprise."

"No. No, you haven't," she says. "I was just thinking for a moment."

"Were you? How dangerous. I try to avoid it myself."

She brushes a stray hair from her eyes. "We haven't been introduced. I am Frau Schröder," Sigrid tells him, offering her hand.

"Firm grip for a woman. I like that," the man says. "My name is Kessler. I think you know my sisters."

"Should I address you as 'Herr Leutnant'?"

The man looks down at the feldgrau tunic he is wearing, as if he may have only inadvertently put it on. Picked it out of his wardrobe by mistake. Then back at her with the gun sight. "You're very beautiful, Frau Schröder, even shrouded in those hausfrau rags," he says. "And I'm a man who can truly appreciate a woman's body. You should let me see you naked sometime." He is still gripping her hand until she whips it away. But she does not break the connection of their eyes.

"Think about it," he suggests, and begins his progress down the steps.

Inside her flat, Sigrid closes the door and stands listening to the rhythmic tri-cadence of the man's gait as he thumps, cane-boot-boot, cane-boot-boot, down the stairs.

TEN

THE ONLY DOLL Sigrid had ever received was as a gift on her eighth birthday. It was such a delicate thing with a china bisque head; hair like spun gold; rose-painted cheeks; and round, pale eyes that rolled open and shut. Too beautiful to touch, really. Sigrid thought it reminded her of her mother. She can recall her mother's beaming face beside the doll's as she presented it to Sigrid after breakfast. The same perfect expression. The star-blue brightness of the eyes.

A waste of good money, she heard her grandmother grumble. *She'll have it in pieces in a week.* Sigrid, however, had learned to dodge the Grossmutter's griping, and turned with a hesitant half smile to her father for her cue. Was it a trick? Should she touch it? Or was it one of her mother's traps? Would it only be swept from her grasp in punishment for some offense in an hour's time? Her father sat at the kitchen table in his immaculately pressed white linen shirt and scrupulously knotted necktie. In those days, he and she could still operate inside a small, unspoken, and expressionless conspiracy with each other. When he set down his coffee cup, she caught the edge of a nod.

When she took the doll into her hands, she thought that she had never before felt anything so unwieldy and yet so fragile. The doll's body was large. The china head the size of a head of red cabbage. But the painted eggshell cheeks were so delicate; they looked like a sneeze might crack them. Sigrid spread a smile across her face, half genuine and half rehearsed. She glanced again to her father for approval of this response, but he had already returned to the frown he wore while reading his newspaper, and had abandoned her to the women's attention. For the rest of the morning before lunch, she was permitted to "skip" her chores in order to "play" with her gift. But she needed coaching. Instead of cradling it, she tried to make it *do* things. Ride the wooden horse her grandfather had carved for her mother, climb from the floor to the top of the grandmother's horsehair settee. When she picked up a hammer, to teach her doll how to drive a tack, her mother was compelled to intervene. *This is no way to play with a doll, Sigrid,* she was assured. *You must cradle it, you see. You must cuddle it and give it kisses, thus so,* her mother instructed, then demonstrated. But though her mother sounded buoyantly confident in voicing her directives, there was some backbone lacking from her demonstration, as if she could only mimic an action that she herself did not truly understand. Sigrid was attentive, and repeated her mother's mimicry with some skill, but honestly, she was relieved when the doll went up in the corner cabinet after lunch, and she returned to her chores, cleaning the squeaking glass windowpanes with soapy water and newsprint.

A week later, to the day, Sigrid bumped into the cabinet while sweeping with the broom, and the doll took a fatal tumble, its head smashing into a starburst of chalky shards, fulfilling her grandmother's prophecy.

IN THE ATTIC she watches Frau Weiss playing with her daughter Ruthi, who is holding her wooden toy. The small tiger, with much of its striping rubbed away. The tiger growls. The tiger prowls up the child's arm, causing her to giggle. Sigrid watches as if peering into an aquarium. No. Rather as if *she* is in the aquarium, peering out. Watching such intimacy in play is shocking. Oddly embarrassing and certainly inexplicably painful. Yet addictive. She cannot help but stare, crouched in the corner of the room, clutching the blanket she is supposedly folding. So close and easy, a mother to her child. The most natural thing in the world. But not so for her.

"Frau Schröder?"

Sigrid's eyes shoot up.

"Are you unwell?" It's Frau Weiss asking. Her little girl holding the wooden tiger, sharing her inquiring gaze at Sigrid. Two pairs of identical caramel brown eyes.

"Unwell?"

Concern levels the woman's voice. "You looked a little . . . " she says, but does not finish the sentence.

Quickly Sigrid must absorb the guilty sickness coloring her face. "No. No, not at all. Just tired," she explains, dutifully returning to her folding of the blanket.

"I think. Well, I *hope*," says Frau Weiss, "that you know what a heroic act you are performing."

Heroic? Sigrid smiles grayly. Eyes averted. "I'm folding a blanket."

"I think you know what I mean. You and the others who risk—" She stops. Glances down at her Ruthi's head and strokes the little girl's curly hair. "Who risk so much," she says in a whisper now. "On our behalf. When so many others have done nothing."

And for this, Sigrid rewards Frau Weiss's gratitude by saying, "She must miss her father."

The woman visibly flinches. A tack inserted into her flesh. "Yes." Frau Weiss nods, covering the girl's ears as she pulls her to her breast, as if to protect the child from her words. "Yes, she misses him very much. For many months she was inconsolable. But now . . . well. Now she no longer cries."

Sigrid lowers her eyes to the child's small face. For the first time she can identify with her. They both have reached a point where they no longer cry. Where they are beyond tears. And then what sometimes strikes her as she watches the child's eyes shine, watches her accept a drink of water from her mother, both of her small hands clutching the glass, what sometimes strikes her, strikes her again. Is this what it would have been *like*? If this child had been hers with Egon, is this what it would have been like? If he had planted the seeds of such motherhood in her womb? If their love had been a sturdy enough structure to support that kind of weight, would she have been able to expose a hidden maternity, and love a child as much as she loved him? A child. *Their* child.

———

She goes to a children's bookshop nearby to look for something she could bring Frau Weiss to read to her daughters. "Something with a tiger in it," she suggests to the hefty female shop assistant, and is pleased to find that there is a series following the sweetly illustrated adventures of a tiger in the Indian jungle named Bollo. She buys two, *Bollo in the Jungle* and *Bollo Follows the River*. But as the shopgirl is wrapping the purchase, Sigrid notices a book displayed on the desk. It is *The Poisonous Mushroom*, the title printed in the Sütterlinschrift, favored by grammar school primers. On the cover is a toadstool with an ugly caricatured face. The Judenstern is stamped on the toadstool's trunk and its cap resembles the round fur hats she remembers on the heads of the immigrant Jews of the Grenadierstrasse. "It's very popular," the shop assistant remarks dimly, with, *What can one do?* embedded in her tone.

Frau Weiss's girls are enthralled with the Bollo books, and Sigrid is shocked at the sight of the tears in Frau Weiss's eyes. "I had forgotten the simple pleasure of reading a bedtime story to them," she whispers. "It seems I'm always thanking you, Frau Schröder."

"Please," Sigrid reminds her blankly, "call me Sigrid."

. . .

THE MOON IS OBSCURED by scudding clouds as they walk down the Uhlandstrasse toward their block, and the street is cold and quiet. Sigrid's torch exudes its blue glow. Her head is a tangle, but she has taken Ericha's arm in hers again, in the way she recalls her mother taking her arm when she was an adolescent, and again, Ericha has allowed her to do so without comment. It feels good to be attached to the girl in a small way. To be anchored by this small affection in the blacked-out street. For a moment the war recedes into the nightly rustle of cold in the trees. For a moment she can find that small crevice of sanctuary.

Maybe that's why the sudden pound of footsteps is so amplified. The man charging in between them out of the darkness, head down like a battering ram. He collides with Ericha with rough intention, unlinking her arms from Sigrid's with force. Sigrid whirls, words in her throat, ready to shout at such an overbearing example of Berlinische manners, when Ericha seizes her arm. "*Don't.* Don't say anything."

"But that oaf nearly knocked you off your feet."

"It makes no difference," Ericha tells her. "I know him."

"Know him?"

"Let's keep walking," she says.

Sigrid opens her mouth, but then doesn't speak. She silences herself until they turn the corner. "So tell me," she says. "He's completely out of sight."

"Do you recall the day in the park when you saw me with a man?"

"Yes," Sigrid replies. "He kissed you."

"To throw off suspicion, he said. To make it look like we're having a lovers' rendezvous."

"That was him?"

"I know him as Johann. He used to supply me with documents."

"You mean," Sigrid begins to say, before executing the German glance, even in the dark. "You mean with forgeries?"

"Maybe. I don't know. Forgeries or stolen. They looked very real to me. He was good at pulling them out of his hat."

"But then?" Sigrid says.

Ericha frowns. "Then *what*?"

"You tell me."

An expulsion of breath. "But then he started trying to touch me. On the arm. On the shoulder. Moving his hand about. Finally, one evening on the train, he leaned over and whispered into my ear, *I have to fuck you*."

Even after Egon taught her how to use the word. Even after it freely filled her mouth. She is sometimes shocked by its sudden introduction. I have to *fuck* you. "And what did you do?"

"I let him." She glances up and then shrugs through the Sigrid's silence. "You must understand, Frau Schröder, how valuable good documents are."

"Valuable enough for a woman to *prostitute* herself for them?" Who is that speaking? Her mother? No. The Grossmutter. That is her grandmother's voice.

"Yes. Valuable enough," Ericha responds without emotion. "People have died for less. So I didn't think spreading my legs for him was such a high price to pay. Only now. Well. You saw. There's trouble there."

"Yes. Trouble. Next time does he run you down with a lorry?"

"He was just making a point."

"A point?"

"That he knows who I am. And what I do."

"And that unless—how did you put it so delicately? Unless you keep *spreading your legs for him*, he'll denounce you to the police?"

"No. Yes. Maybe. I don't know."

"Am I to choose between one of those answers?"

"He's not exactly an innocent in all this. I know where he lives. He took me to his flat in the Heerstrasse. A little man's dump. So I doubt he'll be ringing up the Prinz-Albrecht-Strasse as a lark. Unless it's a suicidal lark."

"Unless," Sigrid repeats.

"So now I'm a whore." Ericha shrugs. "You can add it to your list."

"I have no list." Sigrid frowns.

"Never mind. Let's not talk about it, please. Let's not talk about anything."

They walk for a bit like this, two ends of the same silence. Again Sigrid loops Ericha's arm around hers. And Ericha permits it.

———

The crowd at the cinema is very thin. It's a bomber's night. The moon has cleared the night of clouds. Ericha is scheduled to meet a man about rationing coupons. He's a supervisor at a government printing office and for a price can run off extras. She does not say what that price *is* or how it is to be paid, and Sigrid does not ask. She has posted herself near the door to the balcony, while Ericha sits down in front by the railing. They have agreed on a signal. Sigrid is holding her handkerchief, and if she thinks there is trouble entering, she will pretend to cough. The man beside Ericha is thin and furtive. Sigrid can see him continually glancing over his shoulder. She follows his glance to the entrance, but no one enters. Film chatters in the projector above. On the screen, a spectacle of costumes in an imperial concert hall: women in hooped shirts, hussars in braid, Gustaf Gründgens in a powdered wig seated at a harpsichord. Sigrid attempts to focus on the screen but cannot. Her mind is turning backward. Turning in on itself.

What are you going to do?

I don't know.

That's a lie. I think that's a lie.

The day he left her was hot and sticky. The air filling the flat in Little Wedding was fetid, and she was sweating beneath her dress. He was grimy, his hand rough and unwashed. They undressed each other without words, because they knew that good-bye was the only word left to be spoken. He dug into her body like a cannibal. And when it ended, finally, and they lay on the mattress like two halves of a sliced apple, siphoning breath into their body from the humid air, she closed her eyes and waited for him to say the words.

But she should have known. She should have known that he would not be one to slash the cord between them. That he would put the knife in her hand to make the cut.

She smelled his cigarette smoke. "Anna has been sent a letter from the jüdische Gemeinde," he said. He seldom referred to his wife by name, and Sigrid had learned that when he did so, it was for the sake of impact. A trick to insert the invisible wife between them.

"A letter?" she repeated, flatly as a question, though she knew what it meant. After the war in the East had begun, so had the deportations. This was an open secret of which no one cared to speak, but it was difficult to miss. The SS had taken to marching Jewish deportees through the streets on the way to the train stations. Men, woman, and children, stamped with the yellow six-pointed star. Old silver beards and babies in the arms of their mothers.

"She's been ordered," he said, "to report to the SS transit camp in the Levetzowstrasse in two days' time. With both of our children."

Our children. Suddenly he is claiming his share of them.

Sigrid rolls onto her side and stares blindly at the wall. "What are you going to do?" she asks.

Smoke rises toward the ceiling. "I don't know."

"That's a lie," she says mildly. "I think that's a lie."

She listens to his pause. Then hears him say, "I know a man. For enough money, I can secure a safe place."

"You mean a hiding place," she says.

Silence.

"And you would go with them?"

"What other alternative is left?" he asked thickly and spewed smoke.

Sigrid said nothing. There were other alternatives, of course, that she could think of. At least one. But she did not dare speak it aloud. She dared not even form the thought fully in her head. The two of them together as one. Unencumbered by his wife, by his children. She waited, instead, for him to speak it. She allowed herself to balance on the edge of the razor's blade, waiting to see if he would answer his own question. And when he did not, she let herself tumble from the edge to the safety of irreparable loss. "No other alternative," she finally whispered. "None."

Only now did he touch her. Only now, after she had exonerated him from making the unspoken choice, did he lean his body toward hers and lay his hand on her naked skin. Oddly, she felt his touch only as a weight. She had suddenly gone numb.

"It's not what I want to do," he told her.

She permitted her eyes to flick across the drab pattern of the wallpaper. "I think," she breathed, "that is a lie as well."

A sneeze brings her back. The drab man from the printing office sneezes. Honks into his handkerchief. Sigrid blinks and works to peel away the cling of memory. Suddenly Ericha stands and marches away. Something is wrong. Sigrid readies herself to follow, but as Ericha passes her, the girl rasps out a single word—*Stay*—and exits so quickly, the old usher doesn't even make it to his feet before she is gone. Sigrid feels her belly clench as she glances at the printing office supervisor, who has also risen to his feet, and is now standing haplessly, gazing at Ericha's invisible wake. She watches him clutch the briefcase in his hands as he makes his way through the rank of empty seats. When he passes Sigrid on his way to the balcony doorway, she dares a glance at his face but there's nothing *to* his face but an arrangement of features. A nose, a mouth. Nothing in his eyes. Nothing at all.

Sigrid waits until he is gone, then quickly picks up her bag. Outside, she must cross the street to catch up with Ericha. "What *happened*?"

Ericha shakes her head. "Something was off. I couldn't put my finger on it, but there was something . . . *off*," she repeats. "He was trouble."

"You mean an informant?"

"Maybe," Ericha answers. "I don't know. Just trouble. He was too fidgety."

"Well, perhaps it was simply nerves. He was, after all, breaking the law. Believe it or not, some of us mere mortals still get anxious over that."

"I have to trust my feelings," Ericha replies.

"So no rationing coupons, then, because a man was *fidgety*. Who do we go to *now*? Can you steal enough of Frau Granzinger's food to feed four mouths?" Why does she feel the need to lash out at the girl?

"I'll find somebody. Somebody else." She is struggling to light a cigarette from her packet, but the match does not cooperate.

"Here. Let me help you." Sigrid frowns, but the girls pulls away.

"I don't need your help, thank you. I have learned how to strike a match." And finally she manages. At the steps to their door, Ericha posts herself by the curb.

"What are you doing?" Sigrid inquires.

"I want to smoke for a moment, if that's permissible."

Sigrid exhales and goes up the steps alone. Inside the foyer, she stops to unlock the postbox. Nothing but a thin envelope, which falls out of the box and onto the crumbling tile. When she bends to pick it up, someone enters behind her. Ericha, she assumes, until she feels a hand on her body, and turns to see a face.

"I've been thinking about you," the man inquires. "Have you been thinking about me?"

But it's not the ghost of Egon Weiss. It's the Frau Obersturm-führer's brother, Wolfram, out of his uniform and in a dark wool chesterfield and roll-brim hat. His body close and full of warmth. Leaning into her on his cane. She catches a sharp scent of schnapps on his breath. "Both the ladies of the house are out till ten at least. No one in the flat. And if you're squeamish about using another woman's bed, we can use the sofa. Or the floor." She gazes back at the hunger in his eyes.

The front door opens again, and this time it *is* Ericha. For an instant, the girl freezes at the sight of the two of them pressed against the postboxes. Then, "Pardon me," she offers coldly, before brushing past, head down, shoulders squared as she clomps up the steps.

"You know, if she's jealous, you can bring her along," Wolfram proposes. "I find a threesome to be an efficient use of wartime resources." He has taken her hand in his and guides it firmly inside his coat to the hardness in his trousers.

Sigrid stares. Then removes her hand. He does not attempt to stop her, nor does he follow her, as she begins to climb the stairs, the echo of Ericha's footsteps above her. All she hears him say is, "An empty flat till ten."

She thinks that Ericha might be waiting for her halfway up until the sound of the door thumping closed to Frau Granzinger's flat cancels the thought. Suddenly she feels very angry. Angry at this girl, at the war, at the carpet on the steps, at the wallpaper. At simply everything. She thinks of pounding on Frau Granzinger's door, but before the thought forms fully she has passed it. On the landing outside of her mother-in-law's flat she can hear some Viennese schmaltz playing on the wireless. She's mad at that, too. Mad at the air she is breathing. She starts to claim her key from her bag when she realizes she still has the single piece of mail that fell from the postbox clenched in her hand. A dingy salmon-colored envelope bearing a Feldpost number. She glares at it, then rips it open and refocuses her glare on Kaspar's handwriting. His penmanship was once very neat. Very beautiful, in fact. Ordered and perfectly fluid. But now the writing on the cheap piece of military stationery is tight as a screw, one turn away from threading.

Dear Mother,

I finally received Father's sweater that you patched for me. I am wearing it now. I think about him sometimes, in this sweater, sitting in his chair, smoking his pipe with the newspaper open in his lap. Who knew I would ever be wearing it as a soldier? Best to you. And please tell Sigrid to send some more Pervatin.

He writes to his mother, she thinks. Not to her. Not to his wife. There are only instructions for *her*, to be passed along the chain of command. Tell Sigrid to send more Pervatin.

She finds that she has crumpled the letter in her fist.

From below she listens to Wolfram's three-point thump ascending the stairs. Growing closer.

HE IS EATING HER ALIVE, out of her clothes. Her blouse half off, her brassiere shoved up: naked from the waist down, save for her Kaufhaus nylons. As he gains his rhythm, his trousers down only far enough for him to unleash himself, her skin is scoured by the thick Persian rug. Egon used to take her on the floor like this. She didn't like it then. She felt as if he were trying to drag her down, to demonstrate his dominance, to hammer her like a nail into the hard wood. It would often bruise her, and she hated that. Though sometimes she would observe those bruises in the mirror, alone, and feel love for them. But with Wolfram, the floor is the level she craves. No beds. Nothing so lofty. She digs her fingers into his hair as she feels him working her toward climax, feels the scream building in her, to which she knows she cannot give voice. When it comes, she bites his shoulder to silence it, and listens to the sound of his pain.

ELEVEN

THE TOMMIES COME and the Tommies go. Two raids in three nights, pummeling the factory districts to the north and east. The *Deutsche Wochenschau* shows soldiers serving bombed-out Berliners from portable field kitchens called "goulash cannons." On the screen, everyone is grinning. But at the patent office, there is talk swirling about the aftermath that does not make the newsreels. The school gymnasiums as temporary morgues. Corpses laid out in rank and file for identification. Fragments of bodies in metal tubs on trestle tables.

At the Pension Unsagbar, there's been an addition to the guests. A man in his middle forties. Sallow skin. A wing of greasy hair combed over a balding head and a pair of searching eyes. Grayish stubble on his chin and an absurd Führer mustache on his lip. He owns a dog-eared deck of cards, which he uses to lay out game after game of solitaire. He glares down at the columns of cards on the floorboards. Deuce of clubs on three of diamonds. Red on black on red.

"Who is he?"

Ericha is restocking the pantry shelves with a half dozen tins of canned sugar beets. "You mean what is his name?"

"I mean where did he *come* from?"

"From his accent, I'd say Moabit."

"That's very funny, but not what I'm asking."

"He came through channels like everyone else. He calls himself Kozig."

"And how do you know that he's not a Gestapo spy?"

A look. "How do I know *any* of them aren't? How do I know *you're* not?"

"There's something about him that's different."

"You mean he looks more Jewish."

"I mean maybe he looks more hunted."

"They're all hunted. Are you forgetting that?"

"You have your instincts about people," Sigrid says, "perhaps I have mine."

Ericha glances at the man playing a card, then turns back to the pantry shelf. "He escaped," she says, "from the SS quarantine in the Grosse Hamburger Strasse." A flash of her eyes in Sigrid's direction. "But he left his wife behind."

"You've got to get them out of here." This is Auntie talking. She has cornered Sigrid. "That raid last night was the final straw. Their nerves are stretched. The children especially. Up there, they feel like sitting ducks for the bombers." Sigrid dares a glance at Anna Weiss, bleakly rocking her girls in her lap, covered by a blanket. Both children are staring into some unseen spot.

"You should talk to the young one," is all Sigrid says, nodding once in Ericha's direction.

"I *have* talked to her. Talked until I was blue, and I get nowhere. So now I am talking to the adult," the old woman says. Then swallows her voice. "My brother, maybe you've heard, he's a Party member and he likes to feel important."

Sigrid says nothing.

"He has comrades in the SS," Auntie tells her. "Old Fighters, who brag. So I learn things. And what I've learned is that the noose has *tightened*," she says. "They say that, after Stalingrad, Goebbels was so incensed over Jews still working in the armament factories that he's sworn to make Berlin Jew-free by the end of this month. That means twenty or thirty thousand Jews to be deported."

Sigrid blinks starkly at this. "Thirty thousand?"

"Maybe they thought they were safe working a lathe or a handpress for the war industries," Auntie says, frowning, "but they're finding out differently now. Over a thousand a day are being shipped east in cattle cars. And the Gestapo are *everywhere*. I've seen the same Stapo bull *twice now*, loitering about the grocer's down the street."

Sigrid tastes a drop of dread. "You're sure he's Gestapo?"

"You think I can't recognize one by now? Trilby hat, big leather overcoat. He might as well be wearing a sign," she says, and scowls. "But for every one I *do* see there can be another half dozen I *don't*. *You've* got to get them *out of here*," Auntie declares. "You've got to talk to that girl of yours and make her *understand*."

Sigrid draws a thick breath and shakes her head. The trouble is that Ericha is barely speaking to her since the night before. "I'll see what I can do," she promises dimly.

The room smells of wood rot and leaky plaster and nightly buckets of urine. And underneath, something else. An odor of desolation and chronic fear.

Sigrid kneels down beside Frau Weiss. The woman props up a frail smile in greeting, but it's obvious that her beautiful confidence is starting to fray. "The girls were very frightened last night," she whispers, still slowly rocking the children in her arms. "The guns. They were so loud."

"The Zoo Tower. The gun emplacements have had bigger flak cannons installed," Sigrid tells her. "It was in the newspapers."

"Well." A small shrug. "They are quite deafening."

"I have something for the children," Sigrid says. "Do they like chocolate?" She produces two pieces of bittersweet wrapped in foil from her bag—some of Renate's contraband.

"Chocolate? Oh, yes." Frau Weiss smiles, brushing the hair from Ruthi's eyes. "These little ones *love* their chocolate. Don't they?"

The children raise their eyes to Sigrid blankly, then gaze at the foil-wrapped chocolate. They accept the gift, but without expression.

"Now, what do you say to the kind lady?" their mother prompts.

"Thank you," they chant together.

"Thank you, *Frau Schröder*. Be polite."

"Thank you, Frau Schröder."

Sigrid feels herself smile and, without realizing it, has begun stroking the little one's curly mass of hair. "You're most welcome," she tells them.

"Mama," good soldier Liesl says with innocence, "I want to save mine for Poppa."

"What?" Frau Weiss sounds perplexed.

"I want to save mine for Poppa. Is that all right?"

"I want to save mine for Poppa, too," Ruthi follows. Sigrid removes her hand.

Anna's smile has dipped. "No, no. You needn't do that."

"But Poppa loves chocolate, *too*." Liesl insists, her small face suddenly burdened. "I want him to have it."

Her sister, at this point, has started to cry. "I want to give Poppa my chocolate. *I want to save it for him.*"

"*Shhh, shhh.*" Rocking her girls more tightly. "It's all right. Poppa doesn't need your chocolate. I'm sure there is plenty of chocolate where he is, and he would want you to have yours. Now, this kind lady has brought you a delicious gift. You should enjoy it." But by now, Sigrid has receded. She has removed her hand from the child's head, and can only watch as the woman tries to rebuild the invisible shelter around her children. She catches Frau Weiss's eyes for only an instant before she must look away. She cannot bear to see a mother's terror in the eyes of her lover's wife.

. . .

THEY ARE WALKING to the U-Bahn station past the spires of a tall brick church pointing toward the empty evening sky. Heads down, the cold breath of winter in the air.

"Auntie says you won't listen to her." Sigrid frowns.

"Most people say that."

"Well, she also says that her current pension guests must be moved."

"I'm working on it."

"Are you?"

"Don't you think I *know* how desperate things are? Don't you think I *know*? That pig from the printing office wanted five hundred marks for a single month's worth of ration cards. *Five hundred.* Next month it could be twice that. I know we're running out of resources and I *know* Auntie's getting nervous, but what am I supposed to *do* that I'm not already *doing*? They need *papers*, Sigrid. I can't move them without documents." So seldom does Ericha address her by her given name that the sound has a bite to it.

"But I thought. I mean, don't you *have* a source for that?"

"I did, but now I don't," she says.

"And does that surprise you, considering your method of payment?"

"That's *really* not very helpful," the girl declares sharply. "Really not very helpful *at all.*"

A tram sparks past, its blackout lights glowing like fireflies in the dusk. "So what happened to *you*?" she asks.

Sigrid blinks. "To me?"

"You know what I mean. Your new soldier friend. The Herr Leutnant."

"That's none of your business."

"No? I wonder."

"Nothing happened. Besides, I don't have to explain myself to you."

159

"Does he have a big cock?"

Sigrid stops so suddenly that several Berliners nearly collide with her. "Can't you watch where you're going?" a hausfrau scolds her brashly. "There are people walking, you know."

"I don't expect to be insulted by you," she tells Ericha.

"And I don't expect to be lied to by *you*."

"I have not *lied* to you."

"No, you've simply mislaid a bit of truth. Look, I wouldn't care about whose bed you're filling, but for the fact that you have made a commitment to the work we do. How do I know that you won't let something slip when you're lying under the blankets with this man. He's an officer. You could compromise everything."

"I won't do that."

"How do I *know* you won't?"

"*Because*, little one, you must *trust* me," Sigrid answers. Then removes the edge from her voice. "You must *trust* me."

Ericha's eyes burn fearfully for an instant. Then she turns away. They walk wordlessly forward until, "There's a man been hanging about down the street," Sigrid says. "Auntie thinks he's Gestapo."

Ericha gives her only the briefest of glances. "Auntie sees Gestapo men everywhere," is her only response.

"Are you still in there?"

"*What?*" Sigrid looks up sharply at her mother-in-law across the table.

"I said, are you still in there?"

"In there?" Trying to snap back to the present. "Yes. Yes," she answers curtly. "Still."

"Good. I thought maybe you'd fallen into a coma."

"Only tired," she lies. She rubs at the claw of pain in her head. Stirs the oily cabbage soup in front of her. An official voice yaks at them stridently over the radio, dispensing valuable information about nothing. "Must we?" Sigrid asks.

Blowing on a spoonful from her bowl. "Must we *what*?"

"Have the wireless?"

Mother Schröder looks up from her bowl and dips in her slice of bread. "Why not? Certainly, *you* have nothing to say these days. Why should I be forced to eat in silence?"

Sigrid drops her spoon and shoves herself away from the table. "Never mind. God forbid we should ever have a moment without some squawking jackdaw filling our ears with noise."

"I *happen* to be waiting for my program, if that's allowed," her mother-in-law calls after her reproachfully, but Sigrid is not listening. She tugs open the cabinet above the sink. "I'm taking one of your cigarettes," she announces.

"Well. Nice of you to ask."

Striking a kitchen match, she ignites the tip of one of the old lady's abominations and inhales its poisonous taste.

"Look, there's no reason for you to be hopping up in the middle of supper. If you must have the radio off, *fine*. Turn it off, and sit back down. Your soup is going cold."

Somewhere in the old woman's voice, Sigrid senses an appeal, a thread of need. Is it loneliness? But she is in no mood to accommodate her, in any case, and takes a short, vicious pleasure in squashing the plea. "If you're so concerned, then *you* eat it," she replies. "It tastes like horse piss anyway." Mother Schröder's back stiffens abruptly, but then her eyes drop to hide the injury. The pleasure of the attack dissipates in a blink, and is replaced by a sting of shame, but before Sigrid can say another word, there's a knock at the door that dispels all else as the two women share the sharp ends of the same look. The knock repeats itself firmly. Sigrid inhales smoke, then tamps the cigarette in one of her mother-in-law's tin ashtrays. "I'll get it," she says as calmly as possible. Crossing to the door, she opens it with only a heartbeat's hesitation, then steps back with an audible intake of breath.

It's a soldier. He looms largely in his Landser's uniform, filling up the threshold with a kind of burdened authority. One side of his face is brutally scarred, so that the texture of his skin resembles sandpaper. His nose is crooked and plasticized, and a corner of his mouth is stitched into an artificial grimace. He seems to accept her gasp with practiced tolerance. "Frau Schröder?" he inquires.

Trying to recover herself, her hand at her throat. "Yes."

"My name is Kurtz, Frau Schröder. I'm a comrade of your husband's."

"My husband?" A blankness enters her voice.

"What is it? *What's happened*?" Mother Schröder is demanding anxiously. The Landser's eyes flick toward the old woman, but then back to Sigrid. "He's been wounded."

"Wounded?" she hears her mother-in-law repeat with a swift bleakness. But Sigrid herself can find no words. The silence she craved a moment before now steals her voice.

"Not critically," the Landser assures them tonelessly, and then turns his head as Mother Schröder paces forward.

"What happened? Do you know what happened?"

"He told me his company had orders to hold a position outside of Rzhev. They were dug in for the night when Ivan dropped a few mortars onto their position. He took a dose of shrapnel."

"And where is he?" the old woman must know.

"Recovering. There's an army hospital north of Smolensk. It's where we met. Anyway, I'm sure you'll be getting the notice soon. I've been rotated off the line, but I told him that I would look you up on my way through Berlin. Personally."

Silence. The women stare at the disfigured face dumbly, until the man clears his throat. "Well . . . so I've kept my promise."

At that point Sigrid suddenly finds her voice. "Oh, I'm so sorry. *Please*, come in. Are you hungry? We have some soup."

But the soldier is already waving the offer away. "No. No, thank you. You're kind, but I came here straight from the train and still have to report in."

"Well. *Thank you,*" Sigrid tells him, touching the door. "Thank you for . . ." For what? The words don't want to form. The Landser glances at her hand on the door, and she jerks it away, embarrassed at her desire to shut him out. "For your friendship to Kaspar," she says.

The Landser breathes out, and chucks his duffel bag onto one shoulder. "I'm not sure 'friendship' is the word, Frau Schröder. I'm not sure there is a word for what one front-liner owes to another. In any case," he says with a nod, "I'll say good night."

PREPARING FOR BED that night, Sigrid pauses as she sits on the mattress and gazes at the photo of Kaspar in his dress uniform, but the photographer shot the picture in profile, so he is turning his face away from her. The night before he had reported for induction they had made love. She had wanted to. She had wanted to touch his body. To memorize it with her hands, so that she would remember. At least, she felt, she owed him that much. At least it was her duty to remember. But when he climaxed it was so unlike him; his howl had been so raw, as if he was in agony, and she couldn't help but think: *This is how he will cry out when his flesh is torn in battle.* Bullets, shrapnel, foreign metal ripping through the body she has just committed to memory, that's how he will sound. Afterward, as he slept, she could only see his silent face as a death mask.

IN THE MORNING, leaving for the patent office, she glances briefly at the door to the flat across the landing. Should she feel guilt? Why doesn't she? What is missing from her that she does not feel guilt over adultery? And now Kaspar, a victim of the war. She should be spared by guilt. But mostly she feels confused, as if trying to find her way through some kind of maze.

She stands there for some time until she realizes that she has been holding her breath. Then she exhales and continues down the stairs.

It takes another four days before a letter arrives from the army, informing her that that her husband, Kaspar Albrecht Schröder, Feld-webel, 34. Infanterie-Division, 34. Füsilier-Regiment, Battalion 2, has been wounded while in service to the Führer, Volk, and Fatherland.

TWELVE

Long before the war, the National Socialist bureaucracy had codified its hatred of Jews into legal strictures. The Nuremburg Laws had stripped Jews of German citizenship; barred them from the professions; maligned, ridiculed, and penalized them in statutory language; and segregated them from daily German life.

Distasteful, perhaps, but law were laws. How could a person change them?

And while there were stories of Jews subjected to beatings in the streets, or being torn from their beds and tortured in Brownshirt bunkers, such individual brutality seemed anecdotal. A story of this Jew, a story of that Jew. Terrible, perhaps, but easy to close one's eyes and ears to during the daily routine. What, after all, could be done?

But then, on a November day in 1938, a Foreign Ministry clerk in the German legation in Paris was shot in the stomach. His assailant was a Jewish youth named Grynszpan, who offered no resistance to the French police at his arrest, and declared that he had done what he had done to protest the German persecution of Polish Jews. The legation clerk died two days later, on November 9, which happened to be the fifteenth anniversary of Adolf Hitler's failed Munich putsch, and the holiest day in the National Socialist calendar.

Sigrid had become pregnant. When she was three months along, her mother-in-law complained that she hadn't gained enough weight. That she was starving the baby. Food, however, sickened Sigrid on most days. It was often all she could do to keep a thin gruel down in the mornings. Mother Schröder would sit opposite her at the kitchen table and glare while Sigrid spooned the watery porridge into her mouth, just to make sure that not a single drop was left behind.

"Can you put out your cigarette, please?" Sigrid asked her. "It's making me ill."

"*Everything* makes you ill," her mother-in-law grumbled in response, but then screwed out the cigarette in the small tin ashtray. "Eat," she commanded. "You'll not be shortchanging my grandson on his breakfast."

Sigrid exhaled. "And how do you know it's a boy?"

A shrug. "What else?"

It was a chilly autumn. Sigrid had started working part-time at the patent office earlier that year, and now was under pressure from Kaspar's mother to quit.

"It's absurd that you insist on taking a job."

"I want to work."

"You think my son is not providing for you?"

"I want to do something. I can't devote myself to housework."

"And why not? It's what I've done since I was twelve years old. It's what every honorable woman does."

"Mother," Kaspar interceded glumly from behind the newspaper. "Please. Let it go."

"Let what go?"

"Sigrid is not like you. She needs intellectual stimulation."

"Ah, and what does that make me? A block of wood?" the old woman demanded indignantly, but her son only shifted his expression into a lighter gear.

"No. It makes you a mother."

"Well, what do you think *she* is going to be in another six months? Shall I explain the process to you, my son?"

"Just let it go."

"Is she going to be *intellectually stimulated* right up until the time she drops the baby on the floor of some dusty office?"

"Excuse me," Sigrid muttered suddenly. She knew she wouldn't make it to the toilet, so instead she threw up in the kitchen sink.

Her mother-in-law regarded the scene distantly. "So now I'm supposed to wash dishes in that sink?"

At the patent office she was in pain. A slow discomfort as she sat, preceding sudden cramps that caused her to lose her fingering on the typewriter keys. She had complained to the doctor of these spasms the week before, with Mother Schröder sitting with her in the examination room, but the Herr Doktor had simply dismissed her complaint, as he enjoyed dismissing all of her concerns. *Nervous little mothers*, he would chuckle in a grumpy manner. *I assure you, Frau Schröder, I have been practicing medicine for thirty-seven years, and I have heard it all by now. This is nothing to worry about. Simply the process of childbearing, to which as I'm sure your gracious mother-in-law here can attest, is not all hearts and romance.*

Mother Schröder had raised her eyebrow at the remark, but said nothing.

On the train ride back, Sigrid had said, "I don't much care for him."

"Who?"

"The Herr Doktor. I don't much like his manner."

"You don't have to like his manner. He's the authority. Like or dislike has nothing to do with it."

"He didn't give me anything."

"Such as *what*, daughter-in-law?"

"Such as something for the pain."

"As he said," Mother Schröder said, frowning drably, "it's not all hearts and romance. Life is filled with pain. You can't simply eliminate it. And as far as the good doctor is concerned, he delivered my son, your husband and the father of your child, without a moment's worry. Be grateful for his experience."

Sigrid went silent. She felt suddenly ashamed of herself. Asking for the pain to be eliminated. How weak. Her grandmother would have been appalled. On her deathbed, her mother had begged, pleaded, demanded, and sobbed for something to relieve the agony in her bowels, while Sigrid, in the next room, had clamped her hands over her ears to blot out the sound.

Making her way home from work, she saw a woman on the train. A typical Berlinische hausfrau, with a level, unflappable gaze, and a handbag big enough to fit a manhole cover. Suddenly, peering closely at Sigrid, she boomed, "Say, you don't look so good."

Several nearby faces rose with a trace of squinting alarm. Sigrid opened her mouth and managed to say, "I just entered my third month."

"Well, *of course* you have." The Frau nodded with sudden understanding. "And since when is *that* business anything but misery? You're in your third month? Believe me, it only gets harder from here on out. Five times I've suffered through it. And the worst of them was my first. My Hansel. The little monster made me sick every morning for months, and then took his own sweet time popping out. *Eighteen hours* I was in labor. It felt like I was giving birth to a two-ton lorry," the Frau announced with a cackle. "That was twelve years ago, and he still hasn't gotten any easier. A little devil from birth."

At the Ku'damm, Sigrid left the train, but as she climbed the steps of the U-Bahn, the cramps returned and closed in like a vise. She had to stop and grip the rail to keep from collapsing. At the top of the stairs, she stopped to breathe, just to breathe until the worst of it passed. There was shouting and an acrid tang in the air that tasted like cinders in her mouth. She raised her head and wiped the clamminess from her brow. Several people were pointing. She spotted the thick smear of black smoke ballooning toward the clouds from over the rooftops.

A woman stopped her bicycle in the street and stared with widened eyes. "My God, what is it?" she squawked. "What's burning?"

A plump Berliner volunteered the answer grimly. "The Fasanen-strasse Synagogue."

By the time she boarded the T-Line bus, there were a half dozen smoke columns pluming skyward. A fire engine passed with its klaxon horn blaring. Through the bus's windows she saw an old woman tending to a man, who was sitting on a curbstone, holding a flimsy handkerchief to his bloodied mouth. A handful of boys were gleefully pitching chunks of pavement through the windows of a shop front. On the door was slopped a six-pointed star, yellow paint dripped down over the words *Jews Perish!*

"The Yids are really in for it now!" a fellow at the front of the bus crowed loudly. The silence that followed seemed to agree with him.

Sigrid clamped her eyes shut at another spasm.

Later, she would see it all in the cinema newsreels. The burning synagogues collapsing in a whorl of flame. The black-clad SS men shearing the beard from a shrunken old rabbi, while spectators either sheltered their children from the sight, or held their toddlers aloft for a better look. Jewish storekeepers glumly sweeping up the carpets of glass, glinting like shattered crystal.

But what she would remember most were the ruins of a grand piano that she passed in the street. It had been shoved from a second-floor balcony and smashed to smithereens. The harp split, pointing toward the sky, its strings popped. Keys scattered like broken teeth. The image stayed with her. An image of a crime, somehow more intimate, than the flat, black-and-white violence caught on film. The beauty of the piano, now ruined. She felt the pain of it in a contraction, and turned away.

As she opened the door to the apartment house and stepped into the foyer, the pain struck her like a thunderbolt. Her knees buckled, and she had to grip the door frame to stop from falling. Staring up at the multiple flights of steps before her, she remembered how Kaspar had swept her up in his arms on their wedding day. But Kaspar was still at the bank, no doubt, working late as had become his habit.

On Sigrid's way up the stairs, the cramps seemed to be playing a game with her. Allowing her to shuffle upward, without interference, only to stab her on the next step. By the time she reached the landing of 11G, she was smearing the tears away from her face. Trying to control herself as she fumbled the key into the lock.

"Mother Schröder," she heard herself croak hoarsely as she entered the flat. But then she blinked at the look of horror stamped on her mother-in-law's face.

Marta Trotzmüller shoved back from the table and jumped to her feet, leaving her coffee cup behind. *"Frau Schröder,"* she cried out with a look of pale shock. "You're *bleeding*!"

Only now did Sigrid look down. She watched with an odd curiosity as a dribble of red spotted the well-scrubbed floorboards between her legs.

AFTER THE DOCTOR HAD LEFT, after the pronouncements had been made, when Kaspar entered the bedroom in the evening he was gentle with her. But his face was clouded and distant, like a storm settled over a mountaintop.

She cried, and he sat beside her and held her hand.

She stopped crying, and he continued to hold her hand, but only until he had calculated the earliest moment he could release it. She could see the internal timing in his eyes.

"I'm sorry, Kaspar," she whispered through the fog of the sedative the doctor had finally prescribed her. "I'm so sorry. . . ."

"It's not your fault," he answered. "I don't blame you. Nobody blames you." But it was clear from his gaze that this was a lie.

He stood to leave because she needed her rest, needed her sleep, but she caught him at the door. "Is it over?" she asked with sudden urgency.

He stopped but said nothing.

"The fires. What I saw in the street. It was so terrible."

Kaspar gazed back at her. "You should rest," he said to her. "Don't bother yourself with what you cannot change."

SIGRID FINDS HERSELF thinking about that moment as she sits at her desk in the patent office, staring blankly over her typewriter. How far away from Kaspar she had felt, even though he was so close. Then she hears a voice beside her, and she tries not to look startled. It's Renate, an anxious expression forming her face.

"I heard you got a letter," she says. A letter. Everybody knows what that means. It's standard method used by the army to inform wives and mothers that their husbands and sons are casualties.

Sigrid does not ask her *how* she heard about the letter. This is a type of news that travels. Last November, when Thea Burgel lost her husband at Stalingrad, the entire building knew before lunch. But Sigrid looks up into Renate's gorgeous face without sympathy for Kaspar or for herself.

"Yes," says Sigrid, cranking paper into the hard rubber roller of her typewriter. "But it's not threatening his life. His wound, I mean. A comrade of his appeared at the door last night. He said that Kaspar had been struck by shrapnel from a mortar, but that the wound wasn't critical."

"Well, thank God for *that*," Renate replies with a relief that surprises Sigrid. She has never known Renate to care much for Kaspar. No overt dislike, just blankness between the mention of Kaspar's name and her next word. But now, with a dark frolic of hair hanging over her brow, Renate looks genuinely relieved. Perhaps only relieved that she will not have to suffer through Sigrid's grief.

"Yes," Sigrid replies. "Thank God."

Noise up front as Fräulein Kretchmar claps her hands together. "Ladies! Your attention, please, before the day begins. As some of you may know, Frau Schröder has just this morning received notification that her husband has been wounded in combat on the Eastern Front."

Audible gasps. "Not critically," Sigrid repeats dimly to the room.

Fräulein Kretchmar crimps her lower lip. "Very good to know. But though we all, I'm sure, deeply sympathize with Frau Schröder at this moment in time, we may *not* allow such feelings to interrupt or impede our work. As I have often said: our soldiers have *their* battle-fields and we have *ours*." Standard Kretchmar propaganda. When Inge Voss's husband was shot down in a bomber over the English Channel, Kretchmar's only suggestion was that donations be made to the War Victim Care Fund in his name.

That night Sigrid is stopped by Ericha on the stairwell. She appears to have been lying in wait for her. Her young face is closed, her eyes bottomless. She is starting to look squeezed.

"I heard," the girl says.

"*Wounded.* That's all," Sigrid tells her. She is having difficulty meeting Ericha's gaze.

Ericha stares. "If you need to stop. For a while."

"Stop?" Sigrid looks back at her with a sudden precision. "Why?"

"I don't know. I don't know what it *feels* like to be in your position."

"You've *never* known what it feels like to be in my position, Ericha. Why should that mean something now?"

An almost imperceptible shrug. "Guilt," the girl suggests.

Sigrid keeps her glare rigidly in place. But all she can manage to say is, "Well, it's too late for that."

On a Saturday morning she takes the elevated into the new S-Bahn station at Anhalter Bahnhof. Wolfram has a flat in a house across the Saarlandstrasse in the Askanischer Platz. A squat, nameless collection of walls, with oddly matched furniture, faded curtains, and a floor, well swept, but warped. Even with furnishing, there's an uninhabited quality to the place. She looks around it, slowly tugging off her scarf. She can see the sprawling architecture of the Anhalter rail station through the window. Reclining atop its grand arches, two classical statues: Night and Day.

She turns back around to the flat. "What is this place?"

"A room," he answers, "with a bed." The springs creak painfully as he drops his weight onto the mattress. He has tossed his gabardine coat over a chair, and is dressed in a pullover, leather-chapped jodhpurs, and Rieker riding boots. "I ride once a week in the Tiergarten," he says, answering the unasked question. "It's part of my physical-therapy program."

"I've never been on a horse," Sigrid says mildly. She watches him yank the pullover over his head, followed by his collarless shirt. His upper body is rippled with muscles.

"They're beautiful animals, horses," he says, "though not very bright."

"And isn't that how you like them?" she asks.

He grins back ruefully, then lifts his eyebrows. "So do you want to *see it*?" he inquires with a slight note of mischief.

"I think I already have," she tells him. Still dressed. Still with her coat buttoned.

"No, I don't mean my putz, Frau Schröder," he says, dropping back on the bed to unbutton the breeches. "I mean my stump." Without waiting for an answer, he wrenches down his breeches and skivvies.

His body, naked, is sinewy and long. An athlete's body. But torn also. Clawed by scars. Hauling off one boot with gusto, he must wrestle the other free. On the right, a perfect foot, a perfect calf. But on the left, the leg ends abruptly below the knee. Strapped to the joint is a wooden, calf-length prosthesis, which resolves itself in a hinged wooden foot. "Lovely, isn't it. Courtesy of the Army Medical Service. I have one with a black leather shoe attached, that I bought from a catalog, but wearing boots is more difficult," he tells her, unbuckling the straps. The prosthesis is dropped onto the heap of his clothing. He slides his rump onto the center of the bed, mattress springs crunching as he positions himself for display.

Sigrid stares softly at the rounded pinkish stump of bone and skin, pockmarked by scarring and chapped by the leather strap. "How did it happen?" she asks.

"A Schu-mine," he answers. "One of ours." He smiles grimly, shaking his head at absurdity of it. "Ridiculous. Seventy days of combat, from Poland to the Baltic, and I step on one of our own goddamned mines." This is said without rancor, but with sheer irony. His gun-sight gaze, for an instant, is inverted, staring inward.

"And it still causes you pain?"

"Sometimes. Sometimes it hurts like all that's holy. You don't find it repulsive?"

"I find it sad," Sigrid tells him.

"Ah. That's worse," he says, rolling sideways to shove back the blankets on the bed. "I'd rather be an object of repulsion than pity. Oh, well. You're still in your coat," he points out. "Come, come, Frau Schröder. You watched *me* undress. Now, let me watch *you*."

Sigrid unbuttons her coat and drapes it over a wooden chair. "I wish you wouldn't call me that."

"Then what would you prefer? I must warn you, I have little patience for endearments."

"My name is Sigrid," she says, and undoes the front of her blouse. "You should call me *that*."

He smells of sweated leather and horsehide. It's a smell she likes. A smell of exertion and comfortable animal strength. She finds that she can easily lose herself in Wolfram's body. The riot of her desire blots out the world. When he rolls her onto her back and enters her, mattress springs ringing, she feels only the terrible thrill of the abyss.

But when they are done, collapsed beside one another on the bed, she closes her eyes and sees Egon's face in the ghost light of her memory.

"My husband's been wounded," she says.

Wolfram is silent for a moment, then reaches for a packet of army-issue cigarettes on the bed stand. "Where?" he asks, lighting up.

"A place called Rzhev."

He nearly laughs. "No. I mean where on his body?"

It suddenly panics her that she doesn't know the answer to that question. That she hadn't asked that question when his comrade was at the door. "I have no idea," she answers starkly.

Wolfram expels smoke. "Just curious if he'll be shipped home. You know. A Heimatschuss."

Sigrid stares. Takes in this new term as she steals the cigarette from Wolfram's fingers for a puff. Heimatschuss. A homeward-bound shot. "What a bad person I have become. My husband is wounded, and I don't even bother to find out the details. Meanwhile, I am lying in the bed of another man."

"Not so bad," Wolfram assures her, retrieving the cigarette. "Believe me, if your husband's been in the East, he's done worse. Much worse."

She stares inwardly, as if she might be able to see all the way to Russia, if only she concentrated. But Kaspar and the East remain blocked by an impenetrable cloud, which her brain will not allow her to penetrate. She arches her neck as if the action will shut off her mind. "Do you have an extra?" she asks. "Cigarette?"

He picks up the packet from the side table, then tosses it back. "Empty. But there's fresh ammo in the pocket of my coat," he tells her.

Sigrid climbs from the bed, the room's cold draft embracing her body. "Which pocket?"

"Left or right. One of them."

She feels through the left pocket of his overcoat flopped over the chair back, and feels something hard. But it's not a packet of cigarettes. She pulls it out and looks at a cardboard packet of playing cards with a winking devil on the front.

She sits down on the edge of the bed and dumps the contents on the plain, threadbare quilt. A deck of naked women in four suits stare up at the ceiling. Wolfram looks at her blankly. "Couldn't find the cigarettes?"

"Is this what you think of women?" she asks.

"It's a soldier's diversion," he says, smoking. "One finds them about in the barracks."

"But I didn't find them in a barracks, I found them in your pocket."

"You're shivering. Why don't you come back under the covers?"

"No," is all she says.

"I see. You are offended. You think maybe you're just another card in my deck, is that it?"

"Of course I am. I don't pretend to believe anything else." She picks up the ten of hearts. "Is this how you'd like to see me? With nothing but a milkmaid's cap and a yolk across my shoulders? Or perhaps," she suggests, discarding the card for another, "with a whip and equestrian boots?"

"No. I'm not interested in costumes, Sigrid. If you wish to know about this deck," he says, picking up a few of the cards, only to toss them back down, "my sergeant left it on display on his desk, the idiot, so I picked it up to prevent trouble. Quite honestly, I had forgotten all about it. And as for the rest, I am not so indiscriminate as you are apparently determined to believe. I have no more use for fantasy maidens in naughty positions than I do for bedmates who have no brains. It's boring. Why should I waste my time?"

But Sigrid is staring. Not at him, but at one of the cards.

"Frau Schröder?" he prods. She places her hand on his bare chest as an answer. Her eyes still glued to the ace of spades she has lifted from the bedspread.

"What is it? Have you been transfixed?"

"No. No, it's nothing," Sigrid answers, and begins to gather the cards together. "I'm sorry. Let's forget about it, I had no right to sound so accusatory. After all, we're not here to philosophize. Are we?"

Only after she has left Wolfram asleep in the bed, only after she has left the train, and found a spot on the margin of the U-Bahn rush behind a news kiosk does she open her purse. Only then does she remove the card she took from the deck and stare down at it with . . . *what*? Anger? Shame? Somehow grief.

The thin, dark-headed female nude, adorning the queen of spades, is aggressively graphic in her posture: hands clamped on her hips, pelvis thrust forward. Posed in front of a crudely painted background of the Venetian canals, she is staring down the camera, naked save for the striped stockings gartered to her thighs, and the gondolier's cap raked to one side. Her eyes, so sharp, so challenging, so uncompromising and orphaned from joy.

SIGRID DISPLAYS THE PLAYING CARD, watching Ericha's eyes latch onto it. "Can you explain this?"

Without a millimeter's movement. "Explain what?"

"Explain why you posed for this?"

"Can you explain why you're carrying it in your purse?"

"You're very clever, yes," Sigrid says in a dry voice. "But I want an answer from you." She pokes the card forward again.

Ericha makes no move to touch it, only examines it with a blank pause, and turns away to the street. An army lorry booms past, the soldiers inside hooting and whistling for her attention, but they gain none of it. "A lot of women are doing it. The photographers pay good money."

Sigrid stares. "And that's your explanation? The photographers pay good money?"

"Do I require another?"

"Don't," Sigrid begins to respond, but the words jam up in her head. She must shake them loose before she can speak. "Don't you have any *shame*, child?"

"Shame?" Ericha's eyes are suddenly hard and shadowed. "No, Frau Schröder. No, gnädige Frau, I *have none*. Not a drop. And I will not be held accountable by your obsolete notions of 'propriety.' Propriety died with the first man murdered by the criminals in power, Frau Schröder. The first time a wife received an urn full of her husband's ashes from the Gestapo."

"Yes. Yes, I know you are a fine one with your high talk. But the truth is, *talk* can just be an excuse. A justification to act as you wish, the rest of the world be damned. But there *are* rules. *Still*. Rules about respecting oneself, and one's body. Rules about displaying oneself naked for *payment*!"

"You seem intent on casting me as a whore, Frau Schröder," Ericha observes.

Sigrid blinks, taken aback. "No. No, not at all. I'm simply trying to make you understand," she says, but the girl ambushes her point.

"After the Aufmarsch," Ericha interrupts in a contained voice, "the army was followed into the East by special murder battalions of the SS and police, whose mission, whose *single mission,* was to slaughter Jews. As many Jews as they could find. In Latvia, in the Ukraine, in Russia. Ten, twenty, thirty thousand people massacred at a time. Women, babies, old men. It didn't matter. They were mowed down and their bodies dumped in mass graves."

"Child," Sigrid tries to say, but the girl cuts her off.

"No. Don't interrupt. If you're going to do this work, you should be fully educated. In Poland, they've set up camps. Not work camps, mind you, or 'resettlement' camps, or whatever lie they're telling about them, but *extermination* factories, hidden in the marshlands, with the express purpose of manufacturing corpses by the ton. *That's* the destination of the trains leaving the goods yard of the Bahnhof Grunewald. And *that's* the fate that everyone in Auntie's pension is dodging. *Everyone.* So you'll pardon me," she says, "you must *pardon* me, Frau Schröder, if I'm not too impressed by your flights into the realm of proper behavior for a young lady."

———

The weather grows sodden with rain. The dark building shapes and the gray species of wartime Berliners are bleakly outlined against the downpours. Traffic grinds and slows. Small armies of ragged men have been put to work clearing rubble from bombed buildings around the Belle Alliance Platz. Once Sigrid had seen a newsreel of downed British airmen clearing a sidewalk of slag in the bomb-bruised Potsdamer Platz as grinning Berliners looked on. But that's just propaganda. She's never seen a Brit prisoner of war on the streets. These men are Russian prisoners enduring their punishment in the rain as they are forced to repair a damaged tramline track. Faces like sheared stone. Steel-helmeted SS Totenkopf guards in rubberized cloaks stand by, with carbines slung. One of the Totenkopf men works hard at lighting a cigarette in the rain, stopping only long enough to call out his favorite obscenities to Sigrid as she passes.

The brick apartment block, with its front ripped away, still stands as it did two months before, the interiors of its flats still on display to the street. But somehow the rain makes it seem even not simply abandoned but lonely. Inconsolable.

She shakes the rain from her umbrella in the foyer. Since the notice came from the army, there's been nothing. Opening the postbox, she stares at the empty slot, then closes it. She has been waiting for a letter from Kaspar, but no such letter comes. Where is he? How is he recovering? She has no idea. She has followed the official instructions for wives writing to wounded husbands. Written one letter after the other, each becoming shorter and more succinctly demanding than the last, till finally she was simply writing, *Kaspar, tell me how you are. Tell me how badly you have been hurt.* But no response comes, so the unanswered questions fill up a kind of dead space inside of her. She visits an army office off of the Landwehrkanal, which is charged with knowing such things, but they can tell her nothing new. Only that he was wounded between one date and another, and that he was put on a medical train after being transferred from War Hospital 4/531 Smolensk-Nord. But where this train has taken him, it's simply impossible to say. Records are incomplete. The backlog is gargantuan. The army clerk behind the desk has eyes so deep that she can nearly see the rows of tombstones crowding them.

At the Pension Unsagbar, keeping the guests from freezing has become a problem. Blankets, yes, but there's no way to heat the space properly when the temperatures drop at night. Auntie has taken to allowing the children to sleep with their mother on her parlor floor, which has stirred the pot. The man called Kozig is grumbling. *What claim does she have to warmth that is more legitimate than mine? Because she has children? I have children too. Just not here. Should my children's father freeze? Are her children more valuable than mine? Do they need a parent more?* There have been arguments.

One night Sigrid is leaving as Frau Weiss is listening to her children's prayers. Their little voices reciting the large words in Hebrew. *"Shema Yisrael, Adonai Eloheinu, Adonai Echad."*

"Do you understand?" Frau Weiss asks her with lightness to her smile.

Sigrid shakes her head. "No."

"It means, 'Hear, O Israel. The Lord is our God, the Lord is One.'"

Herr Kozig sneers. "You think God still hears us?" he inquires leadenly, snapping each card as he lays out his game of solitaire. "You really think He's still listening to the Jews?"

Frau Weiss looks at the new arrival, with the gray stubble of beard and the foolish postage-stamp mustache. "I'm sorry if *you* don't think so, Herr Kozig," Frau Weiss replies, though she doesn't sound sorry. She sounds defiant. "I'm sorry if you think God could desert His people."

"*Desert us*? How absurd." He snaps a card from the deck. "He hasn't deserted us. He's served us up on a platter. While you're teaching your children to say the Shema, He's busy with the Nazis sharpening their knives for them, ready to carve up the next Jew for supper."

"Herr Kozig, *please*!" The woman reproves him angrily, her hands over her daughter's ears. "The *children*!"

"They shouldn't know?" He shrugs. "*Say your prayers, my little kinder*," he mocks. "*God is listening*. But what your mama won't tell you is that he is also *laughing*."

"I DON'T LIKE HIM." Auntie frowns, with a sideways glance at Kozig's never-ending game of solitaire.

"It is not for us to like or dislike him, Auntie," Ericha reminds her. "We do not choose favorites."

"And now I get a lecture from the pulpit," the old woman says, smirking. "First you bring me a thief, who steals from my purse, and now *this* one, who's thinking God knows what."

"So shall I write up a morals questionnaire for all U-boats to complete, Auntie? Would that satisfy you?"

"Did you know he has a gun?"

"Does he?"

"A nickel-plated popgun that he sticks in his trousers to fill the void. I've seen him hide it."

"Well, it makes no difference." Ericha shakes her head. "He'll be gone soon. We'll move them *all* out soon. I have a possibility for passports. A man who works in the Interior Ministry."

"And how long have you been saying that? You have *this* possibility or *that* possibility. Some bureaucrat who can stand on his head! Meanwhile, the Gestapo are trying to peer in through the keyhole."

"I'm *working* on it, Auntie."

"Have you heard the old man? His cough is getting worse. Sometimes I think he's choking up the last breath of air in his body. He could be *tubercular*, for all we know."

"I said I'm *working* on it," Ericha repeats in a rebuffing tone as she buttons her coat. "What more would you have me tell you?"

"That you have a *solution*. That's what I would have you tell me."

Then, tugging on her beret, Ericha turns to Sigrid. "We should go."

But on the way out Auntie gives Sigrid a look that isn't hard to read. *Do something!*

ON THE STREETS, the number of flags have multiplied since Goebbels's speech demanding Total War. Patriotic marches jam the wireless and daily broadcasts, assure everyone that the men of the eastern armies are emerging from their winter camps in Russia with iron hearts, and that they will soon unleash such an onslaught that Ivan will simply collapse to his knees and pray for mercy. Oh, yes. *Pray for mercy*. But the BBC broadcasts a slightly different version. According to London, the Russians have retaken vast swaths of territory, and Army Group Center is struggling to re-form its line by withdrawing its forces from the Moscow salients. This, the announcer reminds with cool satisfaction, comes on the heels of the humiliating defeat of all German forces at Stalingrad.

When she reports this to Wolfram, he holds her in his gun sights. "Stalingrad," he says, "was more than just the end of the Sixth Army. It was the end of any hope we might have had of laying our hands on the oil fields in the Caucasus. So there will be no spring offensive," he announces almost casually. "Not really. Maybe by the summer. June or July. At which point, I can only imagine, we'll throw everything we've got into a pincer attack to cut off the salient around Kursk. But it won't be enough. Von Manstein managed to stabilize the southern front and kept it from collapsing because he's a great goddamned soldier, but to breach Ivan's line will mean committing every last piece of functioning armor we have, and draining every last drop of petrol from our reserve. And then, even if we *do,* by some miracle, manage to punch through, we won't have the power to do much more than sit there and wait for the Reds to punch back. Our line will cave in, but this time there'll be no way to rebuild it. No panzers. No fuel. No men," he says flatly. "After that, the eastern armies will begin traveling the glorious road to victory in reverse."

Sigrid looks at him starkly. They have continued to keep the springs ringing in the bed they share in the Askanischer Platz, unfaltering in their pursuit of oblivion. Though she is still a little afraid of the man. There is something of the land mine about him. And now this blunt assessment has stunned her.

"Are you saying," she finally asks, and then must start the question again. "Are you saying that the war in the East is *lost*?"

This prompts a short laugh from Wolfram. "Lost, but far from over. We still have an ocean or two of blood to be spilled before that. Would you believe me if I told you that there are elements of the general staff already planning for the defense of the Reich's eastern borders?" He pokes a cigarette into his mouth and picks up his silver-plated lighter. "It's true," he says, attempting to snap the lighter to life. "What will happen when the Red Army reaches the River Oder?"

Her face is blank, but her eyes are deep. "And what *will* happen?"

A glance up from the malfunctioning lighter. "We'll learn the *true* definition of Total War, gnädige Frau." No fire. "Dammit," he breathes mildly. "Out of fuel, too." And then he asks, "Where are you going?"

"To the WC," she answers. Drawing a blanket from the bed. Out in the hall, she clears the hall with a glance, wraps herself more tightly, and quickly pads to the toilet a few steps away. Inside she locks the door, and sits. She simply had to get away from Wolfram for a moment. The information he is dispensing is so highly potent that she feels drunk from it. Perhaps everyone had their suspicions about the Eastern Front, but no one has ever spoken them aloud like this, not even Ericha. Yet here is this young man, casually calculating the equation of military debacle. No tanks, no petrol, no men equals the Red Army at the Oder.

When she returns to the room from the WC, she finds Wolfram closing the flap of her bag, as if he has just withdrawn his hand from it. "Looking for a match," he explains calmly, cigarette dangling from his lips.

"I don't carry matches," she says.

"So I discovered. But you do carry a sharp little sister in there," he notes, stretching over to the nightstand drawer, still in search of a light.

"I might have to gut a fish," Sigrid answers.

"You're coming back to bed?" he inquires, finally discovering a matchbox in the drawer, and lighting the cigarette.

"No. I have to get dressed," she answers.

"Really? I thought you were staying. We could have dinner."

She shakes her head, gathering her clothes. "I have to go."

"Another man?"

"No. A mother-in-law. I must report in."

"I'm going out of town for several days next week," he tells her. Efficiently slipping into her chemise. "Another woman?"

"Would that make you jealous?"

"I couldn't help but notice that the wardrobe here is filled with a rack of women's clothing. I assume I am not the only one you bring here."

"And if I were to say that you *are*?" His eyes are on her as she dresses.

"I would call you a liar. So where are you going, if it's not another woman?"

"Just reporting in to my own mother-in-law of sorts," he replies, then turns away. "I'm sure you'll miss me dreadfully."

"I will," she hears herself say.

But Wolfram seems to be done with this conversation. He is propped up against the headboard, studying his cigarette. "Take care going home. Keep an eye peeled for dangerous fish."

"Wolfram," she suddenly says. "What is happening to the Jews?"

He gazes at her abruptly, his gun sight returning. "That is quite a loaded question," he says.

"We are murdering them?"

"You mean, you and I?"

"I mean *us*. Germany."

"So you've been listening to the BBC," he suggests.

"Yes, but I'm not a fool. I don't have to listen to the BBC to see what's happening in the streets of my own city. So I'm asking you. Is the objective," she begins, then must swallow before speaking the word, "extermination?"

Only a beat of silence separates them.

"If you're not an fool, Frau Schröder," he replies, and expels a whistle of gray smoke, "and I don't believe you *are*, then why are you asking a question to which you already know the answer?"

THE NEXT MORNING, when she arrives at the police desk in the foyer of the patent office, she finds that her employee identification card is missing from her bag. The old guard at the desk does not make trouble for her. He simply scratches a note with a frown in a logbook. "You'll have to go upstairs to the third floor to have it replaced," he tells her. It's the only full sentence she has ever heard the old man speak. But as she walks down the corridor, she thinks of Wolfram's hand in her bag.

That evening, when she returns to her flat, Mother Schröder is talking to her from the kitchen, where she is washing a plate, and says, "So you're missing your shadow."

Sigrid wraps an uneaten portion of supper in wax paper. A slice of hard Schwarzbrot smeared with fish paste. That will be lunch tomorrow. "My shadow?"

"Your protégée. Fräulein Klink-a-doodle."

The tone tells her that the old lady must have sneaked in a schnapps or two before eating. "Her name is Kohl, and she's not my protégée in any sense of the word. It happens that we both enjoy the cinema. That's all."

"Well, you aren't aware, then? She's . . . what's the expression? She's *jumped ship*?" The china clinks as the old woman places the dish into the wooden drainer. Sigrid glares dumbly, prompting her mother-in-law to smile with satisfaction. "*So*. She Who Knows All didn't know *that*, did she?"

"Know what? What in God's name are you getting at?"

"No need to swear, daughter-in-law. I'm simply surprised that you're in the dark. She didn't come home to her bed last night."

"What?" She must try to sound only mildly alarmed.

"Just what I said. Have you lost your hearing, too, or just your judgment?" The old woman wipes her chapped hands dry with a towel, glaring at Sigrid's stupidity. "I told you that the creature was not to be trusted. But why would you ever listen to me?"

"What do you mean 'not to be trusted'?"

"There were certain items missing."

"Missing?"

"From Lotti Granzinger's flat."

"*What* items?"

"*Certain* items. None of your business what."

Sigrid blinks. Shakes her head to try to free herself from this tangle of nonsense. "Has anyone gone searching for her?"

"*Searching* for her?" Mother Schröder snorts at the idea. "She has found somewhere else to *sleep*. Must I spell it out for you further? She left Lotti no other choice than to report her to the Labor Service." The old woman hangs the hand towel on its hook with finality. "We'll see if a daily dose of close-order drill doesn't check the little strumpet's urges." Then her voice gains an edgy squawk. "And *where* are *you* going at this hour?" Mother Schröder demands.

But Sigrid does not answer. She is snatching her coat and vanishing from the flat.

Forty minutes later she is rapping on Auntie's door. But when the door opens, the look filling the old woman's face kills Sigrid's words before she can utter a single syllable.

"Ah. Good evening, Frau Hoff," says Auntie in a politely formal tone. "I know you said you'd be dropping by, but I didn't realize you'd be coming tonight."

Sigrid stares at her dumbly. *Frau Hoff?* And then she hears it. "Who *is it*, Helene?" a male voice inquires pointedly from within.

"It's Frau Hoff from Herr Schmidt's office. I wasn't expecting her till later this week."

"Well, she's here now," the voice grumbles. "Have her come in."

Sigrid blinks. It takes her an instant to reassemble herself into Frau Hoff. "No, no. I'm so sorry. I must have gotten my dates mixed up. And you have company. I'll come back another night."

"Helene," the voice calls firmly. "Have her come in," it instructs.

Auntie gives her a shrug. "Please. Come in."

Inside, the flat is unusually warm. Or perhaps it's only Sigrid sweating. Planted on the worn-out settee is a worn-out old man. Bald. A face like a prune. An entrenched frown. He appears shrunken inside of the serge suit he wears, and he holds a cane in his hand as if he might use it suddenly to launch himself from the sofa cushion. Pinned to his lapel is a "scary badge" above an Iron Cross from the Kaiser's days. He glares up at Sigrid through smudged spectacles with lenses as thick as ice cubes. "You'll excuse me if I don't rise, Frau Hoff." Not a polite request, more like a direct order. "But I suffered an injury in defense of our Fatherland."

Sigrid stares back for a moment as if the old prune has spoken to her in tongues.

"My brother, Frau Hoff," Auntie interprets. "Herr Brückner. He was wounded during the last war,"

"Frog bayonet," the geezer explains sternly. "Second Verdun."

"Then, please, Herr Brückner, please remain seated. I'm really so sorry to have disrupted your evening."

"Not to worry," Auntie informs her. "I have what you need right at hand." But whatever Frau Hoff needs that is right at hand, it seems to take Auntie an eternity to find it in a cardboard box of papers she has pulled out from under the curtain of the kitchen sink.

"So, Frau Hoff. I've heard your name mentioned before. You work for Schmidt, do you?" the old man suddenly demands.

Sigrid flinches in response. "Yes. For Herr Schmidt."

"How long?"

Sigrid concentrates on breathing. "How long? A while. It often seems longer than it's actually been."

"I can believe that. I'll be blunt, Frau Hoff, I never trusted your employer. I think he cheated my brother-in-law, Otto, for years, and now is making a career of cheating his widow. It's a crime. And someday I'll prove it."

"Reinhold, please. Not again," Auntie begs as she returns from the sink, a dog-eared file folder closed with elastic in her hands. "You must excuse my brother, Frau Hoff. He has made a mistrust of humanity *his* career."

Herr Brückner snorts. "And my sister, Frau Hoff, has never learned to keep her mouth shut in front of strangers."

"An old family tradition." Auntie grins dimly. "So. Here you are," she says, handing over the file folder. I hope this will satisfy Herr Schmidt's needs."

"Yes." Sigrid steps toward her. "Thank you." Removing her gloves, she places them on Auntie's kitchenette table, managing to signal Auntie with her eyes as she pretends to inspect the file folder's contents. "Yes, I'm sure this will be more than adequate. Good night. And good night, Herr Brückner. So very pleased to meet you."

The old man shrugs. Her opinion, not his.

Halfway down the corridor, Auntie appears behind her, flapping the pair of gloves in the air. "Frau Hoff. You left your gloves behind."

Up close, Auntie looks as if she has just been through the wringer. *"What are you doing here?"* she hisses. "I *told* the young one that no one was to come tonight."

"Well, I didn't know that, because the 'young one' has gone *missing*," Sigrid informs her, and watches the old woman's expression fall flat. "She didn't come home last night. That's why I'm here. I thought perhaps—"

"I haven't seen her," Auntie declares curtly.

Sigrid looks at her for a blank moment.

"And I'm not in the business of dispensing sympathy if that's what you're here for. What happens, happens. Nothing to be done."

"I *know* what *business* you're in," Sigrid replies archly, "and I didn't come for sympathy. I came for help."

"Well, help is the last thing I can give you. If the young Fräulein is missing, then it means she may have been compromised. Which means that *I* have been compromised, which means that *our guests* have been compromised, and which, by the way, means that *you* have been compromised, too. So you came to the wrong place for help. Now, if you'll excuse me, I must get back to my brother for further interrogation.

Take your gloves and go. And don't come back unless you've decided that you can be of some help to *me*."

"Helene!" the old fart calls from the flat. "What's taking you? My coffee's gone tepid."

Auntie frowns. Hands over the gloves. "Good night."

THE NEXT EVENING a raw eastern wind skids off the lakes. It rends the snapping banners clinging to their flagstaffs, gusts the thin dry snow in whirling patterns across the asphalt of the Uhlandstrasse, and carries the Gestapo into their apartment building.

"So you have no idea concerning her whereabouts?"

The man's voice is dull. Bored. It matches his expression.

"That's correct," Sigrid replies.

"Yet according to"—he consults his notebook with a frown for the name—"according to Frau Granzinger, the two of you were friendly."

His face is pale and doughy. Thick eyebrows. Dark eyes with only a pilot light burning. "'Friendly'?" Sigrid repeats, as if only vaguely familiar with the concept. "Did she use that word? If she did, then I'm afraid she overstated the matter considerably. I found Fräulein Kohl to be a confused young girl. Perhaps I took some pity on her and tried to give her a steer in the proper direction."

"And what direction would that be?"

"As I said, she was confused. Girls at that age often fall victim to emotional turmoil. Certainly you must be aware of that."

The man looks back at her blankly.

"My advice to her, and how closely it was heeded, I cannot say, but my advice to her was to work and work *hard*. Redouble her efforts. Forget about her personal pains and dedicate herself to the task at hand."

"Which was?"

"Which was the care of Frau Granzinger's children, of course. Keeping them fed. Keeping them clean."

The man's stare is unaltered.

"I told her, you see, that changing soiled diapers might not be very glamorous, but that in doing so she was serving the nation as surely as does the frontline soldier. But then a man in your position must understand that all too well, Herr Kommissar."

The man's eyes flicker ever so slightly. *Must I?*

"Serving as a policeman, that is. Of course, I have no doubt that as a German man you would much prefer to be waging war with a rifle on the battlefield. But you know that there are other battlefields, too, battlefields that are just as important. Fighting the enemies within as well as the enemies without." Sigrid says all this wearing a face of humorless sincerity, her eyes bluntly serene in her convictions.

For a long moment, the man observes her, his gaze illuminated by an infinitesimal glint of scrutiny. Then the door across the hall opens and a man in a snap-brim hat and leather trench coat emerges from the Frau Obersturmführer Junger's flat. But it is not the Frau Obersturmführer showing him out, but the half sister, dressed in her well-pressed nurse's uniform. The woman gives Sigrid a momentary glance, and then offers a, "Heil Hitler, Frau Schröder," in quite a perfunctory manner. A tone that Sigrid mimics perfectly in her reply. "Heil Hitler, Fräulein Kessler," she responds, and then both turn to view the doughy-faced men standing on the landing with the impunity that is the property of the unvarnished heart. Fräulein Kessler shuts her door. The man looks at his partner, who only shrugs; then he stuffs his notebook back into the pocket of his overcoat.

"Thank you, Frau Schröder," he says without gratitude, "for your time. Heil Hitler."

"*Heil Hitler*," Sigrid responds earnestly. She closes the door with a careful thud, then presses her head against the wood, listening to the

191

echo of the men's footsteps as they descend floor by floor. When she tugs off her cardigan, she realizes that she has sweated through her dress. Mother Schröder surveys her darkly, puffing on one of her stinking cigarettes. Only a puddle of schnapps remains in her glass. "I *told* you," she declares sharply. "I *told* you, didn't I? That girl was trouble from the start. Now, look what we've got. The Gestapo at our door."

"The Gestapo," says Sigrid, hanging her cardigan on the hook and wiping her cheek. "was at *everyone's* door. Not just ours."

"And did *everyone* break out into sweat because of it?" the old lady inquires with a sour smirk.

Sigrid removes her hand from her cheek. "They did if they have any brains."

Mother Schröder snorts. Tends to her cigarette. "You're lucky I'm a Party member."

"Yes," Sigrid tells her, crossing to the sink and unscrewing the tap. "Every day I thank God for that."

"You know, you might, for once, think of someone else's welfare," the old woman calls out caustically after her. "If they arrest you, it's your whole family that follows. Forget about me, I'm an old woman. But think about your *husband*, if you can still remember his face. Think about what might happen to *him*."

Sigrid fills her cupped hands and presses her face into the water from the kitchen sink's open tap. She feels it tingle on her skin, then rises up and summons breath. "Kaspar is a soldier. A *wounded* soldier. The army won't let anyone touch him. Besides, I haven't done anything wrong. I work in a patent office. I come home, I go to sleep. I wake up for the bombers when they come, and go back to sleep after they leave. The next morning I start the process over again, just like everyone else. Why should the Gestapo have the slightest interest in arresting me?" Is she reassuring herself with this dialogue? By now she is back into the front room, wiping her hands on the dish towel.

"Because you have no sense," her mother-in-law explains curtly.

"That's always your problem. You think because you're so smart that you can get away with anything. That you're above it all. But you're not, my good girl. And if you're not careful, you're going to find that out, just like that sow Hildegard Remki did."

For an instant the old lady's eyes are searing, then she looks rapidly away. Inhales smoke. A second later she reaches over and snaps on Frau Remki's Telefunken, leaving Sigrid standing there, glaring at her as the Ninth Symphony invades the room. Sigrid feels a chill through her sweated blouse.

In the bedroom, she removes the sweaty garment and picks a dry one from the bureau. Sitting on the bed, she examines the postcard she has secreted from the pocket of her coat. Ericha's eyes are as naked as her body. She regards Sigrid with equally naked appraisal. Eyes steaming wet, Sigrid turns the card over in her hand, and reads the address printed on the back: WILHELMINA VON HOHENHOFF. BEAUTY IMAGES, 146C KANTSTRASSE, BERLIN.

THIRTEEN

SHE KNOCKS but there is no answer, though she can hear a woman's voice. A strong voice, engaged in argument. Quietly she tries the brass door handle, and the door pops open with a smooth click. Peering in, she finds that the loft is full of shadows. Heavy drapes are closed over tall windows, shutting out even a blink of light. Only a table lamp, dressed with a red scarf, burns at the opposite side of the room, where she can see, in the warm, blood-red light, a very tall, athletically trim woman in trousers, pacing back and forth on the telephone, shouting into the receiver with a commanding anger. "I don't *care*, Dieter, I don't care! Those are all *your* problems, *not mine.* Now, we have an agreement and you will stick to it, is that understood?!" But before poor Dieter, whoever he is, can possibly make a reply, she rings off with a slam. Sigrid stands in the threshold, the corridor leaking light behind her. "You're late," the woman announces imperiously. "That's your first and last warning. Keep me waiting again, and I'll sack your ass." She steps away from the lamp glow, and a second later, Sigrid is blinded by a stinging assault of white light.

"Well, don't just stand there, for fuck's sake," she hears the woman demand.

Tentatively Sigrid steps forward, shielding her eyes. "You are Wilhelmina von Hohenhoff?"

The woman steps into the light with an expression of critical appraisal. Her thick bob of curls is dyed henna red. Her eyes are hooded and deeply set. "You're a little old for this," she observes.

"I beg your pardon?"

"Most of my girls aren't much past twenty. But still, you have the eyes, and an interesting bone structure," she says.

Sigrid backs off half a step as the woman fluffs her fingers through her hair. "Frau von Hohenhoff."

"*Fräulein* von Hohenhoff. Good hair. Maybe a braid. But later for the details. Take off your clothes. I want to see your body."

"I am not here to strip down for your camera, *Fräulein* von Hohenhoff."

"*No?* Then why are you wasting my time? I'm sure you were told that I only do nudes."

"I am not here to be photographed. Will you please turn off those lights?"

The woman examines Sigrid with a sudden frown. "Then why *are* you here?"

"My name is Frau Schröder. I'm here about . . . about one of your *models.* Now, if you please, I'm being blinded."

The woman retains her frown, and walks off, the noise of her heels on the hardwood floor echoing into the loft's high ceilings. A metallic click kills the brightness, which is replaced by the glow of a line of studio lights. Sigrid blinks and lowers her hand.

"You have a good look," the woman informs her. "So I won't boot you out the door just yet. But don't get comfortable."

"I'm looking for a girl named Ericha Kohl."

"Yes? And you think she sat for me, do you?"

"Well," Sigrid says, and produces Ericha's playing card, "she wasn't exactly sitting."

The woman observes the card and then Sigrid. "Are you a wife?" Fräulein von Hohenhoff inquires blankly.

"Am I a what?"

"Sometimes wives appear hunting for their husband's bed partner. Sometimes *husbands* appear hunting for their *wife's* bed partner. My girls are not threatened by variety."

"No. Nothing like that. But you know her, correct?"

"Oh, yes. Who could forget the courageous young Ericha?" The woman crushes out her cigarette in a small enamel ashtray overloaded with butts. "Why do you ask, if it's not too much trouble to tell me?"

"Because," Sigrid answers, "she's gone missing."

The woman gazes back at her. Then turns suddenly and strides away, over to a sideboard, without a word. Sigrid follows the echo of her heels. "You have nothing to say?" she asks.

"What would you have me say? A girl has gone missing." The woman shrugs, finding a cigarette to light. "They often do." The room around them is cluttered with cameras and equipment, light stands, props, and assorted Hetzblätter. The smell of developing fluid mixes with the bitter aroma of strongly brewed coffee. On the wall are a dozen or so framed photographs of schnauzer dogs. "My children," she explains. "Arco and Duxi. Dead now. I could never bring myself to have another after them," she explains with wistful efficiency, and then sits and lights another cigarette. But Sigrid is not interested in the dog photos. She is staring at several painted background flats stacked against the wall. Sigrid recognizes the canal scene from Ericha's pose.

"You disapprove?"

"What?"

Fräulein von Hohenhoff nods toward the flats. "Of what I do. You shouldn't. I provide a valuable service to the Wehrmacht by boosting the morale of our troops."

"My approval or disapproval is of no importance," she says.

"Well, I'm glad we can agree on that."

"Can you tell me," she asks, "the last time you saw her?"

Fräulein von Hohenhoff does not have to consider. "Last night. She appeared here in the late evening." The woman inhales smoke, and expels none of it. "I'd hoped she'd come to pose again, because the camera loves her. Strange. To look at her, you'd never imagine, the scrawny thing. But no"—she knocks off a bit of ash into another loaded ashtray—"that wasn't why." "Up close, behind the vigor of her façade, Sigrid sees that the woman is aging. The jawline pulping. The skin of her neck wrinkling, starting to sag. Her teeth and fingers filmed by tobacco stains. "*So*," Fräulein von Hohenhoff says with a cool gaze, "who are you to her?"

"We are neighbors."

"Neighbors. And why should I give a piss about that, Frau Schröder?"

"She works for the woman who lives above me. We've been friends," she says, but suddenly it all becomes a jumble. Too much to explain and not enough. "It's not a joke. The police are looking for her," she announces. "They came to our apartment block last night."

"The police?"

"The Gestapo," Sigrid clarifies.

Fräulein von Hohenhoff takes a breath. Stares at the ashtray and then raises her eyes heavily. "Do you know?" she asks.

"Know?"

"What she does."

A minuscule pause. "Yes."

"Then you must have some idea how useful a photographer might be to . . ."—the woman pauses, to choose the correct words— ". . . to her *hobby*."

Sigrid says nothing

"I gave her my key," the woman tells her. "If she ever needed it. Ever needed a place. But Ericha Kohl is a ghost, Frau Schröder. She appears, she disappears." A shrug. "Like an apparition. If you know her at all, then surely you know that much."

"So, you have no thoughts . . . ?"

"On the contrary. I have many thoughts about our Fräulein Kohl. But where she *is* or *might be*, I have not an inkling."

Sigrid stares for a moment at the woman's face. "Are you lying to me?"

A stony look in reply. Then the Fräulein is up. She steps away, with eyes averted as she rubs a thumb across her forehead. Smoke floats in the air around her. "I was never running a business, you understand. Photos for identity documents? I did them as favors. And only for certain people."

"But you supplied documents to Ericha."

"I am a photographer, not a forger. That work went to someone else. A man she knew in the Heerstrasse," she says, her voice gaining an edge.

"A man, yes. She called him Johann."

"I had no contact with him," she announces flatly. "You say his name was Johann?" A frown. "I didn't inquire."

"Fräulein von Hohenhoff, *please*," Sigrid finally begs. "No more of this piecemeal story. *Tell me what you know.*"

The woman turns, her face transparent and loaded with pain. "I was angry," she declares, her eyes gone suddenly red. "She came to me, not out of any feeling, but only to ask for money. Only money. This *man.* I knew how she was soiling herself with him. I was *angry*," she repeats. "I tossed a hundred marks on the floor and told her to go fuck herself."

Sigrid takes in a painful breath. But the Fräulein turns away.

"Now you may be permitted to judge me, Frau Schröder," she says in a sickened voice. "And then get out."

. . .

SIGRID TRAVELS THE KANTSTRASSE like a sleepwalker, twice bumping into eternally hurried Berliners rushing in the opposite direction. She is headed, ostensibly, for the Zoo U-Bahn station, but is only dimly aware that she has made a wrong turn. "Get your eyes examined!" Her fellow citizens scold her. "Are you blind?" they demand to know. And then a body slams into her with such force that only a pair of hands seizing her arms prevent her from hitting the pavement. The impact forces her to struggle for focus. Then she sees the face, and his name catches in her throat.

"There's someone following you," he whispers. She feels his breath burning her ear. "Black trilby and gray overcoat, a half block back." And then aloud, "Excuse me, gnädige Frau, for my blunder. My apologies." In a heartbeat he is gone, merging into the oncoming pedestrians, but Sigrid is stuck solidly in place, staring after him. Her heart, her brain, her body are in full-blown shock, as the echo of Egon's voice reverberates in her head and heats her flesh. When she lurches forward it is without thought, and this time when she plows into someone she is knocked flat onto her rump. Her head swims. She blinks at the other woman who is bent over her, apologizing, retrieving the contents of Sigrid's purse, which have been spilled on the sidewalk. "Are you hurt?" the woman keeps repeating. A slim, thoughtful face, her eyebrows pinched together with concern. "Are you hurt? I'm so sorry. I simply wasn't watching," she says, gathering up a comb, a compact mirror, a pencil stub and a tube of headache powder, and then stops dead to stare at Ericha's naked postcard. Sigrid snatches it from the woman's hand with a curt "Thank you," and clambers to her feet. "I am unhurt." Then, pushing past without another syllable, she searches the street with a breath of frantic hope, but no hope is found, only strangers. Strangers in front of her and strangers behind her. Though, purchasing a copy of the *B.Z. am Mittag* from a uniformed paperboy, is a hefty Berliner bear wearing a slate gray overcoat and a black trilby hat. Sigrid gulps down a metallic taste of fear, puts down her head, and charges down the walk in the opposite direction, weaving through the midday mob. A block farther, she turns quickly into a small café and finds a chair and a table. Her hands are shaking. Her body shivering. The waitress squints at her. "Sorry, are you ill?" she inquires, but Sigrid ignores the question. Orders coffee. Shock, fear, and unadulterated excitement. The thrill of his voice. The sight of his face. The grip of his hands. So suddenly, igniting her heart. *Alive.* He is not a ghost of her imagination. He is alive and touchable.

The bell over the door jangles, and she glances up with wild hope, but only spots the hefty man entering with a newspaper under his arm. Gray coat, black trilby. He pays her not a whit of attention, but thumps down behind a table, and spreads open his newspaper, ruffling pages, clearing a gummy congestion from his throat. He orders a coffee and a brandy and a Dutch cigar.

Her palms are sweating. She downs a few swallows of the tasteless coffee in her cup and quickly stands. Her coins ring on the tabletop and she bullets for the door. Outside, she sees the E bus, slowing for its stop in the Auguste-Viktoria-Platz, below the zoo. Her pace quickens. She risks a glance behind, only to see the hefty man veering out of the café door with a frown. She picks up her pace again. By the time the bus eases to a halt with a moan of brakes, she is running, and though she dares not turn again, she knows that he is running, too. The last of the passengers are loading themselves aboard, and the bus driver is signaling his return to traffic by the time she makes it to the stop and hammers on the door. This is illegal, and most drivers ignore such desperate actions, but sometimes it works. The bus halts, the doors swing open, and she clambers up. The driver grunts at her, but the young female conductor wearing a striped BdM armlet sets in with an immediate lecture, which Sigrid ignores. She is too busy watching the great bear huffing and puffing as he runs, red-faced, beside the departing bus before tossing up his hands in frustration. The bus grinds into gear and pulls away from the curb, spewing oily exhaust. A car horn sounds in the street. Inside, it is crowded and she must stand. A baby cries over the noise of the motor. An old hausfrau snores. A wordless disgruntlement fills in the empty spaces. She's not even sure where she is going, but doesn't care. The thrill has turned upside down inside of her. Standing there aboard the lumbering bus, jostled and bumped, the odor of unwashed clothing filling her nostrils, she feels Egon's abandonment as keenly as she did the last time they shared a bed. He was there, and then in a blink he was gone. Disappearing into daylight and not throwing a shadow, making his escape, without her. As always. Without her.

AT THE DOOR to the building she is met by Portierfrau Mundt, in her bleached apron over a drab housedress, who holds the foyer door for her as if Sigrid is a truant child. "Awfully late for a married woman to be coming home from work, Frau Schröder," the woman notes. "More delays on the trains, no doubt?"

Sigrid gives her a dark eye. "You were holding supper for me, Portierfrau? Or just spying from your window?"

"My husband and I are responsible for residents of this building," she reminds her archly. "Remarks like that do you no good. As you may one day discover."

Sigrid climbs the stairs, deaf to Mundt. Deaf to herself, beyond the thumping of her heart. At the landing to her flat, she pauses. Digs blindly into her purse for the key. When she doesn't find it, she digs into her pockets. Where had she put the foolish thing? But when she draws out a piece of grayish wartime paper, folded in half, her heart thumps deeply. For a moment, it's too much. She closes her hand over the note and presses it against her belly. Then she steals a breath and opens the fold. Quickly scans the contents once, and then again. It's only a few words. But she reads them over and over, then jumps when the door opens behind her.

"Good evening," she hears Fräulein Kessler say. The woman is dressed in a stiff beige housecoat and wearing wire-rimmed spectacles. The combination makes her look dowdy, older. "I'm sorry, are you all right?"

"All right?"

"You look," Fräulein Kessler considers, "somewhat ill."

Sigrid puts a hand to her forehead as if checking for a fever. "No. No, thank you, I'm not."

"Would you like to come in? I have some brandy. Perhaps you could use a touch."

"No. Very kind, but I'm sorry," Sigrid answers. She sees Fräulein Kessler glance at the note still clenched in her hand. A certain wryness enters the woman's expression.

"So have you screwed him yet?" she asks.

A flash of heat.

"My brother, that is."

Sigrid gazes back at her with loaded eyes. All artifice seems to have abandoned her. "Yes," she answers.

Fräulein Kessler nods to herself as she tugs off her spectacles. "He is irresistible. Even though he's missing a leg, women cannot stop themselves from falling into his bed. A word of warning, though. Don't make plans for the future, because you don't have one. At least not with him."

"Thank you. I'll remember that," Sigrid says thickly.

"You know, Sigrid Schröder, you are missing out on an opportunity. Wolfram may be fickle, but I am not. I can be your friend, even if not your lover."

Only an instant's pause before she says, "Can you?"

"Friends are really of much greater value anyway. Lovers?" She shrugs. "Who can trust them?"

———

At their midday break, Sigrid evades Renate's company, and travels east along the canal toward the Municipal Gasworks, until she drops onto a bench where the dead wands of the willows etch lines in the water's thick blue-green current. Only then does she dare examine the note again. Words scratched at an angle: *cinema* and *balcony*, followed by a time. When a body suddenly shoves onto the bench next to her, she closes the scrap of paper in her fist. A hefty specimen, dressed in a slate gray coat, lifts his black trilby. "Frau Schröder."

Instinctively she attempts to rise, but the man's hand clamps down on her arm. "Please, I'm not who you think," he says, a weighty gaze beneath the bristles of his eyebrows. "I'm a friend of Fräulein Kohl's."

Sigrid stares back, but she settles back onto the bench and the man releases her arm. His hands are calloused, she notes. A workingman's hands.

"You know where she is?"

"I can't say."

"But you know."

"I cannot say."

"You know that she's still alive."

"Yes."

"And safe."

"As safe as any of us can be."

"I want to see her."

"Not possible now."

"Then someone should *make* it possible, because I want to *see* her."

"I can't stay much longer, but you should know that we think the operation has been compromised."

"Auntie?"

"Not arrested, but they're watching her."

"For how *long*?"

"You should listen now, not talk. We're making a plan to get them out. The current guests."

"Get them *out*? How, if they're watching?"

"I cannot say more now. We will need your help, but not now. For now you should stay away. Do you understand? You'll be contacted again," he says, and then he's up, lifts his hat once more, and marches off toward the gasworks.

———

The lobby of the cinema is dim. A single, aging whore occupies a well-worn velveteen chair, staring at the smoke from her cigarette. The old usher's cough webs his lungs. He wipes his mouth with a handkerchief and holds open the door to the mezzanine. The rear of the balcony is empty. No patrons. Her heart is drumming in her chest as the film cranks through the projector. Up on the gray-lit screen, a newsreel camera follows a squadron of condor-winged bombers across a churning Russian sky.

Sigrid unfolds the note again, just to make sure that there are still words written there. Somehow she fears that they may have vanished from the paper, leaving it blank. But the shape of his handwriting is still visible. And then a voice.

"Don't speak."

As if she could.

"Sigrid, I beg you, don't say a word."

As if a word could possibly escape her throat. He is blotted by shadow, only a gray flicker shaping the outline of his face. His grip is desperate as he seizes her arm in his hand, and his body smells of staleness and neglect, and need.

"I have to touch you," he whispers hoarsely. And she lets him. His touch is hunting at first, searching her for something lost. Inside her coat, under her blouse. His mouth suddenly near. Exploring her neck. Her eyes remain pried open. She is too afraid to close them, for fear that the flutter of her lids will be enough to disturb the fragile reality of the instant, that he will vanish into a memory or dream or the darkness inside her own head.

She hurries to unbutton Egon's trousers, with a consuming need that resembles desperation more than desire. Desperate to hold some piece of the past, of her past self in her hand, to give it weight and form.

Hiking her skirt, she climbs onto Egon's lap. He enters her, and she begins to pump herself on him. With slow, hopeful anguish, then with sudden purpose. He has started to gasp. To snort under her assault, so she clamps her hand over his mouth. Presses her head down to his, and takes an ear in her teeth as a hostage. And then it's over, suddenly, in a spasm. And she lets her weight sag against him. Pinning him down.

———

At work, Renate tells Sigrid about her new man. He's a soldier named Heinz, back from the Balkans on furlough. Sigrid listens to the descriptions of their bed sport, thinking of Egon's body, the feel of him inside, with her thighs astride him. She thinks of this, but all she says to Renate is, "So what became of your man in the Potsdamerplatz?"

Renate sighs with a small frown. "Ah, that. There was a scheduling conflict. I arrived at his place one evening, and found him humping a little blond morsel from the Luftwaffeneinsatz." She smiles again and shrugs. "I threw a fit, but really it was only for show. Things had been going downhill. We both knew it was over with. Probably it was the best way to finish it. No sentiment, just a clean cut."

"And now Heinz."

"You know, he's not at all what I'm used to. He's rather rough-hewn. No money to speak of. Just a soldier. We met on the U-Bahn, of all places, when he offered me his seat."

"He offered you his seat, and you offered him your ass," Sigrid says, and then looks up at the pinprick of silence.

Renate is still smiling, but she says. "That wasn't very kind."

"I'm sorry. You're right. I'm sorry. I just don't know what's wrong with me."

"Well. I can have a *guess* at what's wrong. You need a *release*."

Sigrid feels a pause in her throat, then swallows it. "I need a place," she whispers.

It was really too cold for a walk along the canal, but no matter. She has dragged Renate away from the patent office canteen and into the bitter air just to be able to speak this sentence to her. Renate frowns, rubbing her hands together. "A place?"

"A place to *go* to," Sigrid says with muted urgency. "*With* some-one."

And now the light breaks over Renate's face. "*Ahh.*" She grins archly. "Well, it's *about time*, if you don't mind me saying so."

"Please," Sigrid protests.

"So who's the lucky fellow?"

"No one."

"No one?"

"No one you know. Just a man."

"Well, they're *all* just men, dumpling. But surely he has a name. Or do you just call him 'Schnuckiputzi'?" she teases.

"Stop it. This is not a matter for jokes," Sigrid insists, but Renate laughs anyway.

"Of course it is, Liebling. It just seems so serious, because it's your first time in the game. But never mind. I won't make light. I'm just so deadly curious," she says, nudging Sigrid intimately. "It's not that blockhead Werner, is it? God, I hope not. Believe me, he's more crow than cock."

"No. Not Werner. He's not from the office," Sigrid frowns. She stares at the slate of the walk and keeps moving. "I told you, it's no one you know."

"All right, all right, so it's no one I know. At least tell me what he looks like."

"He looks like a man."

"*Pfft,*" Renate snorts with abrupt annoyance. "If this is how you're going to be, you can go tell your problems to the mirror. But if you want my help, you must provide a few *details.*"

The space expands between them, and is filled by the sputter of a motor launch traveling down the canal. Then Sigrid expels a heavy breath. "He's tall," she says.

"Tall," Renate repeats coolly. "Well, I suppose he would be."

"With dark hair."

"And eyes?"

"Brown."

"Just brown?"

"No. Brown like caramel."

"Brown like caramel. Now, we're getting somewhere. A handsome face, I assume."

"Yes. A handsome face. Broad. A bit rough."

"And his body?"

"He has one," Sigrid says, but finds that, against her will, she is experiencing a tingle of pleasure at this. She has never described Egon to anyone before. Never elaborated on his parts in this way. It sends a small thrill through her, which Renate must detect, because her lascivious tone returns. "I'm betting he's muscular. No brains, perhaps, but hard muscles," she purrs, leaning into Sigrid as they walk, throwing her off balance. "A laborer, maybe. Hard muscles, and he grunts like an ape. Like those Frenchmen fixing the rail lines." She laughs, and then the laugh catches in her throat, and her voice drops urgently. "Oh, God. He's *not*, is he?"

"Not?"

"A foreigner?" A problem, the authorities have found. A city full of lonely women meets an army of foreign workers conscripted into the Reich from the occupied lands, often the only males of species around who are not in short pants or walking with a cane. There have been incidents. Some of them highly publicized. The woman shipped off to a concervation camp, and the man, too, if he's from the west, hanged or beheaded if he's from the east.

Sigrid feels her smile die, though she still props up its corpse. "No. Not a foreigner," and then she adds, "He was born in Neukölln."

Renate breathes relief. "Wonderful. A good Berliner proletariat. Is he in the army?"

"*Renate,*" Sigrid complains. "You ask too much."

"All right, I ask too much. But tell me this, at least." And now her lips brush Sigrid's ear. *"Does he fill you up?"*

Her mouth dries, and her eyes go blind to everything in front of her. All she can see is his face below her as she rode him. But words in reply to Renate's question will not come.

"Never mind," Renate tells her, giving her arm a squeeze. "Maybe you don't know yet, do you, Liebchen? So don't worry. Your big sister will fix you up."

"Should I remind you, big sister, that I am older than you?"

"Older? Younger? It's experience that counts here. And in that, strudel, you are a babe in arms."

Sigrid frowns inwardly at this but does not give voice to any objection. "So," she says instead, "I have answered your questions, and we are running out of time. Do you know of a place?"

"I think I do." Renate says, taking her arm and hugs it as they walk. Sigrid does not resist. "I think I know of a place that might serve your purposes quite well."

. . .

THE PLACE TURNS out to be a dreary hotel in the Kantstrasse down the street from the Bahnhof am Zoo. Officially, it caters to out-of-town commercial peddlers. Unofficially, it caters to those who need a room with a bed for just long enough to get the sheets sweaty. So nobody pays too much attention to papers or registration beyond the minimum. The fee for the room is six marks an hour plus a ten-mark "concierge fee." Sigrid has scrounged money from stashes at home, but to her surprise Egon removes a money clip from his pocket, and signs the guest book as Ernst Friedrichsohn and wife, Hannover.

Stupidly, it gives her a small thrill. To be signed in as his wife, even under such ersatz terms. "Identification, please, Herr Friedrichsohn," the dingy old Berliner behind the desk requests, and Sigrid watches Egon produce a brown cardboard booklet. A Mitgliedsbuch issued by the German Labor Front. Full of contribution stamps, but no photograph necessary.

The porter gives the booklet a perfunctory glance. "Very good." He frowns, and makes a notation before he plucks a key from a board of hooks. "Room thirty-three."

Room 33 is cramped. The rooms here are designed to hold a narrow, lumpy bed and little else. No oversize feelings or possibilities. There's a dry sink and a single chair close to the door, where their clothes are draped. Hers on the chair seat, his dangling over the back. Her shoes in a neat duet on the floor, her nylons balled and stuffed into the toes. His shoes, dull from the streets, the leather cracked, lying where they fell, tossed off pell-mell, still laced.

Peeled like a piece of fruit. That's how she feels. Lying in her sweat, feeling the sting of the room's chill on her skin, hearing the windowpanes tremble with the wind. She has so much to say to him, yet she finds she can say nothing at all. So instead she falls into an old habit with Egon. When she cannot bring herself to speak, she asks him what he's thinking.

But Egon is simply staring at the ceiling, as if he can see through it to the sky. "I have to get better papers," he says.

She feels a sharp pinch of distress. He is not thinking about her. About how their heartbeats synchronized as their bodies merge. He's thinking about his damned identification papers.

"What I've got now might get me past a dim-witted hotel porter. But a labor pass won't pass muster with any Sipo man with more than one eye in his head."

She gets the feeling that Egon is talking more to himself than to her. He reaches for one of the cigarettes she'd brought for him. A few of the Bulgarians purloined from the packet she'd given Mother Schröder. She had found them again, hidden in the rear of the dish cabinet, with half of them smoked. He lights up with a wax tip and she watches the smoke rise with his gaze. He makes no comment on the quality of the tobacco. Another disappointment.

"You haven't said."

He barely glances at her. "What?"

"What you think of the accommodations."

"It's a room," he answers blankly.

"Yes," she agrees with a breath. "A room with a bed. I suppose that's all that's required."

"You require more than that, Sigrid? More than a bed we can share?"

"Where are you spending your nights?" she asks with unveiled purpose. But he tosses the question on its head.

"That's a very good question. The place I'm in now isn't working out so well. I need to find something new."

"New?"

"For a few weeks."

"Only that?"

"Maybe a month."

Sigrid feels the air grow thin. "Why only a month?" she asks carefully.

But if Egon hears the interior question that she is asking, he does not respond to it. "Because a month is all I need," he says.

"So where are you staying *now*?" she repeats with an edge. "You're not going to tell me?"

"What difference does it make? I only have a few more nights there. Three. Maybe four."

Nights, she thinks, and is instantaneously jealous. *Is it another woman?* she itches to demand, even though she, herself, is *another woman*. A woman other than his wife.

"I can pay. That's not the problem," he says. "The problem is that it's too dangerous for me on the street. I can be too easily recognized."

"You don't look Jewish," Sigrid hears herself say, and then flinches at the sound of her own words.

But Egon only laughs, hoots grimly at the ceiling. "Yes, I have quite the Aryan puss. No cricked *schnobel* on this Yid," he says with a grin.

"I'm sorry."

"Don't be. Thanks to Juli Streicher, all you good Germans think every Jew looks like a Shylock." That is Julius Streicher, the publisher of a virulent propaganda rag called *Der Stürmer,* who delights in grotesque caricatures of Semitic faces. "In a way, that old bastard has saved my life more than once."

"I'm not a Juli Streicher," Sigrid says, causing Egon to look at her directly. Fully, with assessment.

"No. No, you're not, Sigrid Schröder. You're a woman with a very good heart." He says this and then rolls onto his side, fixing his eyes on hers as the smoke ribbons upward from his cigarette. "So. Will you help me?"

But she is hurt. Wounded by his offhand classification of her, dumping her into the pool of good Germans along with such a notorious

Jew baiter. She may answer Egon's question in her head, but first she must ask him, "Where are your wife and children?"

His expression does not change, but his eyes darken, as if a lamp in the room has been switched off. "I don't know," he answers her.

Perhaps she was hoping to hear something else. A reply that would cancel out the scenario she has built in her head. She, lying here in the bed with him in a second-class hotel, while across town she is hiding his wife and daughters from the Gestapo in a frigid attic. Or perhaps she would like to have heard that he had simply split from his wife. Or that his wife had escaped to some neutral destination—Switzerland, Sweden, the North Pole—and had taken any and all children with her, never to return. Perhaps she may have even preferred to hear that they were dead. At least dead, she could pinpoint them. Reduce them to something manageable.

"You don't know? No idea at *all*?" she presses. And now she can feel him studying her, calculating some inner equation. She does not rearrange the blankness of her face. Finally he looks away, drawing on his cigarette, and tapping an ash into a ceramic tray on the bed stand from Haus Vaterland. He seems to be settling into himself, settling into some version of himself. When he speaks his voice has lost all texture.

"The place I had found. A few rooms above a warehouse in Rixdorf. It worked for a while. I had my contacts for food. There was a roof over their heads. For a time, it all seemed *survivable*. But then I was sitting in a café last summer. I had made arrangements to meet a man about some clothing coupons when I saw someone I recognized. Or rather who recognized me. It was another Jew. A man I had known from the diamond trade, years ago. He stood up and waved his hand at me. I could tell something was wrong, immediately, but I moved too slowly. Before I could make it to the door, there were a pair of Gestapo bulls blocking my path with their cannons out." He stops. Chews a thought for a moment. "They took me to the Grosse Hamburger Strasse and beat hell out me for a night or two. Just for the fun of it." He shrugs.

"And then it was off to the Levetzowstrasse. There I rotted, waiting for my turn to be packed into the cattle cars. Until one morning, after a bombing raid, they picked ten men for a work detail. Hauling rubble." He flicks his eyebrows. "When I saw my chance, I took it. Bashed the guard on the skull with a piece of masonry and ran." He stops again to measure a breath of smoke. "I went straight back to the warehouse, of course, but the rooms were empty. Not a sign of Anna or the girls." He stares, as if surveying the emptied rooms in his head, then jams his cigarette into the ashtray. "Not a thread left behind."

Sigrid does not move as his gaze drifts over to hers.

"So does that answer your questions, Frau Schröder? Is there anything else you require knowing?"

Her eyes go wet. *What are the names of your daughters?* she wants to ask. But the question is suddenly so sharp and dangerous that it threatens to cut her throat if she tries to utter it.

"Good," he concludes at her silence. "Now it's your turn to answer *my* question," he says, sliding his arms around her. "Will you help me?" he asks again.

There is only one answer to this, of course. *Yes.* For a month, for a day, for an hour. If it costs her everything. If it strips her skin down to the bone. Her answer is, as it has always been, *yes.*

FOURTEEN

IN THE MORNING, leaving for the patent office, she steps out of the door to the landing and finds Mundt's husband and one of his cronies muscling the weight of a steamer trunk out of the door and down the stairs. "Mornin', dolly." He winks at Sigrid. "Man's work comin' through." Sigrid steps back to allow them to pass with their burden, then looks up at the sound of her name.

"*Frau Schröder.* What a happy coincidence," the Frau Obersturm-führer announces. She is wearing her Volk's community smile, but her face is bleached and exhausted, and her belly has swollen to the size of a medicine ball.

"It appears you are traveling, Frau Junger."

"To my mother's in Breslau. Just until my little soldier arrives."

"Little soldier" confuses Sigrid for a instant. And then, "Ah, yes. Of course." She quickly snatches the satchel from the girl's hand. "Here, I'm so thoughtless, please let me help you with your bag."

"Oh. Thank you, that's kind. Would you like to go first? I'm afraid I'm rather slow on steps these days. Going down as well as coming up."

After Sigrid had miscarried, the women of the house had gotten on their hands and knees and scrubbed the spots of blood from every step.

"Please. You first, I'll follow."

The Frau Obersturmführer refreshes her smile, and begins her sluggish procession down the stairs. "Getting on the streetcar can take me a lifetime," she says. "But everyone is so understanding and helpful."

"So you think it will be a boy, do you?" Sigrid inquires.

A step, a pause. A step, a pause. "Oh, *yes*. I'm quite sure of it, Frau Schröder. From the strength of his kick, you see." She grins, and Sigrid feels the simple force of her certainty. It pinches Sigrid with some unidentifiable emotion. Somewhere between dread and joy.

That night she leaves her mother-in-law with the wireless and a glass of potato brandy, and knocks on the door across the landing. Fräulein Kessler greets her wearing her nursing shift and her standard sardonic face. "He's not here, Frau Schröder."

"He?"

"My brother, of course. He's in Belgium or Luxembourg, or some such place for a week. I don't know. He tells me these things, but I never know if I should believe him. In any case, he's gone."

"I'm not here to see your brother."

"No?"

"I don't mean to trouble you. Were you on your way to work?"

"Not for a few hours yet. I have the night ward tonight," she says with curious caution.

"Did you mean what you said?" Sigrid asks her. "That you could be my friend?"

A pause. Sigrid watches an internal reorganization of the woman's expression.

"If a friend is what you need," she answers.

"It is."

And now a double-sided glance. The German glance. "I think you'd better come in," says Fräulein Kessler.

. . .

"You know they offered her a place in one of the Font of Life homes," the woman announces from the kitchen.

Removing her scarf, Sigrid glances away from the bronze Führer portrait on the wall. "Font of Life."

"Brigitte. The local Standarte was putting through the paperwork. But I think giving birth in an SS brood mare barn was too much, even for her." She brings the coffee service in from the kitchen. Not the gentrified sterling service that her sister had used, but a sensible, stainless steel press and plain china. "So instead it's off to Breslau and her Mutti. God help her."

"She is difficult, her mother?"

"I've met the woman only twice, but wished to murder her on both occasions." She sets down the tray and pours. "I hope you like it strong. I make it strong, because that's how my father drank it. Cigarette?" she offers, but Sigrid shakes her head tightly. "You seem very anxious. You should relax. You should take off your coat."

"Thank you, I'm fine," she says, and takes a perfunctory sip of the coffee. It scalds her tongue.

"Too hot? No cream to be had, I'm afraid. But you don't take it anyway, do you?"

"No."

"And no white sugar, either. Though, if you'd like, there's rock sugar," she says, offering a small crystal bowl filled with amber-colored rock sugar candy from the table. "You might try it, even if you usually drink it black. Its sweetness kills the bitterness."

"I need to hide someone," Sigrid suddenly blurts out.

Fräulein Kessler pauses, then sets down the bowl and picks up her cigarette case. "Yes. I thought it might be something like that." She ignites her cigarette with a silver-plated table lighter and draws in smoke. "I've heard about your young friend's sudden disappearance.

I'm sorry, I can't recall her name. The police are looking for her, correct?"

"Ericha Kohl is her name. But I'm not here about her. Ericha is gone, and I have no idea where she is. The friend I need you to help is a man."

A stare, then a quick recalibration of her gaze. "Ah. A man," she repeats, and spews smoke. "In trouble with the authorities? Black market or maybe tired of army life?"

"He's a Jew," Sigrid says plainly.

And suddenly Fräulein Kessler's tidy cynicism freezes to her face. She gazes at Sigrid as if trying to see inside of her head.

"I've shocked you," Sigrid points out.

"Well," the woman says, and releases a sigh of smoke, "you do continue to surprise me."

"Can I assume that is said in a friendly way?"

"You're taking an awful chance here, aren't you, Frau Schröder? You think that because I have my . . . " she says, and frowns, "because I have my *proclivities* that I'm not a good German?"

"I said something similar once, Fräulein Kessler," Sigrid tells her. "And what I think is that it is up to us to define what makes a good German good. But you're correct. I *am* taking an awful chance." She gazes back at the woman. "Have I made a mistake?"

· Fräulein Kessler takes another draw from her cigarette and covers a cough. "I'm not sure," she says finally, "what you think I can do."

"Let him sleep on your floor."

"I beg your pardon?"

"Just for a few days. Maybe a week. Until I can," she begins, but then falters. Until she can do *what*, exactly? She makes do with, "Until I can figure something out." As she is speaking, Sigrid is vaguely aware of a wave of tension building in her. Of her throat constricting. Her voice tightening. "I know it's a great deal to ask. A man, whom you haven't met. Of whom you know nothing. But I have no place else. No other ideas. And then I think, since your sister is in Breslau. Since your brother is gone. Maybe a few days. A few days or a week on your floor, till I can find some way—"

"Frau Schröder," the woman interrupts. "You needn't have an apoplexy. I'm saying yes."

"What?"

"I'm saying *yes*," she repeats.

Sigrid looks back at the woman's face. Then suddenly the tears spring from nowhere. A gush that takes her completely unawares. She does her best to stop it up, trawling her bag for a handkerchief. "I'm sorry," she says, choking. "I'm sorry. *Thank you.*"

"Drink some coffee. It'll stiffen you up."

Sigrid nods and takes a sip, wiping her eyes. "Thank you," she says again.

Fräulein Kessler has gathered her elbows together and is leaning forward on them, running the back of her thumb over her forehead absently. "This man. If I may ask, he is your lover?"

Sigrid, mopping herself up, nods. "He is."

"In the same way that my brother is?"

A pause.

"Different."

"Yes, I can see it in your expression."

"I'm sorry," Sigrid tells her. But she shakes her head. "No apologies. Things are as they are. Does anyone else know?"

"No. No one," Sigrid says. Retrieving her breath. Returning the handkerchief to her bag.

"I think," the woman tells her, "if you and I truly are to be friends, and that's the idea, is it not?"

Almost a smile. "It is, Fräulein Kessler."

"Then I think there is something you should know. I'm a Mischling."

The word makes no sense to Sigrid for an instant. And then it does. Mischling. A half Jew. "Ah, me . . . " she whispers.

"Officially, a Mischling, first degree. My father was born Jewish, though he was converted. My grandparents both died in a house fire when he was very small, and he went to the Kessler family in Charlottenburg, who had him christened. When he was grown, he married a Christian woman, who bore first me and then Wolfram, before she died in the influenza epidemic. Wolfram claims he remembers her, but I don't see how. *I* barely do, and I'm four years older."

"And what about," Sigrid asks, "what about your sister?"

"Yes, the dear child. She is the product of wife number two."

"Does she *know*?"

At this, Fräulein Kessler smiles ruefully. "That she is a Mischling, too? Oh, she *knows*, all right. She knows very well. Which is why she goes to so much trouble to portray the perfect Aryan wife. She's really grown quite creative about it. Those letters she reads aloud in the cellar, for instance? Her husband, the great Herr Obersturmführer, never bothers himself to write. He's a thoughtless brute. So she writes them herself."

"But how did . . . ?" Sigrid starts to say, then stops.

"Oh, please feel free to ask the question, Frau Schröder. How did a Mischling end up married to a serving officer in the Waffen-SS in the first place? It's a very good question, and the answer is Wolfram. He's a very resourceful man, my brother. Did he ever mention the nature of his work to you?"

"The nature? He's a soldier," says Sigrid.

"Yes, a soldier, but more than that."

"He's said nothing more."

"No, I suppose not. You had better things to do than talk. Fair enough. Since I'm confessing, I might as well spill it all. Wolfram is a member of the Abwehr. You've heard of this?"

A dull look. "I know nothing about the army other than they have guns and heavy boots."

"Then allow me to educate you. The Abwehr is the clandestine service for the whole of the Wehrmacht," she adds. "I don't know how he did it, but somehow he expunged our family secret from the official registries. On the record, we are one hundred percent Aryan stock, confirmed all the way back to 1750. That's the SS standard for bloodlines, you see. So our little secret of ancestry remains between us and God. As I said," Fräulein Kessler repeats more pointedly, "he's *very* resourceful. Foolish, perhaps, the way he sticks his neck out. But very resourceful."

"Do you have any idea what he might want with my employee identification card from the patent office?"

"What he might *want* with it?"

"I think he may have taken it from my bag."

"Well, I haven't the faintest what makes Wolfram's mind work. Other than to assure you that he does nothing on impulse. Every move on my brother's part is a step in a plan."

"A plan? But what sort of plan could involve a piece of yellow cardboard with my photograph attached?"

"Perhaps he wanted a photograph for his wall. Or, if he took your identity card, then perhaps he thinks you need a new identity," the woman suggests. "Now, drink your coffee, please, I can't abide letting hot good coffee go cold," she says, and heats up Sigrid's cup. "By the way, I do believe you should start calling me Carin now. Considering the topics of our conversation, you and I are far past formalities. Wouldn't you agree?"

———

In the narrow hotel room, Sigrid lies on her back, gazing up at a large brown water stain on the ceiling plaster. Bits of the plaster have decayed and flaked at the corner, where beads of water condense. But the stain spreads out like a great muddy dry bed above her, scalloped at the edges by the outwash of many leaky afternoons. Rain splatters the window-pane outside. She listens to the damp noise of traffic and smells Egon's acrid cigarette smoke.

Is it true? His ghost has been made flesh once more?

"Do you need money?" she hears him ask.

"Money?"

"For this woman. Does she expect to be paid to put me up?"

A disapproving glance. "*No.*"

But Egon only shrugs. Rolls onto his side. Drifts his finger down between her breasts to her belly. "Don't sound so insulted. Most people want to be paid," he says. "You know I do love your body, Sigrid. How strong it is. How subtle."

"Yes. My *body*," she answers.

"You don't think I love you, too?"

"I'm sure I don't know anything about *what* or *whom* you love."

"Still angry," he says with almost a smile, his touch feathering the swell of her breasts. "After all this time?"

"No." She frowns, glaring upward at the stain. "No. You did what you thought you must do."

"No." He frowns. "That's not what I mean. I don't mean you're still angry about *us*. It means you're *still angry*. Under all your middle-class civility, you're still *angry*. It's one of the things that made me fall in love with you to begin with."

"*Egon*," she says, suddenly seizing him by the scruff of his neck and pushing her face into his. "Egon, I want you to stop using that word," she commands. "Do you understand? I want you to *stop*." She watches his eyes. "*I want you to stop,*" she whispers.

A wash of thunder floats above them. Then a knock at the door grabs her in the belly.

"Porter. Ten minutes."

Immediately she sits up and starts dressing.

"So. When will you be ready to make the move?" she asks.

Egon is standing now. Pulling on his skivvies. "Well, that depends on the Royal Air Force."

Fastening the hook of her brassiere. "What?"

"The next time the bombers come. That's when you should expect me. You have a shelter in your building, yes?"

"The cellar."

"Then find some way to stay out of it after the alarms sound, and be ready to meet me by the door." He steps into his trousers.

"You're going to travel through an air raid?'

"It's the best way for Jews to travel. Not even the Gestapo bothers with identity checks when the bombs are falling." Turning his back to her, he shrugs on his shirt. She swivels her feet onto the bare wood floor and picks up her nylon chemise.

"That's a very nice watch," she says.

"What?" Egon grunts, sparing only half a glance.

She picks up the wristwatch from the nightstand. *Cartier* is inscribed on the face. "I said, that's a very nice watch."

He takes it from her and straps it on his wrist. "It manages to tell time," is all he says.

"Always the best. Even now. The fine watch. The mohair coat. How do you do it?" she asks with a touch of awe and, perhaps, a touch of something else. Pride? Pride in her man?

"I do what I do," he replies. She had not expected more of an answer from him. Still, she frowns at the absurdities. Or is it a smile?

"What?" he asks.

"Nothing," she answers. "Women. It really isn't fair what men do to us."

Down in the street, they part, as always, outside the hotel door. She, in her scarf, pushing open an umbrella, he creasing the brim of his hat against the patter of rain. "Good day, Frau Schröder," she hears him say as he leaves her. A smile crossing his face. "You'll understand if I don't wish you a bombless night."

. . .

AT THE DOOR OF HER FLAT, she hears the radio. Lotte Lehmann's trilling soprano voice singing, *Warning*. "I'm sorry I'm late," she calls out as she hangs up her coat, in the most casual voice she can manage. As usual, she finds her mother-in-law planted in the chair beside the wireless, but the look on Mother Schröder's face indicates that she is not listening. In fact, the look indicates that she is considering boring through a steel plate with nothing more that the sharpness of her eyes. Sigrid opens her mouth, but closes it again as a quick electrical pulse shoots through her heart. She sees the dingy packet of letters wrapped by a black ribbon clutched in her mother-in-law's claws. "How did you get those?" she hears herself demand. Her voice is throaty, disconnected. Hoarse, suddenly, with crackling emotion.

"That's what you have to say to me? *How did I get them?*" Mother's Schröder's voice is raw with indignity.

"You violated my privacy."

"I opened a cigarette tin. If you store your *privacy* there, then you should expect it to be violated."

"Give them to me." She makes a move as if to snatch them, but Mother Schröder grips them with both hands.

"No."

"I demand that you *give them to me!*"

"And *I* demand that you give me an explanation of this *filthy trash!*"

"Demand away, it's none of your business."

"You're married to my son. That *makes* it my business. Does he know?"

"Know?"

"That his wife is stashing away this pornography?" she hisses, shaking the letter righteously at Sigrid.

"It was years ago. Before I ever met Kaspar," she lies.

"Yet you keep them."

"They're not pornography."

"They're disgusting. And no woman with a grain of moral character—"

"Oh, can you stuff your *moral character* up your ass, please? I'm sick to death of hearing about it. My God, you're over sixty and what you understand about being a woman would fit in a thimble."

Mother Schröder's face has gone bloodless. "You think that fornication makes you more of a woman?"

"I think that *passion* makes me more of a woman."

Mother Schröder's expression hardens with contempt. "*Passion.* A word used by an idiot. You think you know *me*, yet you have no knowledge of yourself. Passion is the excuse of a whore. And a simple-minded whore at that." She shakes the packet of letters at her. "Is *this* who you are thinking of?"

"*What?*"

"I know what you do. At night. When you're in bed. I'm not a fool."

"You're *spying* on me in my own bed?"

"It's your *husband's* bed, not yours. And I asked you a question."

"You're mad."

"I'm well aware of your history. I know that your father was a philanderer, and left your mother in the lurch. And I warned Kaspar when he married you that the apple doesn't fall far from the tree."

"Leave my family out of this," Sigrid hears herself say coldly.

"Maybe if you had had a decent upbringing, you might have turned out to have a bit of moral backbone."

"Shut your mouth!" Sigrid hears herself shouting. The words rip out of her. "Shut your fucking *mouth!*" she bellows.

Mother Schröder stumbles back a step, as if she has been shoved, her face contorted. "How dare you. How *dare* you use such language toward me," she hisses in rebuke, but clearly, by the expression stamped on her face, Sigrid has frightened her. In that instant, Sigrid sees just how old the woman has become. How hollowed out. She works to force the fire back into her belly, to regain control of herself. "Give me. Those letters," she demands.

The old woman squeezes the packet. Her face reassessing. Reforming itself. "Do you swear to me," she says, "that this man means nothing to you now?"

Sigrid breathes in. Breathes out.

"Can you? *Swear*?"

"I can do better than that, Petronela," Sigrid replies. "I can swear that I meant nothing to him."

A stare, then her mother-in-law frowns. Regains the imperious edge to her voice. "And still you keep his letters? God, but you *are* an idiot." She tosses the letters onto the rug. "My advice? Burn this trash."

RAIN CLOUDS SHEETING BERLIN keep the Royal Air Force away that night, and the next. But on the third night, the sky is a dark, cloudless shell.

She is standing in front of the sink in her apron, washing dishes in brownish tepid water and covertly watching the clock on the wall tick away the minutes till seven o'clock. Seven o'clock is recognized throughout town as the RAF's favorite arrival time. Restaurants have started to time their service by this schedule, and cinemas have started adjusting their showtimes.

As the minute hand closes in on the hour, she realizes that she is holding her breath. Holding it, and then she exhales as she feels the surge of the sirens vibrate through her bones and settle in the pit of her belly.

From behind her comes the scrape of her mother-in-law's chair. The old lady has been sitting over her coffee with a sour-smelling cigarette, still enforcing the silence that has regulated their mealtime. They have not spoken beyond the most basic mechanics of communication since the incident with the letters, but now she hears the old woman say, "What are you *doing*?"

"Doing? I'm doing the dishes."

"Don't be stupid. There's a *raid* on. Dishes will wait. Go see to the fuse box."

"No. I don't think so. I'm tired of hiding in a hole."

"Oh, yes. Always the selfish one. What *she's* tired of doing. Might it occur to you that if a bomb falls on your head, that there would be consequences for *others*?"

"I'm sure you'd manage somehow."

"Perhaps. But what about my son? Wounded. Confined to a hospital bed in some godforsaken corner. Don't you think he has the *right* to come back home to the woman he took for his *wife,* however misguided that decision might have been?"

"If a bomb falls on my head, Kaspar can come home to you," Sigrid hears herself say. "Which is how you've always wanted it anyway."

The old woman scowls. "It's *illegal*. You can't simply *choose* to stay out of the shelter."

Still scrubbing at the dishes in the dirty water. "Yet that is what I'm doing."

"I could have the Hausobman up here to haul you down."

"I'll bolt the door shut."

"Then he'll break it in."

"I doubt it. The door is private property. The landlord would be unhappy at having to replace it. Besides, can you imagine the grist that scene would give to the gossip mills? At your expense, I might add."

Mother Schröder reverts to silence long enough to digest that possibility. Then, "Fine," she blurts. "Let the Tommies blow you to pieces. I won't shed a single tear for stupidity." The old woman marches to the door and begins bustling with her coat and hat.

"Don't forget your sewing bag," Sigrid tells her at the door. Noise drifting up as Frau Granzinger evacuates her brood. Her mother-in-law snatches the bag out of her hand, and exits without giving her a look. But she *does* receive a look from Fräulein Kessler, who is just leaving her flat. It is against regulations to lock your flat during an air raid, in the event that the Hausobman must get in to fight a fire. But just to reassure Sigrid perhaps, the Fräulein leaves the door standing ever so slightly ajar.

THINGS MOVE QUICKLY. Sigrid can hear the muffled drone of bomber engines in the sky and the thudding under-beat of pom-pom guns as she slings open the building's front door, and Egon bursts into the foyer and dashes up the stairs. She hurries to catch up, the sound of their footsteps out of sync, filling up the stairwells as they climb.

"Number 11H," she tells him.

But Egon hangs back. "You go in first. If there's still someone inside, you can make excuses. I could only look like a looter."

She budges the door open. No one is inside. Only the furnishings of the Frau Obersturmführer's model National Socialist flat. She nods to him to enter. When she clamps the door shut behind them, he is standing with his back to her in front of the bronze portrait of the Führer.

"She's a Nazi?" he asks, with an oddly distant curiosity.

"No. It's a complicated story."

He shrugs. Turns away from the plaque and faces her. "Everyone's story is complicated," he says, and shrugs off his overcoat. Then looks up at the ceiling. Above them, the rumble of the bombers is getting louder as she allows him to unbutton the front of her blouse. Then pulls her down. On the floor, her skirt is up, and he has her naked below. He has exposed her to the ghosts of the flat. Frau Remki laying her grief down on her deathbed before seizing up with the convulsions. Her boy, a child again, giggling gleefully as he chases a ball around the room, long before he would grow to be a soldier and be blown to smither-eens. The ghosts in the flat, the ghosts in her mind. Ericha, watching, staring as Sigrid's back arches, her *own* body falling victim to convulsions, but in Sigrid's case, the convulsions of rapture. Ericha staring from the shadows of Sigrid's mind. And Frau Weiss. Frau Anna Weiss, gently shielding her children's eyes from the scene on the floor. Gazing at their coupling in silence from the dim recesses of Auntie's secret room, while above them, the thunder of war shakes the window glass.

———

Total War follows her everywhere. Military marches play continually from the loudspeakers strung up in public squares. Sigrid is deaf to them. She is desperate. *Desperate* to touch him. He has been in hiding in the flat for three nights. Three nights of lying in her bed alone, with Egon across the hall, as unreachable as if he were across an ocean. But tonight, Carin Kessler has promised to take a walk before supper and give her a precious thirty minutes alone with him.

First, however, she must obtain a certain item that they have run short of.

She thinks about this item as she's coming down the steps, on her way to work. Condoms are difficult to come by, at least if you're a female civilian. The Party frowns on contraception. It wants more babies, more good German babies, armies of babies.

The Wehrmacht, however, issues them to the troops by the meter. Every soldier carries them. Wolfram had a pocketful, considered "standard equipment." But not so for U-boats. Not so for Jews in hiding. Egon had organized a small supply from somewhere. Who knows where? She never asked. But it was only a handful, which they have exhausted.

"You know it's illegal," she hears. It's Portierfrau Mundt dressed in her apron, clutching a broom in her hand at the doorway to the concierge flat.

Sigrid turns, hand on the handle of the foyer door. "I beg your pardon?"

"It's *illegal* to stay out of the shelter when there's a raid. So where were you, Frau Schröder? Where exactly were you when Tommy paid us a call?"

She lifts her eyebrows. "My mother-in-law didn't say?"

"What she said was, *Don't ask me.* I believe her exact words were 'As far as I'm concerned, I *have* no daughter-in-law.'"

"We had a row," Sigrid replies. "I left the house."

"And where did you go?"

"Walking. I was angry."

"Walking where?"

"What?"

"Walking *where*, Frau Schröder? The moon? You must have been walking *somewhere.*"

"Not the moon."

"Don't be arrogant, this is a serious matter."

"No, Frau Mundt. I think it's *not* a serious matter. I had an argument with my mother-in-law. Surely *that* is not illegal. I was upset and went for a walk. Surely *that* is not illegal. When the bombers came I went into the Uhlandstrasse U-Bahn tunnel. And certainly *that* is not *illegal.*"

"I see. So you have an explanation up your sleeve, as usual. Such a smart woman you are. But tell me, then, Frau Schröder, if you were out gallivanting, as you say, *why* don't I recall seeing you return before I bolted the door for the night?"

"I can't explain the world for you, Frau Mundt," Sigrid tells her, on edge. "Now, if you don't mind, I cannot be late for work. *That*, I believe, *is* illegal." She turns away, but then a pinch stops her as Mundt literally seizes her arm. The woman's eyes are violent. "I haven't finished with you, Frau Schröder. You've got my back up. I know that you have been cooking up something with that little rag from the Labor Service. *Oh, yes*, I know all about what *she's* been up to."

"*What* do you know?"

And now a smug face. "You think that the Gestapo comes into my building, and I don't know the reason why? She's a black marketeer, and probably a thief to boot. God knows *what* she's looted from the Granzingers' place. And *you*, Frau Schröder. I can't explain it yet. But I know that *you* are her accomplice."

"That's a lie."

"I doubt it."

"Is that what you told the Gestapo?"

"*Nervous*? You should be. But no. I don't need those dunderheads to do my work for me. Men are still men, even in the Geheime Staatspolizei, and I can do quite well without their interference in my business."

"Your business."

"My *building*, Frau Schröder. *Mine.* You think you're protected because your husband's serving, or because my lout of a man wants to squeeze those fine titties of yours? You are *not* protected. My husband is all mouth. When he wants his dirty work, he has his whores in the Augsburger Strasse to sate him. And as far as the Party is concerned, a man's military record does not protect his wife. If the wife deserves punishment, it *will* be meted out. I can promise you that."

"And is that the same promise you made to Frau Remki, before you denounced her?"

"Remki?"

"Yes, I'm sure you recall the lady whom you drove to suicide."

"Ah, so *that's* what you think, is it? Well, you might be interested to know that you have it wrong. I did no such thing."

"You *did*. She may have died by her own hand, but it was only to avoid the *punishment* you called down on her head."

"No. I *mean*, Frau Schröder, it was not *I* who denounced her. Oh, I rang up the Party office, of course, but only to find that someone else had beaten me to the punch."

"What? You're lying."

"You think so, do you? Well, why don't you ask your mother-in-law if she agrees with you?" Mundt says with venomous satisfaction. "Why don't you ask your dear Mother Schröder if I'm lying?"

Sigrid stares dumbly into the hatred flattening Mundt's face.

Then comes the Hausobman's bark from inside the concierge flat.

"Women! Quit your gabbin', will you? You'll wear out your jaw. A man wants his eats while they're hot!"

Mundt maintains her stare. "Keep your tongue in your mouth, old man," she calls back over her shoulder. Then she forms her mouth into a smirk. "Good day, Frau Schröder. And Heil Hitler."

SIGRID FINDS A SEAT on the Elektrische, and watches the rain-dampened street pass by in gray shadows of concrete and granite, asphalt and slate. The tram's noise permeates her bones, and she sits, feeling drained, thinking of her mother-in-law lugging Frau Remki's wireless into the room. The spoils of betrayal.

At the next stop, there are no more seats, so she stands to let a young pregnant woman sit. The woman smiles her thanks. Her face is pasty white. Her hair sticking out from a wool cap, dry and brittle. Her lips colorless. The child inside consuming her, the little cannibal. Sigrid looks away, staring at the nothingness through the window. For a moment she sees Ericha in her mind's eye, and feels suddenly quite lonely, as the tram sparks along on its track.

THERE IS NO midday break today, by order of Herr Esterwegen. His contribution to Total War. It makes it more difficult for Sigrid. She meets Renate at the filing cabinets.

"So I have fulfilled your supply requisition, Frau Schröder," Renate says, suppressing a grin.

Sigrid forces up a small smile in return. "Thank you. Where are they now?"

"In my purse. Shall I create a diversion? Shout *fire*, perhaps?"

"Leave them in the WC."

"I feel like a master criminal. Dropping the loot."

"Yes. It's quite the conspiracy, isn't it?"

"You know, this is really the *man's* job. You should educate him."

"It's hard for him," Sigrid explains.

"Whatever you say, Liebling. I suppose it makes no difference, as long as it stays hard for *you*." Renate smirks.

They look like wrapped candies. Condoms stamped into white cellophane with the brand name Odilei in a red oval. A long snake of them, curled into an old tin of tea leaves, now in Sigrid's bag.

When she walks up the steps to her building, Mundt shoves up her window.

"*Frau Schröder*," she calls.

"Not now, Frau Mundt, please, I have nothing more to say to you."

"Well, we'll see, Frau Schröder. I simply wished to alert you to the surprise waiting for you."

"What? What are you talking about?"

"The *surprise*, Frau Schröder," Mundt repeats, with a hint of mockery. "I'm talking about the *surprise* waiting for you in your flat."

But before Sigrid can muster a response to this, the front door opens, and out steps Carin Kessler in a long coat and brimmed felt hat, toting her handbag.

"*Ah*, Frau Schröder. So glad to see you," she says, grinning stiffly. "I just met your husband."

Sigrid feels the blood drain from her face. "My husband?"

"I knocked on your flat to invite you to join my walk, but when the door opened it was *he*."

Sigrid's mouth opens, but all her words have dissolved.

"I'm going out, so is there anything you need?" Carin asks her. "Any errand I can run?"

"Errand?" Sigrid repeats blankly. "No. No, thank you, Fräulein Kessler. Not as of now."

"Very well. I shan't keep you, then. I'm sure," she says, with a hint of command in her voice, "you must be very happy."

SHE CLIMBS THE FOUR FLIGHTS as if climbing the steps of a gallows. At the door to her flat she stops. She can hear voices on the inside. Mother Schröder gabbling, her normal curmudgeonly tone stripped away. And then the voice of a man. The man to whom she is married.

She looks away to the door across the landing. Only a few steps away. Nothing but that pine door separates her from Egon. Slowly she takes a step toward him. She almost grasps the door handle, but then stops. Her hand will not allow her to do it.

When she enters her flat, it is as if she has walked into someone else's life. Talk ceases. Her mother-in-law is ladling out soup, but the grin she is wearing dies. The man seated at the table turns his head. He is so much thinner now. His jaw angular, honed like the blade of a knife. All the boyishness from his face has been rubbed off. The uniform he wears looks baggy on him. He stands slowly with a scrape of his chair on the floor, and faces her. And in his eyes, she can see the gun sight aimed at the world. He forms his mouth into a smile as he takes a slightly halting step toward her.

"Hello, wife," he says. "Your husband is home."

FIFTEEN

S HE CAN BARELY STAND the happy faces at the patent office. All those smiling wives in the stenographers' pool, so gleeful for her. Her husband has *returned*. She has a *man* again. What's it feel like? It must feel *good*. Sly looks, sly laughs. You must bring him by this Sunday. Yes, you simply *must*. She has a *man* in a world of women, and they want to parse him up. They want to claim a helping of him, as if he were a one-pot Sunday stew. Sigrid grits her teeth.

At the filing cabinet Renate sneaks a moment. She bites her lip and whispers anxiously, "So how is it?"

Sigrid shakes her head tightly. "Very strange. I don't know. He's been away so long. At least it seems so."

"Has he recovered?"

"What?"

"From his wound?"

"He has a bit of a limp. I . . . I don't know how long it will last. If it's permanent."

"He hasn't said?"

"He hasn't *said* much of anything." She shoves a folder into the cabinet and picks through the tabs for another. "In fact, what he *doesn't* say is enormous. He carries what he *doesn't* say like a full field pack on his back."

"And . . . uh"—Renate glances around—"did you *welcome* him home?" she asks, her voice uncharacteristically sheepish over the subject.

Sigrid answers like a good soldier: "I was on bedroom duty, if that's what you mean."

"Was it good?"

A small frown. "It's been a long time. Things were," she says, and then shakes her head. "Things were *awkward*. Honestly? It was as if we were strangers."

"And what about your *friend*?" Renate whispers.

Sigrid plucks a file from the drawer and rolls it shut. "What about him?"

"What are you going to do?"

She pauses, and then answers truthfully. "I don't know."

THAT NIGHT AT SUPPER, Mother Schröder is buoyant. She is yammering on, an old bottle of plum brandy uncorked on the table. Full of stories of her son's childhood, all of which, of course, reflect her own sterling maternal abilities. If she notices that Kaspar is growing bored, she pretends not to, though perhaps it is implicit in the way she continues to try to bribe him with "real coffee," with another "man's share" of the sausage, specially purchased in his honor, with the remains of the packet of "real cigarettes." But he resists as she tries to insert the packet into the breast pocket of his tunic. "*Stop it*, Mother. I have my own goddamned cigarettes," he announces. Mother Schröder looks as if she has been struck with a fire iron. Kaspar tempers his tone. "Those are yours. You keep them," he instructs.

In the silence that follows, he stands. "Thank you for dinner," he says, and solemnly limps over to the coat hooks.

"Where are you *going*?" his mother demands, stricken.

"Out for a while," he answers simply, shuffling on his soldier's greatcoat.

"And when will you be back?"

He buttons his coat closed. "Later" is all he says. Slipping on his field cap, he limps out the door. The thump, as he closes it behind him, occupies the room. Till suddenly, Mother Schröder's voice is like a saber that she wings at Sigrid's head.

"*You* did this!"

"What?"

"This is *your* doing. You've been trying to turn my son against me for years, and now you've finally managed it." Clattering her dishes together with Kaspar's, the old lady marches toward the sink, leaving behind a bloated silence. Slowly, Sigrid piles her flatware atop her single dish and stands.

LYING IN BED, she replays in her mind the sight of the SS herding Jews into the rear of their lorry, and she feels a greasy shame fill her belly. Not just shame over how good Germans could be doing this. Not just shame over her simpleminded denial of "politics" for so long. But also because of the little story that is flickering through her head. *A telephone call would do it.* If the SS were suddenly to sweep Frau Weiss and her children from Sigrid's life, then they would be swept from Egon's life as well. She would be free of them. *He* would be free of them. A telephone call to the local Party office would do it, quite easily. *I know where there are Jews hiding.*

For an instant she stares at the possibility, as if it has taken form outside her head, like an ugly spider dangling above her from a silvered thread. Could she do it? And if she could, how does a person go about her life after such a crime?

When the door to the flat opens, she feels her body tense. She waits. Listens to the aimless shuffling of boots over the drone of the old woman's snoring. A hinge creaks. The toilet flushes. And then the door to the bedroom squeaks open in the darkness. She hears the clump of his boots and then Kaspar's body flops down on the bed beside her. The smell of the schnapps is strong. A moment stretches out before either of them moves. They lie like corpses beside each other.

"I am not what you expected," he says finally.

"It seems so long," she breathes. "It seems like many years have passed."

"Yes, time is strange. A five-minute wait before the order to attack can be an eternity. While five hours of combat will pass in a blink," he says. And then: "I won't ask you if you've been faithful. At the front, there are men who can't stop talking about how they're going to murder their wives for infidelity, but honestly I don't care. We've all done what we have done, and there's nothing for it." He fumbles with a packet of field-issue cigarettes and lights one up, the sharp smoke mixing with the stink of the schnapps. "You know, the army runs field brothels for the front-liners," he says. "Whores shipped in from the Warthegau. They set them up in tents, with blankets draped between the cots. Once we're queued up, the company sergeant hands out small cans of disinfectant spray, and we're required to spray the disinfectant onto the whore's genitals before intercourse. If we don't, and we come out with a full can, we get punishment duty."

"Why are you telling me this?"

"I just want you to know the truth, Sigrid. I don't want any lies between us."

IN THE MORNING, she cannot help but knock on Carin Kessler's door. But she gets no answer. So she scribbles a note on a slip of stationery from her purse, *I must see you*, and slips it under the door.

But as she starts down the steps, she hears the lock turn behind her, and the door to the flat floats open. She feels her breath constrict. When she enters the flat, she finds Egon heaped in a chair.

"I understand your man has returned," he says thickly, "from the front."

She has closed the door behind her, but the wall of Egon's gaze stops her from approaching him. "Yes" is all she answers.

"You must be very proud."

"Egon."

"Have you asked him," he inquires, "have you asked him how many Jews he's murdered?"

"Please don't."

"*Don't?*"

"Please don't do this."

"I'm just curious. Did he have a guess? A hundred Jews? Two hundred? Or were there just too many to keep count?"

"He is not a killer, Egon. Only a soldier."

"Well, what do you think a soldier *is*, Frau Schröder, but a killer in a uniform?"

"He was wounded. In battle. He *did not* murder Jews."

"And how in hell do *you* know? Have you asked him? Have you said, *Excuse me, husband dear, but do you recall slaughtering any kikes while in Russia?*"

She stares back at him. He drains the last drops of whatever's in the glass he's holding. "The truth is, Frau Schröder, that you don't know *what* your husband has done. Whom he has killed or not killed. And the still *greater* truth is, you don't *want* to know."

"This is not my fault," she breathes. "You are blaming me, but this is not my fault."

"It's not my fault that I have a circumcised putz," he tells her. "But the Greater German Reich still blames me for it. Life is not about what is fair." He raises the glass again but, finding it empty, tosses it onto the carpet and watches it roll away. "Don't believe me?" he says, and gestures toward the bronze Hitler relief over the mantel. "Ask *him*," he instructs. "The Führer and I, we understand this. You must live with a stranglehold on the world."

"I have to go to work," she says. "I'll be back. Tonight."

Egon only shrugs. "I'll be here. A rat in its trap."

THERE'S A CROWD at her tram stop, waiting not so very patiently for passengers to climb off so they can clamber aboard. Those with manners wait, those without manners try to push through. When a stout Berliner in a gray coat and black trilby hat bumps into her, she doesn't immediately recognize him. "My apologies, gnädige Frau," the man mumbles, then picks up an envelope from the sidewalk. "I think you dropped this," he says, forcing the envelope into her hand before shoving past her.

She doesn't open it until she arrives at the office. Until she closes the door of the second-floor WC and tugs the bolt into place. Inside the envelope is a single sheet of paper. *Bahnhof Zoo*, it reads. *Under the clock. 6:00 this evening.* After she reads it, she crumbles it into a ball and flushes it down the commode.

At six o'clock, as the city is streaked by a bright violet twilight, she approaches the blind man. "A coin in memory of our sacred dead?" he rasps. Sigrid drops groschen into his cup. "Bless you," he says, then his voice drops a notch. "She's in the station's café."

INSIDE, the loudspeakers are booming out "The March of the Paratroops." The trumpets sound tinny, the voices of the military chorus brassy and warped bouncing off the tiled ceiling. She sees the stout Berliner in his gray coat and black trilby smoking a cigar while getting his shoes shined by a young bootblack. He does not afford her a look, but a short, muscular taxi driver, with tough eyes, silvering hair, and a deep scar cut across his cheek, lowers his copy of the *12-Uhr-Blatt* long enough to give her a nod. She follows his nod, and sees Ericha sitting at a table by the sandwich kiosk. She is surprised when the girl jumps to her feet and hugs her. Surprised at how good it feels to hug her back. "How I've missed you," she hears herself say.

Ericha breaks away. Hurried Berliners march past them to catch their trains. "We must sit down. There isn't much time."

"I WAS FRIGHTENED," Sigrid says with only a small splinter of rebuke in her voice. "You simply vanished."

"I had to."

"Without a word to me."

"There was no time. I was forced to move quickly. The Gestapo came to your door?"

"My door. Everyone's door."

"Then it was better for you that you didn't know what was happening."

"So tell me now."

A lift of her eyebrows. "I was warned that they were coming for me. Nothing more than that."

"Someone turned you in? One of your contacts?"

"Or I made a mistake. Or both," she says. "Only the Gestapo knows."

A whistle, just a few notes, from the taxi driver. Sigrid glances discreetly. "Is that a signal? What does it mean?"

"It's nothing, don't worry."

"Who *are* they?" Sigrid asks. "These men of yours. The fellow in the black trilby, the taxi driver, and the blind man who can see?"

"Comrades, that's all. From no common background. The taxi driver was once a thief. He spent ten months in Oranienburg before the war, and the Brownshirts gave him his scar as a souvenir the day he was to be released. The blind man? He used to be an actor for the State Theater, until he refused to divorce his Jewish wife."

"Is she in hiding, too?"

"Hiding in the grave," Ericha answers plainly. "When she received her evacuation letter from the jüdische Gemeinde, she hanged herself. So you can imagine he has his reasons for what he does."

"And what about the man in the trilby getting his shoes shined? Does he have reasons?"

"Do you?" Ericha asks.

"All right. I get the message. No more questions."

But Ericha answers her questions anyway. "He's just an ordinary man, really. I know him as Franz. He runs a heavy goods delivery business in the Barn Quarter. But he believes in right and wrong, that's all. Those are his reasons."

"He's very protective of you."

"He's appointed himself as my guardian," she says with a bit of irony. But then the irony leaves her voice. "I really couldn't do without him." She recedes slightly and takes a sip of coffee, holding the cup with both hands. Then leans forward by a centimeter. "There's something I must ask you. Something I must be sure of. You've never told Auntie your name, have you?"

"My *name*? No."

"You're sure? Never in passing?"

"No," Sigrid repeats, her eyebrows arching. "Why are you asking me this?"

"Because," Ericha answers, "Auntie's been arrested."

"*Arrested.*" Sigrid feels her breath shorten.

"They came for her at her brother's flat."

"But her brother's in the Party. Couldn't he *do* something? Try to protect her?"

"We suspect it was her brother who denounced her. They took her first to the Gray Misery in the Alex for interrogation, and then transferred her to the Prinz-Albrecht-Strasse."

"Ahh, my *God*." Sigrid breathes out, her palm to her forehead. Prinz-Albrecht-Strasse 8. A well-known address in Berlin. Once it was an industrial arts-and-crafts school, but since '33 it's been the headquarters of the Gestapo.

"And what about"—an instinctive German glance interrupts her—"what about her *guests*?"

"They're safe, if that's what you're asking. We were lucky. Auntie was doing the bookkeeping for her husband's old partner, who apparently was running a swift trade in black-market cigarettes. *That's* why the Sipo picked her up. They ransacked the place, of course, but they were looking for ledger books, not for Jews hiding in the attic."

Sigrid feels the knot in her belly ease. "So, you moved them?"

"Temporarily. But we had to divide them up. And we lost the old man," she says.

"Lost him?"

"There was a place in Charlottenburg, a woman whose father had died in an air raid, who agreed to take him for a few nights. I had him on the S-Bahn with me, when, just past the Knie, he made a kind of muffled noise and simply slumped against my shoulder. I knew of course that he was dead," she says. "His heart gave out, I suppose."

"What did you *do*?"

"What could I do? I got off at the next stop."

"And *left him* there?"

"Old men drop dead in this town every day. Someone took care of him. Gave him a good German burial. Besides, I had other problems. The man Kozig, for instance," she says, pressing two fingertips to her upper lip in a mock Führer mustache. "Full of demands as usual. He must have this, and we must do that. But he's stuck in a rabbit hole for now."

"And Frau Weiss?"

"Frau Weiss?"

"The woman and her children."

"They're safe," Ericha tells her succinctly. "You call her Frau Weiss?"

"I know. Against regulations, but one night I asked. She's Viennese." She sees the face of Frau Weiss and her little daughters inside her head, as if they were sharing the table with them. Egon's wife and Egon's children. Her secret duty and secret leverage. "How safe?"

"After the last raid, six hundred people were bombed out of their homes. Something you won't read in any of the newspapers. So I found a shop in the Berliner Strasse where typewriters are repaired, and while the clerk was in the back room, I filled out the bombing victim's pass."

Paying the bootblack, the man in the trilby clears his throat with gusto and dusts ash from his cigar. Ericha glances at him. "We're running out of time."

"Why? What's going to happen?"

"It's unwise to stay in one place too long. Auntie may be a warhorse, but the Gestapo torturers are experts. We must assume that her endurance and our luck will have limits. Who knows what she might tell them? What she might have *already* told them."

"Isn't there something we can do for her? Someone we can bribe?" Sigrid asks, but Ericha only shakes her head.

"Not at the Prinz-Albrecht-Strasse. We cannot afford *that* level of corruption. No. The Gestapo have her and there's nothing for it. Maybe there'll be time for mourning when the war's over, if any of us are left. But for now we can only keep moving."

"And that means?"

"There's a Reichsbahn superintendent at Anhalter Bahnhof named Zimmermann," Ericha says. "If I pay him enough, he can provide tickets from Berlin to Lübeck."

"Lübeck? You think they're not arresting Jews in Lübeck, too?"

"There is a freighter under Swedish registration that will take them to Malmö. But that costs money, too. A lot of money. So we're scratching for it. Everything we have is invested in the ship's passage, and we're still coming up short. That's one of the things I'd hope you might be able to help with."

"Money?"

"Is there anything you can sell? Some jewelry, perhaps. Clothing? There's a market for good clothing. Especially men's clothing."

"Men's?"

"Your husband. Are there any of his shoes in your closet?"

"Ericha, you should know," Sigrid suddenly says, "my husband's come home."

An uncertain stare. "Your husband."

"Yes. He was wounded."

"And what does this mean?"

"Mean?"

"You have a tone in your voice that makes me very anxious. Does it means that we can no longer count on you?"

"No, that is *not* what it means."

"Is that what you came here tonight to tell me?"

"No. I just thought you should know."

"You haven't said anything, have you? *Told* him anything?"

"My God, of *course* not."

"One wrong word, Sigrid, and we'll all be joining Auntie in the cellar of the Prinz-Albrecht-Strasse."

"I am aware of that, Ericha. You needn't lecture me."

"What else?"

"What?"

"What else? There's something else that you're not saying."

Sigrid pulls her scarf down from the back of her head and takes a breath. "There's a man," she starts.

"I *knew* it. I knew it the moment I saw you together at the door to the building."

"No. Not him. You must button your mouth and listen to me for a change."

Ericha's gaze contracts, but she goes silent.

"A man who once . . ." Sigrid says, but cannot seem to untangle the rest of the sentence in her head. "We were lovers."

Ericha gazes at her. "Were?"

"Were. *Are*." She shrugs. "He's a Jew. I've been helping him. Hiding him."

A silence from Ericha that causes Sigrid to turn her head. She finds the girl gazing at her with a shade of gray uncertainty.

"Why didn't you tell me?" the girl asks, perhaps a little wounded.

"*Because* I thought you'd react exactly as you *did*."

Ericha looks away. Shakes her head. "I don't believe that. I could have helped," she says. "I think you wanted him all to yourself."

"Yes," Sigrid admits. "That's right."

"So. Your husband's return must have been quite an inconvenience," she observes blankly. "What are you planning on doing with him?"

"I don't know. He says he needs better papers. He has a Labor Front membership book, but needs something to travel on."

"And are you going to be traveling with him?"

Brow knitting. "Am I what?"

"You said he's your lover. I make the assumption. Are you leaving with him? Is that your plan?"

"No. *No*, Ericha," Sigrid whispers. "I'm not going anywhere, and I'm not going to abandon you. You must believe me." But before the girl responds, a tin cup rattles its coins beside them.

"Remember the veterans' sacrifice?" the man requests. Then, "Ordnungspolizei coming in," he warns in an undertone.

Ericha quickly drops a coin in the cup.

"Bless you for your kindness," the man tells her, then shoves off, tapping his cane. Behind him, two uniformed Orpo men enter the station. Franz immediately drops his head and jostles past them like any good Berliner in a hurry. It's enough to make them stop and demand his papers.

"We must go. Right now." Ericha stands and heads toward the doors. Sigrid must hurry to follow. She fires a cautious glance at the two Orpo patrolmen, frowning over the stout man's identification as he impatiently chews the butt of a cigar. An ordinary man, who knows the difference between right and wrong. They make it out through the station's bank of doors and into the night air without having to negotiate any hazards more dangerous than pushy Berliners late for their trains.

"Keep walking," Ericha says. "No looking back."

Sigrid fumbles to find her blackout torch and switches it on. Staring at the red beam, she asks, "Aren't you afraid?"

"Afraid?"

"*I* am. I'm frightened all the time."

"I have such terrible dreams," Ericha says, nodding. "Huge machines tearing me to bits. I wake up from them, sweated to the skin, and then lie awake the rest of the night."

Sigrid looks at the girl as they walk. "You look exhausted," she says, but Ericha only shakes her head.

"It makes no difference."

"I've *missed* you," Sigrid tells her. "I've missed you quite a lot."

Ericha gives her a glance. "Even with all those men about you? Lovers, husbands by the bushel?"

"Yes. Even so, Fräulein Kohl."

"This is as far as we go together," Ericha announces, dropping into her voice reserved for dispensing instructions. "When we reach the corner, I will turn left and you will keep going."

"Where are you staying? Just tell me, please. I don't want to lose track of you again."

"You won't," Ericha assures her crisply. "Day after tomorrow at noon. I'll meet you in the Tiergarten. There's a bench by the Luther-brücke. Good night, Frau Schröder," she says. Reaching up, she pelts Sigrid with a kiss on the cheek, before veering away into the twilight of the street.

THAT NIGHT, the Deutschlandsender broadcasts the news from the East. In memory of their fallen comrades of the Sixth Army on the Don, the heroic fighting men of the Leibstandarte SS Adolf Hitler and Das Reich divisions advanced into the city of Kharkov with tanks and motorized grenadiers, and have now completely driven Bolshevik forces from their positions. The German soldiers fought indefatiga-bly as house-to-house combat ensued. Tens of thousands of the Red Army foe have been killed. Tens of thousands more taken prisoner. When the German anthem follows the broadcast, Kaspar stares, then takes a moment to light a cigarette.

"What will happen now?" his mother asks him.

"What will happen?"

"You are the military man, my boy. Can't you tell me?"

"Why, complete and unequivocal victory on all fronts, Mother," he says, without bothering to smile. "Weren't you *listening*?" Then stand-ing, he leaves the room and heads into the WC, leaving Mother Schröder frowning.

KASPAR SLEEPS HEAVIEST in the morning. Sigrid has noticed this. For hours at night, he will toss about under the blankets, but around dawn, he drops off into a thick, corpselike slumber. While he snores, Sigrid climbs from bed and stares into his oaken wardrobe cabinet.

He had been a fastidious dresser once, before the army. He wasn't afraid of spending money on high-quality clothing, though he always pretended that clothes and styles were of little interest to him, and that it was only his position at the bank as an authorized signatory that demanded a certain way of dressing. But she can recall the way he would survey himself in the dressing mirror, adjusting his cuffs, inspecting the lines of his jacket, the seams of his trousers. The vanity reflected in his mirrored face.

The jackets and trousers draped neatly over their hangers are gabardine, English tweed, loden wool, pressed linen. Only a few neckties, but all are silk. His shoes are carefully polished. She brushes the dust from the toe of a pair and reveals a deep burnish that only regularly scheduled buffing can obtain. His current wardrobe, however, consists of a field gray Waffenfrock with a silvered tress on one sleeve that he calls piston rings, two pairs of army-issue breeches, three army-issue blouses, and one pair of hobnailed boots, with a finish of bootblack. A certain way of dressing dictated by the demands of his new posting as a staff clerk in a motor transport company. "A cripple's job," he calls it.

At breakfast, she pours him coffee, and listens to the gurgle as it goes into the china cup. "I'm sorry, it's ersatz," she tells him, but he only shrugs.

"As long as it's hot," he tells her. Then, while his mother is busy whipping batter by the sink, she says, "I'm thinking of donating some of your clothes. To the Winter Relief. Just some of the older things."

"Fine. Take them all," Kaspar answers without interest, glaring at the pages of a copy of *Signal* magazine. On the cover the Führer greets a Romanian officer who lost an arm fighting at Stalingrad. "None of them fit any longer," he says.

That afternoon she feigns an illness. A stomach nausea that she describes to Fräulein Kretchmar as a thunderbolt in her bowels, a common complaint in a city fed on browning vegetables and chemical substitutes. And though Kretchmar views her skeptically, she permits her to leave work thirty minutes early. That allows her just enough time to make it back to the flat and pillage Kaspar's wardrobe before his mother comes back from her weekly kaffeeklatsch at Oswald's, and deposit them in Frau Kessler's flat.

Carin Kessler has started leaving a spare key to the flat under the rubberized doormat. Sigrid inserts the key into the lock and twists it carefully, delicately. She must often battle the feeling that Frau Mundt's predatory ears will be able to detect the tumble of the lock from the ground floor. But as the door slides open, she applies pressure on the handle, and the Portierfrau does not erupt from below in a National Socialist whirlwind. Instead, Sigrid pokes her head inside and finds Egon in a padded chair, staring at the wall.

Closing the door quietly behind herself. "I have clothes for you," she says. "Pick out what you wish. They may be a little long, but they should do."

Still staring at the wall. "They are your husband's?"

"Yes," she says.

"So now you're dressing me up like a doll?"

Sigrid blinks angrily. "Why don't you just *shut up*?" she asks him, which finally prompts him to look at her. "Such a typical Berliner, soaking in self-pity. Think, for a second, of all those *without* somewhere to hide. All those *without* someone to hand them clothes and bring them food."

"All those poor kikes," he says, "without a good Aryan to care for them. You're right, Frau Schröder," he concedes, his voice lacquered with acid, "I am an ingrate."

She glares at him, hotly, but suddenly she cannot hold back the flood from her eyes. The tears overwhelm her as her legs go weak, and she drops to the carpet, unable to stand, unable to speak, unable to stop this sobbing. Then he is beside her. As his arms encircle her, she thinks for an instant that she wants to resist, but then she thinks she doesn't, and folds herself into him. "I am an ingrate," he whispers, but now it sounds like a confession.

SHE HAS ALREADY PUT on the water for the potatoes when Kaspar's mother comes home, wearing her good hat and good wool dress under her coat.

Sigrid wipes the back of her hand across her cheek, as if the streak of a tear might still be visible, but her cheeks are dry now. "How was Oswald's?" she inquires.

"Do you care?"

"No," Sigrid answers honestly.

"Then why ask?"

"I understand that Frau Granzinger has been assigned a new duty-year girl."

Hanging up her coat. "She has." Tugging off her gloves and unpinning her hat. "A scrawny beanpole from the Rhineland. *Why*? Do you plan on ruining her as well?"

"Oh, so is that the verdict? *I* am the source of ruination?"

But her mother-in-law is through talking. She ends the conversation with a brusque wave as if swatting away a bothersome insect, and turns on the wireless in the living room. According to the Reichsfunk announcer, the Afrika Korps has made a strategic withdrawal from the Mareth Line in Tunisia to positions sixty meters to the north of the Tebaga Gap at Akarit. Also, for similar strategic reasons, the Ninth Army has completed its withdrawal from the city of Vyazma, west of Moscow.

"An interesting way of winning a war, advancing by retreating," Sigrid hears herself remark. She hadn't really meant this as a serious comment; it was just that the absurd euphemisms of the Propaganda Ministry had struck her as so ridiculous. And she certainly hadn't meant to speak it aloud. But recently she has found herself simply too exhausted to keep her thoughts silent.

The comment, however, is enough to bring her mother-in-law blowing back in the kitchen like a fireball. *"I will not have that!"* she barks at Sigrid. "I will not permit defeatist talk in my house. *My* house, especially now that my son is home from honorably serving his Fatherland in battle! I rue the day that he married you. I knew it was a mistake then, and I can see now how right I was. So, I *warn* you, my good girl, one more remark like that, one more *insult* to the honor of our gallant Wehrmacht, and, daughter-in-law or no, I will have you up in front of the police!"

"Just as you did Frau Remki?" Sigrid shouts back.

Her mother-in-law's back suddenly goes straight.

"Oh, yes." Sigrid nods vigorously. "Mundt told me all about it."

"So you're listening to Mundt now?"

"We all made the assumption."

"Assumptions are for fools," her mother-in-law declares, retreating toward the kitchen.

"You knew that Mundt would happily take the credit, and keep silent about the truth."

"Well, it doesn't appear that she kept silent enough."

"So you admit it?"

"Admit what? I've committed no crime."

"It wasn't Mundt who denounced Frau Remki, it was *you. You!*"

"And *what of it*?!" the old woman suddenly rails. "She was a *traitor.* She slurred the Führer's name. Whatever she got, *she deserved*!"

"And what did *you* get? Her radio for a few marks. Was that worth her life?"

"She took *her own* life, if you recall. A coward to the last."

At that moment, the door opens and in steps Kaspar. His entrance breaks the argument in half with a wedge of silence. He glances at both of them, then shrugs out of his greatcoat and limps over toward the sink, where he washes his hands, using the nub of a bar of lard soap beside the faucet. "How long till supper?" he asks.

Sigrid lights the burner under the pot of water. "I'm sorry, it's late," she says, sharply swallowing her fury. "Another forty minutes."

He only nods and limps over to the kitchen table, where he sits and takes out his pipe. "Mother, do we have any matches?" he asks, digging the pipe's bowl into a packet of army tobacco. "I'm out."

"Matches," the old woman repeats. Then, "Yes. I'll get you some," she answers solemnly. At the stove, she shoots Sigrid a stiff glare, but her anger does not completely hide a splinter of fear. Her son has come home from the war, alive, but she no longer recognizes him.

SIXTEEN

A SPRINKLING OF RAIN COMES and goes restlessly in the morning, and by the afternoon is replaced by a damp, stolid breeze. Sigrid has made her journey to the bench in the Tiergarten at the foot of the Lutherbrücke, as instructed. As she sits, the breeze is riffling recklessly through the line of poplars as she observes the Berliner's clip of Ericha's slim, dark-clad figure crossing the bridge.

The child looks done in. Her face has been sharpened, depleted of its rounded girlishness. He eyes are shadowed and ringed with blue moons. The crystalline blue of her gaze is now flat and cloudy.

"You look terrible," Sigrid tells her.

"I could say the same of you, Frau Schröder. You should look in the mirror," Ericha replies, then shakes her head. "Sorry, that sounded much more harsh than I intended."

"You're not sleeping?"

"I've been on the move a lot."

"On the move?"

"I catch a few hours here and there."

Suddenly, Sigrid perceives an absence. She looks up and searches the area, but all she sees is an elderly couple propped against each other as they travel slowly down the path. "Ericha? Where's your friend Franz?"

No answer.

"Ericha?"

"I told him to stay away from me for a while."

"Stay away? *Why?*"

Again no answer.

"Ericha, what is going *on?*"

"I'm pregnant," she answers suddenly.

Sigrid stares. Opens her mouth, then closes it again. "How . . . how can that *be?*" she finally manages.

"How can it be? You're a grown woman. You must be familiar with the process. Do I really need to explain?"

"*Ericha.* You know what I'm saying. *How did this happen?*"

"As I said. You must be familiar with the process."

"*Who?*" she demands.

"Does it matter?"

"*Doesn't it?*"

"Not to me."

"I don't understand."

"Listen to yourself. You sound like a typical hausfrau. What is there to understand? There was a man. He had what I needed. So I bounced him for it. That was it. That was the *process.*"

"Only now you end up with a baby in your belly."

"You sound angry with me."

"*Angry?*" Sigrid suddenly catches the pitch of her grandmother's voice. "No. No, of course not. Of course, I'm not *angry.* I'm only, I'm only *shocked.* That's all. Only shocked." She swallows. "I'm sorry if," she starts to say, but Ericha shakes her head.

"It means nothing. Honestly, I wouldn't blame you if you *were* angry. *I'm angry,*" she says, pulling out a cigarette and poking one into her mouth. "I'm *furious.*"

The breeze blows past as Ericha cups her match to light up a cigarette. The smoke she exhales is whisked away. Finally, she says, "You
remember the man named Johann?"

"Your forger? The man who nearly bowled you over in the middle
of the sidewalk? *He's* the father?"

"He was the man I fucked," she corrects.

"And have you told him?"

Now Ericha releases something like a laugh. "*Told him?* No. No, I
haven't *told* him, Frau Schröder. Don't be absurd. This has nothing to
do with him."

"Ericha, I know you have no feelings for him, but if you are carrying his *child*..."

"I'm carrying a tiny kernel in my womb, that's all. A little speck.
If it belongs to *anyone*, it belongs to *me*." She expels smoke and
watches it vanish. With her head turned she asks, "Have you ever had
one done?" When Sigrid doesn't answer her, she turns her head back.
"Have you?"

Sigrid's jaw has stiffened. "You mean...an abortion?" she asks.
Then shakes her head once. "No."

Ericha looks away. Takes another drag from her cigarette. For a
moment she shivers. "Auntie used to do them long ago. She told me
once. She was a midwife working in the factory slums. Delivering
babies, yes. Also, *other* procedures for women. Sometimes after they'd
been raped, but mostly after their husbands had knocked them up for
the seventh or eighth time, and they *just couldn't do it again*. But I can't
get to Auntie now, can I?"

"Is that what you want?" Sigrid asks her.

Ericha swallows. Shrugs. "What else *can* I want? Can you actually
credit me as a mother? I mean, can you imagine it?" she asks. "Me pushing the pram? Me washing nappies? It's laughable," she says harshly,
expelling wintry smoke. "Absolutely *laughable*." Her cigarette is cheap
and the tobacco goes out. "*Shit*," she swears. But as she scratches

another match to life, it trembles in her hand. And when the match is extinguished by an errant breath of wind, her façade crumbles to pieces, and long and terrible sobs seize her utterly. Sigrid clutches her without thought or hesitation. And as she keeps the girl enfolded in her arms, as if trying to keep her from flying into pieces, she thinks for a moment of herself: a motherless child standing at a graveside. Lost.

IT'S GROWING LATE. Dusk gathering above the treetops, darkening the branches. The cemetery warden is hesitant to let her in, but finally concedes to her obvious anguish. "Only a few minutes," he warns, and opens the gate.

Kneeling atop her mother's grave, Sigrid places her hand on the headstone. It is cold. Cold as the ground. Grossmutter had once announced that her mother had been unwanted. Sigrid was still young at the time, seated at the kitchen table with a bowl of black cherries. Still long-limbed and gangly, a scrawny scarecrow with a tousled mess of flaxen hair. Her mother, standing a few feet away, was washing a delicate porcelain bowl in the sink. Grossmutter had been across the table picking at Sigrid's cherries like a poacher. Her face sharp and predatory, as always. One moment she was talking about how she couldn't understand why young women these days were so intent on "keeping their figure," and the next she was announcing that she has never intended to give birth to any more children after her third. "But then along comes your mother." She'd frowned. "Completely unwanted, but there I was. Stuck with another mouth to feed. And back then," she added significantly, "we didn't have a *choice*, if you know what I'm saying. Back then if you had a baby coming, it *came*. And that was that."

Suddenly there was a crash in the sink. The sound of fine porcelain shattering.

"*Now*, what have you broken?" Grossmutter demanded to know loudly.

"I'm sorry," her mother answered, not turning around. "It slipped."

As a girl, she had been angry with her mother at that moment. That she should be so clumsy. That she should break such an important bowl. That she was so weak in the face of Grossmutter's bullying. By that age she had stopped defending her mother, and then after Grossmutter's death, picked up the attack where the old lady had left off.

And when the cancer came, she remembers her mother lying on the horsehair settee, weak as an unstrung puppet, a frail collection of bones wrapped in a thin yellowing skin, pleading for some kind of mercy. And then she was gone. Bundled into the grave. Sigrid's aunt Trudi had come to act as the chief nursemaid, boiling towels and administering old-fashioned remedies, though mostly she just clucked her tongue and shook her head at heaven. At the grave site, she told Sigrid, "At least your poor mother is finally at rest." Sigrid nodded. What a relief death must have been for her.

WHEN SIGRID RETURNS to the flat she finds Kaspar laughing. There are two other soldiers with him at the kitchen table, hunched around a half-empty bottle of corn schnapps, and they are all laughing. It is the first time she has seen her husband laugh since his return.

He stands and steps toward her, grinning, and for an instant she tries to see the man she married, the smiling husband with whom she sometimes passed an easy Sunday afternoon at the lake. But the grin he wears looks more like a distortion of his face. "Ah, my devoted wife. Home from the Battle of the Stenographers' Pool." He doesn't kiss her, but captures her in the crook of his arm and marches her beside the table. She resists the desire to turn away from the stink of schnapps on his breath. "Fall in, comrades," he commands largely. "Salute the Victor of the Reichspatentamt!"

The men leap comically to attention, clicking their boot heels. One is short but built like a tree stump. His head is shaven, and a livid scar draws a crescent across his skull and chops off the tip of his left ear. The other is more like a tree trunk. Long-bodied with willowy limbs. He has no scars on his face, but his left hand, she notes, is shy three fingers. Both of them, like Kaspar, wear the onyx wound badge pinned to their ill-fitting uniforms beside the Ostmedaille, the Frozen Meat Medallion. "Frau Schröder," Kaspar says, continuing his mock drill ground formality, "may I present Unteroffizier Kamphauser and Unteroffizier Messner, two of the best-preserved corpses in the army. Notice there's very little decay. How lifelike they look."

"Only because we're pumped so full of formaldehyde," the stubby one injects, triggering a generous round of guffaws.

"So very pleased to meet you, gentlemen," Sigrid manages, slipping the strap of her bag from her shoulder, and freeing herself from her husband's grip in the process. "Where is your mother, Kaspar?"

"Out somewhere," Kaspar answers without interest. "At ease, comrades!" he commands, returning to the military bluff, refilling the trio of glasses on the table. "Time to regroup." Sigrid prepares herself to decline an offer of a glass, but then no offer is made. She hangs up her coat, thinking of Egon's hands on her skin. "Did your mother start the supper?"

"I really haven't the slightest," Kaspar answers.

"I see. Gentlemen, I assume that you are staying to eat?" she says dutifully, walking toward the kitchen stove, and picking up her apron. But Kaspar waves her off.

"No, no. Nothing special. Just some *pickled beets*," he tells her, triggering another round of guffaws at some private Ostfront joke. Their drunken chumminess makes her feel suddenly claustrophobic. And all she can think of is *Egon*. In the kitchen, there are no pickled beets, but she does find cold fried potatoes and a bit of smoked herring. She quickly puts it on a plate, and drops it off on the table with three forks. "Good appetite, gentlemen," she says. "Kaspar, I have an errand to run." But Kaspar barely acknowledges her. By the time she has slipped back into her coat, they are singing a booming, hideously off-key version of "Lili Marlene."

She steps into the foyer and closes the door behind her, muffling the noise of their chorus. From below stairs, she can hear one of Frau Granzinger's kids screaming. But she is staring at the door of Carin Kessler's flat. A quick German glance, before she tiptoes across, knocking carefully. "It's *me*," she whispers to the door, and the door swings open as if she has just uttered a password.

"Well, Hello, Frau Me," the man in the threshold answers. But it is not Egon. It is Wolfram, in full uniform, silver wound badge, close-combat clasp, Ostmedaille, Iron Cross pinned under the breast pocket of his Waffenrock, tricolor ribbon in his buttonhole. Garrison strap connected to his pistol belt. False leg with the glossy high boot attached. She steps back, fearfully, from the force of his eyes. "Come in," he tells her. "We were just having a game."

Without comprehension. "A game?"

"Yes. Your friend and I. Come in," he says again, but this time it is more of a command. And when she does, she finds Egon seated on the sofa, dressed in his black mohair overcoat over a tweed jacket of Kaspar's, and bent over a chessboard on the coffee table. He looks up at her with the blank concentration of a man defusing a bomb.

"I managed to avoid his Nimzo-Indian defense by conceding my bishops," Wolfram explains, "but it's left me limping into the middle game, if you'll pardon the expression. He's tricky," he concludes, as he shuts the door behind them. "Very tricky. Can I get you a glass of bull's blood?"

"I beg your pardon?"

"Egri Bikavér. It's Hungarian red from the Eger region."

Staring into Egon's face. "No. No, thank you."

"It's really not so bad," Wolfram tells her. Marching with his cane over to the coffee table, he refills a pair of goblets by the game board. Fallen pieces litter its margin, knights, pawns, bishops. "Quite full-bodied. Don't you agree?" he asks Egon.

"It's your move," is all Egon says in return.

Wolfram frowns lightly at the board. "Hmm. I see you are indeed a true disciple of the hypermoderns. Have you heard the story of how Nimzowitsch conceded the Immortal Zugzwang Game to Sämisch? He stood up and slapped himself in the forehead, shouting, '*That I should lose to such an idiot!*' "

"Wolfram," Sigrid says thickly, but he raises his hand to halt her.

"Really, Frau Schröder, you cannot break my concentration if I am expected to have any chance to save my queen from a terrible fate," he orders, with a touch of rawness, and knocks back a deep swallow of bull's blood from his goblet.

"What do you want me to *do*?" Sigrid asks him desolately.

"Well, you could start by taking off your coat and sitting down like a human being." He gives her only the shortest of glances, but she catches the gun sight. She thinks, for only a heartbeat, of the fish knife she keeps in her bag. She looks to Egon, but he is staring distantly at the pieces on the board. So she removes her coat and, like a human being, she sits, balancing herself on the edge of one of the Frau Obersturm-führer's padded club chairs.

"So I understand that my dear sister Carin has developed a big mouth," Wolfram says, glaring at the pieces. "Has she not, Frau Schröder?" he asks, when Sigrid does not respond.

"She told me," Sigrid answers tonelessly, "about your family."

"Yes, a kike by any other name," Wolfram says. "I was discussing it earlier, with our mutual chum here. By the way, if you're feeling awkward, don't," he instructs her.

"Awkward?"

"That you're sitting in a room with two men, both of whom you've fucked. We've discussed that, too. There are no secrets between the children of Abraham, you see."

She looks to Egon for help, but he only offers her a blank glare and takes a swig of the wine.

"Are you," she starts to say, but her throat dries up. "Are you going to call the police?"

"The *police*?" Wolfram squawks. "Why on earth would I do *that*? You know, that's the *trouble* with you Aryan types. Always running to the police to solve your problems." Thrusting a knight forward, he sits back. "There. My brilliant defense," he announces, "Maybe I'll do better than old Nimzo." Opening his cigarette case, he picks one out and jams it into his mouth. "You know, my sister is very fond of you. Which is unusual, because Carin normally despises the world."

"Yes, I'm fond—" she says, but her words are starting to choke her. "I'm fond of her, too."

"Are you *crying*, Frau Schröder?"

Sigrid wipes her eyes. "I *can't*," she whispers. "I can't play this game with you, Wolfram. Please just *do* what you're going to *do*."

"Well, I *did* do what I was going to do, Frau Schröder," he answers. "I defended my queen from a brutal assault by my opponent's rook."

She shakes her head. "*Please . . .*"

Wolfram inhales smoke, and frowns archly at the board. "You need papers?" he asks Egon. "Correct?"

Egon looks up at him. She sees a lightning recalculation change his expression by the slightest measurement. "Correct," he says, in a dead level voice.

Wolfram, nodding to himself as he peers at the pieces. "I can supply them."

Egon's gaze tightens. "And the cost?"

"I'm sure there'll *be* a cost, but it won't be in Reichsmarks," Wolfram answers simply. Slouching to one side, he removes a neatly pressed handkerchief from the pocket of his breeches and offers it to Sigrid. "Here. A gift," he says.

Sigrid accepts the offer. The handkerchief is monogrammed linen. She quickly wipes the remnant of tears from her eyes.

"I really can't stomach tears," Wolfram explains, then prods Egon gamely. "So are we playing or are we playing?" But when Egon doesn't move, Wolfram expels a huff. "Very well, then, if I am to play both sides of this game, so be it." He reaches over to Egon's pieces and hooks the queen's knight to a different square. "There. *That* is the proper response," he declares.

Egon flicks his eyes at the board, then back up at Wolfram's face.

"You think I hate the Nazis because of what they're doing to the Jews?" Wolfram asks him. "I don't. I hate them because they're *stupid*. That's their crime in my opinion. Just so you understand."

"I understand," Egon tells him.

"Do you?"

"I understand that you're the man who can get me the papers I need."

Wolfram's assailing gaze recedes a millimeter. "Ah. A pragmatist. I should have guessed, by the way you play. Taking control of the center board from a distance, while fools rush in with their pawns. You have photographs of yourself?"

Egon reaches into an inner pocket. "These will do, I think," he says, and offers a small paper envelope.

"How efficient you are," Wolfram observes. "Quite an admirable quality. No wonder you can pass for a German." He says this, but instead of accepting the offering, he swallows the remainder of his wine, forcing Egon to set the envelope beside the board, among the carnage of pieces. It's more than Sigrid can take.

"Will you *stop*?" she pleads, her eyes smeared with tears. "*Both of you*, will you quit this, this *warfare*? It's making me sick to my stomach. Just *stop it*."

Silence. Egon suddenly stands. "I am going to the toilet. If you like, finish the game without me. I'm sure you'll hold up my end quite effectively." He says this and then walks out of the room, without giving Sigrid a glance. She sits in the silence he leaves behind, Wolfram's handkerchief balled in her hand. Then comes the ring of the telephone. She looks at it. A sleek black Bakelite instrument. She looks at Wolfram, who is lighting another cigarette.

"Are you going to let it ring?" she finally asks.

"Do you think it's someone important?"

"Shall I answer it for you?"

"Because I am an invalid? Please do."

She stands, sniffing back the tears, the insistent ring scraping her nerves, and snatches the receiver. "Kessler residence, good day." Then she places her palm over the receiver. "It is for you. A man asking for you by rank."

"Which man?"

A blink. "May I ask who is calling?" she inquires into the receiver, then whispers. "Herr Oster."

He holds out his hand without looking at her, and she hands over the receiver. His conversation is clipped. Suddenly, he sounds quite sober and military. "Kessler here, Colonel. Yes, sir, that's correct. No, I shouldn't think that would satisfy the gentlemen in Turkey." He glares and then nods his head curtly. "Yes, sir, I'll be there in thirty minutes." And it's over, without a single Führer salute, and he is prying himself off the settee with his cane. "I must go."

Sigrid says nothing. At the door she tries to assist him with his greatcoat, but he resists. "It's my leg that is missing, Frau Schröder. I still have both arms."

"Wolfram, there is something I must tell you," she says, and shoots a glance in the direction of Egon's departure.

He follows her glance.

"There are more," she says. "More than simply him."

"Really? Are you making a business of it, Frau Schröder? Please, I won't judge you if you are."

An instant's confusion, and then she shakes it off. "No. *No*. I mean more *Jews*," she tells him.

Without expression. "Jews?"

"You are familiar with the term 'U-boats'? I am part of a group who hides them."

Still no expression. "For how long?"

A single-word answer. "Months."

"And *he* knows this?" Wolfram says, nodding toward Egon.

"He doesn't."

"Why not?"

"Because I haven't told him. No one knows unless they need to. That's the way it works."

"How convenient for you. So I am to assume there is a reason why *I* now know."

"There are problems. The Gestapo have arrested one of our people. The woman in charge of our hiding place."

"Then you've been compromised," he concludes evenly.

"It's a possibility," she admits, but Wolfram shakes his head.

"*No*," he instructs. "It's a possibility that it will rain tomorrow, or it's a possibility that a horse will talk. But if the Gestapo have this woman in custody, then it's a *certainty* that *they* know what *she* knows. This is not a game for amateurs, Frau Schröder."

"I'm not aware that it is a *game* at all, Herr Leutnant," Sigrid replies with a glare. "Or is that all you're interested in? Playing games? Is all this just another chess puzzle for you?"

"If it is, then you'd better pray that I am a better player than your friend. I would have trapped him in mate in three moves."

"This isn't about him. It isn't about me." For a moment, she holds the darkness in his eyes.

And then he says, "What is it you need?"

"Documents. We need documents."

"Ah. The world needs documents."

"And travel permits, too. Berlin to Lübeck."

"And what is in Lübeck?"

"Ships."

"Sweden?" he asks, and takes her silence as his answer. "A popular destination, though rather chilly this time of year. How many?"

She tells him.

"I'll need photographs for them as well," he says. "You can arrange that?"

"Photographs? Yes," she answers tightly.

"No snapshots with the family Leica," he warns. "Official standard-sized, full-face shots. No left ears showing, do you know what I'm saying?" By decree, Jewish passport photos always show the left ear. According to the common wisdom of the Interior Ministry, the left ear of a Jew betrays a Semitic shape.

"Yes. Yes, I understand. I know a professional."

"Four different shots in four different outfits is best. They can't appear as if they were all taken at once. Is it men or women?"

"Both."

"All adults?"

"Two small children."

"Small, as in infants?"

"No. Three and five," she answers.

"And how many men?'

"Only one," she says, picturing Herr Kozig, with his stringy hair combed over his bald head and his ridiculous postage-stamp mustache.

"Military age?"

"Late forties."

"Is he the father?"

"No." Only a fraction of hesitation. "Unrelated."

"And how Jewish do they look?"

"How *what*?"

"How *Jewish*? I think it's a simple question."

"I don't know. Not very." Sigrid frowns. But then says, "Except, perhaps, the man."

"Then try to get him in uniform. Any uniform, it doesn't matter. The uniform will carry him."

A flush of the commode rattles the pipes. Wolfram lifts his eyebrows. "As far at *that* one's concerned," he says with a shrug toward the inside of the flat, "I'll get him some exemption papers. He can pass in a decent suit," he says. "And am I correct in assuming he'll need a Reisepass?"

"Yes" is all she says.

"So he'll be traveling to Lübeck as well?"

She keeps her face under tight control. "Traveling, yes. But he has his own plans" is all she says.

"And what about *you*?"

"What *about* me?"

"You have no plans?"

"My plans are to continue day by day," she answers.

"So you are the noble kriegsfrau, is that it?" he asks. "Sticking with you poor wounded husband back from the front?"

"No. 'Noble' is the last word to describe me, I think."

"Good," he answers, "because, I can assure you, nobility is nothing more than an invention of the living to eulogize the dead. The dead are not noble. They are simply decaying in their graves. And if you're not very careful, Sigrid, that is what *you* will be doing," he warns. "By the way, I should ask: What does you husband know?"

"What does he know? About my . . . my many *escapades*, you mean? He knows nothing."

"Does that mean he doesn't know, or doesn't want to know?"

"It means I have said nothing to him."

"*Well*. This may sound perverse, but perhaps you *should*."

"And *why* should I do that?"

"Because, Frau Schröder, if you intend to continue in this line of work, and that seems to be your intent, you're going to require your husband's involvement. If not actively, then at least by implication."

She doesn't like the sound of that word. "Implication?"

"If he knows you're hiding Jews," Wolfram spells it out in a carefully direct tone, "but does nothing about it, he is then, by definition, *implicated*. He can't change his mind later and decide to denounce you to the nearest Party member."

"That would be his mother," she says.

"Even better. If he opens his mouth, if *either* of them do and the Gestapo hauls you away, her standing with the Party will be destroyed. No question about that. In fact, it's very likely that they'll haul *her* away as well. And *he* could end up back at the front, but this time in a penal battalion with a red triangle on his sleeve, clearing minefields by the centimeter with a bayonet."

The picture of this invades her head. She feels herself blanch.

"Now it's *you* who look wounded."

"It never occurred to me," she says.

"That actions have consequences?" he asks.

"The danger in which I've placed Kaspar."

Wolfram gazes at her. "We're fighting a war, Sigrid. What else can you expect?" he asks. For a moment he simply studies her eyes. When he speaks again, his standard tone of irony has returned. "Now, if you'll excuse me, I must suspend further conversation, gnädige Frau. Our Fatherland is calling me." He puts his hand on the doorknob, but she stops him.

"Should I thank you?"

Returning to her face. "Why bother? As you said, it's not about you."

"Do you hate me?" she whispers.

"Because of *him*? No. Hatred is too valuable a quantity to waste.

And if I'm disappointed," he tells her calmly, "it's only because I find most bedmates dull after the first time or two. But you, Sigrid Schröder, are very inventive in the sack. Quite unburdened by convention. Quite at home in your body."

She stares at him. Somewhere in her, she knows, is the desire to touch him, but there is too much in the way for her to find it.

"I'll be in contact," he says, and slips on his peaked uniform cap. "In the meantime, I suggest you grow a pair of eyes in the back of your head," he advises, then makes his way toward the stairs. "My sister will be back in an hour," he announces over his shoulder as he negotiates the first steps downward. "In case you have an interest in her where abouts."

When she returns to the flat, she finds Egon pouring more bull's blood into his glass. "What did he say to you?" he asks.

"He said death is waiting for me."

Egon gazes at her for a moment, unfocused, then lifts the goblet to his lips. "Death is waiting for us *all*," he tells her. "It's only a matter of timing and negotiation. I've taught myself to live with that in order to survive. You should, too."

"How have you done it?" she asks starkly.

"Taught myself?"

"Survived."

His eyes lift and suddenly they are as deep as mine shafts. Without bottom. "Luck," he answers.

"No. No, you don't believe in luck."

He frowns. "There's something I need you to do for me," he announces, setting down the wine goblet.

"I've heard that before," she observes as he removes his mohair overcoat, then unclasps a penknife. Draping his coat lining over his knee, he carefully cuts the stitching loose, and produces a velvet pouch. "There is a man in Schöneberg named Melnikov. He's a Russian. A former tsarist, but now officially stateless. We did business together before the war. I want you to take something to him." Opening the pouch's string, he taps out the contents. Blue-white diamonds. They look like tiny fragments of a star in the palm of his hand. "He's always in the market for decent stones."

Sigrid stares at their light. "So I am to be your bagman again."

He looks at her, waiting.

"How much are they worth?"

"Enough," is all he says.

"I will do whatever you ask," she answers him. "But if you expect me to make a deal with this man, I know nothing about such matters."

"You don't have to. Tell him that Grizmek has sent you to him. He'll give you a good price."

"And who is Grizmek?"

"Me. *I'm* Grizmek," Egon answers, killing the last of his wine. "It's the name I use for this sort of transaction."

"And does this man Melnikov, does he know who you are, *really*?"

"Does anybody know who anyone is? Give me that handkerchief," he tells her.

She obeys, and he opens it into a white square on the sofa next to him. She watches him set about selecting stones from the glimmer in his palm. "You've never said," she breathes.

He affords her a cautious eye. "Said what?"

"Where you're going."

"West," he answers, returning to his selection, holding one small stone up to inspect it in a bit of window light. "I have a contact in the Spanish diplomatic mission. A little man, with a big man's title. For the right amount of cash, he will give me transit papers under any name I like."

He knots the chosen stones into Wolfram's handkerchief and offers her the small bundle, which she accepts. The diamonds feel obscenely light. Star breath.

"To Spain?" she says.

269

"To Madrid. From there I can make my way to Lisbon."

She watches him return the unselected diamonds to the velvet pouch, and stick the pouch into the pocket of his trousers. "And from there?"

He lifts his eyebrows. *Anywhere.*

"What about your family? What about your wife and daughters?"

His eyes grow heavier. "I'm no good to them dead," is all he says.

"And what about *me*?"

A breath. He combs his fingers through his hair. "What *about* you?"

"You haven't said that you want me with you."

"You *are* with me."

"You know what I'm saying."

"Do I, Frau Schröder?"

"I'm just curious how I'm fitting into your plan. Once the bedroom calisthenics are finished, that is."

"My plan is to stay alive," he answers. "Very simple."

Sigrid gazes at him. "With or without me."

"You want me to be your lover, Sigrid? I *am* your lover. You want me to make you happy? I cannot. You want me to complete you? I cannot. You want me to survive? You must help me. I can only offer you what I have. The rest is your choice."

"Yes, I think I've heard that song before."

"What do you *want*? That I proclaim *undying love*?"

"It would be a start."

"It would be a lie. There is no such thing. You dress me up in your husband's *clothes*," he burns, yanking off Kaspar's jacket. "You want me to *play* your husband. You want devotion and fidelity and all those things that, by the way, *you* yourself don't believe in, and you want me to *beg* you to *help me*. The poor Jew, whom you finally have in your power."

"It is not me," she points out numbly, "who will be leaving."

"Makes no difference."

"I think it does."

"So it's 'Come with me, Sigrid.' That's what you're waiting for? If I say, 'Give up everything and risk your life,' you would do it?"

"I've already given up everything. I'm already risking my life."

"So then *come*, if you wish," he snorts. "Why should it be *my* decision?"

"You won't ask me?"

"I am *not responsible*," he bursts. "And I won't be *made* responsible. Not for *you*, not for anyone but myself. That is the way God created me, so if you have a problem with that fact, take it up with Him."

She stares back at him for a moment. So this is the way it will go. He will slip away to Lisbon. And Sigrid will be left to rescue his wife and daughters. Isn't God humorous. She looks at the bundle of diamonds in her hand. Then looks at her watch and says, "Take off your clothes. We have an hour."

AFTERWARD, he goes into the WC as she redresses. When he comes out in his skivvies, buttoning his shirt closed, he asks, "What are you doing?"

She has taken out Carin's darning kit from its basket beside the settee, and is sewing up the hem of his coat lining. "I'm preserving your secret."

"You're what?"

"You left your little bag of treasure unprotected in your trouser pocket, so I'm sewing it back into your coat. See how even?" she says, displaying the freshly sewn lining. "No one will ever notice."

He looks at her with a mix of satisfaction and suspicion. "So you are a seamstress. I never knew."

"I have a question for you," she says suddenly, freezing her needle in mid-stitch.

"A question?"

"What are the names of your daughters?"

She waits in the silence that follows, as if balancing herself on the point of the sewing needle.

"Is this a trade, Sigrid? You carry my diamonds, I answer your questions?"

"No. I simply think about such things. Imagine what their names might be."

"Well," he says, lighting a bitter-smelling cigarette from Carin's silver table lighter, "then imagine I've given you an answer."

———

In the morning, Kaspar is encamped in the toilet. It makes her run late.

"Sorry. It's the Pervatin," he explains blankly, walking into the bedroom in his undershirt and drawers. Pervatin, the little yellow stimulant tablets dished out to front-liners by the army to keep them alert. "It plugs you up." He retrieves his uniform breeches draped over the back of the chair and steps into them. "It's always challenging in the field. By November, the ground in Russia is too frozen to dig a latrine, so you just have to stick your ass out into the wind and grunt. Frostbite is not uncommon."

Sitting on the bedside, slipping on her shoes, she pauses at that image. "So why do you still take them?"

Preoccupied. Lugging his arms into his army blouse. "What?"

"You're not in the field any longer, Kaspar. You're at home. Why are you still taking pills?"

"You never know, Ivan could be hiding in the pantry closet or in the wardrobe, ready for an ambush. I have to stay vigilant," he says, and then shrugs off the joke when he sees she's not laughing. "They keep me going," he confesses drably. Picking one from a pillbox on the dresser, he swallows it dry. "You know? Otherwise I might just keep sleeping one morning."

Unlike Wolfram, Kaspar has not been eager to show off his wound. Even in bed, even during intercourse, he keeps his body hidden under the covers, and he never undresses in front of her. She has seen it only once really. A flash of scar tissue below the left hip, as if he had been clawed. He never complains of pain, but she can see it in his face. As he sits at the kitchen table or walks down the stairs. The minuscule hesitation before a pinch in his expression. No cane, but something in him has been no less crippled.

"So. When we married," she hears him ask, without any particular emotion in his voice, "did you love me?"

The question stabs her. She blinks at his silent face, and then answers. "I thought I did."

"And now? Do you love me now?"

Meeting his eyes. "I don't know."

Turning away, stuffing the tail of his blouse into his breeches. "Oh, come now, Sigrid. That's not a soldier's answer. A soldier's answer is 'yes, sir' or 'no, sir.' "

"I am not a soldier," she says. Shoving her foot into her other shoe, she tries to escape the room, but Kaspar seizes her elbow. "Remember what I said, Sigrid? No secrets between us. Only honesty."

She gazes into the face of the stranger inhabiting Kaspar's body. "I feel sympathy for you. I feel grief for you. But I don't feel love," she says.

"Is there someone else?"

Her lips part before she answers, "Yes."

For an instant, she is unsure what he is going to do. Strike her? Throttle her? He looks as if he is standing on a precipice, gazing downward. But then he simply releases her arm. "Now you see," he tells her as he flops down onto the chair to yank on his boots. "That wasn't so difficult."

She is frozen in place. "Is that all you're going to say?"

"What else would you have me say?"

"Are you going to divorce me?"

"Is that what you want me to do?"

"You're not even going to ask his name?"

"You sound disappointed. It's your business, Sigrid," he says, and stomps his heel into his boot. "Just don't lie to me."

SHE IS RUNNING down the corridor. The train was delayed at the post-bahnof, and now she is late. The noise of flat-heeled shoes reverberating off the linoleum, bouncing off the walls, filling her ears. She flings open the door to the stenographic room, and is met by Fräulein Kretchmar, standing like a stone monument.

"I'm sorry, Fräulein Kretchmar," she quickly pants, but then words stick in her throat. The expression on Fräulein Kretchmar's face is sculpted by a dismal finality.

"You are to report to Herr Esterwegen's office, Frau Schröder."

Sigrid feels eyes in the room stick to her, then peel away. She glances at Renate, who telegraphs her a wet blink of panic before averting her eyes back to the keys of her typewriter.

Eyes continue to follow her in the standard covert fashion as she passes through the lobby of desks that bulwark Herr Esterwegen's private office. His secretary, an old white-headed biddy, offers her a bleak glare as she buzzes the intercom.

"Frau Schröder, Herr Esterwegen."

Sigrid braces herself for the angry noise of a man known for his petty tirades, but all she hears over the intercom's hash is "Send her in."

"Come," he calls when she knocks. The door opens and she finds Esterwegen's pudgy red face scowling at her, chewing on the nail of his little finger, his eye popping behind the steel-rimmed spectacles. "*Sit,*

Frau Schröder. There's someone here to see you," he instructs. But it's not the sight of Esterwegen's anxiety that shortens her breath.

"Herr Kriminal-Kommissar," she declares. It's the Gestapo man from the cinema mezzanine. The same animal fatigue is entrenched in his face. The same sleeplessness fills his eyes. He does not speak to her, however, but turns to Esterwegen instead.

"I'll need your office, Herr Esterwegen," he informs the man.

Esterwegen blinks stupidly. "My office?"

"It won't be for long."

Another blink, before he gets the message. "Of course," he says, his scowl deepening. Standing, he thoughtlessly stuffs papers into an already bulging briefcase, then nods to the Kommissar. "Heil Hitler," he says, showing his palm, but the Herr Kommissar does not respond. He has already blotted out Esterwegen's existence. Shutting the door, he fishes a packet of cigarettes from his coat pocket.

"You don't smoke," he says.

"No," Sigrid answers.

"I've heard that about you. That and a few other things." Lighting his cigarette, he breathes out a jet of smoke. He doesn't use Esterwegen's chair, but rather perches on the corner of his desk, one leg hooked over. "Please, sit."

"Sit?"

"Yes. In the chair," the Herr Kommissar instructs.

Drawing in a breath, Sigrid smooths her skirt and inserts herself into the chair facing the desk.

"So. We have a problem, you and I," he tells her.

She stares.

"It seems your young friend from the cinema has gotten herself into some very serious trouble," he informs her.

Sigrid says nothing, swallowing back the sickly heat coming up from her belly.

"You know she's gone missing, correct?"

"Yes," she answers. "*Yes*, Herr Kommissar."

"But do you know *why*?"

"*No*, Herr Kommissar."

"Were you aware that she was trading on the black market?"

"*No*, Herr Kommissar."

"So I can also assume you were unaware that she was also illegally sheltering criminals?"

"Criminals, Herr Kommissar? She was sleeping on a cot in a pantry closet. Where would she be hiding criminals?" Inhale, exhale.

A frown. "I understand," he says, "your desire to protect her, Frau Schröder. It's only to be expected of a woman such as yourself to have some maternal feelings for a wayward creature. You would not be a woman if you didn't have such feelings. But as difficult as it may be, as *unpleasant* as it may be," the Herr Kommissar says, leaning forward with an intimate lilt, "you must put those feelings aside."

She stares frankly back at him. "I think you have made a mistake, Herr Kommissar."

"Oh, no. No mistake," he assures her, then leans over and lifts open the cover of a file folder lying on the desk blotter. Sigrid's file from the office personnel records, she realizes. He scrutinizes it from an angle, brow furrowed. "Your husband," he says, returning to the tone of a civil servant. "He's been serving on the Eastern Front."

"He was, but now he's home. He was wounded."

The Kommissar nods, expelling smoke. "No children," he says.

"No," she answers.

"Why not?"

A shrug. "Ask God."

The man suppresses a cough of smoke. "Is your husband aware that you have implicated yourself in this ugly business?"

"*No*, he is not, for I *have* not, Herr Kommissar, done any such thing."

For a moment, he seems to be making an appraisal of her, until suddenly he drops his face close to hers. "Have you been informed of the clan penalties for crimes committed against the state, Frau Schröder? If you are guilty, then, by law, so is he. Do you wish his fate to be on your conscience?"

"My husband is a *soldier*."

"Yes, and his mother is a Party member, and all of that will mean exactly nothing. The law is the law. It is very clear on this point. A criminal's *family* is considered equally as culpable as the criminal, *regardless* of circumstances."

"I have done nothing wrong, Herr Kommissar," she says stiffly. "You are not frightening me."

The man stares deeply at her for a moment, an unmoving stare as if he is trying to turn her inside out with his eyes. And then he says suddenly, in a quite level tone, "I've been married three times, Frau Schröder. So, I am aware of how the female mind works. It's not your fault," he says. "You have certain frailties built in, it's part of nature. And if you fall victim to certain misplaced maternal sentiments for a troubled girl, that would only be natural as well. There is no crime in it. Your *crime* is the enshrinement of those sentiments above the laws of the Reich," he says, and his gaze closes in on her. "Now, I'm going to ask you a question. A very important question, and I want you to think *very* hard before you answer," he tells her, smoke ribboning upward from his cigarette. "Are you in contact with Ericha Kohl?"

"No," she answers immediately.

"Let me rephrase the question, and, again, I urge you to weigh your answer very carefully. Are you in contact with the *criminal* Ericha Kohl?"

Sigrid's eyes are level. "Call her what you like, Herr Kommissar. I am not in contact with her."

The Kommissar stares at her vacantly, and then lets out a long, slow exhale of smoke. "Very well. You're free to go, Frau Schröder," he announces. When she does not budge, he repeats himself. "I said you are free to go." He tells her this, grinding out his cigarette in Herr Esterwegen's overflowing ashtray, as if he has lost all interest in her presence. Sitting down behind the desk, he picks up the telephone receiver. "Yes, this is Kriminal-Kommissar Lang, I need to place a call. One moment," he says, and covers the mouthpiece with his hand. "Is there something else you wish to say?" The question is blank, edged only with impatience.

Sigrid blinks sternly. Shakes her head. "No." Her voice is hollow. "No, Herr Kommissar. Nothing else."

"I WOULD HAVE FAINTED were I you," Renate tells her. They are in the cellar of the building, by a window that opens onto the sidewalk. Shelves and shelves, laden with filing boxes, surround them, as well as warning placards: SMOKING FORBIDDEN IN THIS AREA. But it is still a favorite place to steal a quick cigarette. Traffic noises drift in from the window.

"What? Why fainted?"

"Because men cannot abide women fainting. Tears they can withstand, but faint and they'll be on their knees beside you, patting your hand and calling for a glass of water."

Sigrid shakes her head. "I don't think fainting would have changed a thing. There wasn't room to faint."

"And all this was because of your husband?"

"My husband?"

"You said he was asking questions about Kaspar."

"He was. Yes."

"Is it the black market? What has he *done*?"

"Nothing. He's done nothing except serve his country."

Renate frowns. "Then I don't understand."

She asks Renate for a drag from her cigarette. Inhales deeply. Shakes off the sharp touch of light-headedness.

"They're very strong. Ukrainian or something. Heinz smokes them."

Sigrid can tell that Renate's also observing her closely now.

"Thanks," Sigrid says, and returns the smoldering cigarette. "I have something I have to say. Something I have to ask you."

Renate stares. Her expression shrinks slightly. "What?"

"I need to find a doctor."

"A doctor?" Confused. "*Why?* Are you *sick*?"

"No. Not that sort of doctor," she answers.

A small twist of a smile, as if perhaps this is some kind of humorless joke. "What are you talking about? What other kind of doctors *are* there?" she asks, but even as the question leaves her mouth, Sigrid can see that she has the answer. "Oh, good God." She covers her mouth with her hands, to prevent the words from leaving. "Good God, no."

Sigrid keeps her face straight.

"*I gave you condoms,*" Renate scolds in a crushed whisper. "Dammit, I gave you *condoms*. Why didn't you *use* them?"

"Do I really need to explain?"

"Could it be Kaspar's? I mean, is that a possibility? You've been with him, too."

Sigrid knows that she must remove Kaspar from the question in Renate's mind. Aborting an illicit lover's child is different from aborting a husband's. "I was with him, but not in that way," she says. "He wasn't inside of me."

"You're sure?"

"Renate, if I wasn't sure whose it was, would I even be considering?"

"All right. All right. You understand why I must ask these things. I'm sorry, but I must."

"So you've asked. Will you help?"

"I don't know. I have to think."

"This has never happened to you?" she inquires with a tad too much incredulity that Renate seizes upon.

"You mean *even though I've screwed every man in sight*? Is that what you're implying?"

Sigrid shrugs. "I apologize. You don't have to tell me."

"I'll tell you it *hasn't* happened to me, because I'm not *stupid*. I don't *make* stupid mistakes. You *do*, by the way, realize that it is *illegal*. Abortion is a crime. You could end up with two years in Barnim Strasse. And if *I* help you, I could end up joining you there."

"Please forget it," Sigrid tells her. "Please forget I ever mentioned it. I shouldn't have. This is *my* problem."

Renate smokes solemnly. "That's right. *Your problem*," she says, dropping her cigarette onto the floor and crushing it vigorously with the toe of her shoe. Then shakes her head. "I have to get back to work," she says, and frowns. "And you should, too." Saying this, she retrieves the crushed cigarette butt. "After all, there's still a war going on."

Back in the stenographers' pool, Sigrid reinserts herself behind her desk. A glance to Renate yields nothing. The room fills with the chatter of typewriters.

But then the next time she passes by Sigrid's desk, Renate drops a cigarette card beside her typewriter. On the face is a photo of the Reichsminister for Popular Enlightenment and Propaganda, Joseph Goebbels. A simian little man in a brown uniform, posed with his wife at the center of a large brood of golden-haired children. On the back, an address of a clinic in Berlin-Kreuzberg, inked in Renate's neat script. *Identify yourself*, she has written, *as an old friend of Frau Breuer.*

THAT EVENING, she hurries up the stairs of her building. At the fourth-floor landing she can hear the drone of Mother Schröder's wireless through the door. So she knocks on the opposite door instead. This time it is Carin Kessler who answers. "Come in," she says with a weight to her voice.

Inside, Sigrid glances about. Something in Carin's tone has started the acid in her stomach bubbling.

"If you're waiting for him to appear, he won't. He's gone."

She feels the blood drain from her face. "Gone?"

"When I came home from the shops, the place was empty." She takes a small fold of paper off the mantel. "He left this."

Sigrid can only stare, unable to touch it. "Have you read it?" she whispers.

"It was lying open on the kitchen table."

Finally Sigrid manages to reach out and accepts the paper from Carin's fingers. Her heart is thumping in her chest. But all he has written is, *Thank you. Please tell your neighbor that I will be in touch.*

"That's *all*?"

"Do you expect more of men?" Carin inquires.

"Where's Wolfram?" she asks.

"Ah, yes. I heard about the summit over the chessboard. Did he frighten you?" She pours out two measures of brandy from a sleek decanter. "He can be rather terrible when he's been drinking."

"He said he can produce identity documents."

"Well, then I'm sure he can."

"He said I should grow eyes in the back of my head."

Carin gives her a sideways look. "Then perhaps you should," she tells Sigrid. "Here, drink this down," she commands.

Sigrid follows orders without squeamishness. The brandy burns straight through her. "Thank you," she whispers.

A shrug. "I don't accept thanks. Too costly," Carin explains with a veneer of contrariness, avoiding eye contact. "Excuse me, but I think I need a cigarette," she says. But when she picks up the sterling lighter from the coffee table, she frowns. "What's *this*?" she says, and then turns. "Ah, now, here's something rude. Your friend appears to have consumed my entire bowl of rock sugar before he left. Now, *that's* a real crime."

Sigrid can only stare blankly at the empty bowl. "I'm sorry, I must get you some more," she says with a small, vacant voice.

"Never mind," Carin tells her. "I'm just trying to"—she shakes her head—"I don't know what, find reasons to dislike him. Actually, it's rather a hard thing to do. Dislike him, that is. Against my better judgment, I must admit, I found him charming. And if *I* found him so . . . *well*, I can only imagine," she says, with small note of shyness.

Sigrid gazes at her for a moment. "May I ask you a question?" she says.

Carin's face hardens again, though there is something of the same rueful bemusement in her eyes that Sigrid recalls from Wolfram. "Of course," she answers, and takes a sip of coffee without removing her gaze from Sigrid's face. "You want to know *why*, correct? Why I am as I am?"

Sigrid looks back at her but lets her silence be her answer.

"I've been expecting the question, actually. Sooner or later."

"Is it because of the war?"

Something like a smile forms on Carin's face. "The war?"

"All the men in the army. All the women alone."

But Carin only chuckles in a mildly disdainful manner. "You mean: what's left that's not rationed besides sex?" she says. "There are certainly women like that, lonely hausfrauen, bored with their lives and looking for some excitement. But I am not one of them. You wonder, perhaps if I haven't learned my tastes for the female gender simply because there are no men about? The answer is no. I have always been as I am, Sigrid Schröder. Always. It's not a hobby or something I've picked up, like a lingering head cold."

"I'm sorry," Sigrid tells her. "I think I've offended you."

Carin shrugs lightly, and shakes her head. "You haven't. You were curious. You asked a question. Nothing wrong with that." An interior pause separates them awkwardly for a moment, until Carin takes a breath. "But enough of that. I should tell you. I've received a telegram from my half sister this morning. She's coming back to Berlin."

"*When?*"

"Tonight. Any time now."

"I thought she was staying with her mother until the birth."

"Her mother's a drunk," Carin says, exhaling smoke. "Her mother's a drunk who despises her as a half-breed, and her husband's a monster, who fornicates with other women, because it's his *duty* as an SS man to propagate the breed. And if she looks at him wrong, he becomes violent. Fractured her arm once." Then, shaking her head, she says, "It almost makes me feel sorry for the silly little heifer."

———

There's a stretch of the Nachodstrasse in Schöneberg where German is a learned language. A street peddler offers incense for sale, and hand-painted icons of the saints and the patriarchs in their onion-shaped miters. Sigrid finds many shop windows have signs in Cyrillic lettering, but just to make sure there is no misunderstanding, they also display prominent portraits of the Führer, their brown tsar, decked with swastika flags.

The building she enters smells as much of boiled cabbage as does the rest of Berlin these days. An old woman, scarved in black, brushes past her with an unintelligible mutter. Down a poorly lit hallway, she looks for the residence plate, finds a handwritten name, and knocks on the door.

"You are Herr Melnikov?" she asks the large, thickly jowled man who answers.

"And who is asking?" the man inquires with a throaty accent.

"A friend of Grizmek," she replies.

The man clears the hallway in both directions with a look, then peers at her with deeply shadowed eyes. "Please to come in," he tells her.

The flat is neglected and full of clutter, the way the flats of unmarried men of a certain age become. The furnishings are old department-store inventory of the type Sigrid's mother bought at Karstadt twenty years before. There are knickknacks: a small clock with the gilding thinning, a tarnished horse on a bronze base, a souvenir tray from Luna Park, but nothing particularly Russian, beyond the line of gilded icons on the mantel above the coke stove, and two sepia photographs in oval frames hung on the wall.

"My parents," Melnikov explains. Gazing out from the frame is a man with a large, spongy body in a white uniform and peaked cap. His face is disguised by a thick brush of a beard as he poses besides a petite, almost doll-sized woman with frail eyes peeking out from a large bonnet. "My father was a customs official in St. Petersburg, where I was born. My mother, a poetess of sorts, though never very well known." He has opened a bottle of amber and pours out two small cordial glasses. "You'll have one," he says, and puts one of the glasses in Sigrid's hand. "*Na zdorovie*," he toasts, then drains his glass. "Drink. You must," he prods her. Sigrid only takes a sip of the thick, sugary stuff, but it seems to satisfy him. "And *that*," Melnikov sighs, "*that* poor puny *malchik* is me," he says, with a light melancholy, and gestures to the second photo of a scrawny little boy in an academy uniform posed beside a sleek wolfhound as tall as he. "Hard to believe I was ever such a minuscule pip." He sets the glass down and turns on a lamp, rolling open a length of black velvet cloth atop a desk blotter. "So. You will show me what you have brought," he says, then grins at Sigrid's hesitation. "Not to worry. I am too old and too fat to be a thief. Who could run from the police at my age?"

Laid out on the length of velvet, the diamonds become stars in the lamplight. She watches Melnikov handle them with deftness and concentration.

"You are an expert," she observes.

The Russian agrees. "I've been doing this for a very long time," he muses, examining one of the stones with an eye ring. "After the Bolsheviks, there were droves of Russians in Berlin, all trying to unload their ancestral trinkets. Grand dukes waiting tables at the Romanisches Café, pawning the jewels they had smuggled in, sewn into their wives' undergarments. It was quite a time to make money," he reminisces fondly, then nods appreciatively at the diamond he is inspecting. "Excellent. Excellent color, excellent clarity. It's been a long while since I've seen so many top-quality stones. These days, most of what I'm brought is trash. But our friend still has his eye. These will do very nicely. Did he say how much?"

"How much?"

"How much is he asking?"

"He said that you would offer a fair price."

The old Russian snorts. "Then, I suppose I must," he says. "You know, I knew him, before the war, our friend Grizmek. By a different name back then, though," he says, and winks. "I did business with his father and older brother. They were both good men. You know, *honest*. More honest than me," he concedes. "But the young one?" he says. "Like a razor. If you weren't careful? *Slash*, right through to the bone. And then he'd leave you bleeding, but do so with a most disarming smile."

"Yes," Sigrid admits. "I'm familiar with the process."

Melnikov shrugs his understanding. "He has always relied upon his women," he tells her, but then says nothing more about it. Instead he grunts as he bends over to a heavy black safe, which looks as if it has been through more than one war. "You'll excuse me," he says, "if I must ask you to turn your back."

She does, staring at the icons on the mantel, gilded but dust-laden, and listening to the trip of the tumblers and the heavy thunk of the safe's iron door.

"This is what I am prepared to offer," the man tells her, and proffers a kraft paper envelope. She takes it. Inside is a stack of Reichsmarks. She glances at him. What is the protocol? Should she count it? But Melnikov can read her mind, it seems. "Go ahead. Count it. It's no insult."

So she does. Then gazes back at the old man's face with some small anxiety. She has never held this much money in her hands before.

"I am not by nature a generous man," he explains with a shrug. "But there are times when one does what one can do. Tell him it's in honor of his father, God preserve his soul."

"Thank you," Sigrid whispers. Then buries the envelope in her bag. "Thank you, Herr Melnikov."

Sigrid turns, but at the door Melnikov adds a parting thought. "And tell him, please. Tell him I offer my condolences."

"Condolences?"

"Forgive my poor taste for asking you to play as messenger in this case, but please tell him that I was very grieved to hear of his wife."

The words turn Sigrid into cement. She cannot move from the doorway. "His wife," she repeats.

"Yes. I knew her when she was a girl in St. Petersburg. I was partners, briefly, with her uncle in export business."

"St. Petersburg." Sigrid shakes her head. "But that's not possible," she explains.

A blink. "Pardon? What is not possible?"

"His wife is very much alive. And she's not from St. Petersburg, she's from Vienna."

"No," Melnikov corrects in a patient tone. "Vienna is where they *met*. Perhaps," he suggests, "perhaps you've misunderstood."

"No. No, Herr Melnikov. I haven't misunderstood. And I saw his wife only days ago. You're offering *condolences*, but she is very much *alive*."

And now Melnikov's face is starting to darken with caution. He gives the corridor another glance, then clears his throat so that his tone is level and blunt. *"Meine Frau,"* he begins thickly, formally. "Your relationship with Grizmek is your business. I don't know what he has said to you, or what you believe. But I can assure you, I am not so old or so senile that I cannot recall the facts of my own life. I can *also* assure you that what I'm telling you is true. A terrible thing, but *true*. His wife was killed last month on the day she and her daughters were to be transported to Poland."

Sigrid searches the sagging face for some fissure in its certainty, just a small enough crack for her to slip through. But his face is a wall. Finally, she forms the question. "How do you know this?"

Melnikov frowns. "I dislike dealing with the SS, but times being what they are, I have more than one business associate at a certain address in the Grosse Hamburger Strasse. I was aware of Grizmek there. I was aware, too, that they valued his services. Also, perhaps, they were a little frightened of him. I know this sounds absurd, the SS frightened of a Jew? But that was my sense of it. They were very concerned that he never discover the truth about his wife. Especially that *durák* Dirkweiler."

"Who is Dirkweiler?"

"Untersturmführer Dirkweiler. He's a handler."

"A *handler*? What does that *mean*?" she asks, then presses him when he shakes his head. "Tell me, please. What does that mean?"

"It means what it means."

"What about the Grosse Hamburger Strasse? He was a *prisoner* there. What do you mean, they *valued* him? The Gestapo gave him beatings."

"No doubt. In the beginning."

"The beginning? What are you saying, *the beginning*?"

The Russian frowns. "You're telling me you don't know? Quite seriously?"

"Know *what*?"

Suddenly he shakes his head. More worried. "I have said enough.

A little brandy," he tells her, "and a pretty woman has loosened my tongue. That's all." He's trying to crowd her out, but she becomes immovable.

"*No*, Herr Melnikov, I will not allow you to simply shoo me on my way."

"My dear, you have your money, more than I should have paid. What more do you *want* from an old man?"

"I will not leave until you *answer* me."

"Answer you? But I *have* answered you." The door across the hall cracks open. No eye is visible, no listening ear. But it is enough to deepen the frown on the old man's face.

"Shall I scream? I will," Sigrid whispers, her voice gone raw. "I'll scream my head off."

His eyes loom. "You want the police here?"

"Do *you*? I'm sure that I am not the first 'pretty woman' who's come to do *business* at this door. I'm sure they would wonder just what kind of brothel the old Ivan is running."

The Russian's scowl goes black. But then he yanks her back inside with surprising strength, and shuts the door. He glares into her face. "Grosse Hamburger Strasse 26. It's a detention center for Jews in transit. Only there are *some* Jews, like our 'Grizmek,' who have taken up residence there. *Some* who are engaged in a very specialized line of work as a member of what the Gestapo call their 'Search Service.' Do you understand what I'm saying?"

"No. You're not making sense."

"You Germans have a very good word for it. 'Umsatteln,'" he tells her. "To resaddle in midride. Seamlessly so. Search Service Jews are given green permits that allow them to travel freely about town. They sit at café tables," he explains. "They ride the S-Bahn. They don't wear the Judenstern. They sit on a bench in the park, they go to the cinema. And they watch."

"Watch?"

"For other Jews." He shrugs blandly. "And when one is spotted, it only takes a nod. A wave. There's a Gestapo handler nearby who does the rest."

She can hear Ericha's voice in her head. *Jews who hunt Jews.* "Catchers," she breathes.

"So, the gnädige Frau knows more than she lets on."

Sigrid says nothing. There are no words available to her.

"Yes, *catchers.*" Melnikov nods. "Some are trying to save their own lives. Others, the lives of their family, perhaps. And others? I think such work can be very addictive. As a Jew in Gestapo custody, what are you? Nothing. Vermin to be trod upon. As a *catcher* you have *value.* Catchers are privileged. They have independence. They're given special rewards," he says, rubbing his fingers together, displaying the lucrative friction of booty.

"The diamonds," Sigrid whispers.

"Can you imagine? All those Torah-kissing graybeards showing up for evacuation with little fortunes tucked into their clothes and hidden in their satchels? He's of great worth to that gang of Stapo lunkheads, I've no doubt. His eye for stones is very keen. Though, as I understand it, he has quite a talent as a catcher as well. Maybe it's the same keenness," Melnikov suggests. "An eye that can spot the thinnest flaw in the embellishment of a gem, perhaps can spot that same flaw in the embellishment of a man. Or of a woman," he adds. "You know, you're not the first."

Her eyes contract. She can suddenly feel the shame, even before she hears the words.

"There was a little *tichka.* Polish, I think. She used to make his deliveries for him. And then, for a little while, a redhead. Beautiful. Maybe a Jewess. I didn't pry, you know. I'm an old man skating on very thin ice, so when I don't want to know answers, I don't ask questions," he says. And then shrugs. "So, gnädige Frau," he inquires with something like compassion, "do you still wish to scream?"

. . .

SIGRID IS CLAMBERING down the stairs, her stomach heaving. She makes it out of the building, and into the street, before the sickness overcomes her and she pukes bile into the gutter. A Berliner trots up to aid a distraught woman, but she cannot see his face. All she sees is the swastika on his Party pin. "How can I help you, how can I help you?" he keeps repeating. But she has no answer for him. She is beyond help. She has crossed into a territory far beyond the jurisdiction of curbside kindness from a stranger. Beyond the map of her existence. She has vomited out the last dregs of her old self, and is now forming into a different sort of creature. One beyond desire. Beyond mercy.

SHE CARRIES Melnikov's revelation up the stairs toward her flat, as if carrying a mason's tray of bricks on her back. She bleakly surveys the door that only yesterday was a passageway to a doppelgänger's life with Egon, but is now just a plain wooden door. She tries to summon the face of Frau Weiss. Of Liesl and Ruthi, faces she thought were stamped indelibly across her memory, but now her mind is clogged. Thickened and cloudy. She sees their faces as if they have been obscured by a layer of smoke.

When she enters her flat, she finds Kaspar and his comrades from exercise therapy downing schnapps again at the kitchen table. She is relieved to be ignored by this trio as she unties her scarf and slips out of her coat. She wants to be invisible right now. They are drinking and hooting loudly at some front-liner's joke.

Her mother-in-law is snoring in her chair by the wireless. A glass of wine has overturned and spilled onto her lap, staining her dress dark red. Sigrid does not bother to remove the glass or wake her. In fact, she takes some satisfaction in letting the old lady sleep in her own spillage.

Unteroffizier Kamphauser is standing now, his parade-ground voice engorged with hilarity, imitating a particular officer's booming commands, and the trio dissolve into fits of boozy laughter.

When there's a knock on the door that nobody but she seems to hear, she opens it and stiffens. It's Wolfram, in uniform. "Herr Leutnant," she says formally, to warn him. Suddenly the chorus ceases behind her, and there's a noise of chairs. She turns to find that Kaspar and his comrades, in the presence of an officer, have jumped to their feet. Wolfram looks embarrassed. It is the first time she has ever seen such an expression on his face.

"Please, gentlemen. Let's dispense with such nonsense," he tells them, and then leans heavily on his cane, making sure he is displaying the combat credentials pinned to his tunic as he offers his hand. "I'm Kessler."

"Kamphauser, Herr Leutnant," Unteroffizier Kamphauser declares with a heel click as he shakes.

"Kamphauser."

"Messner, Herr Leutnant," Unteroffizier Messner declares with a heel click as he shakes.

"Messner."

"Schröder," says Kaspar as he takes Wolfram's hand. His eyes are wary as if he might be expecting an ambush.

"Ah, Schröder. The master of the house. I can't tell you how highly my sisters speak of your wife."

"Yes. Thank you, Herr Leutnant," Kaspar answers tonelessly.

"In fact, I was just stopping by to deliver a small token of appreciation. We had the good fortune of obtaining a few bottles of French cognac at my office. I thought I should like to share the wealth." He slips a bottle from under his arm and presents it. "Will you accept?" he asks. "Frau Schröder?"

"You'll have to ask my husband, Herr Leutnant."

Wolfram turns his face expectantly. "It is quite smooth," he prods.

291

"Perhaps the French are second-rate soldiers, but they are quite expert at brandy."

"We'll accept, thank you, sir," Kaspar answers. "But only if the Herr Leutnant will stay for a glass."

And now a gleam of bemusement lightens Wolfram's eyes. "What an irresistible invitation," he says. "I can't say no."

Within a half hour one drinks turns into several, as the level of the cognac bottle declines. While Sigrid is drying the dishes for return to the cabinet, Wolfram is amusing his new comrades with an overtly hilarious tale of how his commanding officer had his pisser nipped off by a Red Army sniper while taking a leak. The men howl. And it's only the return of Mother Schröder to consciousness, angered and embarrassed by the spill on her dress, that finally brings the evening to a close.

In the bedroom, Sigrid lies down, still in her clothes, and stares up at the ceiling. The smooth surface is marred by a spidery web of cracks and flaking paint. When she falls asleep she dreams of climbing stairs. She knows that she must get to the top. That everything depends on this, but the stairs never end. Up ahead she can hear Ericha's voice begging her to hurry. But all she can see is darkness.

When she wakes, Kaspar is laid out on the bed beside her, still in his boots.

"Kaspar?" she asks, drowsily.

"Have you been with him?"

She feels the tension at the back of throat. "What?"

"The Herr Leutnant. I don't assume he was actually delivering that bottle of cognac to share with a gang of lowly foot-wrapped Indians."

"If you're asking me to read the man's mind, Kaspar," Sigrid answers quite truthfully, "I assure you, I cannot."

Kaspar says nothing more for a moment. He exhales thickly, and then informs her, "What I don't understand," she hears him say, "what I don't understand is why I am *alive*. I should have been killed a hundred times. But for reasons I cannot imagine, I wasn't. Men died all around me, but I remained alive. One morning, we were just outside of Rzhev. It was snowing. We were up to our knees in it. Pinned down by a couple of Bolshie MGs. I was watching one of my squad mates bleeding into the snow. Bright, *bright* red on the white. The color was so beautiful. So very seductive," he says. "And suddenly I decided I had had enough. So I stood up. Just . . ."—he hesitates—"stood up. I was going to walk straight into the Maxims and let them riddle me to pieces. I refused to survive again when all around me all my squad mates were dead or dying. But then came an explosion. It was a mortar round. That's the last thing I remember before waking up on a hospital cot."

Sigrid is surprised by a sudden feeling of compassion for her husband. A feeling of common mystery. Thousands transported. So many dead. Who decides who lives? Divine calculation? Fate? All evidence aside that neither exists, that life is a random series of numbers. One lives, six die, three live, a thousand die. She cannot help but believe that there is some kind of unknowable clockwork in operation. Some vast pattern, unseen at street level. Perhaps, because otherwise what would be the point? She starts to say something like that. Such things cannot be known, but stops when she realizes that, in fact, Kaspar is no longer beside her. Even though he may be still filling the other half of the bed with his body, he has returned to the East.

"That's a terrible story, Kaspar," she offers quietly.

And for an instant, he seems to actually see her again. Long enough for her to see him drowning in the depth of his own gaze. "No. That's a story of stupidity. But if you'd like to hear a *terrible* story, I have one of those, too."

She is not sure she does, but Kaspar does not wait for her permission. "It was August. Very hot. The air was so heavy with dust it was choking. We had been given orders by battalion to secure a little town west of Zubtsov. Just a village, really, I couldn't tell you its name, but it had cost us. I mean, cost us *dearly*. Ivan simply didn't want to give it up. They were NKVD frontier troops, and they fought like mad dogs.

We took it, lost it, then took it back again. Three days it went like this, back and forth, three days straight, with no sleep, no food, only fighting. Then, finally, the panzers arrive, and the Ivans evacuated. But what they left behind," he says, "it was inhuman. They had taken prisoners. Eleven of them, two from my company. We found their bodies, stripped naked, mutilated. Heads crushed in. Entrails exposed. Genitals sliced off and stuffed into their mouths." He pauses, gazing up at the ceiling, as if he were seeing it all there. "What we felt, when we found them? I can't explain. It was more than rage. It was more than grief. It was something that has no name."

He stares.

"That night we found a cache of vodka that the Reds had left, and got very drunk. Very drunk, and decided that such a crime couldn't go unpunished. So we assembled and went back into the village. Three squads of men. We rousted everyone out of their shacks. Women, children, young and old, and forced them into an empty horse barn. Then we boarded shut the doors," he says, gazing, "and set the barn on fire."

Silence.

"It took an hour before the screaming stopped, though it seemed much longer. At one point, there was a woman. A woman who had dug a hole under the barn with her hands, and tried to squeeze her child out. But when we saw them, we opened up and cut them into pieces."

Sigrid does not move. She cannot move. She can only listen as the tears roll down her cheeks.

"I cannot explain it, Sigrid. I will never be able to explain it. But at that instant, I believed they were *guilty*. All of them. Even the woman and her child. I believed they were all," he whispers, "less than human."

Quietly, Sigrid rises from the bed. Kaspar does not try to stop her. He does not seem to notice. In the bathroom, she manages to turn on the cold water tap to wash her face, but then can only glare at the water swirling down the drain. When she looks up, the mirror above the sink holds an image of a stranger. Hair dangling. Eyes like stones.

SEVENTEEN

THEY HAVE RETURNED to the bench in the Tiergarten near the Lutherbrücke. There's a raw, damp wind blowing, following the Spree up from the lakes and riffling through the limbs of the poplars and black chestnuts. Ericha is bundled in a ragged jacket, and her shoes are starting to display a certain shabbiness from constant wear. The leather cracked. The sole separating from the uppers at strategic seams. She attempts to strike a match for her cigarette. No sign of Franz, but this time Sigrid does not mention him. Finally the match catches and Ericha lights up. A shiver passes through her body like a wire.

"What happened to the warm coat you had?" Sigrid asks, but Ericha only shrugs off such a question. Avoids eye contact.

"Your hands and face are chapped."

"I'm on the move a lot" is all the girl says. "Don't worry about me. What do you have to tell me?"

"I have the money," Sigrid answers. "For the ship passages."

Finally Ericha looks at her.

"Don't ask," Sigrid tells her, stealing a drag from her bitter cigarette.

Ericha shakes her head. "I wasn't going to." Her eyes have taken on the depth of the river as she accepts the cigarette back. Sigrid clears the long sidewalk leading off the bridge with another German glance, then digs into her bag. "Put this in your pocket," she tells Ericha, and presses Melnikov's envelope into the girl's chapped hand. "There should be enough there for everything."

Ericha quickly stuffs it into her coat, then stares into Sigrid's face. "You see, Frau Schröder," she says. "I wasn't wrong about you."

"Yes, yes. You have the Menschenkenntnis. So I've heard. Inside the envelope there's also an address. Written on the back of a cigarette card."

"An address?"

"Auntie can't help you. It's the address of someone who can."

A moment of grayness. "You mean an abortionist?"

"Use some of the money. There's plenty," Sigrid tells her. "All you need to know is on the card." But when she looks back at Ericha's silence, she asks, "It's what you want, isn't it? Isn't it what you *want*?"

But Ericha only gazes at her, her face stamped with dread. "Will you come with me?" she finally asks.

"I can't. I'd be a danger to you," Sigrid tells her, after a German glance. "Do you recall the Kommissar from the cinema? He appeared at my work and questioned me in the director's office."

"Questioned?"

"About my relationship with you. I told him nothing, of course, but you can see how it makes me a liability. Even now it could be dangerous for us to be sharing this bench. I must have changed trains a half dozen times to make sure no one was following me."

"And was there?"

"Not as yet," she says with a glance over her shoulder. "At least not that I could see. But who knows what the Herr Kommissar has up his sleeve? He could reappear at any moment and decide to cart me off. So I think this is the last time we should meet for a while."

Ericha directs her gaze at the cracked slate of the sidewalk and smokes. Sigrid closes her eyes at the silence between them.

Then she hears, "I don't care."

"What?"

"I don't care if you've been questioned. I don't care if Heinrich Himmler is spying on you from your pantry closet. You're no more a liability to anyone than I am. It's *me* whom the Gestapo is after. *I'm* the danger." And then she says, "I've been thinking about turning myself in."

"*Nonsense.*"

"It's *not.* If I give myself up to them, then the danger will be removed."

"And what about the people you are hiding? The *lives* you have been protecting. Who will get them *out*?"

"You will."

Sigrid very nearly laughs. "Now, *that* is ridiculous."

"I think it is not."

"Ericha, you're frightened. I understand. I am frightened, too. But those little girls, their mother. They need *you*. Not me. Not anyone else. Compared to you, the rest of us are just running errands."

Ericha says nothing.

"You are *not* going to turn yourself in. Do you understand me, child? I will not permit it."

Slowly, Ericha drops her cigarette and grinds it out. "You will never," she says, "be a liability to *me,* Frau Schröder."

———

The camera flash bleaches the room as Sigrid turns the key in the lock. There is a pretty girl, her dress hanging loose around her hips, naked from the waist up. She wears a mask of comic shock, clutching a handful of letters as Auntie's former pension guest, Herr Kozig, now costumed in a postman's uniform, cups her breasts from behind. Her hair is wrapped in gooseberry braids. Postman Kozig wears a grin below his postage-stamp mustache, as he leers down at the flesh he is fondling.

It's a bit of a shock to see him so employed, but Wolfram was right. The uniform carries him. Their eyes dart to Sigrid when she enters, but neither breaks his pose. They are obviously under strict orders.

Wilhelmina von Hohenhoff peers up from behind her camera. "Concentrate!" she snaps, then follows their eyes. Her face is still as imperious as a hussar's when she glares at Sigrid's intrusion. "That door was *locked*," she declares.

"Someone," Sigrid answers, "gave me the key." And that's when Ericha shows herself. For a hard moment, the woman's stare does not lessen, until she turns back to her camera.

"One more shot," she announces.

"SO YOU'RE JUDGING ME?

"What, Herr Kozig?" Sigrid says.

The female model has dressed and departed, but Herr Kozig is still in his postal uniform, tugging uncomfortably at the collar. "The photographic pose," he answers. "The young woman in undress. I saw the look on your face."

"And what look did you see, Herr Kozig, exactly?"

"You're not my rabbi, gnädige Frau. This lady," he says with a hand in the direction of Fräulein von Hohenhoff, "this lady has generously agreed to give me a place to sleep. I was only repaying her kindness by assisting her in her work."

"Of course you were, Herr Kozig. And such demanding work, too."

Herr Kozig frowns sheepishly, but then Fräulein von Hohenhoff claps her hands for attention. She has rolled out a rack of clothing into the center of the room. Dresses, coats, hats on hooks, shoes on the bottom rack. "I have nothing that will fit the children, but if anyone is in need, they should feel free to take." Sigrid notes that the woman has yet to speak directly to Ericha, but rather skirts her, including her only in the nonspecific plural. *If anyone is in need.* Frau Weiss steps up to the rack, and touches a coat sleeve. "Oh, this is so lovely. It's been years since I've seen something stylish. I can't imagine."

"You like it? It's yours," Fräulein von Hohenhoff announces without fanfare, and opens up a tall white photographer's scrim. "That stool, please, over here," she directs Kozig, who quickly obeys. "The children," she directs, "must sit very still. No fidgeting. And no talking."

And then each face is frozen by an instant of flash. Face forward. No left ears showing. Frau Weiss looking exhausted, the little girls obedient and blank. Herr Kozig, in uniform, scowls bureaucratically back at the camera. Sigrid looks at her watch, her belly full of acid.

"You're next," Sigrid tells Ericha.

"What do you mean?"

"I mean, you're not exactly going to get very far under your own name any longer, so *you're next*."

"And what about you?"

"What about me? I'm a kriegsfrau. My papers have all been properly issued. What else do I need?"

Ericha looks at her with suspicion. But then steps in front of the scrim.

Fräulein von Hohenhoff raises her eye from the camera's viewfinder long enough to peer at her. Then sinks back down. "Eyes open," she warns, and then pulls the trigger on the flashgun. Ericha meets the burst of sharp white light without blinking.

"Thank you," Sigrid hears. She turns and faces Frau Weiss. The two girls are holding on to her, eyes large, their mother's hands petting their heads. "I know that sounds like such a small thing to say, considering what you are doing for us. What you are risking. But I don't know how else to put it."

Sigrid gazes back into the woman's face. A woman from Vienna and her two daughters. Strangers. No longer part of the story she has been telling herself. "You're welcome. I wish I could say it was because it's the right thing to do. That's why *she* does it," she says, nodding to where Ericha is seated on a chair, covertly trying on a new pair of shoes. "But me? I'm not sure. Guilt, maybe. Hope. I don't know."

Frau Weiss nods with thoughtful eyes. "Well," she replies, "whatever the reason. You're *doing* it. Which is more than most can say." The littlest, with the tiger, tugs on her mother's sleeve and whispers. "Ah," her mother tells her. "Yes. A good idea for all of us. Is there a WC?" she asks.

"WHEN WILL THEY BE READY?"

Sigrid has stepped up to Fräulein von Hohenhoff as she is lifting the scrim. "The photographs."

"I'll print them tonight."

"Good. I'll be by in the morning to collect them." Then, "What about *him*? Your new model?" she inquires, glancing at "Postman" Kozig, who is examining his official identity in one of the floor-length mirrors, his chin clean-shaven now, his postage-stamp mustache neatly trimmed. Shed, temporarily, of the U-boat shoddiness he wore in Auntie's attic.

"He snores. Loudly. I can hear him through the wall. For that reason alone, I want him out. But he can't stay past tonight, in any case. Tomorrow evening there are people coming to my studio."

"People?"

"Clients. Some of them Party members. I doubt I will be able to convince them that he is the butler."

"I understand. I'll collect him along with the photos. Has he said anything?"

"Such as?"

"Such as anything."

"No, I put him to work."

"So I saw."

"Everyone works," she answers in a mildly distracted way. "There is no free ride. Everyone earns their keep."

"Well, he hardly seems to have *objected*," Sigrid observes.

But the tone of Fräulein von Hohenhoff's voice changes. "Do you mind, may I speak with you for a moment?" she asks. Sigrid follows her over to the screened-off area where the photographs of the schnauzers watch with blunt canine inquiry as Fräulein von Hohenhoff lights a cigarette. "I'd like a realistic assessment," she declares.

"Of what?"

"Of their chances."

"Realistically? I don't know. Possibly their chances are not very good. There are certainly plenty of opportunities for things to go wrong. But one hopes otherwise. One must *believe* otherwise. What else can be done?"

"And what about *her*?"

"Her?"

"You know who."

Sigrid can only answer, "I cannot tell the future, Fräulein von Hohenhoff."

"Then what use are you?" she breathes, but then shakes her head. "Look, all I can do is give money. I can't give it to her, but I can give it to you," she says, and presses a pearl gray stationery envelope into Sigrid's palm.

"Thank you. It will help," Sigrid tells her, but Fräulein von Hohenhoff only shakes her head, and glares furiously at the smoke she expels from her cigarette, her eyes gone wet. "It's a fucking crime," she whispers. "How a creature like that can burrow into you, so you can't get her *out*. It's just a fucking *crime*."

Down in the stairwell, waiting for Frau Weiss and her children, Ericha lights another cigarette. She has picked out a new coat and new shoes from the rack, and looks better, less disheveled. But her eyes are still oven pits. "I'm going tomorrow," she says. "To the address you gave me."

"I'll come with you," Sigrid says.

"No. I know I asked you to, but I've changed my mind. This is something . . . It's *my* problem. I'd rather just do it alone."

Voices at the top of the stairs. The children descending with their mother.

"Ericha," Sigrid whispers. "You sound as if you're punishing yourself."

"I'll contact you soon," Ericha replies quickly, and opens the door to the street. "All is clear," she says, and steps out onto the sidewalk.

The next morning is Saturday. Sigrid is making breakfast. Ersatz coffee. Powdered eggs as tasty as powdered laundry soap. Stale bread that she toasts in the oven for Kaspar. Her mother-in-law has left early. She has volunteered to accompany Mundt once a week to the Party office in the Jägerstrasse to sort through the mountains of clothes, shoes, combs, stockings, and coats collected for the frontline troops and for bombing victims.

"Give my regards to the Portierfrau," Sigrid tells her, filling the coffeepot with water. "I'm sure she'll give you an earful of all my antisocial remarks."

Mother Schröder issues her a penetrating look as she is slipping on her gloves. "You think this is a joke?" she asks solemnly. "*Someone* has to maintain our good name with the Party."

When Kaspar emerges from the bedroom, he is dressed in one of the few suits Sigrid has left in the wardrobe. The clothing hangs on him as if he were a scarecrow. "Look," he says, grinning darkly. "I can attend a fancy-dress ball as a civilian."

But the sight pains Sigrid. "You've lost so much weight," she whispers. Kaspar only shrugs and sits down at the table. As she sets his plate in front of him, she asks him, "You have exercises this morning?"

"Yes," he says.

"Do you think they're helping?"

"Tossing the medicine ball with my fellow cripples, all for the greater glory of the Fatherland. Of course it's helping. It's making me a better German. Can't you tell?"

"Will you be bringing your comrades back with you tonight?"

Sawing into the powered eggs on toast with his knife and fork. "My *comrades*?"

"Unteroffizier Kamphauser," says Sigrid. "Unteroffizier Messner."

He shakes his head for a moment. "They're imbeciles," he tells her. He's chewing but doesn't appear to be tasting. His face is devoid of expression. "Only imbeciles survive, it seems." And then he asks, "What about you?"

"Me?"

"What is on the agenda for Frau Schröder's day?"

"Errands." She pours coffee into his cup, then turns away from his eyes, and starts scraping the skillet with the metal spatula. "Shopping and whatnot."

"Are you seeing him?"

Sigrid stops, the spatula frozen in her hand. "I don't know," she says. "I don't know where he is right now. I'm sorry, Kaspar. I can't have this conversation. I simply can't." She abandons the skillet in the sink. He says nothing as she pulls on her coat and ties on her scarf. But before she leaves, she is compelled to kiss him quickly on the forehead.

He stops her, taking her arm. "Are you in trouble?" he asks.

She gazes at him. "Yes."

"How deeply?"

"Deeply enough."

"So tell me," he suggests, but she can only shake her head.

"*What* can I tell you, Kaspar?" she asks sadly. "What good could it possibly do?"

To that he has no answer.

"I'm sorry," she says. "I will do my best to keep you out of it."

But as she turns to go, he still holds on to her arm. "Is he a soldier?" He asks. "There's no shame, Sigrid. There are plenty of men who've simply had enough of this war. If you're hiding him—"

"Kaspar," she says, and nearly spills it. Nearly lets the truth burst out of her. But instead she simply shakes her head and removes his hand from her arm. He does not resist.

A TRAFFIC JAM on the stairwell. As Sigrid descends, she finds that this is *not only* the morning Frau Granzinger is leaving for the country with her brood and new duty-year girl in formation, but that it is also the morning the Frau Obersturmführer returns from Breslau, now hugely swollen. She watches them collide in the building's foyer. Frau Granzinger, looming largely in her monstrous traveling cloak and flat-brimmed hat, is herding the children with her usual impatience, hurling orders at the skinny duty-year girl, in a hurry to make it to the trains before the bombers come. The Frau Obersturmführer is accompanied by a teenaged Hitler Jungvolk toting her luggage, who tries in vain to maintain his military posture in front of the skinny girl, as he is shoved aside by the hefty taxi driver handling Granzinger's steamer trunk.

"*Ah*, Frau *Schröder*," the Frau Obersturmführer calls to her. Her voice is stiffly cheery. Her face bloated, strained, and pale as lard.

"You've *returned*, Frau Obersturmführer," Sigrid observes, hesitantly.

"Yes." The woman nods, trying not to mind the jostling from Granzinger's spawn.

"*Friedrich!* Mind your manners, you little monster," Granzinger barks, and slaps the boy's head. "My apologies, Frau Obersturmführer. We're trying to catch a train."

"You're leaving Berlin?"

"For Eberswalde, yes," Granzinger answers. "Where there are no bombers and no bombs. My sister runs a hotel with her husband. She's always looking for reliable help with the cleaning and cooking. *Helga! Leave your brother alone, do you hear?* I'm so sorry, Frau Obersturm-führer, but we must be going. I'd say welcome home, only you can *keep* this town, as far as I'm concerned. I grew up here, but I'm done with the place now." With that, she bustles out the door, shouting at the taxi driver to mind the steamer.

"Up the stairs to the fourth floor," the young Frau instructs the Jungvolk boy, who only briefly hesitates at the daunting task of hauling the Frau Obersturmführer's heavy cases up the stairs.

Sigrid falls in step beside the young woman, taking her traveling bag and offering her arm as a crutch.

"I must be heavy as a cow by now," the Frau Obersturmführer announces with a painful smile.

"What happened?" Sigrid hears herself asks.

"What?"

"I'm sorry, I don't mean to sound so inquisitive. But I thought you were going to be *staying* in Breslau. For the birth."

"I was. But things," the Frau Obersturmführer tells her, "things didn't quite work out. My mother, you see, she is not the easiest person to live with. We quarreled. It was silly, really. But there it is. And here *I* am."

"Yes," Sigrid agrees. "Here you are."

It takes Sigrid longer to get to the Kantstrasse than she antici-pated. The trains are stalled because of a water main rupture. Or a sui-cide on the tracks. Or because the Feldgendarmerie are combing the cars for deserters. All of these are theories advanced as absolute fact by Berliners trapped in the underground cans with her. But when the train budges forward, further discussion ceases. The train had stopped, and now it's moving again. What more does anyone need to say?

When she finds Herr Kozig near the bronze of Wagner across

from Fräulein von Hohenhoff's studio, a frown stamped on his face below the postage-stamp mustache, he has lost the sullen snugness that he cultivated as a U-boat resident of Auntie's Pension Unsagbar, and is overtly anxious over Sigrid's tardiness. He is out of his postal uniform, with a rucksack over his shoulder and a bandage wrapped around his head that covers one eye. His clothes are still shabby, but whose aren't? And now at least his shoes are in decent order. She greets him formally, in a loud enough voice for others waiting at the stop to hear. "So sorry to keep you waiting," she says, and smiles. "Shall we walk?" Only a few eyes edge briefly in their directions.

"I was worried. I thought you'd been picked up," he whispers urgently to her as they walk briskly past the sculpture-laden façade of the Theater des Westens.

"No, just delayed. Couldn't be helped. You have the photographs?"

"Yes," he says, and covertly hands over an envelope. "You haven't mentioned my disguise," he points out, referring to the bandage. "It was the Fräulein's idea. She thought it would make me look like a bombing casualty."

Sigrid quickly inserts the envelope into her bag. "Very genuine." Across the street she spies Ericha's stocky taxi driver with the scar, leaning against the door of a green-back cab. He gives her a quick look, lifting his eyes from a folded newspaper.

"She's really a very remarkable woman, Fräulein von Hohenhoff," Kozig tells her enthusiastically. "Don't you agree? And not unattractive for her age."

But Sigrid does not answer. She has spotted Franz waiting for them, shed for once of his signature coat and trilby, and dressed in a heavy oilcloth jacket and worker's cap. Parked at the curb is a rickety Ford lorry with a gas generator attached. But when she turns her eyes to Herr Kozig, something is wrong. He has stopped in his tracks, his face suddenly drained.

"What is it?"

"That man up ahead by the lorry. He's Gestapo."

"What?"

"He's *Gestapo*, I said."

"Don't be absurd. That's impossible."

"I *know* what I *know*. And what I *know* is that *that* man works for the *Gestapo*. We've got to get out of here." And before Sigrid can attempt another word, he breaks away in a panic. Sigrid swivels back to look at Franz. He has taken a step forward with uncertainty, but then freezes up. She follows his eyes, and feels her color drain as well.

Two men in leather trench coats are jumping out of a black Benz sedan. She hears a popping noise, and one of the headlamps on Franz's lorry bursts. Everything is racing around her, but at the same time moving very slowly. She can see the gun now in Kozig's hand, the tiny nickel-plated revolver producing its little puff of smoke. "Halt! Halt!" the trench coats are bellowing. The pistols in their hands are much bigger. When they discharge, Kozig shudders and drops to one knee. And that's when Franz moves. He seizes one of the trench coats from behind with his bearlike arms. All it takes is a twist of the neck and the man dangles in his grip. One of the big guns is now in Franz's fist. He fires twice. The second trench coat crumples, but not before discharging a final round. The cap flies from Franz's head with a splatter of red, and the big man drops like a felled tree. Sigrid's mind is swirling. Noise everywhere. Screaming. Shouting. A whistle blowing. Car horns honking. Someone shouting. She turns to see the scar-faced taxi driver, shoving Kozig into the rear of his cab. *"Get in!"* he is shouting to her. *"Get in!"*

KOZIG IS BLEEDING in the rear of the taxi, and gulping breath. *"Find the wound and put pressure on it,"* the driver orders as he barges the vehicle through the streets. *"Put pressure on it or he'll bleed to death."*

Sigrid is rummaging through Kozig's clothing. "Where are you shot?" she keeps repeating. "Herr Kozig, *where are you shot?*" But Kozig only groans. There is so much blood, but finally she discovers the bullet hole drilled into the man's thigh.

"I found it! It's in the thigh!"

"*Press down on it!* Hard! Both hands!" she hears, but when she does, Kozig screams.

"It's hurting him!"

"Of course it's hurting him. He's got a goddamned bullet in his leg. It must have chipped an artery. You've got stop the bleeding or he's dead."

She forces herself to ignore Kozig's pain, and does as commanded, but blood is oozing through her fingers. "It's not *helping*. He's still *bleeding*."

"You'll have to make a tourniquet. Use your scarf!" the taxi driver yells over his shoulder to her. "Tie it tightly around his leg above the wound. *Tightly*! So it cuts off the flow."

Kozig gnashes his teeth against the agony as Sigrid follows the taxi driver's direction, but instead of her scarf, she has removed the silly bandage wrapped around the man's head. The back of the cab is pungent with the odor of blood. Everything is drenched red. But she manages to knot the bandage, tight, around the man's thigh. *"Done!"* she shouts.

"Now *pressure* again."

Sigrid clamps her hands back down over the wound, but this time Herr Kozig's reaction is less sharp. More internalized. "Where are you driving?" she calls to the cabbie.

"There's a doctor. Not far from here. We've used him before."

"He said," Sigrid begins. "He said that *Franz* was working for the Gestapo. That's why he broke."

"Well, he was right. Franz *was* working for the Gestapo."

"What?"

"His trucking business. He cleaned out the flats of Jews who'd been taken for transport to the Grosse Hamburger Strasse. He was always looking for strong backs, so I'd help him when I wasn't in the cab." He hits the horn, cursing at another driver. "I know it may sound ghoulish," he admits, "but we made money. Money for food, for ration cards, for bribes. Clothes for our U-boats."

"Well, if that's so, then tell me why was the Gestapo waiting for us with guns?"

This question the driver cannot answer. "I don't know," he admits. "Franz was having troubles. Money troubles. His wife is very sick. In a sanatorium that costs plenty. Maybe," he starts to say, but doesn't finish the sentence. "I don't know."

Herr Kozig gurgles. Attempting to speak. "Don't talk," Sigrid tells him, but he keeps trying to reach into his coat. Finally she bends her ear to his mouth. "In my pocket," he whispers. "Coat pocket. Please."

"Herr Kozig, I *can't*. I can't let the pressure off your wound."

His face is bleaching white. His mouth works. His eyes trail away for a moment and then focus on something only he can see. He starts to whisper. Something foreign to Sigrid's ear. Something ancient. *"Shema . . . Yisrael . . ."*

"Not much farther!" the taxi man shouts as he wings around a turn and bumps into an alleyway. The bump jolts Sigrid enough that she loses her perch, and by the time she regains herself and presses back down on the wound, something has changed. Herr Kozig's stare has gone still as stone.

The cab jerks to a halt. *"We're here,"* yells the driver. He leaps from behind the wheel, and hammers on a rear door of one of the buildings. A stout matron answers, and he argues with her. But Sigrid is looking at Herr Kozig's face. His mouth is hanging open. His teeth are stained brown. An eyelid has drooped so that only the white shows. The other eye no longer absorbs light. She reaches into the inside of his coat with her bloodstained fingers and removes a small folded photograph with scalloped edges. The crease down the center divides him from the two children. Herr Kozig, well fed in a tailored suit and spats, trimly barbered, posing by a garden wall. The children plump and smiling, a bow in the girl's hair, the little boy in lederhosen. She gazes at the image, then returns it to the dead man's pocket, just as the cabdriver yanks open the rear door.

"No point," Sigrid informs him bleakly. "There's no point."

THERE IS A SINK outside of the doctor's surgery, with a deep basin and a goose-necked spout. Sigrid has stripped down to her slip. The rest of her clothing is stained crimson. The water from the spout is hot, the lye soap burning and abrasive. It feels good. As she scrubs away the blood it feels as if she is scrubbing off her old skin. She can hear the taxi driver arguing again, this time with the doctor. But she can't make out the words until the door pops opens and the matron enters.

"I cannot help you. I am not an undertaker."

"So what am I to do with him? Dump him in the Landwehr when nobody's looking?"

"If that's what you decide. It's really none of my affair. I treat only the living."

The door shuts. The nurse is an obese, unsmiling woman, with an expression as stiff as her starched apron. "I am to bring you these," she announces, and plops a bundle of clothing with a paper sack on a laminated tabletop. "They won't fit," she informs Sigrid with stern satisfaction, "but it's better than walking the streets half naked. The contents of your pockets you will find in the sack. You should change behind the screen."

"Thank you," Sigrid tell her, and the woman grunts. "And *my* clothing?"

"Into the incinerator," the matron says, frowning. "The Herr Doktor is not running a laundry service." With that, she exits, thumping the door shut.

Sigrid opens her bag. Everything looks in order. She opens the envelope of photographs and meets Kozig in his postal uniform, his camera stare unblinking. Then thumbs through the rest. All there. Behind the screen she changes into the clothes. They are very baggy, but she covers them with a putty-colored raincoat and binds the belt tightly. She turbans her hair with a blue flannel scarf like factory women do. There is a rectangular mirror hanging on the wall above a chair, and the reflection it displays is of an anonymous Berliner Frau. There's a knock, and the taxi man sticks his head in.

"You are decent?"

"Come in," Sigrid tells him.

"Good. You have replacement clothes," he says, his face drawn, running his fingers through his hair. "I'm going to have to dispose of the body. The bastard doctor won't help me, not even for cash."

"How?"

"I don't know yet. I covered him with a blanket and parked the taxi behind the building. But it can't stay there long, it'll draw too much attention."

"I'll help you."

"No. No, the Fräulein would have my nuts if she knew I put you in further danger." He says this with a kind of smile.

"The Fräulein?'

"You know the one I mean. Skinny as a stick, with eyes like Judgment Day. Besides, you have your own work cut out for you."

"Yes. The photographs," Sigrid says.

The man tugs on his cap. "I'm sorry we couldn't save him."

Sigrid nods blankly, thinking of those two plump children. "Yes."

"And too bad about Franz. He was always a very good source for very bad cigars," the fellow laments, but only briefly. "Well. I shall say good-bye, gnädige Frau. And wish you the best," he says, shaking her hand.

"Good-bye," she answers. "I don't know your name."

"Call me Rudi."

"Then good-bye, Rudi. Thank you. You probably saved my life."

"No. Thank Franz. *He's* the one who saved you," Rudi says, and turns to go. But Sigrid stops him. "I have to ask you," she says. "The Grosse Hamburger Strasse."

Rudi's expression dims.

"When you went there, did you ever deal with a man named"— and she must dig out from her memory the name of the Gestapo man whom the Russian claimed ran the Search Service—"with a man named *Dirkweiler*?"

"Dirkweiler?" Almost a smile, but not a nice one. "Oh, yes. A genuine hangman. Doesn't have shit for brains. Why? You have an interest?"

She doesn't answer. Instead she asks, "Do you also know of a man called Grizmek?"

And now the smile gains a trace of bitterness. "Sure. He was a catcher," Rudi replies. "And if you know his name, then you know what that means."

"You say he *was*?"

"He was until he escaped." Rudi shrugs. "Grizmek was privileged."

"Privileged." The same word the Russian has used.

"Because he was so talented at what he did. Plenty of tobacco, plenty of food. Dirkweiler had started rewarding him with nice clothes, silk ties, watches, even cash. All confiscated from the Jews he was netting," Rudi points out. "He was partnered with this tasty redhead named Freya. A sweet piece of pie, if you'll pardon me. Together they were quite a successful couple. But then something happened. The last time Franz and I arrived with the lorry, the whole operation was in an uproar, and Dirkweiler was through the roof. Grizmek had vanished along with a sack full of diamonds from the safe. Not only that, but he had stuck a knife into his Gestapo handler. Killed him while they were on the U-Bahn, and then just stepped off at the next stop." He says this, and then gazes thickly at Sigrid. "That's all I know. Does it answer your question?"

Sigrid swallows. She picks up her handbag from where she has left it under a chair. She'd given Ericha all the money from the diamond sale, but there was still the envelope from Fräulein von Hohenhoff. She opens its flap and removes half of its contents. "Here. Take this," she tells Rudi. "This is three hundred marks."

"Well. That's impressive," Rudi observes.

"Maybe you can give it to Franz's wife. Or just use it as you see fit."

Stuffing the money into his pocket, he tells her, "Good luck to you, gnädige Frau," and climbs behind the wheel of his cab.

"Wait," Sigrid calls. "Rudi. One more thing."

Rudi looks up from the steering wheel. She had never noticed before the kindness in the man's eyes that the scar tended to mask.

"If I need to. I mean to say, if it's essential. Is there a way that I can contact you?"

"Not directly," Rudi says. "But if it's essential, you can always get in touch through the blind man."

"The blind man," Sigrid repeats.

"Zoo Bahnhof, under the clock. You'll find him there every afternoon, rain or shine."

THAT NIGHT, she takes a long soak in the bathtub. As hot as she can make it. As hot as she can stand. Her mother-in-law bangs on the door, complaining, "Are you drowned in there?" but Sigrid ignores her. In a little while, music from the wireless floats by. Mozart's Piano Concerto No. 21. She can recall her mother playing Mozart on her phonograph on a Sunday afternoon. Those pearly notes rippling through the piano's harp, and sweetening the air with its placid melancholy.

Sigrid closes her eyes, opens herself to the music, and lets herself drown in the memory of something exquisite.

EIGHTEEN

SHE AWAKENS, SEEING the dead man's face. Herr Kozig's half-eyed stare into death. The sight of Franz as his head splinters red. The images flicker inside her mind. They spot her vision as she dresses, as she fills the coffeepot, as she scrubs her teeth with powdered tooth cleaner, as she tries to insert death into the routine of her life.

"I was just about to knock on your door." Carin says, dressed in a sensibly cut coat and felt hat, coming out of her flat as Sigrid is leaving hers. She does not inquire about Sigrid's "friend." She does not even inquire about her brother. She only says, as she buttons her coat, "Would you mind stepping in for a moment?"

Sigrid hesitates, but then does as she is asked. Carin shuts the door behind them.

"I have a favor to ask of you," she announces in the sheepishly painful tone adopted by people who never ask favors. "I have to go to a funeral on Thursday out of town," she says. "I should be back by nightfall, but could I ask you? That is, would you mind looking in on Brigitte?"

Sigrid blinks. *It's not helping. He's still bleeding!* "Mind?"

"I find I'm somehow concerned about the silly cow," Carin admits. "She seems unwell. Nothing serious, of course. On and off with a fever, and a bit of nausea. That's common enough, considering how far along she is. Only, her color isn't good," she says. And then, "Now that I mention it, *your* color doesn't look so good, either. Is something the matter?"

"No. Just a lack of sleep. Isn't she seeing a doctor?"

"Yes, but the old quack thinks the cure for all ailments is a chorus of the 'Horst Wessel Lied.' You know the type. Pictures of the Führer in every room. Party pin on his medical coat. Belligerently condescending toward his female patients. I think, honestly, she's afraid of the man."

"Afraid?"

"That she'll be *discovered*," Carin whispers with arch confidentiality. "That he'll see the invisible J stamped over her private parts. *Something*." Carin shrugs. "Spending a week with her mother has addled her brain. I should have anticipated that, I suppose. I may have mentioned, her dear 'Mutti' is not only a heinous human being, but has become an equally heinous anti-Semite, ignoring the fact at she was once *married* to man of Jewish blood. That's what makes her company so enthralling. She thinks she's Goebbels in a dress now, and sometimes so do I. But I should have anticipated that a delicate piece of porcelain like Brigitte would go to pieces after a few days. In any case, if you could just look in on her."

"Of course," Sigrid answers.

Carin takes a breath. "Thank you," she says, with a touch of awkwardness. "I really have no one else to ask."

"I'm sorry, you said you were going to a funeral, and I didn't offer you my condolences. Was it someone close?" She asks this and then realizes that perhaps the question is too large for a small exchange. Carin shakes her head.

"No. Not any *longer*, at any rate. A woman I once knew," she says, straightening her coat. "Or *thought* I did. We lived together for a year."

"I'm sorry," Sigrid repeats.

"Ancient history." Carin sighs dimly, and reopens the door. "Really nothing more."

. . .

THE U-BAHN IS CROWDED and gray with the standard silence of the commute. Only the rumble of the rails fills the carriage. Sigrid takes the undercoating of noise into herself. She looks at her hands covertly. No blood. But if she closes her eyes, she can still see it there, her fingers drenched in red.

At her job, no one speaks to her any longer beyond what is absolutely necessary. News travels fast, and Kommissar Lang's visit has turned her into a pariah on the scale of Frau Remki. She doesn't mind. Mostly she prefers to be left to herself, except for Renate. It stings that Renate also seems to have forgotten her name. Finally at the filing drawers, she whispers, "So you are never going to speak to me again? Is that it?"

Renate gives her a close glare. Then turns back to her filing. "I have a suspicion about you," she says, and frowns.

"Do you really? What kind of suspicion?"

"Why were you sent to Esterwegen's office?"

Sigrid inserts a file firmly in place. "There's a girl in my building who's gotten into some trouble. Too many stoop transactions, I think."

"So why was the Geheime Staatspolizei interested in *you*?"

"Because I was foolish enough to befriend the child. She seemed lonely."

"That's all? A girl in your building?" Her voice is bluntly skeptical.

Sigrid responds with a direct look. "What else you would you like me to say, Renate?"

Renate shrugs. "I don't know. The truth, perhaps."

A frown as she continues filing. "And what does *that* mean?"

"Who was the man?" Renate asks evenly.

"What man?"

Only a tick of her eyes suffices for the German Glance. "The man you were bedding."

"I told you."

"No. No, you *didn't* tell me. In fact you made a point of not telling me."

"Perhaps I thought it was my business."

"Or perhaps there was something about him you didn't want me to know. Something that shamed you."

And now Sigrid's eyes ignite. "I think that this conversation is over," she says, gathering her folders together.

"Is he a Jew?" Renate asks bluntly.

Not a blink. Not a breath of hesitation. "Of course not, that's absurd."

"Is it?"

"Where would I meet a Jew, Renate?"

"I don't know. But I've been giving it some thought, and it all makes sense. Why did *you* have to get the condoms? Why couldn't *he* get them? Why wouldn't you answer me when I asked if he was in the army?"

"Renate, listen to yourself. You're not making any sense at all. Why would I look for such trouble?"

"I don't know. Maybe you wouldn't. But it would explain things. Like why you've been so edgy about him."

"I'm a married woman, Renate," she points out.

Renate shakes her head. "It's more than that, and you *know* it." And then she says, "I think that you and I should discontinue our friendship for a while, Frau Schröder."

"Because I don't brag about the details of my bedroom escapades?"

"Like *me*, you mean? No. That's not it. Because you won't tell me the truth. And what good is a friend if there is no truth between them?"

Sigrid picks out a file and sticks it under her arm. "Now, that's funny."

"You think so?"

"And if I *do* tell you what you want to hear, just to satisfy you? If I pretend your 'suspicion' is correct, *then* what do you say?"

Renate's eyes are fixed on her. "Then I would say I am ashamed for you. I would say that you have polluted your body, *polluted your womb* with some Jew's dirty spunk. And I would say that, were it me, I would sooner abort such a growth with a table fork than give birth to a half-breed."

Only the smallest of shrugs as Sigrid absorbs this. "Then what good is the truth?"

"*Is it* the truth?"

"No." Sigrid shoves the filing drawer closed. "It's not."

IN THE KU'DAMM there's a weinstube, a wine resturant, with a view of the tall spire of the Gedächtniskirche. It's the sort of place that Kaspar might have taken her for a birthday or anniversary years ago. The sort of place where Sigrid would have dressed to patronize. Gloves, her good dress. A stylish hat with a veil. But since the total war decrees were issued by the Propaganda Ministry, the windows have been shuttered, the awning rolled up, and the door locked. And she is dressed in the out-of-fashion coat from the doctor's office. She knocks, as instructed, as a splash of rain spatters the sidewalk. No answer. But when she knocks again, the door cracks open and an old uncle pokes out his head with a pair of soggy, looming eyes.

"Closed," the old uncle tells her.

"Yes. But I was told to come here," she tries to explain quickly. "By the Herr Leutnant."

"The Herr Leutnant?" A thick, boggy voice.

"Yes. He said I should knock and that you would let me in." A German Glance, and the old uncle opens the door just wide enough for her to squeeze through. Inside, she finds the dining room gloomy and lit only by the daylight that filters through the shutters. The bar is covered by a long canvas tarp, and chairs are stacked on tabletops. The old man is wearing a dirty apron over a wool pullover.

"Is that her, Otto?" a voice calls.

"It is, Herr Leutnant."

"Good. Show her over, won't you?"

The cover has slipped to reveal a bit of glass on a shrouded mirror. She pulls off her scarf and runs her fingers through her hair, covertly peering into her reflection.

"This way, please." The old man frowns.

She spots Wolfram first through the forest of chair legs, seated at the single table in the room set with linen. He is dressed in mufti, a cashmere coat and well-blocked roll-brim hat on the table beside his elbow. He doesn't exactly smile at the sight of her, but she likes the light in his eyes. "You made it," he observes. "You'll pardon me if I don't stand. My leg is killing me today."

"I'm sorry," says Sigrid, "but Wolfram shrugs it off." The old uncle suddenly adopts a proper hausherr's bearing and offers Sigrid a seat. She accepts, listening to the delicate scuff of the chair. "Thank you."

A correct nod for the gnädige Frau.

"Do you want something to drink?" Wolfram asks, screwing out a cigarette in an enameled ashtray that he's already dirtied.

"Oh, um. A coffee would be nice."

"Nothing stronger?"

"Coffee."

"You'll regret it," he says, putting aside the copy of the *Vossische Zeitung* he'd been smoking over. "A coffee for the lady, and I'll have another Gilka."

The old uncle shows them the shadow of a bow, then quickly removes the empty glass and the dirty ashtray. There is no fussing with ration cards.

"So, such an extraordinary establishment, and it serves only you," she notes. "I'm very impressed."

But Wolfram reacts as if perhaps he's only now noticed that he's the only patron and that he does not find this astonishing in the least. "Not me, personally, but it does serve my office," he says, lifting a leather briefcase from the floor beside his false leg and setting it on his lap. "I have a gift for you," he says, thumbing open its clasp. Out of the case comes a box the size of a book, wrapped in colored tissue and ribbons.

The old uncle arrives. "Gnädige Frau," he says, and sets the coffee on the linen tablecloth, with a sugar bowl and small cream pitcher filled with a chalky liquid that is nothing like cream. "And for the Herr Leutnant," he says, setting down the glass of Gilka with a clean ashtray.

When he shuffles away, Sigrid looks down at the package, then up at Wolfram. "Shall I open it?"

"That's normally the procedure with a gift," he says.

Carefully, she removes the tissue from the box and opens the lid. It is a book. A newly minted edition, bookshop fresh, with the author's Charlie Chaplin face glowering up at her from the dust jacket. His eyes like pellets of coal. The fetlock of hair slicked over his brow. The postage-stamp mustache. Sigrid stares into the face. The title is in heavy script: Mein Kampf.

"I thought this was an appropriate choice. Have you read it?"

"No."

"Then I won't tell you how it ends," he says, and then assures her, "You should find everything required within."

She gives Wolfram half a glance, trying unsuccessfully to read his face. Then lifts the book's cover only long enough to see the thick envelope fitted securely into the hollowed-out pages.

"I see. Very clandestine."

"I think you'll find that all is in order," Wolfram tells her. "Except I was expecting a man with a Jewish face. You left him out."

"He's dead."

"Really? What happened?"

"It doesn't matter," she says as she replaces the book into its box, then inserts the box into her bag. "He's dead. That's all."

"How different you've become," Wolfram observes. "So much tougher than you were."

But Sigrid only shakes her head. "No. Not tougher. Just numb." Then she frowns at her cup. "This coffee is terrible."

"I tried to warn you. The Kümmel, on the other hand, is very smooth. Smoke?"

"I'll share one," she tells him, and watches him light up. The patrician's profile. The damage reflected in his eyes. "I'm sorry, Wolfram," she suddenly says, observing him.

He exhales smoke, and lifts an eyebrow. "Sorry? For what are you sorry?"

"I don't know. Something."

"For breaking my heart?"

Almost a smile. "Is your heart broken? I doubt that. I hear you go through women like you do cigarettes," she says, cheating a drag.

"Again. You cannot believe everything my sister tells you," he repeats. "So you haven't mentioned."

"Mentioned what?"

"Our friend the chess player. I hope he has been improving his game."

"He's playing well enough to beat me," she tells him, staring archly at a spot on the table linen. Then shakes her head. "I don't know what to do about him."

"Then I think that you had better drop him."

She lifts her eyes.

"Please understand, I say this not out of jealousy, Sigrid," he tells her. "I don't believe in jealousy. But he is dangerous. Dangerous because he has nothing to live for. And even more dangerous, because he doesn't yet know it."

She takes a breath. "And you can tell all this, Herr Leutnant, from a chess game?"

Wolfram shrugs, and taps his cigarette ash. "You will do what you will do, Frau Schröder. That much I have learned about you. But remember, you ignored my warning about the coffee." Picking up his snifter of Gilka, he clinks it against Sigrid's coffee cup in a toast. *"Prost,"* he offers efficiently, taking a deep swallow, sets down the glass, and removes a creamy white envelope from his coat, sliding it across the table.

A look, and then she removes the envelope's contents and pauses. Another Reisepass. Lifting open the document's linen facing, she is confronted by her own glum expression. "So. You *did* steal my card," is all she says.

"I needed a photograph. And I knew you would never stand for one. So now, Frau Schröder, should you ever decide to take a holiday outside the borders of our Fatherland, you have the Reisepass necessary to satisfy the rubber-stamp brigades."

"I see," she says, and reinserts the booklet in the envelope, but as she does a small brass capsule tumbles out onto the table linen. "And what is this?"

Wolfram reaches over and picks it up in his fingers. "Remove the brass cap like this," he instructs, exposing the tip of a tiny glass vial. "Insert the glass vial into the back of your mouth, and bite down. In case," he tells her quietly, "you ever need to make a *different* decision."

Sigrid gazes deeply at the vial as if gazing at a hole that has suddenly opened up in front of her. "Is it . . . Is it painful?"

"Painful?" he repeats. The muscle in the line of his jaw twitches lightly. "It's instantaneous." Slipping the brass cap back into place, he reinserts the capsule into the envelope. "Are you sure you won't have that glass of Gilka now?"

"Wolfram, I think I may be under surveillance," she says suddenly. His response is unperturbed. "Yes, that's right," he nods. "One of the bloodhounds of the Burgstrasse Gestapo office has your scent in his nostrils. A Kommissar Lang, I think."

Sigrid feels a jolt. "You mean you *know* this?"

"The Abwehr doesn't exactly have a brotherly relationship with the Geheime Staatspolizei. But I try to keep a few of their number on our payroll. There's a fellow named Rössner. Not so bad. He's an old-time Kriminalpolizei bull, who thought the Gestapo would be good for his career. In any case, he's been very cooperative."

"*Cooperative*? I don't understand what that means."

"Keep an eye peeled for him. Medium height. Not much of a chin, but more off a belly. Ears stick out like a monkey's. He favors a brown snap-brim fedora. You'll spot him, I'm sure."

"And he's *watching* me?"

"Yes, but I pay him to have very poor eyesight. Also, he much prefers stopping off at the corner Kneipe for a short one to traipsing about town wearing out his shoe leather."

She gazes at him with gratitude and regret. "Once again, you are my champion, Herr Leutnant," she says.

But Wolfram only turns up his wrist to frown at his watch. "I must go," he says. But outside, he turns to her. "Here, take this. It's the key to the flat in the Askanischer Platz," he tells her. "In the event that you have use of it." The street is chilled by a sharp breeze.

"Yes. Thank you," she tells him. "It could be handy." And then she asks, "Will you kiss me?"

The gun sight. "Why?"

"Because I'm asking you to. Because I want you to."

A small bob of his Adam's apple and the gun sight lifts. He kisses her once, as if he might steal a breath from her, then breaks away. She watches him quick-march down the Ku'damm with his cane, as the clock in the Gedächtniskirche chimes the hour.

Two o'clock.

She must head for the zoo.

. . .

FOR SEVERAL MINUTES she pretends to be examining the posters plac-
arding a *Litfass* column across the street. Paper drives are advertised.
Clothing drives. *Get rid of old clothing and shoes!* A bloated toadlike face:
The Jew—The inciter of war, the prolonger of war, the caption incites.

She is watching the street. Watching the pedestrians on the sidewalk. But there is no monkey-eared fellow with a big belly and wearing
a snap-brim hat. So she crosses at the signal and enters the Zoolo-
gischer Garten through the Gartenufer gate. Passes the beaver dam,
now vacant after bombing, as well as the rabbit hutches and the bear
den. She has a memory of standing in front of the bear den, holding
her mother's hand, wondering if the huge brown sow, named Berlonia, frisking with her cubs, was really as hungry for bad little girls as
her mother had always claimed. Now Berlonia, if it is still she, is alone.
Her snout silver. She appears listless and apolitical. No matter, Sigrid
is on the lookout for a different species of wild beast. For an instant,
she thinks she sees him, prowling the path. But when she looks again,
he is gone.

The Grosse Raubtierhaus is still intact. Still warm and smelling of
animal needs. Animal hopes. She finds Ericha stationed in front of an
enormous white Siberian tiger, pacing off the length of his cage. There
are many words she could speak. Too many to actually fit into a work-
able sentence. So instead she simply asks. "Am I late?"

Gazing at the cage. "Yes."

"I'm sorry," she answers. Then her voice dips, and she pulls off her
gloves. "There's a man over there watching us."

"Yes. He's a friend. Call him Becker."

"And what does he do, Herr Becker?"

"He says he once trafficked cocaine in Friedrichshain. Maybe that's
true. All I know is that he's been expert at losing the Gestapo."

Sigrid gives the man a glance. Tall, reedy, chinless. In his thirties, wearing a fur Alpiner on his head. He's smoking while studying a racing form.

"I see," Sigrid says, thoughtfully. "And where did you find a gentleman with such a skill?"

"You know the rules," Ericha reminds her. Then, staring forward, she says, "I spoke to Rudi. He told me what happened in the street."

"And what do you think it means?" Sigrid asks.

"I think it means Kozig panicked. He recognized Franz from the Grosse Hamburger Strasse and assumed the worst."

"But that doesn't explain how the Sipo came out of the woodwork."

A shrug. "Maybe they thought they were onto something and were simply shadowing Franz to see what turned up."

"There's also another explanation."

"That Franz betrayed us?"

"You think that's impossible."

"I think nothing is impossible. But it makes no difference now. Besides, he knew only so much."

"He knew about *you*," Sigrid points out.

"I've already switched to a different location. Even if the Gestapo *did* turn him, their information will be useless to them."

"So. What next?"

"We continue as planned, what else?"

Sigrid takes a breath. She looks into the tiger's face, and the tiger looks back. "I have something for you," she tells the girl, and hands her the box. "But don't read it until you have the necessary privacy."

Ericha takes the box. Lifts the lid on it, then closes it again. "That's quite a joke," she says without smiling.

"Not mine. But appropriate, I think. It contains everything that's required."

"Everything that's required," she repeats vacantly, turning her attention toward the tiger. "Do you feel sympathy for him?"

"For the tiger?"

"For the tiger in a cage." She gives a shallow sigh. "When I was a child, I thought I *was* a tiger. My mother assumed it was a game. That I was pretending. So at first she indulged me. Then she became frustrated when I wouldn't stop. And then angry, I remember, when I refused to use a knife and fork at the table, because tigers ate with their paws and fangs. She exploded. It was the first time she struck me. The first time," she says. "But not the last." And then she stares into Sigrid's face. And Sigrid sees the tiger in it.

"Ericha, you know I must ask you."

"It was a trap," Ericha announces, cutting her off.

Sigrid turns her head. "What?"

"The address on the cigarette card. That's what you were going to ask about, correct? The abortionist? It was a trap. I spotted them as soon as I stepped off the tram. A pair of them in the front seat of a sedan, waiting."

Sigrid is feeling an abyss open up in her. "You're *sure*?"

"You think by now I can't recognize the Sipo when I see them, Frau Schröder? I'm sure. Very sure. It was a black Mercedes 260D. The standard Gestapo hearse. I pretended to be waiting to catch a transfer just to see what would happen. Then there comes a woman, alone, going up the steps and through the door. They wait for a few minutes. Give her time to pay her money, I suppose. That must be part of the arrangement, so they can get their cut. Anyway, they wait for another moment, then out of the car they come. Tossing away their cigarette butts. Up the steps and through the door, too. I wait until I see them reverse the process, out of the door and down the steps, only now they have the woman between them in wrist manacles and she is sobbing. She collapses at the bottom of the steps, so they drag her on her knees into the rear of the car."

"Ericha," Sigrid whispers, her eyes steaming.

"I don't blame you," Ericha says, staring back at the pacing tiger. "I don't blame you," she repeats. "I only," she says, but then can't say any more. The tears roll coldly down her cheeks, until Sigrid envelops her.

WALKING DOWN THE TAUENZIEN STRASSE, she keeps her arm clamped around Ericha's shoulder. Becker is close behind, but, crossing at the light, she picks up something else behind them as well. A feeling. A presence. She risks a glance at the dusky shadows of pedestrians, head bent against the cold, and for an instant she catches him. Far back, but there.

"What is it?" Ericha asks.

"Nothing."

"You've started walking faster. Is there trouble?"

"It's nothing."

"We should split up."

"No. No, we're not splitting up." Hurrying Ericha down the steps to the U-Bahn platform, they catch a train as it is about to leave the station. The doors close. She searches the car and sees that Becker has made it aboard, standing, holding on to a handle, eyes still glued to his racing form. But no sign of Egon in pursuit of her.

"Where are we going?" Ericha whispers.

"Never mind," Sigrid tells her. "You'll find out."

THE FLAT in the Askanischer Platz is cold, and the air inside is stale. Sigrid turns on a lamp by the bed, illluminating the room's drabness in the pale output of a wartime lightbulb. Without Wolfram in the bed, the place seems squalid. "Sit," she commands Ericha, and sets about lighting the coke stove. It stinks of coal dust and sulfur but produces a few fingers of warmth. Ericha draws in a breath and holds it before finally exhaling.

"We're getting them out," the girl says, sluggishly crawling out of her coat. "The mother and her children."

"When?"

"In three days."

"And how will it happen?" Sigrid asks from the window, peering around the edge of the bulky blackout curtain.

"They'll take the train to Dresden first, then from Dresden to Lübeck. It's the longest way, but the cheapest. Also the safest. The Gestapo comb the express trains. Anyway, that's how we have it arranged. I'll meet them at the Nollendorfplatz, pass on their documents, and escort them to Anhalter Bahnhof. The intercity to Dresden leaves from platform B at five past two."

"Then this spot is perfect. You can stay here till then," Sigrid says. Down in the street, ghost lights illuminate the arches of the station's façade. She tries to catch Egon's figure in the settling twilight, but figures populating the Saarlandstrasse are no more than silhouettes. "I don't see your man Becker," she says.

"He's out there," Ericha assures her leadenly. "Whether you see him or not."

"You should tell him to be on the lookout for a man with a brown snap-brim who has a pair of ears that stick out. He could be Gestapo."

But Ericha says nothing in response to this. Only stares into the air.

"What time have you arranged to meet them?" Sigrid asks.

"What?"

"What time have you arranged to meet them? The woman and her children."

"An hour before the train. But I should mention. There's been an addition."

"An *addition*?"

"Not another U-boat. Just a man who needs to get out of the country."

Sigrid suddenly feels off kilter. "But we have no papers for an *addition*. No plans. No money for the passage . . ."

"He has his own resources. We are simply to transport him to Lübeck with our group and get him on the ship for Sweden."

Sigrid narrows her eyes. "Say that again?"

"Why? I think you must have heard me."

"Heard you, yes. But the way you put it: 'We are simply to transport him'? Are you following *orders*?"

She frowns "No. Of course not orders. But I've made connections with another group. A better-funded group, with a much broader network. Not just in Berlin. We can increase our effectiveness tenfold if we work with them."

"Work with or *for* them?"

"It's cooperation. *Please*, Sigrid."

"I don't understand."

"You don't have to understand," the girl suddenly bites. Her eyes flash blankly, and then cool. "I'm sorry," she offers. "I'm sorry, I just can't answer questions. It *is* what it *is*," she says. "Can you accept that?"

Sigrid looks into the girl's face. She looks suddenly childlike.

"Yes," Sigrid whispers. "Yes, of course I can. If that's what you need me to do." Ericha holds her gaze for an instant longer, then turns away.

"I'm very thirsty," the girl says with a small swallow. "Do you think," she asks, "that I could get a glass of water?"

"Water?" Sigrid repeats. Then stands quickly. "Yes. Yes, I'll bring it to you." She goes into the small kitchenette across from the bath. There's a window over the sink and a large rip in the blackout curtain. As she fills a water glass from the tap, she can see a flicker of light down in the alleyway. A match touching a cigarette, which glows red and then vanishes.

Ericha accepts the water glass without words, and Sigrid watches her drain it in two long drinks, then takes away the emptied glass and sets it on the nightstand.

"You must rest," Sigrid tells her. She expects resistance to this, but is surprised when Ericha slumps sideways on the mattress.

"Rest," the girl repeats. "That's a foreign word."

Sigrid slips off Ericha's shoes and lifts her feet onto the bed. Drapes the bedspread over her and perches on the edge of the mattress.

"I want you to promise me something, Frau Schröder," Ericha says. "When the day comes to do this, I want you to promise me that you'll stay home. Press your husband's shirts like a good hausfrau or argue with your mother-in-law. Better yet, go to your lover."

"Ericha."

"Everything will go smoothly without you. It's all planned out, and there's no reason why anything should go wrong. But if it *does*, then there's no reason they should get us all. So you will promise me that you will stay away from the Anhalter Bahnhof."

"And if I don't?"

"You must."

"So now *you're* giving the orders?"

"Someone will have to continue, Sigrid. If we're taken, then someone must be left."

"What about your new friends with their broad network. *They* won't be continuing?"

"They're not interested in saving people. They're only interested in politics. So you must agree. You must promise me."

"Close your eyes," she whispers, and brushes a strand of hair from the girl's forehead. "If I *must* promise you, then I *will* promise you."

Ericha nods lightly. "Thank you," she breathes as her eyes drift shut. But when Sigrid starts to stand, the girl squeezes her wrist.

"Stay," Ericha whispers. "Can you? Just for a bit?"

Gently, Sigrid places her hand over Ericha's. "Yes," she whispers. "I can stay."

. . .

SHE IS STANDING on the landing, the walls shake with the bombing. Fire scorches the ceiling, and all she can think of are the *sand buckets*. *Where are the sand buckets?* When the floorboards beneath her feet separate, she latches onto the railing, but the railing is attached to nothing, and she is falling, plummeting into a swirling black hole.

Sigrid awakes with a start, settled in the padded armchair by the bed. She blinks, dimly trying to decide where she is, and then wipes her face with her hands. The stove has gone out, and the room is cold. She can see daylight edging through a crack in the blackout curtain, so she shoves it aside, and the Berlin morning invades the room. Her heart falls when she sees that bedclothes are twisted in a heap but the bed is empty.

SHE LOCKS THE DOOR to Wolfram's flat and travels down the stairs, excusing herself around a young female Ostarbeiter scrubbing the tile floor of the foyer. The woman mumbles contritely in Polish and keeps her eyes on her scrub bucket. Outside, the chill of the morning awaits her. She carefully glances about, checking for idling autos or any men loitering innocuously about the newspaper canisters, but sees only a few Berliners minding their own business as they travel the sidewalk. So she is shocked when a hand seizes her from behind by the hair, and yanks her to one side. "This way, Liebste," Egon tells her and guides her painfully into the narrow alley around the corner.

"You're hurting me."

"*Hurting* you? You're lucky I don't wring your fucking *neck*." He pushes her roughly against the alley wall and presses his face into hers. Holding up the diamond pouch, he turns it upside so the contents spill out. "*Rock sugar*," he seethes. "You took my diamonds and left me *rock sugar*."

"That's right," she breathes.

"*Why?*"

"Because there are those who have needs greater than yours."

"Sigrid," he says, pronouncing her name as if he might bite it in half. "Sigrid, I *want* my *diamonds.*"

"Go to hell," she tells him.

"You *bitch*," he swears, and cracks her across the face with the back of his hand. She expels a yelp of pain, as he seizes her chin in his hand. "*I want my property!*"

"It's not," she manages. "It's not *your* property."

"It *is*! It belongs to *me*!"

"*No.* No, it belongs to the Jews whom you sent to their *deaths.*"

Silence.

"It belongs to *them*! Like that pretty watch you wear. Like the money in your pocket and the fancy coat on your *back.*"

His face hangs in front of her, still contorted.

"I know what you *are*," she assures him. "I know what you've *done.*"

His teeth grind. "You know *nothing.*"

"How many *lives*, Egon? How many lives did you trade for your own?"

"So now you think you are the expert. But you're not. *You're an idiot!* A silly cunt who knows *nothing*!"

"Tell me about Freya."

"Freya," he repeats.

"I hear she is quite the dish. Was she good in the *sack*?"

"My God, is *that*—" He simply can't believe it. "Is *that* what this is? A *woman's jealousy*? You make me ill, Frau Schröder."

"You're a *murderer.*"

"*No.* I'm an animal. A simple human animal. If I kill, it's for the sake of survival."

"You mean *your* survival."

"Yes, my survival!" he blasts her. "You know, you are so *thick*. Such a fucking hausfrau. I think I would like to *crack* your stupid skull open! Do you know *that*?" he hisses, and then freezes up.

She watches his expression go rigid. Her breathing deepens. "Do you feel that?" she asks him.

He stares. "Yes."

"Then you know what it's for," she says, pressing the muzzle of Kozig's revolver into his belly.

"You won't use it," he assures her. "Though I wish to God you would."

"Take a step back," she commands.

He waits, but then steps back. She digs something out of her pocket and then drops it on the damp black paving stones. A brown envelope and a fold of Reichsmarks fastened together with a thick elastic. "That's for you. A Reisepass, a new Arbeitsbuch, a commercial registry card, and travel permit, plus a letter of exemption from military service due to your *essential* war work. Your name is Hans Richter. You're an assessor for the National Insurance Office," she says, still gripping the revolver. "Everything you'll need to get to where you're going, including two hundred marks and an up-to-date subscription record for the *Völkischer Beobachter*."

"May I pick it up?" he asks grimly.

"Yes."

He does so, stuffing the envelope into his coat pocket. "Two hundred marks," he says, "isn't going to get me far."

"It's what you've got. You should count yourself lucky that you're traveling west instead of east."

"And what if I were to push you against this wall right now, and kiss you hard on the mouth?"

"First you want to kill me, then you want to kiss me. You should make a decision, Egon."

"You're the one who is aiding my escape with one hand, while pointing a pistol at me with the other. I think it's *you* who should make a decision."

She stares into his darkened face. Then thumbs back the revolver's hammer. "I don't know much about guns," she admits. "But I believe the next step is to squeeze the trigger."

Egon lifts his eyes from the pistol. "Becoming a killer takes courage, Frau Schröder. Not fairy-tale courage, but the courage to leave it all behind. To become a different sort of creature." For a moment, he gazes at her. "I'm not sure you've reached that point yet."

She tightens her grip on the revolver's handle. She knows that if he tried, he could wrench the thing from her hand. She wonders if he knows it, too. His gaze tells her nothing. It is like staring into a face cut from stone. Then a noise comes from the end of the alley. The Polish scrub girl opens a door and dumps her pail of dirty water. She looks up at them, holding her bucket, and pauses. Speaks a word in Polish. Egon frowns. "Next time," he tells her, "you'll have to be stronger," and then gathers his coat closed and stalks away.

WHEN SHE ENTERS the flat in the Uhlandstrasse, she finds it empty. The door to 11G creaks open into silence. She takes off her scarf and hangs it up. Slips off the coat and hangs it up, too. The wind rattles the taped window glass briefly. She smooths her skirt as she surveys the room's emptiness. Then walks over to the stove. Drops in three briquettes of coal with the shuttle, and strikes a match. The fire catches. It burns evenly, obediently. She feels the heat on her face grow.

In the bedroom, she checks the mirror. Touches the spot on her cheek where he struck her. A pinkish imprint of the force of his knuckles. It hurts, but she feels numb to the pain. She turns away and retrieves the cigarette tin. She wonders for a moment if Kaspar has ever discovered the tin's contents. She certainly hadn't made much of an effort to hide them, even after her run-in with Mother Schröder. A few pairs of flannel stockings, and a nylon chemise in a drawer constitute their only camouflage.

The stove is hot by now, emitting a stinging heat into the air. She must lift the lid with the iron tongs. A bright orange fire fills the stove's belly. Sigrid opens the tin, and tugs open the ribbon binding the packet of letters. She opens the flap on the top envelope, revealing the heated upstroke of his handwriting. The words *without mercy* are all she can read. Then she closes the flap and drops the letter into the stove. The envelope writhes, then blackens as she watches it disintegrate in flames.

It takes only a matter of minutes before all of them are ashes.

NINETEEN

S HE SPIES THE MAN with the monkey ears and the snap-brim brown
fedora on the train. After the Nollendorfplatz, she sees him, standing a few meters away, a newspaper tucked under an arm, as he clings to
the handrail, intentionally paying her not a whit of attention. When she
leaves the train at the Hallesches Tor, she catches him briefly behind
her, but then he disappears.

Inside the patent office, she hurries past the old guard, who must
call her back to look at her identity card. She is late. Impatiently waiting. When she enters the stenographic room, there is a brief cessation
of typewriter chatter. When Fräulein Kretchmar calls her into the office
in the corner, all eyes remain locked in their proper places, and the rattle of keys on the paper sounds like a kind of thunder. Only Renate lifts
a glance from her desk, but her eyes are expressionless.

In the office, Fräulein Kretchmar closes the door and seats herself
behind a steel desk. "Sit, Frau Schröder," she instructs.

"No, I don't think I will, thank you," Sigrid answers.

The woman gazes morosely at her through the lenses of the pince-
nez adorning her nose. "Very well, as you wish. I'm afraid I must
inform you, Frau Schröder, that I have been directed by Herr Esterwegen to dismiss you from your position. This to take effect imme-

diately. If you have any personal effects, you may retrieve them from your desk."

"And may I inquire, Fräulein Kretchmar," Sigrid asks thickly, "as to the reason for my dismissal?"

"It has been determined by those in superior positions that your continued employment by the Reichspatentamt would be a detriment to productivity, and a risk to the good name of the office."

"I see," Sigrid says dully. "And is that your opinion as well?"

But Kretchmar only shakes her head, her mouth clamped in a tight line. Choosing a rubber stamp from a rack, she thumps the file on her blotter. "Take this to the second floor," she says, handing it over. "Your final wages will be issued to you."

Sigrid pauses only an instant before accepting the file.

Kretchmar's attention turns to the papers stacked on her desktop. A vein pulses in her neck as she says, "Best of luck to you, Frau Schröder. Heil Hitler." But then, as Sigrid turns her back on the woman and slips her hand onto the door handle, Fräulein Kretchmar finds the words she could not speak a moment before. "You *understand*," she says, "you understand that I had no say in this matter. The decision was made by higher authorities. I can only do as I've been instructed."

"I *understand*, Fräulein Kretchmar, that someday," Sigrid replies, "someday you will open up your eyes and wonder what has become of your life. And the only answer will be that you have *squandered* it, trying to prove something to these men. These *higher authorities* of yours. Trying to elicit from them some minuscule measure of respect or equality, which you will never receive. Not ever."

Kretchmar gazes back. Behind her, the message canisters whoosh through the pneumatic tubes.

ON THE TRAIN, Sigrid burrows into the silence beneath the rattle of the cars. She doesn't think of the patent office. She doesn't think of the singular blankness of Renate's glance. She doesn't even think of Herr Kozig's bloodless death mask. She thinks that, if she closes her eyes, she can still imagine Egon's hands touching her body. The pleasing roughness of his fingers on the skin of her shoulder. His palm lightly dancing across her nipple.

Suddenly there is an intrusion. A body squeezing into the space beside her, too close. For an instant she thinks Egon has returned, but the body is the wrong size. Too stringy. No meat on it. She gazes into the angry, hawkish face of the U-boat youth from Auntie's pension.

"Where is he?" he demands in a scrubby whisper.

She gazes back without words.

"I have a knife," he hisses, "so you'd better tell me."

"I don't know what you're talking about."

"Yes, you do. The catcher named Grizmek. I've seen you with him. Where is he?"

A blank glare. She thinks for an instant of Herr Kozig's little pistol she has wrapped in a handkerchief at the bottom of her bag. "I have no idea," she says.

"You're lying."

"I'm not."

"Tell me. Tell me or maybe I'll slit your throat right here."

"No," Sigrid says, not removing her eyes from the boy's. "No, I don't think you will."

The boy's face clenches like an angry fist, but his eyes are suddenly enraged with grief. "He murdered my sisters. They're dead, because he turned them in to the Gestapo. He might as well have killed them with his own hands."

"Frau Schröder?" a voice inquires with a sharp concern.

Sigrid's eyes twitch toward a stubby soldier who is leaning forward from the opposite side of the carriage. It's one of Kaspar's drinking comrades from the kitchen table, though it takes her a moment to summon the name. "Unteroffizier Kamphauser," she says.

"I thought it was you," he says. "Are you all right?" he inquires more closely, his voice gaining weight as his eyes roll toward the youth, training the gun sight gaze on him. "Is this Schurke giving you trouble?"

But before she can answer, the train bursts into the station, and the boy is up, shoving into the crowd exiting to the platform. The soldier stands abruptly, as if to give chase, but Sigrid waves her hand. "No. No, please. It's fine. Just an overly excited boy." The doors are rolled closed, and the train ambles forward. She gains a glimpse of the boy's face on the platform for a moment, staring with anguished rage.

"Thank you, Herr Kamphauser," she says, her hand pressed to her breast, slowly breathing in, slowly breathing out. Recovering.

The soldier sits down, then nods his head. "No need for thanks. Though, actually, I'm Messner. Kamphauser is the tall one."

A blink of confusion, then, "Oh. I'm so sorry."

"No need."

"My head, you understand, is so full of cobwebs these days."

"It's nothing. I answer to anything," he grins. A joke. In the gloom of the U-Bahn, his complexion has lost its fermented ruddiness and gone muddy. "Frau Schröder, please excuse me. I don't mean to talk too much. Or to bother you. It's just that there's something I feel I should say. It's something I've been thinking about, and since we've met like this . . ."

She looks at him carefully. "Yes?"

"You know," he begins with a slightly uncertain note in his voice, "I just want to say that your *husband* . . ."

"My husband," she repeats blankly.

"Your husband," he says, "is really the sort that keeps a mutt like me going."

Another blink. "He is?" she replies, surprised by a sudden urge to listen.

"Oh, yes. I mean, I *know* what I am, Frau Schröder." He chuckles bleakly. "I'm dirt. I'm nobody. But a man like your husband, who

339

worked as a bank officer. Who has a nice flat and a good wife. For him to invite me to his home, it *means* something," he says. "It truly does. I don't mind admitting that I'm going to miss him greatly."

Something in her stops dead. "Say that again."

"I said, I'm going to miss him," Messner repeats. "When he returns to active duty."

She hears this, then watches the impact of her expression on his.

"You knew this, didn't you?" He is sounding suddenly anxious. "I mean, you *must have* known this already."

"Are you saying," Sigrid breathes in. "Are you saying that he's been recalled to the front?"

"No. No, not recalled," Messner frowns. There's a helpless insistence to his voice. "But surely you *know* this, Frau Schröder."

"Know *what*, Herr Messner?"

"He volunteered." A crooked pain shapes the man's face. "When he heard that his regiment was being redeployed to the Ukraine, he volunteered to rejoin them."

"But. But he *can't*. You must be wrong about this. He's been *wounded*. He's still going to the hospital for therapy, for God's sake."

"One of the doctors at the hospital certified him as fit."

"*Fit?* And is this doctor *insane?*"

"I'm . . . I'm certain they won't put him on the line," he tries to reassure her. "There are plenty of jobs in the rear. He could be clerking for a transport company, just as he's doing now," he says with hope.

"No." She shakes her head at the floor of the carriage. "No, this is too much."

"I *apologize*, Frau Schröder. I opened my trap when I shouldn't have, obviously, and I'm sorry. Please don't tell him it was me who spilled the beans, will you?" he pleads. "I wouldn't want him to think ill of me."

Sigrid looks back at Messner, but really she has stopped seeing the man. Stopped hearing what he is saying.

KASPAR OPENS THE DOOR, and stops long enough to survey her at the kitchen table. Then shuts the door and hangs up his greatcoat. "What are you doing?" he inquires.

"Having a drink. Would you like one? I have a glass ready for you."

For a moment he does not respond. Then he sits down and faces the glass as Sigrid dumps out three fingers of schnapps. *"Prosit,"* she offers, and empties her glass in a swallow.

"I've never seen a woman do that before," he remarks, then downs his own.

"Never?" She takes the bottle and pours two more measures. "Not even your whores from the Warthegau?" When he doesn't answer, she says, "You know, I happened to see one of your comrades from the hospital on the U-Bahn."

"And he was sober?"

"He told me that you are the sort that keeps him going."

"Me? *I* am the sort?"

"You, yes. Because you worked as a bank officer. Because you have a nice flat and a good wife."

He stares at her and she stares back.

"Why didn't you tell me, Kaspar? I thought you said you wanted only the truth between us."

His mouth turns downward at the edges. "I didn't think it would matter to you," he answers.

"My husband has volunteered to return to the front, and he didn't think it would matter to me?"

"Why would it? You have your man tucked away to keep you satisfied. Why would you care what I do?"

"So that's *it*? It's male jealousy? The mortar wounded your body, but I've wounded your pride, so you're marching back to Russia to make yourself a target for all those machine gunners who missed you the first time?"

"How much of this kerosene have you swallowed already?" he asks, examining the bottle.

"Never mind. That's beside the point. The point is that you lied to me."

"No, I simply omitted the truth."

"A fine distinction."

"One with which you're familiar."

"I've tried to be truthful with you, Kaspar."

"No. Perhaps you haven't *lied* outright, but you've tried *not* to be truthful with me, unless absolutely necessary. Another fine distinction, I know, but an important one."

"All right, then, since you're asking for the full truth? The truth with no holes in it? You'll get it. More than you'll have wished for," she assures him. Killing her shot, she exhales a flat breath. "I'm hiding Jews from the Gestapo."

Kaspar's face is unmoved for a moment. Then he almost smiles, as if his hearing must be playing tricks. He looks at her again with incomprehension. For an instant she can recall the puzzled expression of the young man she had married. It's the expression he would wear when faced with a dilemma outside the prescribed lines of his experience. An expression she had always found at once irksome and endearing. "Is that a joke, Sigrid?" he finally asks. "Are you trying to shock me?"

"Not a joke, Kaspar. Just the truth you were asking for. I'm part of a group."

Incredulous. "A group hiding Jews."

"Not restricted to Jews. Anyone who needs help."

"*Help?*" A wire of anger is weaving itself into his voice. "Well, this is rather insane," he says, with his teeth clenching into a humorless grin, as if he might decide to chomp on the air. "This is really rather insane."

"Yes. I'll agree."

"*Will* you? Well, very nice. How very nice it is that my wife *agrees* with me," he steams, "on the subject of her insanity."

"Not my insanity, Kaspar."

"And by *help*, when you say the word *help*, what does that mean? You help them evade the police?"

"Yes."

"Criminals."

"That depends on your definition of the word."

"*Criminals.* People who have committed *crimes.* People have broken the *law*."

"Unjust laws."

"But the *law*, just the same." His eyes are darkening.

"Yes."

"Deserters, too?"

"You mean men who have 'simply had enough of this war'? Weren't those *your* words?"

His voice gains volume. "I mean men who have abandoned their *posts.*"

"Probably. I often don't *know* their reasons for having gone underground. Only that they have them."

"And is that where you've found your lover? Among these men?"

"It's not just men, Kaspar. Also women. Also children."

"Women, children, yes." He nods starkly. "But that doesn't answer my question, does it? Please, Sigrid," he says, with a hollow, almost manic note entering his voice. "Please tell me that my wife is screwing a criminal or a deserter. Please tell me that *at least* she's screwing a *German* and not a—"

But he doesn't finish the sentence. The look on her face has stopped him, so the unspoken word of the unfinished sentence weights the air between them. Kaspar drops his head and shakes it at the table.

Sigrid says nothing. She is watching him around the edges, where the hidden heat of his temper has always been signaled by a twitch of muscle, a flex of his fist. But there is an eerie animal stillness to him now that she does not recognize. She can hear him breathing. Thin, measured breaths. As if he has gone in to a kind of hibernation inside himself.

Finally, she touches his knuckles with the tips of her fingers. It's a gesture that, after years of marriage to him, has become unconscious. "Kaspar," she says. But the touch of her fingers is a trigger, and he detonates, ripping the tablecloth from the table, and sending everything flying. The schnapps bottle smashes on the hardwood floor. On his feet, Kaspar glares furiously at the bare table, and then overturns it with a wounded groan.

Sigrid has shoved herself back from the violence, and sits, clenching the chair as if desperate to keep it in place, as if Kaspar might next rip up the floorboard. An echo of the noise of his outburst is stuck in Sigrid's head. The sound of the crashing bottle. The crashing table. He is breathing roughly now, but he doesn't appear to see her any longer. Instead, he is gazing wildly into some dark hole. There are tears streaming down his cheeks.

They are motionless like this, both staked to their positions, unmoving.

Until slowly, carefully, Sigrid lets go of the chair, and rises. Her heart thumping. The tears draw her to him. "Kaspar," she whispers.

That night, she removes her clothes, with the dim bedside lamp still burning, and climbs beneath the blankets as Kaspar watches her. His uniform is already laid out for the morning, draped over the chair. They lie together naked. Not touching, but still sharing the bed while Mother Schröder snores on the other side of the flat.

"So what are you going to do?" she asks in their careful voice. Over the years, they had developed a way of talking in bed, so that Mother

Schröder could not hear, even if she was trying to. Not really a whisper, but more like an undertone.

He takes a breath slowly and exhales it. "You mean, am I planning on telling the police? Telling them that my wife has made a hobby of smuggling deserters and Jews? No," he tells her. "I think I'll forgo that pleasure."

She fixes his eyes. "No. That's not what I meant. You know, Kaspar, if you're intent on committing suicide, you don't have to travel all the way back to the Eastern Front. You can simply step in front of a double-decker."

"I'm not going back to commit suicide."

"You are. Why else would you be doing it, if not to die?"

"Because I can't *live*. Not here. I have no purpose here."

"Because you won't permit yourself to have a purpose here. Because you can no longer make sense of your world, you have decided that the *world* no longer makes sense."

"No. Honestly, the world has never made sense to me." His voice picks up a beat of distance. "I have always felt that I was playing a game of catch-up."

"Well, it doesn't have to be that way."

He looks at her with a strained weariness. "Yes, of course. My wife has the answer to everything," he says with muted bitterness.

"When are you leaving?"

"I'm to report to the mustering officer tomorrow morning. We ship out from Anhalter Bahnhof the next day."

"Goddamn it, Kaspar," she whispers. "What were you planning to do? Drop me a note in the Feldpost from the Ukraine?"

"I've written you a letter. I planned on leaving it."

"For me to read after you were gone. *Dearest Wife: Sorry to say, but I'm off to die for the Führer and Fatherland. Please send Pervatin.*" When had she started to cry? She jams her palm into her eyes to wipe them clean. Even with their door closed, she can hear her mother-in-law's snoring. She swallows. "I'm assuming that you have not yet told the *other* Frau Schröder in the household?"

"I've written her a letter as well. I must ask you, Sigrid, not to say anything to her."

"Are you joking? You think *this* is the sort of news I would break to your mother? She'd only blame me. Of course, she'll blame me in any case. But that makes no difference. Blame is what keeps your mother alive." She takes a breath free of tears. "I won't be waiting for you again, Kaspar," she tells him.

"Were you waiting for me the first time?" he asks.

The truth of this silences her for a moment. "No, I suppose I wasn't."

A shrug. "Then what's the fuss?"

"You have another choice," she says.

A blank look dangles from his face. "And what does that mean?"

"I could get you out."

"Out?"

"I could get you to Sweden."

"Sweden." He almost smiles at this absurdity. Kaspar Schröder of Berlin-Wilmersdorf among the Swedes. "No."

"No one will know you. No one will expect you to be anyone other than who you tell them you are."

"No one will know what I've *done*. No one will know about my *crime*. Isn't that what you are really saying?"

"I'm not saying that. Because it's not true. *You* will still know. And if suicide's your answer, then you can kill yourself in Sweden as well as in the East. But if it's not, if what you're telling me is true, then perhaps you can begin to expunge your crime by living a different life."

He stares. Shakes his head lightly. "Sounds like a fairy tale."

"It doesn't have to be. But you have to be willing to try. To try to forgive yourself."

"So. Is that what you have done? Learned to *forgive* yourself? Hiding Jews illegally, helping soldiers desert their companies? What crime are *you* trying to expunge, dear wife?"

"The crime of complicity, dear husband," she answers.

"And you think what you are doing will cleanse you of that? It won't. We are all dirty, no matter what we do. Life is dirty."

"So that is why you are choosing death?"

"I don't think I've ever understood you, Sigrid," he says. "There was a time when I thought I did. I always knew you were different from other women I had met. And I appreciated the fact that you had your own mind. In some ways it made our life together easier. I didn't have to try to figure out what you wanted from me. But I always thought, I always *assumed* that there would be boundaries. Now, I see that there are none at all. That boundaries do not exist." He says this, and then looks at her. His face close. "These children you are hiding," he asks. "They are how old?"

Silence. She does not respond. She can read his mind.

"Do you ever think," he asks. "Do you ever think about how old our child would be? *Would have been?*" he corrects.

Had she not miscarried. Had she not failed to carry their baby to term. She does not answer, but Kaspar does not seem to be waiting for her to. "I never used to. But," he tells her, "I see the pictures other men carry. How they show them off. And it makes me think about these things." He is silent. And then, "I know you believe I blame you."

"Don't you?"

"Yes. Somewhat. But I also blame myself," he tells her. "Honestly, Sigrid, the idea of a baby terrified me. I had no idea how to be a father, and assumed I would become a very poor one. Also, it made me jealous."

"Jealous," Sigrid repeats.

"We had built a very balanced life, you and I. I knew a baby would turn that upside down. So I let my mother take over your care, when

I should have listened to you. I knew you didn't like her doctor. Perhaps if I had interceded," he says but doesn't finish the sentence. Instead, he gazes up at the ceiling. "I was relieved when you miscarried, Sigrid," he tells her. "Angry, ashamed. But relieved. I blamed you because it was the simplest option. And because I was frightened that, otherwise, you'd see through me, and realize the sort of man you had married. I blamed you and allowed you to blame yourself. And for that, I am sorry. I should have done better. I should have been a better husband to you."

"Kaspar," she whispers. Her body is stationary, but her voice moves closer to him. "If I asked you," she says.

He turns his face to her. "If you asked me what?"

"What would you do if I asked for your help?"

"My help? I don't believe you've ever made such a request."

"Well, I'm making it now."

"What's his name?" he suddenly asks.

"What?"

"Your Jew. I'm assuming he has a name. What is it?" She can hear the boyish hurt hidden by the flatness of his voice.

"Why do you ask me such a thing?"

"Because I want to know. You ask for my help. Perhaps, that is the price I require you to pay."

"His name is Egon," she finally answers him.

A breath of silence, as she can feel him stamping a name to a face he has created in his head.

"And is it your plan," he inquires, "to run away with him?"

A swallow. "Oh, no," she answers quietly, and feels her eyes go wet. "No. That's not in anyone's plan."

IN THE MORNING, when she wakes, she finds the imprint Kaspar has left on the sheets. The chair is empty. His wardrobe is empty of his uniforms and gear. In the bathroom, she dresses quickly. When she enters the kitchen, Mother Schröder is still snoring in the other room. Only one envelope has been left on the table and it is marked for her mother-in-law. She picks it up for a moment, but then drops it and walks over to the sink. By the time the old lady emerges from sleep, she is already boiling the water for coffee.

"What is it? Why are you up so early?" she hears the woman ask suspiciously.

She lifts the top of the coffeepot and spoons in three measures from the tin. "He's gone."

A thick glower. "What does *that* mean?"

"It means he's gone. Your son. My husband. Feldwebel Kaspar Albrecht Schröder is gone." She swallows. "He left you a letter."

Mother Schröder's eyes drop with acid suspicion to the table. She glares at the envelope, then sits. Splits open the flap with her finger and unfolds the single sheet. She reads it, then sets it down. She claims a cigarette from the pocket of her dressing gown and lights it up with a wax-tipped match and inhales smoke deeply. When she turns her eyes to Sigrid, they are damp and loaded. "You are responsible for this," she announces with murderous brevity.

"Of course you would like to think so." Sigrid pours the hot water into the pot. "If only I had made him a decent wife."

"If only you had."

"Well, I didn't. I couldn't. Blame me for it. Despise me for it. There's still nothing I could have changed."

"Your husband goes back to war *just to get away from you*, and all you can offer is this glibness?"

"Is that what he told you in his letter? That the front is preferable to life with his wife?"

"He didn't *have* to tell me. It's *obvious*. He left to escape you."

"To escape me, to escape you, to escape all of us. But mostly to escape himself."

"More fancy talk that's simply *rubbish*. The *truth is*," she starts to say, but Sigrid cuts her off.

"The *truth is*, Petronela, that the Kaspar we knew never made it back. That the man the army sent back to you—to *us*—was a stranger. An Ostkampfer."

"He was still my boy."

"He was a *casualty*," Sigrid snaps. And then, with a softer edge, "That's all . . . another casualty."

She watches the old woman across the table swallow hard, her eyes wet with fury and grief. "So that's *it*? He's *gone*? My only son. We erect a tombstone and move on? Is that what you're advising, daughter-in-law?"

Yes. She thinks it before she says it. "Yes."

Sigrid watches her mother-in-law age before her eyes. The woman's face clouds, and she stands with a brittle quality, lifting herself from the chair by leveraging her weight with the palm of her hand clamped on the table. She picks up her son's letter and turns her back, but her step has taken on a shamble. "There's a tin of powdered milk in the pantry," she tells Sigrid as she shuffles in her bed slippers. "I'd like some in my coffee, please."

THAT DAY SIGRID GOES to the films. She tells her mother-in-law this, but her mother-in-law is silent, planted in her chair by the wireless. Some popular tune babbles, but she seems not to hear it.

On the way to the Elektrischetram, she spies her shadow. Brown, snap-brim fedora. Beer belly. Ears like a monkey's. She sees him on the tram, and again when she exits. It feels strange being followed. To know you are being followed. So she decides to give the fellow a test, and lead him on a bit of a chase. Down one block and up another. At some point he vanishes. Either he's doing better at camouflaging himself, or has nipped into a lokal for a quick glass or two.

At the cinema there's no sign of him. Hans Moser's petulant expression on the poster fills the display case by the ticket booth. *Love Is Duty Free: A Comedy of Vienna.* The interior of the lobby smells of cold wool and singed wiring from the portable heater. The patrons file into the auditorium with funereal silence. Sigrid passes a girl in an usher's uniform and follows the carpeted runner up to the mezzanine balcony. There's a hefty Berliner in a fur-collared coat seated in the front row by the rail. Squinting, he turns his head to inspect Sigrid, but then frowns, disappointed. In the back row, she takes a seat at the end of the aisle. When the lights go down, she tries to claim comfort in the darkness, but this time there is none to be claimed. She feels simply alone. Then light shudders from the projector and the screen silvers. She opens her eyes to a roar of newsreel *Heils* and Wagnerian thunder. It's *another* petulant Austrian. The Führer speaks in honor of Heroes' Remembrance Day in the courtyard of the Zeughaus, flanked by captured Red Army flags. His peaked uniform cap is jammed down onto his head, and he resembles a curmudgeonly family uncle, slumped into his greatcoat and favoring his right arm as he grumbles into the microphone.

When another patron finds a seat in a row by the balcony, his silhouette blocks her view. Sigrid feels her breath shorten. The man is wearing no hat, and she can recognize the shape of the back of Egon's head. Recognize his shadow. He sits beside the only other occupant of the row, the fellow in the fur-collared coat. There's an exchange of some sort, and Sigrid watches the other man suddenly stand and make his way out. But when she watches Egon stand a moment later, he stops. She can feel his gaze penetrate her. She is at once terrified and overjoyed when she watches him close in on the spot where she is seated. His silhouette cuts its contours out of the Führer's face on screen. When he dumps himself into the seat beside her, she can smell the aroma of his cigarette tobacco.

"So, this is a surprise," he states. "Since you haven't shot me on sight, am I to assume that you have discarded your shiny pistol?"

"I have it still," she answers.

"Then I should assume you simply prefer point-blank range."

"That depends. Do you still intend to throttle me?"

"No. I'm here on business, as you witnessed."

"The tubby gentleman."

"A small cog in the great machinery."

"More diamonds stolen from Jewish coat hems?"

"No, contraband stock certificates, actually. Not really my market, you understand. I deal in stones, not paper. I'm just earning a cut of the proceeds as a go-between."

"A bagman. How demeaning for you."

"You didn't leave me much choice. I couldn't blow my nose on the money you left me. Two hundred marks. Perhaps I will throttle you, after all."

"And who will remove the bullet from your belly after you try?"

He actually laughs at this. A thick familiar chuckle. In spite of herself, she feels her skin tingle at the sound of it. She turns her eyes to the screen, but can feel his gaze attaching itself to her, as a squadron of Stuka bombers dive murderously through the air, sirens shrieking. "There's a boy who is stalking you," she says.

"A what?"

"I don't know his name. But he was one of the U-boats I was hiding. He's been trailing *me*, apparently, hoping to find *you*. And he does not have kind intentions."

"And who am I to him, this boy?"

"He's under the impression that you are the responsible party in the deaths of his sisters at the hands of the Gestapo." Her voice is detached. Almost mild. "Can that be true?"

A panzer column speeding through a burning townscape fills the cinema's screen. Egon's silence at the end of her question is crushing.

"I can't forgive you, Egon," she hears herself say.

"I haven't asked you to. Forgiveness means nothing to me in any case. Just more words."

"Can you tell me why?" she asks. The ground explodes on the screen, spewing whorls of dark earth.

"Why?"

"Why you *did it*?"

"You mean, why did I betray my fellow Jews to those pigs in the Grosse Hamburger Strasse? You think maybe it wasn't just my love for the Führer and Fatherland?"

"Were you afraid? Did they threaten you? Did they threaten your family?"

"So." He laughs again, but this time there is nothing appealing about the sound. "All that bravado, Sigrid. 'I can't forgive you, Egon.' Yet you're still trying to. Still trying to give me a way out. A moral escape route. 'Did they threaten your family?' the lady asks." He shakes his head at the joke. But then a silence follows. She can feel something inside of him ebb. "I'm going to tell you the truth this time," he says finally, with distance. "So that no one is operating under any delusions."

Sigrid is a stone, waiting. She watches him swallow, staring into the truth before he can consider speaking it.

"Just before the war started, my wife," he says. "My wife had begged to go to Palestine. *Begged*. She'd had a cousin, you see, who liked to style himself as a Zionist. He'd paid a fortune for a berth on a Portuguese freighter, and had been smuggled into the Mandate right under the noses of the British. But *I* thought, a *kibbutz*? Not for me. Thank you, no. I was *not interested* in eating sand for breakfast with the zealots. And, anyway, I was already working on visas, and not to some salt bed on the Dead Sea. My brother had made a contact in the American embassy. He claimed he was bouncing the wife of a legation secretary, but I never got the truth out of him. The Gestapo picked him up before I had the chance, the stupid schmuck. Maybe *they* got the truth out of him. I don't know about that, either, because three weeks later they sent an urn full of ashes to my sister-in-law, along with an itemized bill to cover the cost of his execution." He says this as the gray-white flashes from the screen mottle his face. "I tried to pick up where he'd left off with the visas, but it was too late. The Americans were through talking to Jews. And then the Wehrmacht stormed over the border into Poland, and the lid clamped shut on emigration." He draws a breath and then expels it. "That was when Anna came up pregnant. She was so angry with me," he says, as if seeing her face. "She said it was *my* doing that her baby would be born in a concentration camp. I told her she was being hysterical. I told her the Nazis were swine, but they understood the value of money. I could deal with them. And for a while I could. One year passed, and then another, and I managed. In fact, I was rather impressed with myself. We'd lost the flat in Schöneberg, but I'd found a spot down by the docks. Noisy, though not so bad, I thought. It wasn't a dump. There was food, and coal for the stove."

I saw your face, and I knew that I simply had to hear the sound of your voice.

"And that's where you were living," she asks, "when you fucked me here in the back row?"

"It was that seat over there, wasn't it?" he says.

"You have no idea which seat it was, so please don't try to pretend."

He shrugs. "Maybe, maybe not. But I'm willing to bet that *you* know which seat it was."

"Your arrogance does not promote your case," she says, then brings him back on track. "So your wife received a letter from the jüdische Gemeinde, ordering her to report to the SS with the children? Isn't that the next line in the story?"

"Yes."

"And you made the arrangements to go underground. A few rooms above a warehouse in Rixdorf."

"Yes. A few rooms above a warehouse in Rixdorf," he repeats. "I paid plenty for it, too, but apparently the good German I was dealing with was running a side business with the Sicherheitspolizei. First the Jews paid him, and then the Sipo paid him. Anyway. They came while we were sleeping. I kicked out a window, and made it out over the rooftops, but I was the only one to escape. It probably would have been better if I had simply flung myself off one of those rooftops," he considers. "That would have been the noble thing, wouldn't it?"

"So there was no arrest in a café. No desperate escape from a work detail. No return to empty rooms above a warehouse. All that was a lie."

"A man runs away, while his wife and children are ensnared? Not exactly anyone's idea of a heroic action. But then I thought, *I could get them out.* I could work the system. What could the Stapos *really* want with a woman and her two children? I could *buy* them back. I took up a name I had used once years before, and started working. I found where they were being held, and set up a transaction with a bull named Dirkweiler from the Gross Hamburger Strasse Sammellager. It really wasn't difficult. The Stapos are greedy old whores when it comes to what fills up their pockets. But Dirkweiler was greedier than most. He made promises, always boasting about how he could free a hundred Jews with the stroke of his pen but then always asking for more.

"And then," he says, "came the end of February. The Sicherheitspolizei arrested more than ten thousand Jews over the course of a single morning, mostly out of the factories. It was a massive operation. Gestapo, Kriminalpolizei, even squads of Waffen-SS men, stuffing Jewish factory workers into the lorries. All the collection areas began to overflow, the Gross Hamburger Strasse included, so the decision was made to clear out some room. Three days later, Dirkweiler informed me that he had ordered my wife and children transferred to Theresienstadt in Bohemia. The 'paradise camp,' he called it. And there they would remain, alive and well fed, as long as I *cooperated* with his operations." He stares dimly into the light from the screen. "That was the day I became a catcher." A shrug. "I was good at it. In the diamond business you learn to read people's faces, as well as the stones. I would pick out a man in a café and stare at him, until he caught my eyes, and then I would know. I became an expert at betrayal. Finally, one morning Dirkweiler calls me into his office. He was happy. I was making him look good with his bosses in the Burgstrasse office, and he wanted to show his appreciation. He'd laid his hands on a bottle of Napoleon brandy from some old Jew's cellar, most likely. It was second rate, but he thought it was a prize, and wanted to *share* it with me. A great honor, at least in *his* eyes. An SS officer inviting a Jew to share a bottle of cognac. *Unheard of.*"

Sigrid grits her teeth. "And what did you do?"

Egon gazes at her for a moment. "I told him that I wasn't interested in his brandy. Or his cigarettes, or wristwatches, or any of his trinkets any longer. I told him that if he wanted me to continue to make him look good with his bosses, then he'd have to do something for me."

"For you," Sigrid repeats.

Egon slowly breathes in, then exhales. "At first he didn't react. Maybe he was curious about what I might want. About what a man like me might consider to be valuable, beyond the daily contraband. So I told him. I told him he'd have to bring my wife and daughters back to Berlin."

Sigrid feels herself go still. Perfectly still. Egon's eyes are fixed as if he's still staring into the SS man's face. "Suddenly, the Herr Untersturmführer didn't look too happy any longer," he says. "A minute later he was on his feet banging his fist and shouting about how he didn't take orders from a fucking Yid. But it was all a front. I had already read the truth in his face." He says this and swallows. "Maybe I had always known it."

There's a pause. Egon takes a long and distant breath to finish the story. "The next day I was on the train with one of the Stapo bulls. His name was Purzel. Not so bad a sort, really. I've certainly known worse men. In his way he was a *thoughtful* butcher. He liked to perform card tricks. Maybe he actually thought he was doing me a favor by telling me.

Anna and the girls had never been sent to any sort of a 'paradise camp.' They'd been put on transport to a camp in Poland on the twenty-sixth of February. A place called Auschwitz. Apparently, Anna had grown hysterical when one of the girls was separated from her in the crowd at the station platform. The SS don't like panic during a transport, of course, and have no patience for shrieking women. So a guard struck her in the head with his rifle butt, hard enough to kill her, and then tossed her body onto the train."

He says this with an even, toneless voice, but then stares blankly for a moment. "This was the story Purzel told me. As I said, maybe he thought he was doing me a service. Maybe he thought he was being *humane*. I don't know. He looked rather surprised when I shoved the knife blade into him. Even disappointed. In any case, that was the moment I ended my career with the Geheime Staatspolizei."

Tears are rolling freely down Sigrid's cheeks. She would like to touch him. She would like to feel the texture of the grief on his face. But she is afraid that if she touched his skin, she would burn her fingers. There is something of the furnace about his expression, so all she can do is wipe her eyes and say, "What about your daughters?"

"How will I ever know?" he asks the darkness into which he is staring. Then he turns his head and regards Sigrid for an instant as if regarding one of his gems. *"Come with me,"* he breathes.

She feels, for an instant, as if she has been hollowed out. "That's not possible."

"It *is*. Anything is possible. I would have thought you'd have learned that by now. Come with me."

She shakes her head. "How?"

"How? We get on a train. Madrid is how many hours away by rail? Less than a day."

"No. I have work here. There are people who *depend* on me."

"*Depend on you?* For how long? How long until the Gestapo come banging on your door one night? I've *seen* what they do in the cellars at

357

Grosse Hamburger Strasse. There are cellars like that all over the city. Torture is not a strong enough word for it."

"You can't frighten me, Egon."

"I'm not trying to, Frau Schröder. I'm trying to save your *life*."

She gazes at the light beading in his eyes.

"Meet me here. Tomorrow. There's a matinee," he tells her.

"I can't."

"I have a plan I've been working on. It's a bit risky, but if I can pull it off, it'll put some money in our pockets. Enough to buy you a dozen passports. All I need is that little spitter you've been carrying."

"What?"

"The revolver, Sigrid."

"What are you doing to do with it?"

"Nothing. Just hand it over."

She hesitates. Her stomach crawling. "What if I need to shoot you later?" she asks.

"Then you can always ask for it back," he tells her, and holds out his hand.

She shifts, finally, and passes over the shiny piece of nickel plating and watches him stuff it into his pocket. "Don't wait for me," she tells him. "Tomorrow. I won't be coming."

"We'll see," he replies. "A lot could happen between now and then. The world could shift on its axis, Sigrid. Mountains could spring from the seas. Pigs could fly. A woman could change her mind," he says, and exits the seat beside her.

Outside in the street, she searches for the monkey-eared Kommissar, and spots him at the news kiosk buying a paper from an old veteran. Only this time he's exactly the man she wants to see. It actually takes some effort to make sure she doesn't lose him in the crowd on the U-Bahn platform. Inside the carriage, he takes a seat on the opposite side of the aisle and glowers at his newspaper. Not a good Nazi rag like the *Völkischer Beobachter*, but a spicy illustrated known for its salacious stories and its "beauty" adverts featuring undressed women. The front page features a pile of muddy skulls with the headline RUSSIA'S GUILT!

She stays on past her stop. Far past her stop, in fact. Past the stop for the Deutsche Opernhaus-Bismarckstrasse, past the stop for Sophie-Charlottenburg-Platz, past the stop for Kaiserdammbrücke and the circumference of the Ringbahn. At one point, as the train is pulling away from the platform at the Adolf-Hitler-Platz, the monkey-eared Kommissar stretches his neck and frowns out the window with a perplexed expression. He must wonder what sort of a ride this woman is taking him on. Finally, two stops later, it's getting a little embarrassing. They are quite nearly the only ones left in the carriage when it heaves through the tunnel for the Reichssportfeld platform. Sigrid stands and he buries his nose in his newspaper, but when she suddenly crowds into the seat beside him, he jumps as if she's shocked him with a bolt of electricity.

"I'd like you to look inside my bag, Herr Kommissar," she tells him with polite force. Her handbag is open, and inside, her hand is gripping the handle of her fish knife. She watches his expression freeze. "Please believe that I don't wish to hurt you," she assures him. "Just the opposite, in fact. I want you to remain very healthy. And least for another day."

He says nothing, only stares at her with blank stupefaction.

"I see you wear a wedding ring," she observes. "That's very good. What is the date of your anniversary?"

His eyes narrow. "My *what*?"

"Your wedding anniversary," Sigrid repeats.

Eyes still narrow, a glance down at the knife, but now perhaps he's a bit curious. "April twenty-seventh," he answers.

"Not very far away," she notes as she brings out something enclosed in her fist from her coat pocket. "Show me your palm, Herr Kommissar," she tells him.

He hesitates.

"Go on."

His frown deepens, but covertly, he opens his palm. "And has your wife ever received a diamond from her husband?" Sigrid inquires. The small stone she releases from her fist gleams for an instant, before the Kommissar's hand closes over it. Quickly it disappears into his pocket, and he turns a page of his newspaper.

"You have a leak in your bucket," he tells her.

"A *leak*," she repeats.

"A Judas, gnädige Frau," says the kommissar. "In your little group. You've been betrayed."

She stares blankly at him, but he only frowns at his paper. *"Who?"* she whispers darkly. "Did you have a *name*?"

"Yes," the kommissar answers, and rattles the paper as he turns another page. "I have a name."

"And?"

A sniff. "My wife's *birthday* is May fifteenth."

TWENTY

"WHAT ARE YOU DOING?" her mother-in-law demands to know.

"Packing a suitcase."

"I can *see* that. Where do you think you're *going*?"

"On a holiday."

"A *holiday*?" The old woman nearly swoons at the very idea. "And what about your *job*?"

"What about it?"

"You cannot miss work. It's illegal."

"I don't have a job, Petronela. I was dismissed."

"*Dismissed?* Oh, my God in Heaven," her mother-in-law bleats mournfully, "I *knew* it would come to this. Your defeatism and quick mouth finally caught up with you."

"That's right." Sigrid stuffs a pair of shoes into the sides of the case and closes the lid. The snaps don't work properly, so she finds one of Kaspar's belts to strap it securely. In the other room, the wireless plays a tune by Charlie and His Orchestra. "You Can't Stop Me from Dreaming."

"And what about *me*?"

"You?"

"Off you go, leaving me behind to live on a widow's pension?"

"I'm sure that the Party won't let a devoted dues-paying member starve."

"*You see!* You see, that is *exactly* the sort of remark that lost you your position, I'm quite sure of it."

"Just think, Petronela, of the freedom you'll have. You can play your radio whenever you like."

"You can't *do* this."

"Can't I?"

"You can't just *leave.*"

"You'll miss me?" she inquires, throwing on her overcoat.

"I *won't* be left alone here. I'm warning you."

"What are you going to do? Ring up the police? Denounce me for packing a suitcase?"

"There's plenty more I could talk about, I assure you."

"Maybe that's true." She picks up the case by the handle and jiggles it to test the binding job. "But if the police arrest me, then I'll still be gone, and you'll still be alone."

In the next room, Charlie and His Orchestra are suddenly interrupted by a sharp, syncopated beeping.

"I'm going," Sigrid declares.

"You can't. There's an air raid."

"Churchill sent me a telegram. He said I'd be safe."

"You can't go outside, you're insane. You won't be *allowed.*"

But Sigrid is not listening. The voice of the Portierfrau Mundt is sharply audible in the stairwell. *"Into the cellar. Everyone into the cellar."* When she spots Sigrid, her voice gains an edge as the sirens yowl. "Frau Schröder. What do you think you're *doing*?"

"Getting out, Frau Mundt."

"That is not permitted. All residents—" she begins, but Sigrid cuts her off.

"Oh, please. Won't you just shut your hole, you dried-up old bitch?"

"How *dare* you speak so to a member of the Party!"

"Yes. You think you're the Führer's favorite, do you? You think he gives the slightest shit whether you live or die? Whether *any* of us do? *He doesn't.*"

"That's *treasonous*!" Mundt actually sounds shocked. "Insulting the *Führer*."

"Get out of my way."

"Oh! My *God*," they hear a woman gasp painfully, and turn to see Brigitte, with a belly as big as a drum, waddling down the steps, hugging her air raid blanket. Mother Schröder grips her arm. "It's coming soon. She could drop at any moment," the old woman announces. A bolt of guilt strikes Sigrid squarely in the chest. Her promise to Carin had flown out the window.

"Don't just stand there gawking," Mother Schröder chides. "*Help* me with her!"

Sigrid drops her suitcase.

The young woman's face is chalky and coated with sweat as they help her down the stairs. "I'm sorry," Sigrid whispers. "Your sister asked me to keep an eye on you while she was away. I'm afraid I haven't done a very good job."

But Brigitte appears beyond caring about apologies. She bites her lip to suppress a cry as they guide her down the next step. "He's kicking up quite a ruckus tonight," she says, rubbing her belly. "Isn't he? So impatient. Just like his father."

CRYING FORBIDDEN, the sign still reads, but the Tommies are close tonight. Too close for speculation, too close for jokes. There's only room for fear between the bomb blasts.

In the cellar, the kaffeeklatsch has taken charge of Brigitte, assembling benches into a makeshift bed and covering her in blankets. Sigrid looks at her wristwatch in the swinging lamplight. *"Christ!"* an old uncle from the first floor is calling plaintively at the tremors from the bombs blasts. *"Jesus Christ!"*

Then Mother Schröder seizes her roughly by the arm. *"Her water's broken. She's going into labor!"* she shouts into Sigrid's face.

THE FRAUEN IN THE BUILDING have abandoned their mending, and separated the girl completely from the men. The members of the kaffeeklatsch prop her up. Frau This and Frau That. In the blinking light, the girl's face gleams with sweat, even as her breath frosts. Frau Trotzmüller whispers nonsensical encouragements as she mops at the sweat with a handkerchief. Brigitte's legs are splayed wide open, her dress shoved up past her waist. Sigrid is one of the women holding up a curtain of blankets to guard the Frau Obersturmführer's modesty. The men peer blankly at the action. Outsiders looking in. But when she turns her head, she can see the crown of the baby's head emerging from the birth canal. *"Push!"* Mother Schröder commands the girl as she prepares to receive the infant in the folds of her apron. "Now is the time, girl! Push! *Push!*"

"It's coming out!" Frau Trotzmüller shouts with a gleeful panic. "The head is out, little mother!"

"Almost there!" Mother Schröder shouts over the girl's agonized screams. "Keep pushing! That's it! *Keep pushing!*"

"It's coming out! It's coming out!"

And it is. A tiny pinkish thing covered in maternal goo. Sigrid stares.

"It's out!" Frau Trotzmüller crows with ecstatic relief. "Thank God, it's *out!*"

Lifting it by the legs, Sigrid's mother-in-law administers the slap that draws air into the baby's body. Its first exhale emerges in a sharp, high-pitched whine that is so full of life it stings Sigrid's eyes with tears. And for a single moment in that dingy cellar, there is crying, but there is also cheering.

"Daughter-in-law, get me a shears, I need to cut the cord," Mother Schröder instructs with some spark of satisfaction.

"My sewing basket is against the bench there," Marta Trotzmüller declares with excitement. "Use *mine*. You'll see it!"

She bolts over to sewing basket and returns with the shears. The sound of a snip is heard over the mighty squalling coming from the tiny mouth. "It's a *girl*," Mother Schröder announces to all as she swaddles the child in her apron. But something is amiss. The Frau Obersturmführer's face is still an agonized twist. "No. *No*, you are *wrong*!"

"Child?"

"No, you are *wrong*. It must be a *boy*. A *boy*. It *must* be!"

"Blood!" Frau Trotzmüller suddenly squawks. "Blood!"

"Good God, she's hemorrhaging. Sigrid, take the baby," her mother-in-law commands, and before she can refuse, Sigrid has the child in her hands, wrapped in a kitchen apron. This tiny little thing that's nothing more than a loud noise, but that fills her arms with the weight of promise. The weight of existence.

WHEN THE RESCUE WORKERS and the fire police are hauling the bodies from the cellar the next morning, they will find the child's mother intact. Undamaged by the collapsing beams that crushed the Portierfrau Mundt into something quite unrecognizable. They will find her unbroken by the small mountain of masonry that buried the remains of others. Frau This and Frau That. They will remove the Frau Obersturmführer's lifeless body from the wreckage of the cellar as if it's a holy relic. "Her eyes were gazing toward Providence," one of the local papers will write. "A bloodless Madonna." It will be the SS who take charge of her corpse, and they will

*bury it with standards unfurled, and torches crackling. This little Mischling
Sleeping Beauty casketed like a Martyr of the Movement. Her husband,
the Obersturmführer, just returned from the front minus an arm below the
left elbow, will raise his remaining limb in stiff salute above the open coffin
as a chorus of BdM Jungmädel sing, "High Night of Clear Stars." Beside
her bier, the tiny white coffin is closed. Closed, though all it contains is the
bloodstained kitchen apron which swaddled her daughter at birth. It's all
the rescuers could find of the child.*

*Two things will be determined from the crater in the street. One, that
the bomb was probably a standard British GP, a "general purpose," set
for impact demolition. It will also be determined that the blast was not the
result of a direct hit. It was clearly this last fact that allowed for survivors,
when the façade of the building was sheared away and collapsed into the cellar. Of the fifteen people jammed into that small, dank underground space,
fully half of them managed to escape through the special brickwork passages that lead into the cellar next door. When interviewed days later by a
police captain, Herr Mundt, the local Party warden, denied vehemently any
possibility that he could have allowed the newborn of a serving SS officer
to be stolen. That, regardless of what some of those loopy women in the
cellar might have to say, they were simply balmy, and that there was no
chance—absolutely no chance—that such a tiny little baby, no bigger than
a thumbnail, could possibly have survived.*

ABOVE THEIR HEADS is a thunder, like a thousand trains, like a thousand pianos dumped from a great height, like a mountain collapsing in
on itself. A scream and flash of light, and then nothing but the roar of
darkness. For minutes, maybe hours, maybe seconds, Sigrid is unsure
if she is alive or dead. Her body is embraced by a thick black numb-
ness. But slowly, slowly, she is aware that her heart is beating. Slowly,
she is aware that she is breathing. And then she hears the impatient cry
of the baby shielded in her arms. Shielded by her body. Light comes a

few breaths later. The beams of electric torches. Shouting. Moaning. Somebody sobbing and somebody giving orders.

"Frau Schröder. You must come!"

It's a voice she recognizes. A woman's voice. Beams of light are bouncing off broken beams, shimmering through the dust. She is coughing on the heavy air.

"Frau Schröder. You must leave her." A voice coming closer. "She is *dead*, Frau Schröder, you must leave her."

But no, she wants to say. *No, You're wrong.* And maybe she does say that, as she holds the baby tightly. *She's alive. Can't you hear her? She's crying? Can't you hear?* Then a shaft of light catches a face in the rubble. Mother Schröder glowers back at her in blunt astonishment. Unblinking. Her expression frozen, like the face of a watch that has stopped, its last second suspended in time. A dark trickle of blood extends the corner of her final frown.

Another noise. Loud banging, and then a crack. "It's open!" she suddenly hears Mundt's husband holler in triumph. "We're *through!*" the man whoops. And the beams of light shift. She can see Marta Trotzmüller's face, blood smeared across her forehead. Eyes moony. "Come, now, you cannot argue," the woman begs. "The men have breached the escape way. We must *go*. If this little doll is to survive, then you must get her *out*."

THE BUILDING ACROSS the street is burning, throwing off waves of heat. Silhouettes dash across the blinding, orange flicker. Sigrid is still cradling the baby, wrapped in one of the air raid blankets, as she staggers into the street. Clutching the little squalling being to her breast to protect it from the dust and smoke. Someone is calling her name, but it takes a moment for her to realize it. It takes a moment for her to realize that it is Carin, negotiating the chunks of rubble littering the asphalt street.

"I'm sorry," Sigrid tells her. "I'm sorry. Your sister," she says.

"Brigitte?" Carin gazes wildly at Sigrid's face, the dance of the firelight reflecting in her eyes. Then she turns back a flap of the bundle and shifts her gaze to the tiny face screwed up with infant bawling. "My God..."

"She is unhurt, I think. But I cannot stay. You must take her, Carin," Sigrid says, and transfers the bundle into Carin's arms. "Take her to the hospital. Get her treatment, then get her *out*."

"Out?"

"She will need a mother now, Carin."

"A mother? Don't be absurd. I mean, how *can I*?" Her face is stricken. All of its usual cynicism gone. "*How can I? A* woman like *me*, alone?"

"A woman like you is exactly whom she needs. But you are not alone. You have your brother. Go to Wolfram. Find a way, Carin," Sigrid tells her. "Get her out of this nightmare."

TWENTY-ONE

S HE REMEMBERS THE TUNNEL. There's a tunnel that connects the
Anhalter Bahnhof, rising imperiously in stacks of yellow Grep-
piner brick above the Saarlandstrasse to the equally imperious Hotel
Excelsior, with its massive columned façade. Sigrid remembers the
tunnel from her childhood because of the row of underground shops
where her mother once bought her a velvet frock, dark blue, like a night
sky. She thought it was so very sophisticated, and was worried when
her father wanted to know how much it was going to set him back. The
shopgirl told him, and he snorted as if the price had blown up in his
head like a sneeze. Her mother, however, intervened. *It's important,
Günter, that she have something nice.* Her father acquiesced, as he usually
did, with a sigh that filled and then deflated his cheeks, making them
resemble a gasbag. Later that afternoon they had lunch at a small café
in the Pariser Platz that served a fruit cup that included oranges, and
then rented a toboggan to go sledding down the drive of the Reichstag
Building with a multitude of Berliner families. She remembers her
father's laughter as the two of them careened sideways into a snow-
bank. A boy's laughter. A happy, unfettered chuckle. It made her feel
good to hear him laugh, but also sad in a way, because his laughter was
all about his own snow antics. It was not shared with her.

. . .

Outside the station, a brass band of middle-aged Brownshirts has assembled in the open plaza with air-raid sandbags as a backdrop. The brassy clash as they tune up echoes in the vaulted ceilings of the bahnhof's main portal.

Inside, the grandly appointed booking house, built for empire, has taken on a grimy, patched-up wartime face. Sandbags, boarded-up windows, chips, and cracks in the masonry. An immense swastika banner, edged with grime, hangs above the heads of the hordes of drab travelers, who grumble as they are herded by the loudspeakers.

Sigrid moves through the crowd with the same colorless sense of destination, but her eyes are crisp and alert. She has left her baggage behind in the rubble of the bombing. She had bathed and changed in the flat across the Askanischer Platz, picked out a clean dress from the wardrobe rack, scrubbed the residue of the bomb blast from her skin with a scouring brush in the tub down the hall, and then slept like a stone on the bed, without dreams. The bloodied, smoked, stained clothes she has left behind like a discarded skin. She has been born into a new entity. Part human, dressed in Carin's sensible blue topcoat; part machinery, which armors her with purpose. When she spies Ericha loitering by the schedule cabinets she snatches her arm. Ericha snaps around with a dangerously cornered expression. "What are you doing here?"

"I've made some adjustments to the plan," Sigrid answers. "Come," she orders, and hauls her to a spot by the long row of schedule tables.

"I thought we had an agreement," the girl hisses at her.

But Sigrid is covering the area with an extended German glance. "Where are they?"

"Where are who?"

"Frau Weiss and her daughters?"

"In the restaurant. They were hungry, I thought they should eat."

"Are they alone?"

"Alone? It's a crowded restaurant at lunchtime."

"You know what I mean. Do you have someone with them?"

"No. No one. Look, you still haven't explained—"

"What about the 'addition' you told me about? Where is he?"

"He's hasn't arrived yet."

"Then there may still be time."

"Sigrid."

"He's a traitor, Ericha."

"*What?* What are you *saying*?"

"I'm saying whoever you *think* he may be, he's either a fraud or he's been turned. These people in this other group you're connected with, they're not to be trusted, do you understand? They've been compromised by the Gestapo."

"No. No, you're wrong."

"*Not this time,*" Sigrid insists. "I know you'd like to believe that your instincts are infallible, but you're not the pope. You've made a mistake. Now, come. We've got to get moving. Where is your man Becker? I don't see him."

"*No,*" Ericha repeats. Her voice has grown full and dark.

"No? No, *what*?"

"No. You are *wrong*," she says. "The *addition*," she says, and shakes her head. "He's a German-speaking Czech. The British parachuted him into the protectorate to organize sabotage cells in the arms factories. He's been on the run from the Gestapo for months, all the way from Prague."

Sigrid stops. Stares sharply into Ericha's face. "So, that's *his* story. We all have a story," she says. "How do you know it's not a lie?"

"I *know*, Frau Schröder," she whispers blankly, "because *I* am the traitor."

Sigrid goes silent. Closes her eyes and then opens them. Ericha is glaring straight ahead. "What I told you," she says, "about the address on the cigarette card. It was not completely accurate. The Sipo detectives were waiting there. But the woman they arrested was me."

"Child," Sigrid whispers. But Ericha is still glaring like the tiger in its cage. "They took me to the Alex first," she says. "But my name must have been on a list, because after a few hours, they trucked me over to the Prinz-Albrecht-Strasse. I was told they had prepared a little show for my benefit. A little show that should also be very educational. So I was taken down into the cellar, and manacled to a chair. Then in came two big Stapo men, dragging a woman between them, and I was made to watch while they stripped her, chained her to a table, and proceeded to beat her body with rubber truncheons." The tears come only now, one followed by another, as the girl replays the scene inside her head. "At first she screamed. Sobbed. But after a while there were only these horrible animal grunts as the blows fell. Only then," she says, "did they explain their proposition to me. It was very simple, really. All I need do is help them spring this trap. All I need do is betray *everyone* and *everything*, and I would not be harmed. Otherwise, I would be next on the table."

She shakes her head at the unseeable point of her gaze. "I should have resisted. I should have let them pummel me into a spot of grease. But I didn't," she whispers. "I *couldn't*. Because all I could think," she says, and then must restart the sentence. "All I could think was that the *baby* would never survive the beating. It's *ridiculous*, I know. Only a few hours before, I was going to pay a man to scrape it away. But at that instant—I can't explain. It had come to life inside me." Turning her head, she suddenly looks Sigrid in the face. "And now, I am a murderer. I have murdered all those who have trusted me. All to save myself and this little tadpole growing in my belly. So you understand. You must *go*, Sigrid Schröder. Right now. Before I murder you as well."

Sigrid stares. Then smears a tear from her face. "Becker?" she asks.

"My watchdog. But he's not alone. I recognize one by the stairs with the newspaper, and another smoking by the news kiosk."

"That makes three."

"*Please*, Sigrid," she starts to say, but Sigrid won't let her finish.

"I'll handle this now, if you don't mind, Fräulein Kohl," she announces. "What do you think they're going to do with you when their little trap is sprung? Set you loose, or drop you into some hole you'll never climb out of?"

"They won't. I'm still of some value to them."

"And when you're not?"

Ericha gazes at her with eyes like wind tunnels.

"You're a fine one for moralizing, Fräulein," Sigrid continues. "So if you're going to *have* this baby, don't you think you have a *moral responsibility* to keep its mother out of some godforsaken camp in the marshes of Poland?"

From outside comes the noise of a brassy march struck up by the SA band, an anthem, popular on the radio, called, "Onward to Moscow!" It turns heads and prompts a pattering of applause, which suddenly swell as a company of troops come marching into the concourse with rifles, greatcoats, and full packs.

Sigrid peers starkly. "This man from Prague," she says, "can the Gestapo identify him?"

"No. Only I have seen his photo."

"Fine. Where are you supposed to meet him?"

"By the schedule table."

"And what are supposed to do when you see him?"

"Ask him for a light for my cigarette."

"All right," Sigrid says. "Let's see what we can do with that." Quickly searching faces, Sigrid picks a stranger from the crowd at random. Just the first male traveler her eyes find, who happens to be standing in the spot where she needs a male traveler to be standing. "Now, do you see that man at the end of the schedule cabinet, smoking his pipe? Go ask him for a light."

She stares.

"*Go.* I'm right behind you."

The man is a dull Berliner mensch with a bland, midwinter face. He carries a worn valise, and is peering at the schedules with a stiff frown, the stem of his pipe locked between his teeth. He looks at Ericha in a perplexed manner when she asks him for a light for her cigarette. Sets down his valise to search his pockets for a lighter. Sigrid notes a swastika pin attached to his lapel. *Even better*, she thinks.

"Let's go," she says to Ericha, pulling the girl away by the arm, as she spots Becker and a Stapo trench coat by the kiosk closing in. "Just keep walking."

Behind them, they can hear the anonymous pipe smoker stammering loudly. Protesting his innocence. "This can't *be*! I'm a Party member! A *Party member*!" he repeats fervently. Then suddenly there is a man in front of them, blocking their way, his eyes hard as steel balls, glaring from beneath his snap-brim fedora. Sigrid can feel Ericha's urge to break away, her urge to flee, but she holds her arm tightly.

"*You have five minutes,*" the man hisses, his monkeylike ears flushing red. "I can't delay them longer." And then he pushes past.

Ericha looks astonished, but when she starts to speak, Sigrid cuts her off. "No explanations now, please, only action." The SA band has marched into the station behind the troops, and the drum major has struck up an old military chestnut, "Watch on the Rhine," squeaky with brass, solemn and ponderous. Sigrid plows straight into the crowd that has gathered to listen, with Ericha in tow, not looking back. The restaurant is crowded with grim-faced patrons, girding themselves for wartime rail travel. Waitresses negotiate the piles of tableside luggage as children wail above the rumble of conversation. Sigrid brushes past the young hostess at the entrance, and starts giving orders. "Come! Come! You're going to miss the train!"

The expression on Frau Weiss's face freezes up, but Sigrid is already at their table, handing their suitcases to Ericha. "Is your meal paid for?"

A glance to Ericha from Frau Weiss. "Yes."

"Then let's go. You can have a second cup of coffee in Frankfurt. No more dawdling," she insists, and hoists the youngest girl up into her arms. "Come, little one, to the train. Don't forget your tiger."

Outside the restaurant, she sees Becker and his man in the trench coat furiously searching the crowds. "To the boarding platforms," Sigrid instructs Frau Weiss. "Follow me and don't stop for anyone." Behind them a whistle blasts. Someone shouts, "Halt!"

"Keep going!" She is heading for the troops. They are out of formation now, crowding the platform as they are being boarded by harried transport officers. Wives and sweethearts are saying good-bye. Babies are being handed up to the windows to be kissed. BdM girls are decorating the soldiers' backpacks with flags and tossing handfuls of tiny white swastika confetti.

"Kaspar!" she shouts, and one of the soldiers turns around. He blinks at her, his cap and shoulders dusted with the swastika snowflakes.

"Kiss the little one good-bye," she prompts.

The man blinks again. But kisses the little girls on the cheek, giving the terrain a soldier's reconnaissance. "Be good! Do as your mummy says," he instructs loudly enough for everyone to hear. Sigrid grips him by the collar of his greatcoat. "Now, kiss your wife good-bye," she tells him. The kiss, in that instant, contains all that she has to give. When she breaks away, she tells him, *"They're behind us."*

The child has started to whine uncomfortably in Sigrid's grip as they cross the platform to the waiting train. Frau Weiss steps up, carrying her elder daughter, and coos at the child in Sigrid's grip to reassure her. "It's all right, Liebchen. It's all all right." A pair of rail porters are loading bags from trolleys onto the baggage car.

"Ericha," Sigrid says, "leave the suitcases and keep walking."

More whistles blowing behind them. Heads turning. She can hear Kaspar's voice like a barrier, barring the way of their pursuers. "You pig. You desk coward. You think you can just shove past a frontline soldier without a word?" More voices join in, and a flood of angry invective chafes the air.

"My God," she hears a woman bleat to her companion. *"Did you see? Those soldiers just knocked that man to his knees!"*

Sigrid closes her eyes long enough to swallow a beat of her heart, but does not slow. More whistles are blowing. More voices are raised. Track signals clang. "Sigrid, this is the wrong train," Ericha tells her, with a buried frantic note. "We can't put them on this train. We don't have the correct *tickets.*"

"No one is traveling on this train, child. No one is traveling on *any* train. Up ahead, you'll see a certain ticketing superintendent with whom you've done business. Only now he's been paid to open a door. So keep moving."

The superintendent is a chubby old bear in an old-fashioned Reichsbahn uniform and a peaked cap set too low on his brow. He avoids eye contact, frowns as he unlocks the door at the end of platform, and steps away, seeing nothing.

The cold air and noise of the Möckernstrasse hit them stiffly as they step out onto the sidewalk, and the door thunks shut behind them.

"The tunnel," Sigrid commands, and heads for the concrete stairwell below the sign that reads PLAZA PASSAGEWAY TO THE HOTEL EXCELSIOR. SHOPPING IN THE TUNNEL. The stairwell leads downward to a bustling corridor, dull yellow with the glow of subterranean lighting. Sigrid has a flash of her mother gazing into a dress shop window, while her father frowns at his watch, but the shops are closed now, NUR ANTRAPPEN notices in the windows.

"Follow me. Hurry, but don't run," Sigrid instructs. But Ericha suddenly seems frozen.

"Frau Weiss," Sigrid calls, and hands off the little girl to her. "Go straight. We'll catch up."

When Sigrid turns back, all Ericha says is, "I can't."

"You can and you will, if I must *drag* you, Fräulein Kohl," Sigrid informs her. "Now, *move*, please."

Halfway through the tunnel, Sigrid risks a glance over her shoulder, but there is no sign of the Gestapo. Ahead, a circus clown with a painted red grin is collecting for Winter Relief beside a Party man in full brown regalia and a swastika armband. The clown gives Frau Weiss's children a jaunty wave, and they gaze back at him widely. "How goes it, little ones?" the clown calls to them. "Can you give up your ice creams today so Mutti can make a donation?" Sigrid quickly intervenes, dropping coins into the collection urn.

"Heil Hitler," the Party man says, and smiles, flapping her a German salute.

"Heil Hitler, and good afternoon," Sigrid says, smiling back, but keeps everyone walking, slowing only to pick up the older girl. Good soldier Liesl. The trusting weight of the child in her arms touches something in her, but all she says is, "At the end of the corridor, go left up the steps."

The stairs leading upward are many, though Sigrid keeps her gaze aimed at the rectangle of hard white daylight waiting for them. As they emerge into the Saarlandstrasse, her eyes search, but only for a instant, before she spots Rudi, crushing out his cigarette on his boot heel, and stuffing the unsmoked butt behind his ear. Flinging open the rear door of his cab, he asks, "Taxi, gnädige Frauen?"

Frau Weiss into the rear first with the little one, and then Sigrid deposits Liesl. "In, please," she tells Ericha next.

"You knew," Ericha concludes in a penetrating whisper; her voice sounds as if it is drilling through a deep fog. "You knew that it was me, didn't you?"

"You're aware of the rules," Sigrid answers. "No questions. Now, *in*, please," she repeats.

And this time Ericha offers no resistance.

. . .

THE DILAPIDATED CANVAS-TOPPED LORRY sits in the dim recesses of an alley beside a bombed-out Handwerk warehouse on the south side of the canal.

"It was just where you said it would be," Rudi announces. "An Opel Blitz three-tonner."

"It meets your high standards, I hope?" Sigrid says

A shrug. "It's a bit of an ogre. The three-tonner handles like a barge full of rocks. But at least it has new tires. I haven't seen new tires since 1938."

"And the papers were in place?"

According to the registration, your driver will be a civilian contractor, with a permit to transport a war widow and her children from Berlin to Lübeck, after the family's flat was bombed, Kaspar's letter to her had read.

"All in order," Rudi assure her. "Very neat."

"Yes," Sigrid nods as she surveys the lorry, thinking of Kaspar as she lightly touches the high, side-view mirror. "Very neat."

Climbing into the cab, Rudi turns over the engine and leaves it idling, the tailpipe stinking of diesel smoke, and then hops back down to the asphalt. Lowering the rear gate, he shoves back the canvas flaps, revealing a conglomeration of mismatched furnishings.

"So should I ask where all the furniture came from?" Sigrid inquires.

Rudi lifts his eyebrows. "I had a chum help me. If a family is moving, I thought it should look convincing. Which means furniture." He tosses away the nib of a cigarette. "There's room up front for the lady and her children," he says. "And a bench in the rear for the Fräulein. We should load up."

Sigrid peers into a small shack by the taxis' shed, where a coffeepot sits on an electric hotplate. Frau Weiss clutching a tin cup, with Liesl on her lap. Little Ruthi with her wooden tiger tapping across the wooden floor. Ericha lowers her cigarette as her eyes rise, but Sigrid still avoids her gaze. "It's time to go," is all she says.

Rudi lifts the little girls up onto the front seat. Sigrid watches them scoot to the middle with a mixture of uncertainty and anticipation. Then she speaks to Frau Weiss in a confidential tone, handing her a small envelope. "I picked these up at an apothecary. Sedatives. Mild enough for the girls. It's a long trip to Lübeck, and it'll help them sleep."

"Thank you, Frau Schröder," the woman replies, gripping Sigrid's hand, her eyes warming with tears.

"Keep your children close, Frau Weiss," Sigrid tells her.

"I will. *Thank you*," she repeats.

"Mama," the little one calls, and waves the wooden tiger.

"When they reach Lübeck," Sigrid says, "give them this kiss for me," she smiles, and carefully kisses the woman's cheek and watches her climb aboard.

Only now, when there is no other choice, does she look Ericha in the eyes.

"And so it's you next," she says. "Come, come. We don't want the lorry to run out of petrol idling in the alley. Climb aboard."

"Sigrid."

"If you're stopped, which you won't be, but if you are, tell them that you're visiting your fiancée in the Kriegsmarine. Heinrich. I think that's a good name for a fiancée, don't you? Heinrich Schuler of Third Port Battery Command. Now, climb aboard, or shall I have Rudi lift you up like one of the children? You'd do that for me, wouldn't you, Rudi? Tell her."

"I follow the gnädige Frau's orders," Rudi confirms. He raises one of the lorry's hood covers and makes an adjustment, which causes the motor to growl impatiently. "But we must get moving. Lübeck isn't exactly a Sunday drive."

"Exactly so. Therefore, no delays, please. I've given Rudi your

Reisepass along with your travel papers and money for your passage. For once, Fräulein Kohl, just *do as you're told*. It'll be a new experience for you."

"You haven't answered me," Ericha says. Her eyes like shattered blue shards of crystal.

"What I *knew*, child, is that I wasn't going to allow that baby inside of you to be born in a concentration camp. Nothing else. Only that."

"I can't."

"Yes."

" I can't simply *leave*."

"*Yes*. You *can*. It's an uncomplicated process. You ride in a lorry till you reach a ship. Then you sail in that ship till you reach the shore of Sweden. And then you are safe." She feels her eyes heating up. Going damp.

"You think I *want* to be safe?"

"I think that regardless of what you *want*, Fräulein Kohl, we must *have* you safe."

Ericha stares. "And what about you?"

"Me?"

"Yes. Frau Schröder." She swallows. "What about her?"

"She will continue," Sigrid answers. She looks away to wipe the tears from her eyes. "What else can she do? Now, there's nothing more to be said," she declares, and clasps Ericha close. "Except good-bye." Her eyes suddenly sting. "Think of me often, my dearest girl," she whispers as she hugs her so very tightly. "I will always think of you."

"*Ladies,*" Rudi prompts.

Sigrid breaks away and stands back as Ericha accepts a hand from Rudi and climbs into the lorry. Rudi raises the tailgate and chains it shut, and then unlaces the canvas flaps, closing the curtain on the depth of Ericha's gaze. "Tschüss, Chefin," he says to Sigrid, as he climbs into the cab.

"Tschüss, Rudi," she answers. The engine coughs, then turns over, sputtering irritably. But as the old junk heap jerks forward, Ericha parts the canvas flaps. "It'll never work out," she calls, tears streaking her face, "between Heinrich and me!"

And Sigrid watches her face as the lorry pulls out into the silvered daylight and turns onto the street.

———

The feature has started as she steps into the mezzanine balcony of the cinema. On the screen, a squad of soldiers is crouched in a circle around a fallen comrade. There are a few faces in the audience, hard to read in silhouette, staring at the screen. She knows she is late, and is ready to believe that he did not wait, though the thought rips at her heart.

But then she spots him. Under the projector in the back row.

"So," she hears him say in graveled whisper, "pigs fly."

"I'm only here," she tells him, her words thickening in her throat. "I am only here to say good-bye."

"Then, Frau Schröder," he tells her, "your timing is impeccable."

As he shifts, she sees his hand pressed against his side. Sees the pain shaping his face in the flickering glow, and the dark stain on his fingers.

"You're hurt," she whispers sharply.

"I suppose one could say that."

"My *God*, Egon, we must get you to a *doctor.*"

"No."

"It's all right. There's a doctor who keeps his mouth shut. No questions. I know where his surgery is."

"No, Sigrid. No doctors. This is not a matter for doctors," he says, and swallows pain as he tries to reach into his coat. "I *can't*," he breathes. "I need your help. There's an envelope."

"Egon."

"Please, Sigrid, just *get it.*"

Carefully, she reaches into his coat. Hand brushing across his chest. An intimate dip into the recesses of his clothing. Then there's the envelope. Wartime paper, rough against her fingertips. She draws it out.

"Don't open it until you're somewhere safe. You'll find a claim ticket inside," he tells her, then his face twists. He chokes back a cry. "Fucking hell," he whispers. "That's the last time I order the Stammgericht at the Kranzler."

"Tell me what happened. Tell me," she whispers her command.

"Your young U-boat."

A flash of the hawkish eyes, and the angry voice in her ear: *Grizmek. I've seen you with him.* "He found you," she breathes.

"Well, his knife blade did."

"And I led him to you," she says with damp horror, but Egon shakes his head.

"No. Not you. It was *my* mistake. Like most animals, I'm prone to habit. I foolishly made a return to my old hunting grounds around the Gedächtniskirche, and there he was, waiting. My personal angel of death. He must have spotted me on the street and followed me into the U-Bahn. I didn't see him till the knife was out." He nearly smiles. "Justice, isn't it? A kind of justice? You can't disagree," he insists. "Maybe that's what I was looking for. But never mind. What's important now is the claim ticket. Take it to the baggage desk at the Bahnhof Zoo. The clerk will give you a leather kit bag in return. Inside of it," he says, and then must stop to breathe in the pain. "Inside of it," he repeats, "you'll find eighty thousand marks."

"Egon." She whispers his name. Maybe just to hear it aloud.

"I think, with that kind of wire, you can smuggle out a lot of Jews, don't you, Frau Schröder? Call it my contribution." He tries to grin, but then lurches forward for an instant, like a wrestler trying to establish a superior grip on his opponent. When he falls back into the seat, there is blood where he has bitten into his lip. "*Go*, will you?"

"*No.*"

"Yes. *Please*, Sigrid. It isn't safe here. Besides. I don't want you to watch me die. Not like this."

Tears wet her cheeks. "I won't leave you."

"You've never *watched* a man die from a belly wound. But I have. It's ugly. As ugly as it gets. And I'd rather your last memory of me not involve any puking of blood. So, please. *Go.*" He says this as the pain cuts into him again, and he shudders angrily, trying to contain it. "*Go,*" he repeats.

But she knows that for once she will not do what he asks of her. "No, Egon," she says, and wipes the tears from her eyes efficiently. She has given him her breath and the pulse of her body. Given him her passion, her hatred, and her love, her past and future. Given him all that is essential in her, so that she will never be whole without him. But it hasn't been enough. She knows she must give him one final gift. His freedom.

"I have something for you. Something that will help," she tells him gently. She had pinned it into her hair in case she was taken. In case she was tossed into in a prison cell with nothing. The small brass capsule. She removes it from the prong of the hairpin and opens it up. "Something that will act very quickly."

The film projector mutters above them, beaming sterile, blue-white light. He gazes thickly at the glass vial in the palm of her hand. "Your resourcefulness, Sigrid Schröder, continues to astound me." Then he raises his eyes to hers. "But I can't," he says. "I can't let you waste it."

"Waste it," she repeats.

"What happens. what happens when the day comes that you need it for yourself?"

"It won't come," she says.

But he manages to shake his head. "You don't know that. In fact. If you've learned anything—it should be how *easy* it is for people—for people to betray one another. That day may come. And then you'll have"—he breathes in raggedly—"no way out."

"I don't care. I won't let you suffer like this."

"*Suffer?*" He almost smiles. "It's the least that I deserve. Ask anyone. Ask yourself. Is the selfish bastard worth it?"

"Yes," she replies. "That's my decision. He is. Now, no more argument, if you please, Herr Grizmek." And then, "Please, Egon," she whispers. "Let me. Let me help you."

His eyes have closed.

"Egon."

When they open again, he says, "My daughters." Staring ahead. "My daughters. When I close my eyes, I can see their faces." He says this as if it surprises him, or haunts him. When she speaks his name again, he doesn't answer her. Only stares ahead and grits his teeth through a spasm. Then blinks his eyes once when it ends. The tears steam her eyes as she carefully parts his lips with her fingers. He does not resist as she inserts the vial into the back of his mouth and whispers heat into his ear. *"I love you. I will love you always."* The last heat she will ever offer him. He hesitates, infinitesimally, before he bites down. She feels his body flinch. Nothing more than that. A flinch. And then she feels its stillness enter her heart.

She is not sure how long she remains beside him in the darkness. Nor can she determine exactly the point when she separates herself from him, unclasping her hand from his. Closing his eyes, she kisses each lid. A painless calm has formed his expression. Gazing at him, she remembers how only sleep could quiet his face.

AT THE BAGGAGE CLAIM in Bahnhof Zoo, she exchanges the chit in Egon's envelope for a hefty black leather kit bag, heavily worn around the seams. When she cracks it opens, she sees the hundred-mark denomination of the bank-fresh stacks. Quickly she closes the bag's clasp. As she passes through the station she witnesses a man coming home to his family from this travels. Two little girls in their mother's arms chirping happily at their father's arrival. A small shudder passes through her like a thin length of wire, but she does not slow her pace.

Outside, under a hard white dome of light, she finds the blind man, beneath the clock. A passing rinse of afternoon rain, typical for Berlin, has turned the pavement into a slick mirror, throwing back a distorted reflection of the day.

"A coin in memory of our sacred dead?" the man rasps.

She can feel him gazing at her from behind the dark lenses of this goggles, and peers into their black reflection. "Yes. For the dead," she agrees. Though as her coins ring in his cup, she bends her head toward his, as if to tell him a secret. "But I am working for the living now."

WHAT WOULD ANY OF US DO?

Writing *City of Women*

This book came about from my desire to write about history and about ordinary people thrust into extraordinary circumstances.

I have always been captivated by history. Not just its broad sweep, but also its intimate corners, where the shadows gather. And Berlin, during the Second World War, was a city defined by its shadows. It provided the perfect setting for people making difficult decisions in their daily lives that could reshape their future in a heartbeat.

When I visited Berlin for the first time, just after the Wall came down in 1989, I intended to search for what was left of the city from before the war. What I discovered was that much of that city was gone. Just gone. Berlin's busiest corner in the 1930s, the Potsdamer Platz, was nothing more than an open field studded by bits and pieces of shattered brick and tile. Its greatest rail palace, Anhalter Bahnhof, where Sigrid meets Ericha at the climax of the novel, was nothing more than a shattered remnant of its once grand façade. It sits, to this day, like a tombstone, at a subway stop that bears its name. And of the tunnel linking the station to the hotel across the street—that tunnel of shops through which Sigrid races with Ericha and the Weiss family, pursued by the Gestapo? The hotel is gone, the rail station is a ruined wall, but the tunnel is down there still, sealed beneath the streets. Inaccessible and forgotten. Through fiction, however, I found I could unearth it. I could resurrect the entire city, and the people in it. That's where the characters of *City of Women* live. In the shadows of a lost city's architecture.

So I travel in time. I close my eyes and open them in 1943. After a year's hiatus, the British bombers return to Berlin. It is a shock. The Nazi regime has assured its people that the war is all but won. Just hang on for a little bit longer, they say. Make a few more sacrifices. Bury more of your sons and husbands, but don't worry—victory is just around the corner. Yet by the time Sigrid returns to the bomb shelter in the cellar of Uhlandstrasse 11 at the beginning of the book, it is very difficult to ignore the fact that the war is *not* almost won. Not only is the RAF raining bombs on the rooftops again, but an entire German army has been annihilated in a place called Stalingrad, by an enemy who was supposed to be on the brink of utter defeat. And though no one dares voice the words, it is becoming apparent that Germany is *losing* the war. The Nazis try to distract the population from this bitter truth by intensifying their anti-Semitic campaigns. The Gestapo sweeps through Berlin's factories, deporting Jewish workers and their families en masse: men, women, children, the elderly, the infirm, it makes no difference. They all go. And those who try to dodge arrest? Those who've found a place to hide? For them the Gestapo has dispatched the catchers of the infamous Search Service, Jewish inmates of the SS transit camp in the Grosse Hamburger Strasse, whose only job is to comb the city and track down other Jews—the so-called U-boats—who have submerged beneath the surface of the city's daily life.

But what about those people who are not being arrested and deported? People who claim they are simply trying to feed their kids, keep a roof over their heads, and stay out of trouble? How do these people respond to the crimes being committed in their name by the regime? That is the question at the heart of *City of Women*. It's about ordinary people making hard decisions in extraordinary times. It's about small decisions leading to bigger decisions. And it asks, At what point does one arrive at a moral commitment? Sigrid Schröder helps a young woman whom she barely knows evade an arrogant police detective, simply because she doesn't like bullies. A few months later Sigrid is being chased by the Gestapo through a train station, with the lives of four other people in her hands. How did she get there?

I created the character of Sigrid because I wanted to write about a woman who has capitulated to the slavish routine that defines her daily life. Her present has become so mind-numbing and tedious that she has given up on her own future. But when circumstances change, so does she. In fact, when Ericha Kohl seizes her arm in the cinema, and begs for her help, Sigrid is already primed to break free from her passivity by a passionate nature she has been taught since childhood to keep in check. Soon she is making one dangerous choice after the next, driven by . . . by what? Desire? Excitement? Conscience? All of these? Certainly, she has watched as the casual anti-Semitism of the German middle class in the 1930s has transformed into state-sponsored persecution, and state-supported pogroms. She has witnessed the Night of Broken Glass in Berlin, and its aftermath, when thousands of Jews were arrested, beaten, and murdered. For years she may have disapproved, she may have felt shame for her nation, but she did not resist, even as Jewish Berliners were marched through the streets on their way to "resettlement" in the East. Did she feel helpless to act? Most probably. (What, after all, could one woman do?) Did she feel relieved by the fact of her helplessness? Very likely. If she *could not* act, then she did not need to feel a responsibility to act. So when she finally breaks free of this self-imposed trap, how much of Sigrid's transformation is due to love or moral choice, and how much is due simply to her sudden need to recognize her true self?

Of course, the overarching question—the question I continually asked myself as I was writing *City of Women*—was and is: What would *you* do? It's easy to watch from a comfortable distance as people make choices with life-or-death consequences. Characters in a book make their decisions and roll the dice. They succeed or fail, they live or die. But the question is: If you were Sigrid, and a young woman seized you by the arm as you sat in a cinema, and begged, *Please say that we came here together,* what would you do? What would any of us do?

—*David Gillham*

ACKNOWLEDGMENTS

There are a number of people whose guidance, support, and rallying spirit were instrumental in bringing *City of Women* to fruition.

First, I want to offer thanks to my agent, Rebecca Gradinger of Fletcher and Company, who has labored ceaselessly on my behalf, and has the ability to routinely make the impossible possible. I can count on her encouragement when the work is on track, and, more importantly, her unflinching critical eye when it's not. I also want to thank Christy Fletcher, who maintained her faith in my work for over ten years, and was willing to give me the break I needed when I finally had the material that could crack a long cycle of glowing rejections.

Then there's my editor and publisher, Amy Einhorn. I could not have imagined a better fit or a more generous and supportive editor had I made her up myself. Fortunately, I didn't have to. Amy is brilliantly meticulous in her work (she still does a complete line edit) and both my characters and I owe her a deep debt of gratitude. Thank you, Amy.

I also want to thank my copy editor, David Koral, for burnishing every syllable of every page; Liz Stein at Amy Einhorn Books for all her invaluable assistance; my writing consultant, Carol Epstein of the Vernon Street Writing Group, who acted as my sounding board throughout the drafts; my first writing teacher at USC, Shelly Lowen-kopf, who set me upon this course of novel-writing; and my parents, Charles and Marcia Gillham, plus my sister, Lisa Curtiss Gillham, for providing me with a childhood home where artistic accomplishment was truly valued.

And, of course, I must thank my wife, Ludmilla Pavlova-Gillham, who continues to be my touchstone in all things.